⟨ **P9-CEC-718**

Through the back window of the cabin Kate saw her.

Her best friend lay on a blood-soaked mattress, a knife protruding from her chest. Her eyes were open, staring at Kate, accusing her.

A blink of something green caught her eye. Next to the door a digital clock. All at once, Kate took in the entire room, not just Paige's dead body.

The wires. The plastique. *The time.*

The clock was counting backward: 1:11, 1:10, 1:09.

Kate broke the window with her gun and jumped through. She wanted to get Paige out, but didn't have time.

Using her windbreaker as a glove, she reached over and pulled the knife from Paige's body, wrapped it in her jacket, and leaped out the window.

She didn't care about contaminating evidence. She just wanted a print. A print that could lead to the real identity of Paige's killer.

You didn't need evidence if you never went to court.

Also by Allison Brennan

The Prey
The Hunt
The Kill
Speak No Evil
See No Evil

FEAR NO EVIL

A Novel

Allison BRENNAN

BALLANTINE BOOKS • NEW YORK

Fear No Evil is a work of fiction. Names, characters, places, and incidents are the products of the author's imagination or are used fictitiously. Any resemblance to actual events, locales, or persons, living or dead, is entirely coincidental.

A Ballantine Books Mass Market Original

Copyright © 2007 by Allison Brennan

Published in the United States by Ballantine Books, an imprint of The Random House Publishing Group, a division of Random House, Inc., New York.

BALLANTINE and colophon are registered trademarks of Random House, Inc.

ISBN 978-0-345-49504-4

Printed in the United States of America

www.ballantinebooks.com

OPM   9   8   7   6   5   4   3   2   1

For the 151 sworn officers killed in the line of duty in 2006 and their families, especially Sacramento County Deputy Sheriff Jeffrey Mitchell (1968–2006).

The generosity of professionals, friends, and fellow authors continues to amaze me, in particular Pia Berg-qvist of the Cessna Aircraft Company, Rae Monet, Karen Rose, Candy Calvert, Rex Moen, Cheryl Zoe Thomas, and Gordon Hinkle. While I tried to keep the facts of computer technology and small plane craft accurate, if I got anything wrong it was due to my own error and certainly not because of these help-ful people.

To Karin Tabke for always listening when I panicked, then telling me to get back to work because I didn't have time to wallow in self-doubt.

And of course the fabulous Ballantine and Trident teams, without whom I wouldn't be penning these ac-knowledgments.

I especially want to recognize and thank businessman and philanthropist Bill Simon, who has been a special friend to my family, for all the good works he and his wife Cindy do.

PROLOGUE

Five Years Ago

THE SICK AND DEPRAVED HAD VOTED: death by stabbing.

"No."

Kate Donovan's whisper became a cry as she pocketed her cell phone, unable to respond to the text message her only remaining friend in the FBI had sent.

Unable and unwilling. She was so close, dammit! She knew it, sensed it, but no one believed her. Why should they? Less than two days ago, she'd led her people into a trap, and an agent—her lover Evan—ended up dead. Another agent—her partner Paige—kidnapped.

She had been tracking the webcam of Paige for twenty-four hours. The sick reality of what had already happened to her partner live on the Internet propelled her forward. She'd called in every favor, stolen expensive equipment from FBI headquarters, and hacked into private companies all in what she feared was a futile effort to save Paige's life. Saving

Paige had become her sole goal, so she wouldn't think about Evan's death.

She breathed heavily through her mouth as she ran even faster through the woods. An internal clock audibly ticked in her ear, pushing her forward. Fear crawled up her spine and slithered into her heart, constricting her chest until every breath hurt. She wasn't going to make it.

An all-too-human scream echoed through the wooded canyon, then was abruptly cut short.

Kate tripped, caught herself, and was surprised to feel moisture on her face. She couldn't be crying. She wiped her forehead and came away with blood. The gash on her head from the failed sting operation had needed stitches, but she'd had no time. No wonder it had started bleeding again.

Wiping her bloody hands on her jeans, Kate tied the bandanna tighter around her forehead and continued running, gun drawn.

The grand, two-story cabin stood in a clearing. She stared at the satellite dish on the roof and knew this was it. Her training and instincts had paid off: she had been right about where Trask had taken Paige. The dish opened onto the clear blue sky, enabling Paige Henshaw's rape and murder to be bounced from satellite to server to satellite, broadcast live for all to see. Kate almost ran across the open field to storm the cabin, but that could possibly have gotten her killed.

Don't be stupid, Donovan!

She circled the property, staying behind the tree line, ignoring her vibrating cell phone. The FBI knew where she was. If they had really been determined to save Paige, they would have listened to her, come with her instead of trying to arrest her for disobeying orders.

A black Suburban was parked next to the cabin. No other vehicles were in sight. Trask wasn't stupid enough to be out here alone, without security. Even though he lost men the night before last when he'd ambushed her and Paige in the warehouse, he still had at least two other men in his employ.

Her skin tingled. Someone was watching. Swallowing, she looked around, keeping low. She thought she had bypassed all his security traps. Had she unknowingly triggered something? A camera, a microphone? What kind of technology did this monster have?

She crouched in the bushes, still as a hunter with prey in sight—yet she felt more like a deer in a rifle sight than a tough FBI agent.

Nothing. No sound from the cabin. No sound from the woods except the soft *whish-whish* of the breeze rustling the pine needles. Frogs. A bird.

Where was he?

Dammit, Trask! Where are you?

Sixty yards away, the cabin door slowly opened. He stood, framed in the doorway.

She didn't know his real name, only knew him as "Trask," the founder of Trask Enterprises, an online pornography company. Kate hadn't known his race, his nationality, or his age. Now she studied him. He was Caucasian or light-skinned Hispanic, perhaps European from his high-chiseled cheekbones and strong chin, darker than Scandinavian, lighter than Mediterranean. Thirty? Older?

She might not know anything personal about him, but she'd never forget his face. She had stared into his icy blue eyes thirty-six hours ago as he aimed a gun at her head.

He stared at her hiding place, as frozen in time as she. Her mouth went dry, her hand itched to fire her gun. She swallowed and training won out. There was no way, even with her excellent marksmanship skills, that she could assuredly take him down with her service pistol at this distance.

He stepped outside, and two larger men followed. One carried two suitcases. The other carried a semi-automatic rifle and eyed the horizon. He didn't see her, but his eyes swept back and forth as the three men walked purposefully toward the Suburban.

There was no hope. She couldn't take down all of them by herself. And while she might get a shot at one of the guards, she wouldn't get to the leader, the man who had come up with the plan, who had executed it, and who took perverse pleasure in killing.

If she could kill the bastard who called himself Trask, Kate would be willing to die—already the pain of losing Evan was eating at her. But if she couldn't get Trask, her sacrifice would be for nothing. And Kate refused to die in vain.

She watched the Suburban drive away, deep anger and remorse clutching her heart. She'd lost Evan, lost everything because she had moved too quickly, too soon, at the warehouse. She hadn't verified crucial information. If only she hadn't been so eager to capture Trask and prove to everyone that she was right, she wouldn't have lost her career, her best friend, and her freedom.

Being right meant nothing when everything you cared about was destroyed.

The Suburban disappeared around the bend. Kate left her hiding place and ran to the main door of the cabin. Instinct told her everyone was gone, but she had to do a perimeter check anyway.

Through the back window, she saw her best friend.

Paige lay on a blood-soaked mattress, a knife protruding from her chest. Her body was in shreds, her eyes open, staring at Kate, accusing her.

You promised you'd find me.

Paige had saved her life at the warehouse. Trask had Kate first and brought his gun to her head.

"You're coming with me," he'd said.

Paige had attacked him from behind, stunning Trask just long enough for Kate to dive behind crates and retrieve the gun she'd lost in the struggle. Sirens had then cut through the night and Kate had looked up just as Trask hit Paige over the head and his partner, Roger Morton, carried her from the warehouse.

Kate didn't shoot out of fear of hitting Paige.

Paige had given her life to save Kate's. A cry escaped from her and she swallowed her pain and failure. Kate almost ran into the room, just to shut Paige's eyes. To call their boss and blame him for not backing her up. To turn off the damn video camera in the corner, broadcasting Paige's mutilated body to the thousands of sick bastards who had paid to see her raped and murdered.

A blink of something green caught her eye. Next to the door a digital clock. All at once Kate took in the entire room, not just Paige's dead body.

The wires.

The plastique.

The time.

The clock was counting backward: 1:11, 1:10, 1:09.

Looking quickly around the window for any booby traps, she broke it with the grip of her gun, cleared the glass as best she could, and jumped through.

The countdown turned from one minute to fifty-nine seconds. Fifty-eight. Fifty-seven.

She fired a round into the video camera lens, then took off her windbreaker and approached Paige's body. She wanted to get her out, but she didn't have time.

So much blood.

I'm sorry, Paige.

Forty-one seconds.

Using her windbreaker as a glove, she reached over and pulled the knife from Paige's body. It was stuck in bone. She grimaced as she used all her strength to remove it, then wrapped it in her jacket and leaped out the window.

All the evidence was about to be destroyed and this knife might be the one thing that could implicate the murderer.

"I'll find him, Paige," she promised then glanced at the clock.

Nineteen seconds.

Kate ran as fast and far as she could. The explosion shook the earth, knocking her off her feet. Her jacket fell from her grasp and the wind was knocked out of her.

She didn't care about contaminating evidence. She just wanted a print. A print that could lead to the real identity of Paige's killer.

You didn't need evidence if you never went to court.

ONE

LUCY'S GRADUATION CEREMONY was being held outside on the high school's football field. On the cusp of adulthood, nine hundred eighteen-year-olds sat surprisingly still on the risers framing each side of the temporary stage. Dillon Kincaid shielded his eyes against San Diego's morning sun, scanning the crowd for his family. He was late because of a last-minute psychiatric assessment of a prisoner who was being arraigned that afternoon.

The principal called the next graduate. "Monica Julian." A tall, lithe blonde walked up the steps to the platform and accepted her certificate.

Good. He hadn't missed Lucy receiving her diploma. He'd keep an eye on the audience for the largest burst of applause, and that would be where the Kincaid clan had saved him a seat.

The principal went through fifteen more names before announcing, "Lucia Kincaid."

Dillon smiled, anticipating his beautiful dark-haired baby sister walking up the stairs. She'd worked hard for her grades, and her acceptance to their father's alma mater of Georgetown was icing on the cake. He heard a loud raucous cheer in the middle of the right seating section, saw the tallest Kincaid, Connor, standing and hooting.

Circling the field and making his way to where his family cheered, Dillon watched the stage for his sister.

"Lucia Kincaid?" The principal repeated her name and Dillon stopped to scan the graduates. Where was Lucy? He reached the edge of his family's row of seats as Carina emerged.

"Robert P. Kinney." The principal went on to the next graduate.

"I'm going to look for Lucy," Carina told Dillon when she spotted him. Her fiancé, Nick Thomas, was right behind her.

Dillon fell into step next to Nick while Carina made a beeline for the nearest girls' restroom. She'd graduated from the same high school fourteen years before and knew the campus well. Wearing graduation robes, two girls came out, adjusting their hats. Carina asked, "Is Lucy Kincaid in there?"

"I don't think so," one responded.

Carina brushed past her and went into the girls' room, calling Lucy's name. "She's not there," she stated tersely when she came out.

"Is there another bathroom?" Nick asked.

"Way over on the other side of the field."

"Let's check it out."

They crossed the field behind all the proud families. "I can't believe she ditched her own graduation!" Carina sounded both worried and angry.

"You don't know that she did," Dillon said. "There's a logical explanation. Lucy could be sick."

"And she didn't come and tell us?" Carina frowned, picked up her pace. "No one's seen her since eight o'clock this morning. She went to Becky's house to get ready, saying she'd meet us here."

"Carina," Dillon said, "stop being a cop for a minute. Don't assume the worst."

"I can't help it."

Dillon had the same fears as his sister. Both siblings worked with violent predators every day—Carina as a homicide detective catching killers, Dillon as a forensic psychiatrist trying to understand them. The two had been sent down their career paths by the murder of their nephew. Justin Stanton would also have been graduating today had he not been murdered eleven years ago.

Carina took a deep breath as she walked under the bleachers and toward the restrooms. A group of male graduates was smoking cigarettes around the corner. "They're at the 'N's now. You'd better get back," Carina told them.

"Whatever," one of the kids dismissed her.

Carina glared at him, and Dillon pulled her back, reminding her what was important. "Let's find Lucy."

The restroom was vacant except for a mother and daughter.

Standing outside the restroom, Carina said to no one, "Where is she?"

"You said she went to Becky Anderson's this morning, right? The petite blond girl who was at her birthday dinner?"

Carina nodded. "She's in the third row on the left."

"Let me go talk to her. You and Nick check the campus."

Carina looked like she was about to argue with him—Dillon knew she wanted a crack at interrogating Becky—but he held firm and Nick guided Carina toward the parking lot.

Dillon walked over to the graduates' seating. He spotted Becky halfway down the third row and waved to catch her attention.

A teacher approached. "I'm afraid I'm going to have to ask you to leave. You can speak to your daughter after the ceremony."

Dillon cringed. He might technically be old enough to be Lucy's father, but he knew Lucy was sensitive to being much younger than her six siblings.

"I just need to talk to Becky Anderson. It's important."

"I'm afraid that's not possible."

Dillon caught Becky's eye and motioned her to come over. She started down the aisle, her face revealing that she knew exactly why Dillon was asking to speak with her.

"Sir—" the teacher began.

"This is about a missing girl. I have to speak with Becky."

Without giving the teacher another word, Dillon took Becky by the arm and led her away from the crowd.

The petite eighteen-year-old had guilt written all over her face.

"Do you know why I want to talk to you?" Dillon asked, trying to maintain calm while his concern over Lucy continued to grow.

"I—" Becky bit her lip. "I don't know why Lucy's late."

"An hour late?" Dillon asked.

"Well, I . . . she'll be here," Becky said lamely.

"What happened after Lucy arrived at your house this morning?"

"Um, she didn't."

"*What?*" Dillon exclaimed. "Where was she going?"

"Please, you don't understand."

"I need the truth, Becky. Now."

"She went to meet someone."

"Who?"

"A friend."

"Name?"

"Trevor Conrad."

Dillon frowned. "That doesn't sound like one of her boyfriends." But he admitted to himself that he'd been too busy lately to keep up with Lucy's love life.

"He's in college."

Dillon tensed. He didn't like where this conversation was going. "Where did she meet him?"

"Starbucks. The one right around the corner," she added as if that made it safe. "We always go there."

"And you lied for her?"

"I didn't really lie," Becky said.

Dillon raised an eyebrow, but didn't have to say anything. "Lucy knew everyone would throw a fit if they found out she met someone on—" Becky shut her mouth.

"Online?" Dillon prodded.

Becky nodded.

Dillon pulled out his cell phone and dialed Lucy's number.

"*Hola!* It's Luce. I'm either talking or sleeping! Leave a message. *Adios.*"

"Lucy, it's Dillon. Call me as soon as you get this message. It's important."

He hung up.

"What do you know about Trevor Conrad?" Dillon asked Becky.

"He goes to Georgetown. He's a freshman and from Los Angeles. Lucy met him through an online group at Georgetown. It's all legitimate. You have to be a student to join. She's not stupid."

She doesn't have to be stupid to be in danger.

Dillon was now as concerned as Carina had been earlier. Trevor Conrad may be a student at Georgetown and still a threat. Or he could be impersonating a student. Dillon needed to get to Starbucks as soon as possible and talk to the staff.

"When was Lucy supposed to meet this Trevor?"

"Nine," she said.

"Is there anything else you're not telling me, Becky?"

She bit her lip, tears rolling over her lashes. "She promised to meet me here fifteen minutes before graduation started. I don't know what happened. Lucy should be here by now. I'm so sorry."

Lucy regained consciousness when a reverberating motor changed pitch.

Her eyelids wouldn't open, her limbs were numb, and she was bone cold. She shifted and discovered she'd been tied to a metal pipe.

She was sitting in a low puddle of ocean water, its distinctive salty aroma permeating her senses, waking her fully. The low rumble of a motor and the rise and fall of the floor told her she was on a boat. It wasn't a big boat, she could tell, but it was big enough to have a couple of rooms beneath the deck.

Her new suede jacket—the one Carina had given her for high school graduation—was torn. Lucy felt a flap of material hanging from her elbow. That angered her for a split second, before she realized that something else was very, very wrong.

Someone was in the hold with her.

"So you're finally awake."

She jumped at the unfamiliar male voice.

"Who are you?" Lucy tried but failed to keep the panic out of her voice.

No answer. Though it hurt her head, she forced her eyelids open. Faint, orange emergency lights glowed dimly. It was indeed the hold of a boat, a small room with pipes and storage bins. The engine was behind her, its sound vibrating off the metal walls, making it seem like it was coming from everywhere. She swallowed thickly, coughed.

A big man with blond hair sat on a chair by the door, staring at her with dark eyes. In his right hand was a gun.

She swallowed again, feeling nauseous. "Who are you?" she repeated, fear bubbling in her gut. How did she get here? What had happened? Everything seemed fuzzy, her head felt thick. Had someone hit her over the head? She couldn't remember. No, her head didn't hurt like that. Just tired.

Had she been drugged?

The stranger stood, then knocked on the room's closed metal door. A moment later, it opened. "She's awake," he said to someone Lucy couldn't see.

"I'll get him," another voice replied, and Lucy heard someone walking up metal stairs.

"What's going on?" Lucy tried to sound brave, but she was terrified.

The last thing she remembered was leaving the house to meet Trevor. They'd spent the past year talking online and more recently on the phone.

She'd never even made it into Starbucks. What had happened? She honestly couldn't remember.

Think, Lucy!

It had been crowded, nine o'clock on a Thursday morning. She'd had two hours to get to the school, more than enough time. Parking at the far end of the lot, Lucy had been nervous. What if Trevor didn't like her? What if he thought she was too young or immature?

She had opened her car door—

Then nothing. Lucy couldn't remember anything after that.

The metal door of the hold reopened and another man walked in. He dismissed the hulking figure with the gun as he said, "Circle the island until all is clear, then let me know before you dock."

Island? Lucy shivered. This man wasn't as old as the big lug with the gun, but Lucy wasn't sure exactly *how* old. Maybe thirty-five, maybe forty. He was also blond, but with windswept hair. Handsome, too, until Lucy looked in his eyes.

Cold, hard, blue. Even in the dim light, she saw how icy pale they were.

"Hello, Lucy."

"Who are you? Why am I tied up?"

He put on an expression of mock surprise. "I'm shocked you don't know who I am."

She shook her head. "I've never met you."

He smiled, but it didn't make her feel any safer. "I recall you told me once, 'We're soul mates. I can feel it. I'd know you anywhere.'"

Lucy dry heaved, her words coming back to her. The words she'd typed to Trevor Conrad. Her online boyfriend. But Trevor was a freshman at Georgetown, where she would be starting college in the fall. They'd met in a Georgetown student chat room. He was nineteen. He wasn't this man who was older than her brothers.

"You're not—"

He laughed and touched her face. Lucy recoiled as if burned and he scowled, bringing his hardened face an inch from hers. Fear Lucy had never known before gripped her and she began shaking uncontrollably. "You should have listened to your family and not met with someone you didn't know."

"Why?" Her voice came out a squeak. She hated being afraid. "Why are you doing this?"

"You're going to be a star, Lucy."

"I want to go home. My family has some money. Call them. They'll come."

He laughed, stood, and walked back to the hatch door. "Lucy, do you think everything is about money? You don't understand now, but you will. Very, very soon. Your family might try to find you, but you'll never see them again."

He opened the door.

"What are you going to do?"

Trevor looked over his shoulder. "Trust me, sweetheart, you don't want to know."

*   *   *

She was perfect.

Trevor Conrad wasn't his name, but he'd once known—and killed—a man named Trevor Conrad. In fact, were Trevor still alive he would have fallen head over heels for the dark-haired beauty. But Trevor was, deservedly, in his grave. As far as Lucy was concerned, he was Trevor Conrad, a freshman at Georgetown. Trask was fine with that identity for the time being. After Lucy was dead, he would step into another dead man's shoes. He had plenty to choose from.

Trask wasn't his name, either, but he'd grown used to it. He liked it. The name commanded respect. *Trask.* Strong, forceful, in charge. He'd particularly enjoyed the way Special Agent Kate Donovan spat it from her mouth, with such venom, right before he disappeared from the warehouse with her partner. He loved women who fought back. They were the most fun to kill.

Unfortunately, he hadn't been able to get to Kate in the warehouse, a minor failure. Ever since she and her partner had started investigating Trask Enterprises, they'd been a problem. On the surface his corporation had been legitimate, but they had dug too deep. They'd never be able to prove he killed April Klinger. First, his face had never been shown on screen. Second, there was no body. The acid would have eaten away every identifiable piece of April even if they were able to find where he'd buried her.

But his other operations were at risk. While Trask Enterprises was legitimate and aboveboard, his more entertaining sideline was not.

The bigger failure of that night was Kate Donovan

killing two of his men. He couldn't forgive her for that. Good men who took orders were hard to find. And because she'd seen him, he'd had to disappear, putting his legitimate business in the hands of pathetic investors who were now raking in the dough from Trask's own cyber masterpiece: sexual fantasy role-playing. And Roger had had to go underground because he was wanted for murder.

Just thinking of all he'd lost, the money he'd been forced to spend to stay in hiding these past five years, enraged him. He'd taken care of Paige Henshaw, but Kate had slipped away. The bitch. He couldn't wait to someday get his hands around her little neck.

But for now, he'd let pretty little Lucy think whatever she wanted. And she thought he was Trevor Conrad. Although it really didn't matter if she knew his real name; she'd be dead in two days.

"All clear?" he asked Ollie as he went on deck.

The sun had set, and its dim light was fading fast. The evening breeze this far north was cold, but he didn't put on a jacket. He enjoyed the sensation, the freshest air in the world empowering him. He'd always felt at home here.

"Yes, sir," Ollie said.

"Dock next time you come around. Is the house ready?"

"Yes. Denise did a terrific job."

"I knew she would."

He had planned on killing Denise years ago, but she was so perfectly submissive she had ended up becoming a necessary partner. Special Agent Paige Henshaw had died in her place. It was better that way. Denise would do anything Trask asked, though it wasn't as much fun *pretending* to rape a woman as it was to take a woman who didn't want him.

Paige. She'd been satisfying, though because of her arrogant partner tracking her to the cabin, he'd had to rush her kill, resulting in a loss of more than a million dollars.

He'd lied to Lucy Kincaid: it was *always* about the money. The rest, well, that was just plain fun.

This island had become his sanctuary five years ago when he'd had to go underground. His network had temporarily fallen apart and he had tried, unsuccessfully, to find that bitch who'd fucked him. But Special Agent Kate Donovan had her own problems and she'd disappeared herself.

How does it feel to be on the run, Kate? Someday I'll come for you. You can't hide from me forever.

Killing Lucy Kincaid would be fun.

Killing Kate Donovan would be ecstasy.

TWO

JUST AFTER MIDNIGHT the alarm sounded.

Kate leaped from the cot, sliding her feet into boots before they touched the frigid cement floor. She strode to the computer bank that filled an entire wall of her barren room. She didn't need additional lighting. The computer screens provided enough illumination for her to use the keyboard.

Typing in her personal codes, she watched the computer security program she'd enhanced identify the latest webcam that had gone live.

She didn't get her hopes up that it would be Trask. For the past five years she'd been running and watching, always on the lookout for him. She was keeping strong, staying smart. After Paige, he'd killed two others, and they, too, weighed on her conscience. If only she'd taken him down when she'd had the chance.

But now she had better technology, more equipment, and time. After finding this hiding place two years ago, she was no longer running. That gave Kate an edge. She didn't have to watch her back as vigorously.

Her alarm went off at least twice a day, sometimes

more. She ran through the protocols she'd set up to triangulate the signal, not missing a step. The methodical process kept her heart rate steady, her mind engaged.

She knew that if she could find the signal quickly, it wouldn't be Trask. He was too good.

Feed not found.

She sat up straighter, flipped on the coffeepot to reheat what was left from earlier in the day. Her resources were at a premium, drinking stale coffee part of the routine. Her blond hair and blue eyes stuck out in Mexico, so she didn't make the daylong trip to Monterrey often. She didn't want to have to disappear again. Besides, between government factions both good and bad, and the bands of criminals and drug smugglers, the whole area was dangerous—except here. This mountaintop observatory was an ideal place to monitor Trask's movement. High enough to get rid of chatter, to tap into national security networks, to monitor every live webcam she found the feed for. Remote enough that she and ancient Professor Fox didn't get visitors or tourists.

She usually bribed one of the local kids to bring her supplies. Sometimes they left with her money, but sometimes they came back for an opportunity to look at the stars.

Sometimes she looked at the stars as well, on nights when she didn't feel that everything she did was hopeless. That Trask was going to kill again, another woman was going to suffer a violent, miserable death so Trask could rake in millions of dollars from the perverts who jerked off to the rape and torture and slaughter of women.

Kate wanted to kill him with her bare hands, wanted to make Trask suffer like he had made, by her count, nine women suffer. She would use a knife or a gun or any other weapon at her disposal. He needed to be *dead*.

She pushed her emotions to the back of her mind and tried her second protocol.

Feed not found.

She poured lukewarm coffee into her mug, dumped in a spoonful of sugar, and stirred, watching the strings of numbers, each representing a satellite frequency and corresponding land-based server. Legitimate webcams would route the information to the satellite and then to specific servers around the globe. They used the same system, so they were easy to identify.

Trask, like most cyber criminals, piggybacked on legitimate transmissions and repeatedly bounced the data he sent from server to satellite to server so that it was virtually impossible to track where the feed originated. By the time law enforcement tracked it—which could take days, if they found the physical location at all—the suspect could disappear. Or, like Trask, they might use a randomly generated protocol that made it impossible to track, unless federal law enforcement had a warrant. And even a warrant didn't always help. Criminals often set up a false signature behind the feed so that it looked like it was coming from somewhere else.

Kate was no longer concerned with things like warrants. What she was doing was highly illegal. And her goal was *not* putting Trask in prison.

Feed not found.

She hesitated a moment, then logged on to the dummy account she'd created five years ago to monitor Trask. If someone at the Bureau was watching in real time, they might be able to track her. So it was imperative that Kate get in and out fast.

Her dummy account profile was that of a wealthy Texas businessman. She had a credit card with no limit, though the cost of watching a woman die was twenty-five thousand dollars. She'd used it once before, but she'd been too late.

Five years ago, Kate and Paige had been assigned to April Klinger's disappearance. She had run away when she was seventeen. A private investigator her grandmother hired had discovered that April was an online porn actress. He had found one filmed segment that disturbed him, and he had brought it to the FBI's attention.

It looked like April had been murdered, and the rape-fantasy scenario and her death had been posted online. Downloads of the segment numbered in the hundreds of thousands.

Problem was, they had no body—dead or alive. The FBI investigation led to Trask Enterprises, run by the slimy Roger Morton. He denied that "Trask" the person even existed.

Trask Enterprises had its tentacles in many so-called legitimate Internet pornography sites. The corporation was set up to rake in the money with willing participants and hundreds of thousands of regular-paying customers. At anywhere from $9.95 to $29.99 a month, sexual deviants could watch live sex, fantasy role-playing including rape, men and women stripping, and more. No longer was pornography a male-only spectator sport. During Kate's tenure on the sex crimes task force of the Violent Crimes/Major Offenders unit—VCMO—she had investigated numerous claims, most of which ended up being consensual sex, advertised for the world to see.

But this case sent Kate's instincts into orbit, and when witness after witness turned up dead or missing, she knew she was on to something. Or someone. Trask.

She and Paige had managed to get to one person inside Trask Enterprises, a terrified woman named Denise Arno. They had promised her immunity, anything and everything, to set Trask up.

But something happened that night in the warehouse. Kate still wasn't sure why their backup was missing, or how Trask discovered that Denise had turned on him. But suddenly it was Paige, Kate, and Evan against five well-armed men, and poor Denise was presumed dead.

After that failed operation, Trask and his sidekick, Roger Morton, went underground. But Kate had seen *him*—the man behind Trask Enterprises. They could no longer be public in their pornography operation because the FBI wanted both Trask and Morton for questioning in the death of two agents. Roger Morton himself had even been captured on camera raping Paige.

Still, five years later, they had enough money, shell corporations, false names, and real people to keep all the balls in the air while they stayed in the shadows. Kate knew Trask was still behind many of the major sex sites out there, pulling in millions of dollars, all to pay for his one big show every year.

Her computer beeped, bringing her attention back to her computer. She looked at the screen. It was him, Trask. The countdown had already begun.

47:35:09.

She took only small pleasure that it had taken less than twenty-five minutes to isolate his feed.

The first four hours were free. After that, the audience had to pay to keep watching.

It cost twenty-five thousand dollars to watch the psychological and physical torture of a young woman. Watch her fear grow. Watch her be raped.

Watch her be killed.

An added bonus to those who paid was a "best of" series of highlights from previous rapes and kills.

Rapes that were under the false disclaimer of "fantasy role-playing." Kills that Trask claimed were staged. But Kate knew the difference between fake blood and real blood. She knew the difference between the eyes of the living and those of the dead.

The first four hours cost nothing, to draw in the perverts and give them a taste of what was to come. Encourage them to mortgage their houses, cash in their retirements, steal from their friends and family to pay for the privilege of actually watching a woman die.

The room where it happened was usually plain, devoid of identifying features. Wood paneling, like in the cabin where Paige Henshaw had died. Little or no natural light.

Trask's latest victim looked college age and was very beautiful—Trask preferred to kill pretty girls. This girl was still clothed, her face both terrified and strong under the glare of two spotlights from behind the camera. Kate stared into her eyes. This one was a fighter. She would not give in.

Kate ran to the bathroom and vomited into the toilet. She puked until there was nothing left, and still dry heaves wracked her body.

Trask was back and he had another victim. Forty-eight hours and this defiant girl would be dead.

Correction, forty-seven hours twenty-two minutes and ten seconds.

Kate sat back at her computer terminal and brought up her secure e-mail server. She sent a message to the only person she still trusted in the FBI.

HE'S BACK. CLICK HERE FOR THE FEED.

K.

She hesitated just a moment. There was always a chance the authorities could find her. Extradite her and bring her before the Office of Professional Responsibility—the FBI version of Internal Affairs. Losing her job was the least of Kate's concerns. She'd been running for five years; she had no job to return to. It was losing her freedom, being prosecuted for the botched operation that resulted in her lover, Evan, and her partner, Paige, being killed.

Her former boss, Jeff Merritt, had threatened her before she went after Paige alone all those years ago. *"It's your fault Paige was kidnapped. If she dies, it's on your head and I will make sure you end up locked in prison for life."*

For five years she had quietly sent the FBI everything she had learned, but every lead had turned into a dead end. Two years ago she'd been close, but Trask had set up a trap and a team of top federal agents had nearly lost their lives, further setting Kate's former boss against her. He wanted her head, and Kate knew he'd gladly sever it from her body.

But could she do nothing? It wasn't her fault that the previous locations she had isolated had become dead ends. Trask was a computer genius. Even when she thought she'd uncovered all his tricks, he came up with new ones.

What else could she do except analyze every trick he used and keep looking for him through the vast Internet? There were millions of satellite transmissions, but only one was his. One would lead to him. She'd been close many times, but he was always a step ahead. When she slept, she heard him laughing at her failures.

Kate stared at the live feed. Watched as the dark-haired beauty was tied to a chair. Watched the camera zoom to her face. The fear in her young eyes, the strength of her profile. A knife at her neck, menacingly wielded by a man Kate didn't recognize. She captured his image for analysis.

The sound suddenly came on, loud, vibrating. Music. Then it was cut off, replaced by Trask's voice, low, proper, formal. "Meet Lucy. Watch her for free until the countdown hits forty-four hours. Then click on the link for a secure business transaction. Isn't she lovely?"

Lucy gasped, her breath coming fast, louder, her body shaking. The onscreen creep moved the knife away and Kate watched a small trail of blood flow from the poor girl's neck. Down to her jacket.

"Let me go!" Lucy screamed.

Laughter was heard in the background.

A disclaimer scrolled along the bottom of the screen:

"Kill the Whore" is fantasy rape role-playing. All players are actors. No one is seriously hurt during the production of this special.

Kate hit Send. Then she grabbed her coffee mug and threw it against the far wall.

THREE

THE KINCAID FAMILY mobilized to find Lucy. The detective, Carina, pulling in law enforcement personnel; the computer e-crimes expert, Patrick, creating an online timeline; PI Connor working his sources.

And Dillon was asked the same question a dozen times.

"Who would do this?" his mother asked this time. "Who would take our Lucy?"

"We'll find her," he grimly replied.

Dillon knew all too well the type of psychopath who took a girl like Lucy. As a forensic psychiatrist, it was his job to get into their heads, to listen to their abnormal fantasies, to learn what made them hurt people, in the hopes that someday the authorities could reduce violent crime, make society safer.

And all Dillon's insider knowledge made sitting here, in the kitchen, trying to console his mother, that much more frustrating.

He knew what kind of person would kidnap Lucy. He knew what kind of fantasies he harbored, what he would do to her simply because he could. Killers didn't feel remorse or emotion or guilt like normal people. They enjoyed inflicting pain. That Lucy was with such a person terrified Dillon.

Nick Thomas walked into the kitchen, making eye contact with Dillon.

"What?" Rosa Kincaid asked. "Did you find her?"

"No, ma'am. Not yet. I'm sorry. Where's the Colonel?"

"In his office. On the phone. Calling everyone we can think of." Rosa looked at Dillon. "It's been sixteen hours. That's bad, isn't it? Justin was killed immediately after—"

Dillon pulled his mother into a fierce hug. "We're going to find her. You can't compare this with what happened to Justin." Eleven years ago Dillon's seven-year-old nephew had been kidnapped from his bedroom and murdered. The random act of violence had changed everyone in the family. Dillon had planned to go into sports medicine; instead, he became a forensic psychiatrist in an attempt to make sense of what was so wrong in the world.

Nick motioned with his head that he needed Dillon to follow him upstairs. Dillon nodded. "Mama, let me take you to Dad's office."

"No, I need to make coffee. And something to eat. When Carina and Connor get back they'll be hungry."

"Are you sure?"

"Go. Find Lucy," said Rosa Kincaid, her Cuban features fiercely determined.

Dillon followed Nick upstairs to Lucy's bedroom, where Patrick was working on Lucy's computer. "I got a call from a friend in the FBI. They found Lucy."

From his tone, Dillon was certain Lucy was dead. "What happened?" His voice cracked with emotion.

Nick rested a hand on his arm. "She's still alive."

"Where?"

As soon as Nick opened the door, Patrick let out a vicious curse. Dillon stared at the computer screen.

Lucy.

She was tied to a chair, her long dark hair loose and tangled, her dark eyes looking wild beneath smeared makeup. When she jerked her head up, Dillon said, "It's a webcam."

"Live," Patrick said, "and the fucking FBI doesn't know where it's coming from!"

"What are those numbers?" Dillon asked. In the bottom right-hand corner there appeared to be a digital clock of some sort with the numbers running backward.

46:02:36. 46:02:35.

"I don't know yet," Patrick said. "Nick's FBI contact sent us this link and asked if she was Lucy."

Though technically the FBI wouldn't get involved in a typical missing persons case this quickly, Nick's best friend was the special agent in charge out of Seattle, Quincy Peterson. He had unofficially put the word out about Lucy.

Nick dialed a number from the house phone and put it on speaker. "Peterson," the voice answered.

"Quinn, it's Nick Thomas. I have you on a speakerphone with Dillon and Patrick Kincaid, Lucy's brothers."

"Is it her?" Quinn asked.

"Yes," Patrick said through his clenched jaw. "Shit."

"Agent Peterson," Dillon asked, "what's going on? How did you find her?"

"A friend found the link."

"And you don't know where Lucy is being held?"

"No. The webcam feed is masked. He bounces the data all over the world before it's fed into a server and shown. That server is rotated continually to prevent us from tracking him. We have Quantico putting all their best people on it, and my friend is working on tracking the feed as well, but it's difficult."

Patrick interjected, "That doesn't make me feel any better. Does this 'friend' have a name?"

"The FBI is getting involved. We're assembling a task force of the best agents in the country to find your sister."

"What can we do?" Dillon asked, realizing Peterson had avoided the question about his "friend." "My brother Patrick is the head of e-crimes. We can—"

"What I need is a recap of exactly what happened when Lucy disappeared. Any witnesses?"

"No," Dillon said. "She disappeared between nine and eleven yesterday morning. She was supposed to be meeting someone at Starbucks before her graduation, and her car, with her purse and keys inside, was found in the parking lot, but no one saw anything. The employees didn't think she'd been inside."

Nick spoke up. "We learned she'd planned on meeting someone she met online."

"Who?"

"His name is Trevor Conrad and he's supposed to

be a student at Georgetown, but we can't find any record of him."

"I need her computer," Quinn said. "I'll send someone from the local FBI office to pick it up."

"No," Dillon said.

"Hell, no," Patrick concurred. "We'll bring it to the task force. Consider yourself working very closely with the San Diego Police Department."

"I don't think—" Quinn began, then relented. "All right. We're basing operations out of the San Diego field office. I'm on my way down there now."

"Agent Peterson," Dillon said, "what are those numbers in the bottom right corner?"

When Quinn didn't say anything for a minute, Dillon prompted, "It looks like a countdown."

"It is," Quinn finally said.

Dillon was almost afraid to ask, but he did nonetheless.

"A countdown to what?"

"Murder."

Kate monitored her bank of computer screens as her enhanced programs attempted to triangulate the location of Trask's signal. The largest screen, the one in the middle, was the live feed of the victim.

Kate did pull-ups on a bar she'd installed in her room as she watched the young woman on the screen. The girl sat frozen, defiant, scared. Trask wouldn't let her stay like that too long. But for now, he was still whetting his viewers' appetite, showing them the prize. He'd probably give them something before the first free hours were up, something to entice them to pay the twenty-five thousand.

At four hours, FBI Agent Paige Henshaw had been raped.

Sweat coated her skin, but Kate continued the pull-ups until her arms shook. She dropped and did crunches. The air was too thin up here in the mountains to run, so she'd modified her routine, keeping it intense, building her strength.

She came up on a crunch and caught movement in the center screen. One of Trask's goons had untied the victim and was holding her from behind. Another man, Roger Morton—the man who'd first raped Paige—held a knife.

Kate jumped up and touched the screen. *No!* If the power of her will could stop what was happening, the earth would stop rotating on its axis.

Roger held the knife in front of the girl's face. Her eyes went wide and she visibly shook. He put the tip of the knife at her throat, then in one swift motion ripped her blouse with his other hand.

She flinched, the knife cutting into her throat just enough to draw blood. Roger and the goon laughed and pulled off her blouse. She wore a black lace bra. Something she had probably picked up with a girlfriend at the mall, enjoying the feeling of maturity, of growing up, of femininity.

Now its sexy lace was her humiliation.

"Show your fans what you've got, Lucy baby." Roger stepped aside so the camera could pan the girl's chest.

She pulled away from the grasp of the bastard behind her and punched Roger in the face. She almost got in another jab, but the men wrestled her to the ground. She fought and cried out, not in pain but in rage.

"Keep fighting, honey," Kate said to the screen. "Keep the spirit alive. Don't let them defeat you."

Roger slugged the girl and a voice from off-camera said, "Don't."

Trask.

Goose bumps rose on Kate's arms. Her scalp tingled. Her chest tightened. The bastard was watching. Why should she be surprised? Why would it be any different from how it had been five years ago? Three years ago? She'd slowed down Trask's operation, but hadn't ended it. Other girls had died after Paige.

Kate double-checked her programs, helpless to do anything but wait for the computer to find a weakness, and pray that it wasn't another clever trap. Each girl Trask had killed had provided her with more tools to locate him, but he was improving his security at the same rate she was improving her hacking ability. Last year the FBI had almost lost another agent based on her intelligence.

Or lack thereof, she thought with dread. After she'd sent that last set of data, she had discovered that Trask had set a trap for the federal rescue team. Jeff Merritt hadn't wanted to use Kate's information in the first place, but when she sent him her analysis, he had jumped at it, walking right into Trask's trap, ignoring Kate's warnings to be cautious, that it might be another of Trask's ruses. If only she'd had more time, more resources, more help.

Her instant messenger beeped. Only one person had her IM identity.

She sat down and read the message.

Kate, it's me. I know you're there.

She typed.

> You don't know. You're just guessing.
> I know you're there because you won't leave until she's dead or you locate him.
> What do you want?

She didn't need any of Quinn Peterson's crap. He typed,

> The hostage is Lucy Kincaid. She's eighteen and was supposed to graduate from high school yesterday. Trask used the name Trevor Conrad to lure her out. We need your help.
> I already helped. I sent you the link less than twenty-five minutes after it went up.
> I know you're tracking him. You can't go after him alone.
> Do I have immunity?

A long pause on the screen before Quinn typed,

> You know I can't do that. But I'm on your side. I'll do anything and everything I can.
> I'm not coming back until I find him. Otherwise everything I've done since Paige died will have been for nothing.

She shut down the IM so Quinn couldn't argue with her. He'd been her only link with the outside world during the last five years, and she would always be grateful to him. But the truth was, he couldn't give her freedom. And last year he had been as frustrated as Jeff Merritt that her information had led the feds into a trap.

She'd rather be in a prison of her own making than railroaded into a jail cell by her own people. They should have listened to her when she had told them it might be a trap. But Merritt was as headstrong as she was about bringing Paige's killer to justice. He'd jumped the gun. Was that Kate's fault? She'd warned them.

It was just Kate now. Her versus Trask. She wasn't about to jeopardize any more lives. If Merritt and the others had been killed, their deaths would have been on her conscience, no matter what she'd tried to do to protect them.

The center screen showed that Roger and the goon had wrestled the girl—Lucy—to the floor. She was positioned on the ground, tied to metal hoops protruding from the beige carpet. The camera panned over her breasts and face.

His voice, Trask or Conrad or whatever name the bastard was using now, came over cyberspace clearly.

"Only thirty more minutes to enjoy the free show. If you'd like to continue after that, log on to my secure server and use your credit card to purchase the entire forty-eight hours for only fifty thousand dollars."

He'd doubled his prices.

"Once you register, you'll be able to vote on how our lovely guest will be treated. Isn't Lucy just perfect? Fiesty. And I have it on very good authority that she's a virgin.

"For your enjoyment, and for a limited time, you can download highlights from our past shows for a small fee. Simply click on the box in the lower left-hand corner of your screen."

Kate swallowed. She didn't want to see them, but she had to force herself.

She clicked on the box and bought the compilation, saving the server information to analyze, though she knew he would keep this particular server at a location far from his hideout.

The video was ten minutes long.

Play.

Meghan was first. Her humiliation of being stripped and put on all fours. Kate knew Meghan had been told that if she cooperated, she'd be spared.

She had cooperated but hadn't been spared.

Trask didn't show Meghan's death. Kate didn't know whether to be relieved or terrified.

She dreaded the thought of watching Paige be stabbed to death, but her guilt would force Kate to watch if he showed it. She hadn't seen Paige's death; she had been just minutes away in the woods, desperately trying to reach her in time. She had failed. She'd only seen the aftermath, touched her partner's blood, smelled her fear.

Trask didn't show Paige. Of course he wouldn't, Kate thought. Paige had been his one mistake, and hers. He couldn't show her death again because of who she was, an FBI agent who most certainly didn't consent to the so-called fantasy rape role-playing. Her death connected him to the murder game, and he couldn't pretend there weren't people still looking for FBI Agent Paige Henshaw.

Rayanna was next. There she was on-screen, her

chest marked by cigarette burns. Her eyes terrified, her lips quivering, her expression fighting with the need to give in. A knife came down toward her, her mouth opened to scream . . .

Cut. One of Trask's men was raping another victim. Joanna. They'd spliced the tape, making it appear that Joanna enjoyed her assault. It was all part of Trask's tightrope walk: to make everything appear somewhat legitimate.

Other girls flashed by, Angela and Carol and Christy. Over time the photography improved, but Trask's cruelty was the same. He'd started in snuff films—DVDs—but technology had given him a boost with webcams and untraceable downloads. Kate didn't know how many young women Trask had actually murdered before Paige, filming their agony to share with other sickos, but he'd been at his grisly task for years. She may have only identified a fraction of his victims, and they had so little evidence they'd never been able to build a solid case. That's why she and Paige had come up with their plan five years ago. The plan that had ended in death and failure.

The "sample" ended. Kate slapped the tears off her cheeks. She had no right to cry. No right to suffer for the women who had died at his hands. The emotional pain she harbored was nothing compared to what they'd endured: the humiliation and torture. Their deaths were probably a relief.

Consensual role-playing? Who did Trask think he was kidding?

Unfortunately too many people. Including many of her superiors back then. Now they believed her, but only because Paige had died.

If only Kate hadn't acted so soon . . .

If only she'd followed her instincts . . .

If only Paige hadn't lied to her . . .

A lot of good all that did her now. And how could she blame Paige? Kate couldn't very well yell at her partner about backup that never arrived. Because Paige was dead.

If Kate saw Trask again, he would die.

Even if she had to die along with him.

His first kill had been an accident.

It was early morning. Far too early for the sun, too early for the birds. The time he liked best, alone, to think.

Remember . . .

They'd been sixteen, two young lovers exploring as only eager amateurs could. Not really knowing what they were doing, but enjoying the thrill of being sexual, of tasting forbidden fruit.

He'd wanted her forever, and he always got what he wanted. He was the son of wealth and power; few dared to say no. And Monique had loved being his girl. She had a mouth on her that wouldn't quit, knew how to use it. He'd suspected she'd practiced giving blow jobs on other boys—or maybe men—because she was too good to be a novice. But in bed, she had been a virgin, her telltale blood marking his sheets.

For six months they joyfully had intercourse, and were inseparable. But for him, it was never enough. He pushed Monique for more. Role-playing. Pain. *Her* pain. At first she was amicable. Anything to please him.

"Not like that," she told him that last time, panting. They were in the pool house at his family's estate. He had her on all fours, wearing a leash. He wanted her from behind. Her ass was so firm, so round, so perfect.

"You'll like it." He pushed her down.

"No, I won't."

Defiant. A bubble of anger surfaced. He would not let her say no.

"Are you jerking me around?"

"Of course not, I—"

"If you don't want to play, get out."

"You don't mean that!" Monique's voice quivered. She glanced over her shoulder, hurt, a little fear in her eyes. He stared, his entire body reacting to that faint panic on her face. He wanted more of that.

"Please," she whispered. "I love you."

"Bullshit. You don't know what love is."

"Maybe *you're* the one with the problem. Can't you get off without stupid games?"

How dare she talk to him like that! He had no problems getting off. She had liked the games, until they became too much for her, and then she had the nerve to say *he* had a problem?

She stood up, naked but for the collar and leash. She looked around for her clothing.

He slapped her. A red welt rose on her cheek. It didn't surprise him that he'd hit her. What surprised him was that he felt no regret.

"I'm sorry," he said automatically. His penis was rock solid again.

She glared. "Don't *ever* do that again."

"I won't. I promise."

He kissed her. Touched her where she liked. At first she protested feebly, but he knew what she wanted, knew the words that made her bend to his will, and soon she was all over him. He pushed her down to the floor and fucked her the way she asked for it. She moaned.

"Just. Like. That," she begged.

His eyes fell to her smooth, white neck. He stared at the silky skin, a sheen of sweat glistening in the sunlight streaming through the windows. The dip in her throat, her muscles straining as her hips met his, working herself up to an orgasm, the sleek outline of her clavicle as she arched her back.

"Don't stop," she panted.

Her neck looked so good.

His hands went behind her head and he kissed her. Then he moved them down, brought his thumbs around. Caressed that hollow of her neck.

Slowly he squeezed. She didn't know what he was doing at first, didn't know until it was too late.

She grabbed at his hands but couldn't speak.

The fear that had touched her face earlier now exploded, her terror real. He watched her eyes as his hands maintained the pressure. He continued fucking her, his orgasm building, her eyes panicked, her fists pounding on him.

He held on too long. Later he had tried to tell himself that he didn't do it on purpose, that it had been an accident. That he had just wanted to maximize his pleasure. And he had. He'd never experienced such a high. Every inch of his skin radiated with power, as if every cell orgasmed as one, his entire body immersed in a forbidden pleasure.

She was convulsing beneath him when he finally let go, his body one with the universe. He saw everything with a clarity he knew he'd attempt to re-create. By then it was too late for Monique. He'd crushed the bone in her neck.

He watched her die.

Trask found it ironic that Monique's death all those years ago had come around full circle. He'd enlisted the help of his friends to dispose of the body. He should have known Trevor Conrad was weak. He'd had to kill Trevor, too, but Trask couldn't make Trevor disappear as easily as Monique.

And now "Trevor" had brought Lucy to him. Lucy, who looked so much like Monique that Trask felt sixteen again.

He couldn't wait to relive the experience.

FOUR

DILLON PACED the small room the task force had set up to find Lucy. Special Agent Joseph Garcia was working with Patrick to pore through code on Lucy's computer, as well as the feed that was coming in from an unknown server. The feed that showed Lucy in her bra and jeans, tied to the floor, terrified. Though he wanted to, Dillon couldn't take his eyes off her.

Connor had left the room immediately after Lucy's shirt was ripped off. Carina went after him. That was nearly an hour ago. Time was not on their side.

It was a countdown to murder.

They had less than forty-five hours to find Lucy. Though saving her life was their number one priority, Dillon wanted to find her *now*, to save her from what was about to happen—what his sixth sense, his experience, told him would inevitably happen.

Dillon turned when the door opened, expecting Connor and Carina to return. Instead a tall, lanky cop entered the room. Special Agent Quinn Peterson's professional attire was rumpled and he carried a jacket over his shoulder and a thick file folder under one arm.

Nick Thomas made the introductions. Nick had worked with Peterson on the Butcher investigation in Montana. It helped that Nick trusted the FBI agent, but Lucy was not *their* sister. They didn't have to face Rosa and Pat Kincaid and tell them that their daughter was about to be raped in public for the sick pleasure of everyone who ponied up the money to watch.

Peterson dumped his jacket and paperwork on the table and turned to Garcia. "Any developments?"

Garcia shook his head. "Just what I told you on the phone. He raised the ante."

"Any headway on the feed?"

"He has better security than the Pentagon. But Kincaid here is a pro."

Dillon spoke. "Agent Peterson, what do you know about the man who has my sister? You've obviously dealt with him in the past."

At that moment, Carina walked in with Connor, who saw Peterson and made a beeline for him. "What the hell is going on? Where's my sister? Why was she taken?"

Dillon tried to give his brother a look to steady his temper, but it failed. Connor was acting out what Dillon felt inside: a deep rage and sense of failure in protecting their youngest sister.

"Sit down, Mr. Kincaid," Peterson said, unfazed.

"I'll stand." Connor crossed his arms.

Dillon sat, wanting answers. Peterson seated himself across from him. "You're the forensic psychiatrist, right?" Peterson asked Dillon.

"Correct."

"This is for you." Quinn pushed over the file folder. "A copy of everything we have on Trask."

"Trask?"

Peterson nodded. "That's the name we know him by. He's calling himself Trevor Conrad now. His name has changed a half dozen times that we know of, but his real identity remains a mystery. We have his prints from a case five years ago, but they haven't matched anything on record. He's not in the system."

"He's been doing exactly *what* for how long?"

Peterson took a deep breath, glanced at everyone in the room, then focused on Dillon. "I'm not going to lie to you. Trask has killed at least nine young women over the past ten years. Before he went underground five years ago, he was a semilegitimate businessman running an online porn website."

"How'd you get his prints?"

"Off a murder weapon. We have no name, but we have matched them to a long-standing snuff-film distributor who ran a company called Achilles Film Distribution."

"Arrogant," Dillon said. "He knows he's not in the system so he doesn't even try to hide his identity."

"Trask is the walking definition of arrogance," Peterson said. "We know he still runs—through shell corporations, fake identities, and some real people— legal pornography websites. Live webcam sex acts, stripping, pornographic downloads, things like that."

"And you haven't been able to track him from that?"

"A task force worked for a solid year trying to unravel his network after one of his actresses disappeared and it appeared she'd been killed online. There was no proof, however, and the employees of his company claimed she'd just quit.

"The task force was dismantled, but two agents continued to investigate on their own time. Trask's organization came apart when he abducted one of those agents during an unsanctioned sting. He made a federal agent part of his show. He and his crew raped and murdered her live on the Internet, knowing the FBI would see it. Then he disappeared. Our team was"—he gestured helplessly with his hands—"torn apart. And because Trask went into hiding for two years, every trail we had turned cold.

"He popped up three years ago with another live murder and has killed five more women since Agent Henshaw died. The bodies of three earlier kills—April Klinger, Denise Arno, and Erica Gomez—have never been found, but we have evidence that they are in fact dead."

"And you can't find him?" Connor leaned over and put his hands on the table. "That doesn't say much about our federal law enforcement, does it?"

Peterson dipped his head in partial acknowledgment, but his clenched jaw told Dillon he was angry. "We lost two good agents five years ago. We're not going to lose more."

"But you're willing to sacrifice my sister!" Connor pushed himself away from the table and ran a nervous hand through his hair.

"We're not *willing* to sacrifice anyone," Quinn responded.

"So what is the FBI doing?" Dillon kept his voice composed while his stomach churned. He was trying to keep things calm even when he felt anything but.

Peterson slapped a hand on the thick folder now in

front of Dillon. "*This* is who we're up against. A man without remorse, a man who gets his kicks from raping, torturing, and murdering women. But make no mistake about it, he's in it for another reason, too: to make money. The legal porn industry is a multi-billion-dollar business; the illegal porn industry is worth even more. He thrives on the risk, on taunting us, on being smarter than anyone else. You read his file, Dr. Kincaid, and let me know what you think."

Dillon kept his voice low, but his tone radiated his own anger and helplessness. "From what you've told us so far, we have less than forty-five hours to find my sister before she's dead. This isn't pornography or sex slaves. This is *murder.*"

Peterson curtly nodded.

"What do we need to do? Between all of us we can pull together a million dollars, maybe." Dillon glanced at his siblings.

"He isn't holding her for ransom," Peterson said.

"But we need resources to find him, don't we? You're basically saying that you don't have the time, money, or manpower to track him down before Lucy's time is up."

Peterson opened his mouth, then closed it, then said, "To be perfectly honest, by the time we found out about the women after our agent was murdered, the countdown was too tight. We tried and failed to isolate the feed. And by the time the girls were dead, he had closed shop. He sends out false leads that we follow, wasting time. But we can't *not* follow up. We found one of the victims the day after, but by that time he'd cleared out completely and the rape and murder were already available for download. We have more time now—more time than we've ever had. That's in our favor. This is the number one priority of our e-crimes unit."

"What about tracking the money?" Patrick spoke up. "The credit cards, the bank accounts? No one can funnel millions of dollars around the world without drawing the attention of the IRS and FBI."

"True. Remember how Capone went down. Money. We're working that angle with the Treasury Department. But this guy is good. Off-shore accounts, lots of cash, lots of movement. Every time we think we're close—and we have seized several of his accounts—he changes tactics."

"Like a chameleon," Dillon said. "Constantly changing to blend in with the environment."

"For all we know, he could be the CEO of a major corporation, or a self-employed accountant."

"He would have to be financially savvy," Dillon agreed. "Someone with expert knowledge of banking, investments, money exchange, tax laws. He knows too much about the system to be an amateur."

"Absolutely," Peterson said.

"Which would suggest he went to school, has a degree, possibly worked in, still works in, the finance arena."

Peterson nodded. "Our top profiler indicated the same thing."

Dillon opened the file in front of him as Carina asked, "You said you found out about the feeds of the other victims too late to stop him. But we have time with Lucy. How did you find it so quickly?"

Peterson said nothing and Dillon looked up at him, read his expression. "An informant?" he asked.

Peterson dipped his head. "Of sorts."

"Can this person help us isolate the feed? Someone willing to help?"

"She's more than willing to help, but not us."

"Why not?" Carina demanded. "Doesn't she know a life is at stake?"

"More than anyone," Peterson said, "but I don't know where she is. She feeds me information and I forward it to the appropriate people."

"She can't be hard to find," Patrick said.

"She doesn't want to be found," Peterson said. "I tried to bring her back with this case, but she's not buying it. If she learns anything, she'll let me know."

"That's not good enough!" Connor exclaimed.

Dillon listened to what Quinn Peterson said—and what he didn't say. "Who is she?"

"A former FBI agent."

"And?"

Joseph Garcia spoke up. "Kate Donovan is notorious in the department. You either love her or you hate her. Agent Paige Henshaw was Donovan's partner. They set up the sting after Trask was suspected of killing a teenage girl online. But—and no one is exactly sure what happened because Donovan disappeared—apparently she and Henshaw set up a sting without any authority. They walked into a trap. Henshaw was kidnapped, raped, and stabbed to death. Donovan missed saving her by minutes."

"Or getting herself killed as well," Peterson mumbled.

"Why is she a *former* agent?" Dillon asked. "Did she quit?"

Garcia raised his eyebrows, glanced at Peterson. "That was before my time. I only know the rumors."

Peterson sighed. "When Agent Henshaw went missing, Kate was told to step back. The Office of Professional Responsibility wanted to talk to her about why they set up the sting without backup and in direct violation of their orders. Instead, Kate went underground to find her partner. She resurfaced only to ask for backup, but when teams were sent to two false locations and she claimed she'd finally isolated the feed, it was the case of crying wolf. No one believed her, and after the death of one agent and Henshaw still missing, the powers that be refused to act on unsubstantiated data. After Paige Henshaw died, Kate disappeared. She was right that last time, but the FBI had acted too late."

Dillon stared at the documents in front of him, pages of reports about the activities of "Trask." The films, rapes, murders. Suspected and proven. His extensive pornography network.

"Trask thinks of himself as playing a role like an actor. But he considers himself superior to Hollywood types," Dillon said slowly. "He's smart, probably a genius-level IQ, but for him I think this is more a game, a sense of grandstanding, showing off his intelligence. But why not fraud? Theft? Hacking into banks? Something about this manner of gamesmanship, this online show, fuels his fantasy. There's something very personal in his choice of murder."

"Yeah, he gets his thrills from killing women,"

Connor spat out. "Talking about this bastard isn't getting us any closer to finding Lucy."

Dillon stared at Connor, wishing he could release his own rage and frustration, but he would leave that to his more volatile brother. "If we don't understand him, we'll never find him."

"Fuck that! We're sitting around doing nothing while Lucy is . . . is—" Connor couldn't finish. He stared at the computer screen, drawing all their eyes to a half-naked Lucy. Scared and vulnerable. Tears coated Connor's eyes and he ran a hand over his face. Carina squeezed his arm.

"I'm sorry, Dil." Connor's voice was thick with emotion.

Dillon caught his brother's eye, nodded. "I want to talk to Kate Donovan," Dillon said to Peterson. "Do you have any way to reach her?"

Peterson looked uncomfortable. Garcia spoke. "I need to take a leak. Can I get anyone coffee?"

"Thanks, Joe." Peterson watched him leave. "He knows I've been talking to Kate. He wants plausible deniability, and I don't blame him. Her former boss wants her head on a platter."

"Why does she trust you?" Dillon asked.

"We were in the same class at the Academy. And I wasn't working the case five years ago when Paige Henshaw died. She considers me neutral."

"And are you?"

"Hell, no. I'm on Kate's side. Always have been. But I can't give her the one thing she needs."

"Which is?" asked Dillon.

"Immunity."

The complexity and sensitivity of the situation was

becoming clear to Dillon. But Lucy's life was at stake, and if Kate Donovan could help save her, Dillon would find a way to convince her to help.

"Kate Donovan's been tracking this killer for over five years," Dillon said. "She has the answers. I just need to ask the right questions."

"You should know that some of the information she's turned up was false. No doubt a setup by Trask, but the Bureau doesn't like wasting resources setting up rescues or stings when there's no one to rescue. Two years ago we almost lost a team of agents in a trap. Kate warned us it might be, but, well, it was just the case of crying wolf all over again. We had her analysis and methodology, but didn't have time to run the scenarios ourselves. The FBI won't do that again, but being methodical takes time."

"Time that Lucy doesn't have," Dillon said quietly.

Peterson stood, walked over to where Patrick was sitting at the computer station in the corner. Five screens had been set up, two for the FBI, Lucy's computer, and Patrick's laptop. The fifth screen showed Lucy via the webcam.

There'd been little movement for the last twenty minutes. Every few moments Lucy tried in vain to break free from her chains. Her jaw was clenched, her neck taut, as she stoically held up against the terror that glistened in her dark eyes. Her mouth moved, but sound had been turned off at the source.

If Lucy died, Dillon didn't know if he could hold everyone together. His family was already fractured, yet even under tragedy they'd managed to stay together. Lucy's death would break them. Dillon couldn't let her die, especially like this.

Peterson brought up an instant messaging system on the FBI computer and typed in a code, then wrote:

I need to talk to you.

A moment later.

User not online.

"Dammit!" Connor exclaimed. "I can't sit around here and do nothing."

"What do you suggest we do, Mr. Kincaid?" Peterson said. "Where would you look? The world is a big place. We've narrowed his network down to the North American continent, but from Canada to the Panama Canal? A lot of territory to cover. Kate shares her technology with me, and I give it to the powers that be. They're tracking him just like Kate is. Thing is, she's on it twenty-four/seven. She eats, sleeps, and breathes this bastard. If anyone is going to find him, it's her."

"Even with all her mistakes?" Connor questioned. "The traps and the dead ends? Sounds like she *should* be ignored."

"It sounds bad, but you have to understand the environment we're in. Kate provides information with reservation. She doesn't *know* if it's legitimate, but she can't in good conscience withhold it. In the past, some people have jumped the gun and then blamed her when the operation went south."

"She'll go after him on her own if she believes she knows where he is," Dillon said quietly.

Peterson impatiently tapped his fingers on the table as he stared at the screen. "You have her pegged."

"May I?" Dillon motioned to the computer.

"Be my guest."

Peterson walked to where Nick and Carina stood in the corner. They spoke quietly as Dillon put himself in the mind-set of a vigilante FBI agent ridden with guilt and anger. And pain. Lots of pain.

He began typing.

> Kate, my name is Dillon Kincaid and I'm Lucy's brother.
>
> User not online.
>
> I think you are online. I think you're waiting for word from Quinn Peterson. Listen to me. We need your help.
>
> User not online.
>
> Lucy is eighteen years old. She graduated from high school yesterday. She's smart and beautiful and the youngest of seven kids. I'm her oldest brother.
>
> User not online.
>
> Lucy's going to Georgetown in the fall. She wants to be a diplomat. She's well versed in languages, speaks four fluently. She loves Irish folk music and Cuban rock.
>
> User not online.
>
> Eleven years ago my nephew was murdered. Justin and Lucy were best friends, seven years old, and Justin was kidnapped from his bed and killed. My older sister Nelia never recovered from Justin's murder. My family was changed forever. My sister Carina and two of my brothers became cops, wanting to stop predators like the one who killed Justin. I became a forensic psychiatrist. I get into the heads of killers. I think I can find Trask. I can find this predator who kills women for pleasure and profit. But I need your help.

Nothing.

Dillon's heart pounded. Had he hit a nerve?

Belatedly,

User not online.

"You're online, Kate," Dillon mumbled, "and you're going to talk." He turned to Patrick. "Start a trace."

FIVE

No one was in the room. It was just her, half-naked, and the damn blinking red eye of a camera. Filming her.

Lucy didn't know exactly what was happening, but she feared her life was on the line. After all, she'd seen their faces. Isn't that what she'd always heard? If you can identify them, they won't let you go.

They're going to kill me.

Her face burned remembering how Trevor had told someone that she was a virgin. He'd been standing in the corner, talking into a phone, as if he were a game-show announcer, talking about paying to watch her.

She might be a virgin, but she wasn't so naive that she didn't know exactly what he meant. He was going to rape her.

She swallowed, a sob escaping before she could stop the betraying sound of fear. She didn't want to show him anything. No emotion. She'd lie there and let him do whatever he was going to do. She remembered Carina teaching her how to fight back, giving Lucy a top-notch self-defense class every couple of months. Kick, scratch, scream, run. Get away.

None of it helped when you were already tied up.

But she'd also learned that rapists got off on the fight, on subduing their victims. He'd called her "feisty," as if that were a good thing, a *fun* thing. She wouldn't do it. She'd bite her tongue before she screamed or begged for mercy.

The blinking eye bothered her, though. The camera. They were recording her. Why? To watch the rape over and over again? So he could show it to his sick friends?

Bile rose in her throat and she swallowed it uneasily, the vomit burning. She swallowed again.

Hold it together, Lucy. Think.

Someone would find her. They had to. By now her family knew she was missing. It was dark, late at night or early morning, she didn't know.

They would be looking for her. Connor and Carina and Patrick and Dillon—and they had friends in high places. She had to hold on to that hope. And anything that might happen; well, put that aside. Put that away. Surviving was the most important thing. Everything else, she could deal with in time, right?

But her life—she had to survive, whatever brutality they had planned for her.

Where was she? The room was dimly lit, probably just bright enough for her body to be filmed. There was a single window, but the blinds were drawn. Two doors. She knew one led to a hall. The other? A bathroom? Closet? She didn't know.

Trevor had brought her here on a boat. She'd heard something about an island. One of the guys said they were approaching an island.

What island? Catalina? Avalon? How could that be? Too many people and tourists. Maybe he'd taken her south, to an island off Mexico. Away from America, from safety.

The blinking eye of the camera mocked her. *Lu-cy. Lu-cy.*

"Enjoy the show for free" Trevor had said.

Was that camera *live*?

Her body involuntarily shook and she groaned out a cry of misery. How? What was he doing with it? Could people see her right now? Like *this*?

She pulled at her restraints, but they were tight.

"You fucking bastard!" she screamed. "Let me go!" Lucy strained and pulled.

On the other side of the door, someone laughed. It wasn't Trevor.

It was a female voice. And it didn't sound completely . . . right.

That scared Lucy even more.

Kate typed.

User not online.

Dillon Kincaid was persistent, she would give him that. Why was she even reading his pleas? She should have turned off the monitor when he first tried to draw her into conversation.

She was punishing herself. *You want to know everything about the girl who's going to die next.*

Punishment? Where the hell had that thought come from? Kate was trying to prevent Lucy Kincaid's murder. She still had a chance. Every one of Kate's computers was working at full capacity. She had all the server space and computer resources she needed. The fastest drives, hundreds of gigabytes of memory. Nothing was slowing her down. Kate would find Lucy and she would save her.

Like she couldn't save Paige and the others.

Dillon Kincaid was still writing.

My brother Patrick is a computer genius. He can help you. With your skills and his skills, together we can find Lucy before it's too late. Talk to him, please.

There were good computer people, but no one was as good as Kate Donovan. All Patrick could do would be slow her down asking stupid questions about why she did this, why she did that. And he had a vested interest, his attention would be split. He wouldn't be focused on the task, instead watching what was happening to his sister.

She typed.

User not online.

She glanced at Lucy Kincaid on the center screen. She was tugging at her restraints, yelling something. *Fucking* was one of the words. Kate smiled bitterly. Lucy was a fighter; Kate liked her.

Dammit, Lucy, I don't want you to die.

Eighteen years old, her entire life ahead of her. Kate wanted to put a bullet in Trask's head so badly she could almost feel her finger press the trigger, see the bullet enter his skull, picture his brains splatter on the wall. He deserved torture, but she'd be content with a quick death.

Dillon Kincaid sent another message.

Kate, I know you want to help. You've been helping for five years. You lost people you cared about. You've been running all this time, but still haven't forgotten the victims. I have Quinn Peterson's file here. His private file. I know what you've done, and I'm in awe of you. I also know what Trevor Conrad has done to these women—you know him as Trask.

Kate, together we can find him. As I read Peterson's notes and your messages to him over the last five years, I see who this man is. Arrogant. Ruthless. Remorseless. He's done this many times. Before Paige. Technology gave him the ability to broadcast his sick fantasies, but don't think you pushed him into murder.

He'd been killing for years before you and Paige uncovered his crimes. You were going after him because of a missing girl. Well, guess what? If we dig further, we'll find dozens of women he's killed. You sent him underground. You've already saved lives.

Paige did not die in vain.

Please help me find Lucy. Don't let her be his victim. Talk to me, Kate.

Her hands shook. She wanted to talk to Dillon Kincaid. He seemed to understand things even her friend Quinn Peterson didn't.

But she couldn't. Who was he, really? She couldn't be stupid. Kate already had a plan, it was solid, she had to execute it.

She typed.

User not onlone.

She didn't notice her typo until after she hit enter.

Hello, Kate.

She shut down the program, her heart pounding. He'd gotten to her, dammit.

Movement on the center screen caught her attention. Roger Morton walked into view.

The countdown read 44:05:00. Roger unchained Lucy, held her in front of him, his head close to hers. Kate reached over and turned on the volume.

". . . pretty for the camera, Lucy."

"Fuck you," Lucy said.

"Oh, we'll do that, sweetheart, I promise. But for now your fans just want a sneak peek."

With a flick of his wrist, Roger extracted a butterfly knife and sliced open Lucy's bra. Kate gasped, watched a thin trail of blood where the tip of the knife had nicked her breast.

Lucy stifled a scream and said, "Y-you bastard!"

She struggled. Roger laughed as he easily held her hands tightly behind her. Her struggles made her breasts bounce in the camera, perfect titillation for the sick perverts who watched Trask's show.

Roger kissed Lucy's neck and she used her head to wallop his. The hard crunch of bone hitting bone made Kate's head ache.

"Bitch." Roger was pissed. He liked feisty, but he didn't like getting hurt.

Suddenly Roger cried out and Lucy ran out of the camera frame. The shot had been a close-up, but there was no mistaking that she'd kicked him in the balls. She was out of view for one, two, three seconds. Then she fell into view, pushed roughly onto the thin beige carpet.

Trask didn't show his face, but Kate knew him from his broad build and the short-cropped blond hair. He bent over Lucy, slapped her once, then again, then kneeled as he tied her back down. She fought him, and Roger grabbed her legs. Lucy shouted obscenities, her hand working furiously. She bit Trask on the forearm and he slapped her so hard the side of her head hit the mat, her cheek instantly red with his handprint.

Her hand. Something about Lucy's hand. She was repeating the same motions over and over. It looked like sign language.

Then the feed stopped, froze.

The countdown read 44:00:00.

"Dammit, I paid, you bastard!" Kate spun around to another computer, frantically typed until she brought up Trask's secure server and paid him again to watch the feed. It took her nearly ten minutes to get through. His server was getting a lot of traffic today, she thought bitterly.

A message popped up on the screen.

Hello, Kate Donovan. Just wanted to make sure it was you, sweetheart. This one's free. Enjoy.

"What happened?" Dillon asked. "Why did it freeze?"

Peterson sat at a vacant terminal and typed in a bunch of codes. "We have to pay to watch. I thought this was taken care of."

A message came up on the screen several minutes later.

Hello, FBI. I see you've gotten much better at hiding your identity, but you're not as good as I am. I don't think I want you watching this one. You might get the wrong idea. Remember, this is consensual fantasy role-playing, but I'd rather not have to explain it to a jury.

Too bad you don't know where Kate is. I gave her the feed for free. It's ironic. All these years she's been trying to find me, getting close, very close, but all she did was lead me right to her door.

"Shit! The bastard!" Quinn typed frantically, then the computer froze. Blue screen.

Quinn spoke quietly yet frantically on the phone. Dillon read Quinn's file as he paced, feeling more helpless than at any other time in his life.

Thirty minutes later Patrick said quietly, "I have it."

"How'd you do that?" Quinn and Dillon stood over Patrick's shoulder.

43:31:45.

Again on screen, Lucy was restrained on the floor, tears running down her cheeks. She was looking straight up at the ceiling. Her breasts were bare, blood on her stomach, a bruise already forming on her cheek.

Dillon didn't know if he was more relieved he had missed witnessing his sister's humiliation or furious that it had happened in the first place.

"I hacked the feed, falsified the DNS so he doesn't see it coming from a government server, and sent in Nick's credit card information. I didn't want him running names to numbers and seeing a 'Kincaid' on the list," Patrick added.

Peterson was trying to text message Kate to warn her. "Dammit! Kate shut down her system. She's in danger."

"Lucy is in danger!" Connor exclaimed.

"Kate will contact us," Dillon said.

"How can you be sure?" Connor threw his arms up in the air. "I can't stand around and do nothing."

"So don't," said Dillon.

"Stop playing shrink and tell me straight."

Tensions were high, and Nick stepped between the two brothers. "I think what Dillon is suggesting is that we try to track him through other means."

Connor sighed, rubbed a hand over his rough face. "The money."

"Exactly," Dillon said. "The payments need to be going somewhere. And, frankly, I don't care about the law right now." He glanced at Peterson. "Find the financial institution, get the DA, Andrew Stanton, to write any warrant we need, and see what trail we can find."

Peterson went through the file he'd given Dillon and handed Connor a stack of paper. "These are the known bank accounts on this guy. Most have been shut down, many are inactive. We haven't found a pattern to them, only that he opens them right before a live feed, and closes them immediately after, transferring the funds to another account. Last time we seized most of his money, and now we don't know what he'll do. Our profiler thinks he'll withdraw the money every couple of hours to prevent losing it all."

Patrick said, "Have Nick's credit card company track the payment. Get every confirmation number you can, contact information. It'll be a dummy company, but eventually it'll lead somewhere. It has to."

Connor wasn't happy, but it gave him something to do. Nick clapped him on the back. "Where can we work?" he asked Peterson.

"I'll get you set up." They left with Carina.

Dillon and Patrick were alone. Dillon watched Lucy on the camera and admitted to his brother, "I'm scared for her."

"So am I." Patrick was reading code that seemed to fly by on the computer, his eyes darting back and forth. Focused, determined.

Dillon paced. What good was it to understand why someone kills when he couldn't prevent him from doing it?

Kate was the key. She had confronted Trask, faced him. If Dillon could bounce theories off her, it would help him put together a better profile, one that could lead Dillon to Trask. And to Lucy.

If he could find his first kill, Dillon was certain that it would lead to his identity. A killer's first victim almost always led to him. The FBI had to have run like crimes.

Dillon needed to put together a visual time line. He flipped open Peterson's file and had just started creating a time line on the white board when Peterson's computer beeped. Dillon looked at the screen.

"It's her," Patrick said.

Does Lucy know sign language?

Dillon typed.

Yes.

I'm sending you a feed of the last thirty seconds before it was cut off. Watch her hands. I think she's signing in Spanish, but my Spanish is rusty.

Kate, you need to be careful. He knows where you are.

A long pause before a link came through and the words:

I know.

Dillon clicked on the link. He tried to focus on Lucy's hands, but both he and Patrick tensed as they watched their sister brutalized as she was wrestled to the floor by two men. They replayed it, watching only her hands.

Kate was right. She was signing in Spanish.

Boat. Island. Before sunrise. Boat. Island. Before sunrise.

"She's telling us the time. That the sun hasn't come up yet."

"It's four thirty in the morning right now," Patrick said. "She could be close by."

"In the same time zone." Which meant she could be thirty minutes away or hours.

"On an island. There are dozens of islands off the coast."

"In this time zone, hundreds," Dillon corrected. "I don't think he's close," Dillon added.

"Why? You're basing it on a hunch, not on fact." Patrick was getting agitated. "She could be on Anacapa or San Miguel. An hour or less from where we are by helicopter! We need to check the Channel Islands right now."

"We have less than two days to find her. We can't possibly storm every island off the coast. And your hunch that it's the Channel Islands? Filled with tourists this time of year."

"There's a lot of small islands in the chain. They could be on one of those."

"But what if we're wrong? We have no evidence, and it would take days to search every island even with the manpower of the FBI behind us."

"Dammit, we have to try!"

Dillon tamped down his own temper, knowing his brother was teetering on the edge. First Connor, now Patrick. Well, so was Dillon. He was just better at holding back. Assessing. Being the reasonable, responsible, mature Kincaid. Sometimes he wished he could explode with the injustice he saw in humanity. But he couldn't. People depended on his stability, particularly his family.

He tried to calmly explain his reasoning. "He had Lucy for more than twelve hours before putting the webcam on her. I think the bulk of that time was getting her to his destination. They went by boat, at least for part of the trip. Twelve hours on a ship could get them all the way to the Canadian border, or to the tip of Baja California."

"Or he was waiting for midnight," Patrick said. "Which is when the feed started. Are you willing to put Lucy's life on the line for a theory?"

"Are you?" Dillon responded.

Peterson walked back in, immediately on alert when he felt the tension between the brothers. "What happened?"

Dillon told him about Lucy's clues.

"I'll get the Coast Guard on alert up the entire

West Coast. I think he went to Mexico or Canada," Peterson added.

"Why?"

"We've never found one of his sites in the United States. When we found Meghan, it was on a small island near Prince Edward Island in eastern Canada. But if that's the case, the sun would already have risen. He used a private, secluded estate on a Caribbean island at one point, but we raided it and seized all his property."

"So Lucy's right? She's on an island?"

Peterson nodded. "Very likely."

"But we still know next to nothing," Patrick mumbled, clicking frenetically on his keyboard.

"We know she's on the West Coast, which is more than we knew five minutes ago," Dillon said.

"I found her," Patrick said.

"Lucy?" Dillon and Peterson said simultaneously.

"Kate Donovan. At least I've isolated her general area. Mexico, near the west Texas border. A couple hours out of Hidalgo, in the mountains, north of Monterrey. But she went off-line as soon as you downloaded the feed."

Peterson looked at the map. "Dammit, that area is full of rebels, drug smugglers, gunrunners. We can get into Monterrey, but that means a couple hours' detour. Direct? Virtually impossible."

Dillon stared at Patrick. "I can find her."

Patrick shook his head, mixed emotions crossing his boyish face. "Don't."

"I have to. For Lucy. Just get me a more accurate location by the time Jack calls back."

"He might not even call," said Patrick.

"He'll call me," Dillon insisted.

"Who's Jack?" Peterson asked.

"Our brother," Patrick said. "Jack is Dillon's twin."

"Another Kincaid?" Peterson mumbled.

Jack returned Dillon's call thirty minutes later.

"Hello, Jack," Dillon answered.

"What's wrong?" Jack asked without preamble. They hadn't seen or spoken to each other in eleven years, but Jack got right to the point.

Dillon didn't waste time. "Lucy has been kidnapped. I need your help finding an ex-FBI agent who's hiding out in the eastern Mexican mountains."

"Are you sure? Lucy's an adult. Maybe she just walked."

"If you have an Internet connection, I can send you the feed where she's half naked and tied to the floor." Dillon's voice vibrated with anger. Jack had gone off to do his own thing twenty years ago and came home only for funerals. He didn't know Lucy, and he wanted to believe she had just left the family without a word?

"Of course I'm sure she's been kidnapped." Dillon suppressed the complex emotions that talking with his brother Jack inevitably stirred. "The FBI has a task force in place. Her kidnapper has done this before. And if we don't find her in forty-three hours, she'll be dead. Murdered live on the Internet. Do you think I would call you if it weren't a life-or-death emergency? If I didn't think you might be in a position to help?"

"And you want me to track this FBI agent down why?"

"She has some sort of compound where she's been tracking this killer for the last couple of years. She has her own issues with the FBI and won't come back voluntarily."

"So you want me to kidnap her and bring her to you?"

"No. I want you to bring me to her. She's on a mountain, about an hour north of Monterrey, which according to the FBI is dangerous territory."

"Dangerous is an understatement," Jack said. "I'm not bringing you anywhere. I'll find the agent myself and compel her to return."

Dillon said, "No, Jack. You'll bring both me and Patrick to her. She has computer files we need and the ability to find Lucy. She thinks she can do it on her own, but I think our killer might just *want* her to find him, that he might leak her information to trap her. And Lucy is his bait."

"Why do you care about this renegade FBI agent? Who cares about the damn feds? Nothing but backstabbing bureaucrats with guns. I'll help you find Lucy. I have friends all over the world."

The quiet arrogant confidence in Jack's voice was typical.

"No," Dillon said. "Why is it always your way, Jack? You know very little about this situation. I'm certainly not putting Lucy's life in your hands."

"But you're putting her life in *your* hands, Doctor? Since when were you in the military? Or the police academy? Do you even know how to shoot a gun?"

"Forget it, Jack. I'll find Kate on my own. I'm sorry I called you. I guess you really are no longer family."

Click.

Dillon stared at his cell phone. He didn't like to gamble, but he also believed he understood his twin. He hoped he did.

For twenty years, Dillon had wondered what had happened to Jack that he would turn his back on his family and devote his life solely to the military—whatever the hell it was Jack did for them. Jack had only come home for Justin's funeral, a sad testament to a man who as a boy had been Dillon's best friend.

But Jack was fiercely loyal, had been from early childhood. They'd moved every six to twelve months while Colonel Kincaid was moved from military base to military base. They could only count on themselves and their family, because friendships were fleeting.

Jack joined the military when he turned eighteen and then something happened. Something that seemed to prevent him from keeping in touch with his family. Jack never spoke of it, never even acknowledged that anything *had* happened.

But Dillon knew his twin brother. Family used to be important to him.

The phone rang five minutes later.

"I'll meet you in four hours at a bar called La Honda in Hidalgo, Texas," Jack said. "Don't bring anyone with you."

Dillon wrote down the information Jack imparted and hung up. He was glad he was right about Jack, that he would come through after all.

Don't bring anyone?

"Patrick, we're going to Texas. I'm going to find Agent Peterson and see how fast he can get us out there."

SIX

"Good morning, sunshine."

Trevor Conrad walked into the room, staying out of view of the camera. Lucy must have dozed off. She startled awake.

How could she have even fallen asleep?

She jerked at the ties around her wrists. Her skin was chafed and sore.

"Fuck you, Trevor," she said.

He chuckled. He was *laughing* at her. Lucy's face grew hot with humiliation and anger. Fear was there, too, cold and hot at the same time, making everything in the plain room sharper, with fewer shadows.

Light.

The one covered window blocked the sun, but the quality of light told Lucy it was morning. How long had she been sleeping? It couldn't have been long.

"Lucy, I'd like to reintroduce you to Roger," Trevor said. "You remember him, of course."

The big ugly jerk she'd kicked in the balls when he'd cut off her bra walked in behind Trevor. She watched as he unzipped his jeans.

"No. No no no no!" She shook her head back and forth, as if she thought that if she said it long enough, loud enough, they would go away. She fought her restraints, but they held fast. Warm blood coated her wrists from the chafing ropes.

Trevor laughed softly. "You're such a fabulous actress, Lucy. You may have a future in film." He shrugged. "Or not."

Roger approached and knelt over her, his penis growing rigid. She closed her eyes.

Pretend you're far away.

He pulled her jeans down to her ankles, where they tangled in the ropes at her feet.

The beach. The ocean is rolling up the sand. Seagulls. Kids. Friends. Volleyball.

Something cold and hard touched her skin and her underpants were cut from her body. The hard reality of her fate slapped her and Lucy couldn't pretend it wasn't happening. She couldn't be anywhere else.

She screamed.

Kate tried to ignore what was happening to Lucy Kincaid as she scoured data for any clue that would tell her where the satellite feed was originating. It was hard to avoid it, to avoid remembering Paige. Her eyes watered and her teeth ground together as she tried to suppress her own primal scream at what Lucy now endured.

Damn bastard Trask knew she was watching.

Power.

The enormity of his power structure is what confused Kate. He'd had money at his disposal, even before his online porn sites began to flourish. His corporations paid taxes, filed reports, had a board of directors—all of which had been thoroughly investigated by the FBI and deemed legitimate. In fact, at one point her boyfriend, Evan, also an FBI agent, had told Kate she was chasing a ghost, that Trask didn't exist. That the disappearance of the women she and Paige had been trying to find was unrelated to their jobs as porn stars. That April Klinger hadn't been killed on screen. It had all just been an act, he said.

She'd fought with Evan the week before the sting, before Paige was kidnapped.

They had been in the living room of the small town house they shared near Quantico. She worked at headquarters, while Evan was a special agent in charge out of Washington, D.C. She was in Violent Crimes/Major Offenders, he was in Public Corruption. But he'd served in VCMO for years and had been a great sounding board for her and Paige when they'd been assigned a missing persons case related to the online pornography they routinely monitored for the VCMO unit.

Kate paced as she verbalized her reasoning on the case. It was Sunday, a rare day off for both of them, and Evan had wanted to take his boat out. He was annoyed that she was still in work mode.

"What if April *was* murdered during the play-acting?" Kate asked. "Maybe it was an accident. They didn't mean to kill her. But if they reported it, a half-dozen agencies would be all over their ass, ready to shut them down. So Trask and his people covered it up."

Evan sighed, rubbed a hand over his face. "You interviewed every actor employed by Trask Enterprises and everyone said April was alive and well after the shoot."

"Then where is she? No one *outside* of their studio has seen her. She's no longer working for them."

"The CEO, what's his name, said she quit. Said she was going to Hollywood to do real movies." Evan rolled his eyes.

"The CEO is Roger Morton. You haven't taken my case seriously since the beginning, have you?"

"I've listened to you for *months*, helped analyze data, took my own time to interview witnesses. Don't tell me I haven't taken you seriously. You've spent more time watching online porn than spending time in bed with me. What am I supposed to make of that?"

"That's sick, Evan. This is my *job*. I need to find out what happened to April. Her grandmother deserves to know."

Evan walked over to her, put his hands on her shoulders, looked her in the eye. Evan had been good to her, ever since they'd met two years ago when assigned to the same special task force. Last year he had moved into her town house. He'd been tolerant of Kate's obsessive personality, how she took her cases personally, and up until April Klinger went missing, she'd begun to share her past with him. He knew things about her no one else knew, things she'd lied about to get into the FBI Academy in the first place.

"This is all about you, isn't it, Kate?"

She froze. The last thing she'd expected of Evan was bringing up her past, especially now. Especially like this.

"It has nothing to do with me. You once told me you admired my dedication. If it weren't for me being such a pit bull with evidence, we'd never have found the Williamette Strangler two years ago. You said that yourself."

"I know, but—"

"I *feel* that there's something here. I can't prove it yet. But I know there is. Something about her eyes— don't you see it?"

She pulled out a file and shoved a picture of April under his nose. It was her eyes that told Kate she was dead. The split second of film before the tape was cut.

She didn't know what was sicker: strangling April to death while having sex, or running the segment on the website for months after the murder. It was only after she and Paige started interviewing employees of Trask Enterprises that the download went off-line.

And it killed her that when she'd fought tooth and nail to get a subpoena of the original digital file, it cut off at the exact same spot.

"Kate, I love you." Evan touched her hair, ran a finger lightly over her cheek. "You're a fantastic agent and even now you're becoming a legend in the agency with your computer skills. You've spent the last four months of your life working on a case that has gone nowhere. Put it on the back burner. Other violent crimes out there need your attention. Or maybe you should consider the offer you got last month from the e-crimes unit. They want you. You'll get a raise, you'll get a promotion, and you'll love it. You told me that."

It was true. She'd wanted e-crimes because it was a challenge. But her heart—her soul—was in VCMO. She'd once told Evan that she'd been born to do this job.

"I just can't let April go." Kate implored Evan with

her eyes, took his hands in hers. "You understand, don't you?"

He kissed her hand. "I understand. I just think the case is cold. And you can continue to monitor it, I wouldn't expect you to drop it completely, but it's been *four months*. There's a new hot case every day. This isn't helping you. You've already strained your relationship with everyone else in the unit, including your boss. And Paige isn't making any friends, either."

"She agrees with me. That April was murdered."

"Let's say that she was. That they were filming one of those rape-fantasy scenes Trask is known for. Things got out of hand. April died. Prove it."

"I can't, but if—"

"You can't because they covered it up. Got rid of her body. It could be at the bottom of the Atlantic Ocean for all we know. Unless there's a body or a witness willing to come forward, you got nothing. You're spinning your wheels. And it's hurting *us*. I love you, Kate. I want you to be happy." He kissed her.

The front door opened and Paige burst in. "Kate, guess wh—" She covered her eyes. "Sorry, didn't mean to catch you making out."

Evan swore under his breath.

Kate squeezed his hand. Evan and Paige had butted heads since they'd met. "What's up?" she asked her partner.

"I have someone willing to talk. Remember Denise Arno? She's one of the actresses at Trask. She just contacted me. She quit and is scared to death. Wants to meet with us tonight. She has evidence that April was killed, and that they're planning on smuggling illegals into the country to use as victims."

"When and where?" Kate dropped Evan's hand and grabbed her notebook.

"Ten tonight, at the Jefferson Memorial."

Evan shook his head. "I don't like this."

"Come with us," Kate said. "Maybe you'll understand why this is important."

"I understand," Evan said. "Are you going to have backup?"

Kate tensed. "You think I'm stupid? Or a maverick?"

"No, but—"

"No buts. You don't trust me."

"I think this case has blinded both of you."

"I'm not going into this blind."

Paige interjected. "I already talked to Jeff. He's waiting for us to debrief him. I think we'll get everything we want."

"Jeff Merritt agreed to this?" Evan frowned.

"Of course." Paige pouted. "I outlined the game plan."

Kate turned to Evan. "Please, Evan. It's important to me that you're with me on this. If you don't want to be involved, I understand. It's not your case. But don't turn your back on me."

Evan touched her. "Oh, Kate. I'd never turn my back on you."

Beep beep beep beep beep beep . . .

Kate shook her head, ridding herself of the bittersweet memories. She typed in a series of numbers and stopped the computer from beeping at her.

Five days after that conversation with Evan, he'd

followed her to the sting operation she and Paige had set up. Evan had informed Kate that there was no backup, Merritt hadn't authorized it. He'd looked at Kate as if she'd lied to him. But she hadn't.

She'd repeated what Paige had told her just that morning. She'd never thought to question her partner. She'd never thought her partner would put them in jeopardy.

Evan had died believing Kate had lied to him. It still hurt.

She glanced up at the screen just as Roger climbed off Lucy Kincaid, a crooked grin on the bastard's face. The poor girl was crying, then the picture was cut off. Trask's voice came over the speakers as another "best of" compilation began.

"Lucy wants to clean up after her first act. Wasn't that fabulous? Lucy definitely has a future as an actress. So while she takes care of her business, here are highlights of our past shows."

Kate didn't watch, not this time. She was frantically trying to isolate a frequency. But as soon as the highlights began, Lucy's feed was off the network. Kate was tracking phantoms.

She buried her head in her arms. She'd been so close, then he cut her off. Did he do it on purpose? Or was he trying to set her up, give her a false location like he had with Paige? Could Kate even trust her skills anymore? She was better, much, much better, than five years ago, but so was Trask.

Again, it was all about power. Trask had all the money he could ever want from his pornography trade. He didn't need to kill women to increase his cash flow. And on top of the legitimate money, she suspected he had a number of illegal schemes going on.

So why kill? And why kill online? Why show the world what he was doing?

He thinks he's God.

For five years the FBI had been trying to find Morton and Trask, but they didn't even fully believe Trask existed. The Bureau wanted vengeance for the murder of two federal agents. They'd take anyone and everyone they could. Some believed "Trask" was an alias of Roger Morton's, and no matter how Kate tried to convince them that they were two different people, they'd found no proof that Trask was a separate individual. Through her contact, Special Agent Quinn Peterson, she knew they'd raided Trask Enterprises, arrested and interviewed everyone on staff. But Roger Morton had disappeared, and no one else in the company had ever heard of an individual named Trask. They all believed it was just the name of the company, not related to a living, breathing person. Then, a new CEO was appointed by the board, a man above reproach—other than the fact that he ran a strip club in New York.

There was no evidence that Trask Enterprises had anything to do with Paige's murder.

But Kate knew the truth, even if she couldn't prove it.

SEVEN

THE DIVE BAR in the depressed border town of Hidalgo, Texas, was open from six a.m. until two a.m. Dillon suspected it had never been cleaned. Stale beer, cheap cigarettes, and sweat assaulted his senses as soon as he entered. He approached the bar, sat on a stool, the knowledge that he was far from his comfort zone hitting him hard. He should have brought Connor. He would have fit in better with this rough-and-tumble crowd. And Connor knew how to use a gun. Dillon didn't own one, and hadn't been comfortable with Connor's offer of his backup piece.

The fact that he was the only Kincaid who didn't know how to shoot wasn't lost on him. What was he doing going after a renegade FBI agent? What was he doing trekking through dangerous Mexican territory, enlisting the help of the twin brother he hadn't seen in eleven years?

Lucy. She would die if he didn't do something, and even with all the gun power the Kincaids had—and their ability to use it—only Dillon could think like Trask. And understanding the mind of the killer might just be the key to saving Lucy.

"I told you to come alone."

Dillon hadn't heard Jack approach. He turned to face him. They were not identical, and at first glance one might not think they were brothers at all, aside from the fact that they were both six feet two inches tall. Dillon had light-brown curly hair that he tamed by keeping short compared to Jack's black military cut. Dillon was fair-skinned, green-eyed, lean, and athletic. Jack was dark-skinned, black-eyed, and muscular—not a man you would want to encounter alone. How many men had Jack killed?

Dillon didn't want to think about that. He didn't know why the thought had even come to mind. Jack had been in the military for more than half his life, and in special operations for a decade. Whatever he did, he did with the sanction of the United States government. At least Dillon hoped that was still the case.

"Hello, Jack."

Jack had aged, as evidenced by the lines on his face, the experience in his eyes.

"Deal's off."

Jack started to walk past.

"Don't."

Jack turned, stared at Dillon. "I told you to come alone."

"I'm here alone."

"Connor and Patrick are outside."

"I'm surprised you recognize them."

If Jack was embarrassed or guilty about that fact, he didn't show it.

"This isn't a family reunion," Jack said.

Dillon was slow to anger, but Jack had always been the one to set him off. His voice was low and hard. "The bastard raped Lucy, and people paid to watch.

Are you going to help her or protect your damn pride and ego?"

Jack flinched almost imperceptibly, but Dillon saw it. He'd hit a sore point. Good.

Dillon said, "I need Patrick because he's a computer genius and Agent Kate Donovan has a setup on the mountain that's trying to track the kidnapper's satellite feed. And I couldn't have kept Connor home if I'd tried." He raised an eyebrow. "Connor's a lot like you."

He'd almost not been able to keep his future brother-in-law Nick Thomas back home as well. But Nick had undergone knee surgery three months ago and wouldn't have done well on what promised to be a tortuous trek up the mountain. And they couldn't go slow. Lucy had only thirty-nine hours left.

"You keep them out of my face and out of my business, Dillon."

"Understood."

Jack assessed him, dipped his head. "I have my team ready. We'll escort you up the mountain, then you're on your own."

"So that's it?"

"That's it. I'm not a fucking tour guide, and I have a job to do."

"Right. You have places to go and people to kill."

Jack took a step toward him but Dillon stood his ground.

Jack said, "Stay out of my head."

What had Lucy done to deserve this? She'd gone to church every Sunday with her parents. More or less believed. Tried to be good. She liked that commandment, the one that went "love your neighbor as yourself." She used that as her philosophy of life, and had a lot of good friends. She tried to be a good daughter, a good friend, a good sister.

Why would anyone want to hurt her?

Lucy went back to what she'd heard her older brothers and sisters tell her ad nauseum. There are bad people in the world. They hurt others just because they can. Because they like to. She knew it, intellectually. She was a straight-A student. She had a life, a future she wanted, desperately wanted. All her dreams, everything she wanted to do, had been within her grasp.

But her heart, her soul, couldn't help but think that something she'd done had created this awful situation. Had she hurt someone and not known it? After all, she'd lied to her parents, to everyone, about her online boyfriend.

And look what had happened.

It was her own fault. She'd gotten herself into this disaster. Still, Lucy didn't want to die.

Dear God, listen to me! Don't let him hurt me again. Please. I want to live. I'm sorry I lied. I'm sorry I was stupid. Please don't let me die.

The shame of what had happened hit her, and her body—involuntarily, repeatedly—shook. The red eye of the camera was off. What did that mean? Were they through with her? Would they let her go?

She wanted to believe the answer was yes, but her mind told her no, don't get your hopes up, Lucy. They're never going to let you go.

They're not done with you. They may never be through with you.

Her jeans were still caught in the ropes around her ankles. Vulnerable, exposed, and terrified. She hated herself right at that moment. Hated what had happened to her, what had become of her. She was changing, it wasn't a sudden shift, but a process. Something unexplainable was going on inside her. What it was she didn't know, didn't understand. She didn't want to think about it.

A woman came into the room. At first Lucy thought she was going to help her, but Lucy quickly dismissed that thought. The woman's cruel eyes held nothing but contempt for her.

The woman was short and skinny, and wore her mousy brown hair tucked behind her ears. She'd been pretty at one time, but not today, and probably not yesterday. She strode over to Lucy, took out a knife, and before Lucy could say anything, cut the ropes.

"Can I go?" Lucy's voice was small, lost in her ears. She swallowed, her body shaking.

The woman laughed.

"Get up," she said, her voice surprisingly soft. As if she had laryngitis without the hoarseness. The tone was almost as scary as her piercing pale eyes, so pale blue they looked virtually colorless.

Look for an out.

She didn't care if she was naked, she would run. Go anywhere.

You're on an island. Where do you think you'd go?

She was a championship swimmer. She could handle the water. Ocean, lakes, whatever. She didn't care how cold the water was, she'd rather trust her own swimming ability than leave her fate in the hands of the horrible men who'd hurt her.

The humiliation of the rape rushed over her again, like a hot wave, but one that left her cold and shaking.

Forget it! Dammit, Lucy, cry about it later. You have to find a way out.

The woman kicked her in the kidney and Lucy couldn't suppress the gasp of pain.

"I said *get up*." That unnaturally low voice got under Lucy's skin, bringing forth goose bumps.

She rose slowly, her legs stiff. She tried to pull up her jeans, but the woman slapped her hand away. "Drop them, or you won't get a shower."

"I couldn't care less about a shower. Just let me *go*."

"You'll shower, you'll clean yourself, and you'll do exactly what I tell you to do."

With a sudden movement, the woman stepped forward, grabbed Lucy's hair, and pulled her head back. The knife that had slashed her bindings now touched her neck. "You don't know how much I want to kill you," the woman spat out. "You think you own the world, so pretty, so perfect with your perky breasts and your *virtue*. How does it feel to have your precious virginity ripped from your body? Taken with force? No man will want you after this. No one will want to touch you. You'll beg to die before this is over. And I will be happy to—"

"Denise!"

The command was sharp. The woman released Lucy and pocketed the knife.

"She wasn't complying."

Trevor Conrad stood in the doorway, his blond hair damp from a recent shower or swim. His billowing shirt was reminiscent of a pirate, his tan slacks pressed and creased. He looked more like the handsome CEO of a major corporation, or a movie star, than a sadist.

He smiled.

Lucy would not be tricked by his appearance like she'd been tricked by his online words.

"Come, Lucy. You probably want a shower after the show."

"It wasn't a show," she said, her heart pounding so hard in her chest that she thought for certain he could see it beating through her skin. "He raped me." As she said it she remembered that she was naked. She heated from embarrassment, wanting to cover herself. She didn't want to show her fear, her humiliation, to the man in front of her.

But she couldn't stop shaking.

Trevor smiled. "The first time is always the most difficult." He held out his hand. "Come."

Lucy didn't know what his game was. He'd been cruel on the boat, now he was nice? Was this some mind game to get her to comply? To brainwash her? She'd been such a fool to believe everything he'd told her online. That he was a student at Georgetown. That they liked the same music, that they both loved romantic comedies—what guy her age likes romantic comedies? Her boyfriends only wanted to go see action movies. She had thought she'd been so smart, so safe, but she'd been stupid.

Lucy started toward Trevor, but didn't take his

hand. For an instant, anger flashed in his face, a cold hardness that hadn't been there when he'd stood in the doorway. She wasn't going to give in to his game.

He let her pass him in the doorway. She froze. Four men sat in a large room. They stared at her and whistled. One of the men was Roger, the man who had raped her.

She turned and walked straight into Trevor's hard chest.

"They've already seen everything. No sense being modest now," he said, his light tone further humiliating her.

Tears sprang from her eyes. She didn't want to cry in front of these men, didn't want to cry at all, but she couldn't stop the tears from pouring out. Head high, she walked through the room at Trevor's direction. Tall windows showed only pine trees beyond. No water, no people. They were on an island in the middle of nowhere.

Trevor opened a door on the far side of the room. A large bathroom with a skylight in the roof but no windows. A stack of fluffy towels sat on the counter. A cheery photograph of a whale hung on the wall, reflected in the cabinet mirror.

"There's shampoo and soap in the shower," Trevor said. He snapped his fingers and Denise was at his side holding clothing that wasn't Lucy's. She thrust the garment into Lucy's hands. Lucy let it fall to the floor.

Trevor scowled. "Put those on when you're done. You have twenty minutes. Use them wisely. You don't want to see me when I get angry."

He shut and locked the door.

Lucy picked up the clothing. It was a white filmy layered dress with a wide belt with studs and hoops. There were no underclothes, just the dress and belt.

She turned on the water, almost in a daze. Maybe there was something she could use as a weapon—against five men? Hardly. Her self-defense skills hadn't even done damage to one.

Still, she looked through the cabinets.

They were empty. Not even a bobby pin. Not only empty, but unused. Not a stain of toothpaste or perfume in the drawers, not even a strand of hair.

The shower beckoned. It wasn't only her legs that were sore. She now saw the blood on her stomach, the blood on her thighs, the dried semen. She looked in the mirror and saw the spot on her neck where Roger's knife had cut her, the deeper cut on her breast.

She climbed into the shower, sat on the tile floor, and cried as she scrubbed herself, ridding herself of the scent of violence, trying to reclaim her dignity.

And failing.

EIGHT

JACK AND HIS TEAM had driven them to the base of the mountain in two hours; then two more were spent trekking up the mountain to the observatory at the top. The morning had started cool, but as the sun rose so did the heat. The dust from the dirt roads coated Dillon, and he drank heavily from his water bottle.

"I made some inquiries after your call," Jack had told Dillon. "Learned that an old man up here, Professor Fox, has had some female company for the last couple of years. No one knows who she is, but she's treated the locals well so they haven't bothered her."

Dillon absorbed the information. "You could have gone for her yourself," he said. "You didn't have to wait for me."

Jack shrugged. "I promised I'd meet you." He stared Dillon in the eye. For the first time in many years, Dillon saw a real complexity to Jack. He couldn't say if it was good or bad, but Jack was a man of his word.

Without comment, Jack motioned to his team. They'd already circumvented one group of rebels who'd been camping at the base of the mountain. They faced another up ahead.

Dillon was completely out of his element. Both Patrick and Connor were armed and taking orders from an older brother they barely knew. As cops, they were used to a command structure. Jack's team of soldiers acted as a unit with a mere hand signal. Dillon had no weapon to protect himself or anyone else. Being physically fit and able to keep up with the others was a small consolation. He was being protected, he sensed it even though Jack didn't say it.

The position made him uncomfortable. Dillon was used to being in control of any given situation. People came to him—cops, prosecutors, doctors—for his advice and opinions. He had the respect and admiration of everyone he worked with, his family, and his friends. He was good at his job, his vocation, his ability to crawl into the mind of society's most sick and depraved and find justice for their victims.

And until now it had never touched him. Until now he'd believed he was providing a service. After someone had been killed, he helped find the killer by *thinking* like the killer. Before there was another victim, before the killer struck again.

He'd never been responsible for finding a victim alive. His analysis largely came from the kill itself, looking at the body scientifically, the life and death of the victim, understanding the victimology, determining through an almost empathetic process—the antithesis of science—what human makeup had done such an evil act. Then peering into the shadows of the victim's life, narrowing suspects using logic and experience. Forensic psychiatry was as much a social discipline as a scientific one.

His inadequacies came crashing down. The sheer enormity of what faced them over the next thirty-six hours, that they might not be able to save Lucy, that only through her death might he be capable of finding her murderer.

"Connor," he said quietly, "can I have your backup weapon?"

At first Dillon thought his brother was going to balk. Connor knew Dillon was a novice with firearms.

But he handed it over, butt first. "Safety's on," he said.

Dillon hoped he wouldn't have to use it. He'd prefer to use words and diplomacy to finesse any tense situation.

But an arrogant, remorseless killer had Lucy, and if talking couldn't save her life, a gun just might.

The dress Lucy wore was identical to the one April Klinger had worn during her final show. It seemed fitting, Trask thought, to have Lucy wear it. They had a lot in common. Not so much the way they looked—April had been petite, curvy, and blond, while Lucy was tall, lithe, and brunette—but Lucy was a dancer, Trask knew that from their months of online conversations. Twelve years of ballet. So was April, until she ran away from home after her grandmother told her she was sending her to drug rehab.

Trask had liked April, and had used her drug addiction to keep her compliant. He liked April because the girl hated what she did. Her fake rapes were popular because she wasn't faking most of the time. She was feisty. Still, her drug addiction kept her in line, kept her coming back every week for another live show.

He remembered when he killed her. As with Monique, he hadn't planned it exactly, but once his hands were around her neck, he couldn't stop himself.

For years, he'd been distributing snuff films through Achilles Distribution. Nervous, because mailing them was dangerous. Still, that was how he learned to hone his sixth sense, to discern what mail drops were monitored by the feds, and whom he could trust. When the Internet bloomed, he created Trask Enterprises. No longer did he need to risk exposure by mailing the films—he could have customers download them.

But snuff films were dangerous because someone died, and while most of the women he killed were society's throwaways—prostitutes, drug addicts, runaways—there was always the chance someone would be looking for them.

With the Internet, the niche market for snuff films was irrelevant. *Millions* of people would pay him ten dollars a month to watch sex on their computer. He made even more money selling the downloads.

He'd carefully planned the show. April would play a dance student. Her instructor would call her in for after-class lessons. Denise had always played the lesbian role well. They'd have a little lesbo action, whet the viewers' appetite, then three men would burst in and rape them both.

Trask knew it'd be a bestseller.

But as he watched April dance, he grew hard. In the

porn industry, sex was business. It took a very special woman to make Trask feel anything. Unless of course she was chained and fighting him, then he had no problems.

He let Denise and April go at it, let them titillate the audience, but he stopped the three actors from storming in.

He walked onstage instead, a mask on, naked.

One look in April's eyes and she knew.

"No."

He took her every way he wanted, her fighting egging him on. The act that wasn't an act. And then she was beneath him. His hands went around her neck. And just like Monique, he knew that only in April's death would he achieve pure ecstasy.

The fact that the entire scene was being filmed turned Trask on even more.

He wished his father could watch. See what he had created. Women would no longer dominate him; he was in control. He would always be in control. He had the power, the money, the brains to have his pleasure and not pay a hypocritical legal system that thought what he did was illegal.

His father, who had stolen his inheritance, who had humiliated him, who had told him he would be nothing.

Trask was something. He had more power than his pathetic father had. He had money, three times the wealth of his family—and growing. He was *somebody*. People feared him.

Then April was dead.

Trask watched Lucy dance, the anticipation building. He turned to Roger, who stood next to him. "I want the vote to go my way."

"But everyone likes the blood," Roger whined.

Trask glared at him, fists clenching and unclenching. "My money, my show."

As Kate watched, the girl danced. The filmy white gown shifted and shimmered, revealing her naked body beneath. Lucy was elegant, poised, as if she'd danced her entire life. And maybe she had. If it weren't for the anger on her face, the terror in her eyes, Kate would have thought Lucy was dancing because she wanted to.

Kate knew better. Trask had ways of forcing women to comply. And most women did what he demanded in order to save their lives. Not that it helped, in the end.

Kate stared at the data that had just come in. She didn't believe it could be that easy to find Lucy. One minute, nothing. The next minute, the coordinates of the feed.

She searched the Internet for the coordinates to see if she saw anything from satellite photographs. The area was off the coast of Baja California, south of San Diego, where Lucy had been abducted. A string of islands, some with structures, some natural. Kate bit her lip. Was this a trick? Another ambush like two years ago?

It was too easy. She hadn't done anything different from when Rayanna had disappeared, but she hadn't found Rayanna's location until an hour before she was killed. And the FBI hadn't arrived for three hours after that.

Something was off. She should send Quinn Peterson the data, let him make the decision. Because if she was wrong and Lucy *was* on that island off Baja California, Kate would never forgive herself for not acting to save her.

But *she* wanted Trask. And she wasn't confident that he was on that island.

Trust your instincts.

If only she had trusted her instincts before, Evan wouldn't have died. She had believed Paige, maybe blindly. Jeff Merritt had told both of them to back off of Trask. Then the next day Paige said Merritt had agreed to their plan and was providing backup. Despite some initial doubts, Kate had believed Paige because she had wanted to. She hadn't trusted her instincts and Paige had ended up raped and butchered.

Dammit!

She didn't think Trask was there. But she couldn't ignore the evidence, even after being wrong before. She typed a message to Quinn.

> Either Lucy is here, or Trask has put out another trail of bread crumbs for me—or you—to walk into his trap. I'm sending out all my data and methodology. This one is in your hands.
>
> K.

Mick Mallory watched Lucy dance. She was beautiful.

And she was as good as dead.

If he could have, he would have slit Trask's throat in his sleep. The bastard deserved nothing less than death. If he could have, the feds would be all over this island.

But he had no fucking idea where he was, and no way to contact anyone. Deep cover? Hell, he'd been written off the planet.

Roger had always been suspicious of him, and Mick didn't dare attempt anything. He had no phone, he was hired security. Had done one job, proven his worth at the expense of the life of another beautiful innocent girl.

He'd never be able to live with himself. Even killing Trask wouldn't remove the stain of sin on Mick's soul.

Roger had called him two days ago. Then the bastard had fucking *drugged* him at the rendezvous point. Brought him to the island to handle patrols.

Mick had no way of contacting anyone. It was just like the nightmare when Rayanna had died because he had done nothing.

Lucy would die over his dead body. And maybe, just maybe, his death would mean something.

But he'd much rather get off the damn island alive. Fuck orders. Saving Lucy Kincaid was more important than arresting Trask, or whatever his name was.

He'd wait until Trask and Roger were occupied. And that wack-job, Denise. She really creeped him out.

"Sexy bitch, isn't she?"

Roger came up behind him as Mick stared at the monitor.

"Hm," Mick grunted.

"Trask said you can have her next. Thinks you're ready for the big time."

Mick tensed. He'd never thought—

"What?" Roger said.

"You're fucking with me."

Roger laughed, slapped him hard on the back. "Trask doesn't joke around, not with his bitches. You can have her at the twenty-four-hour mark." Roger leaned forward, whispered. "Or maybe I'm right about you."

"I don't know what the fuck you're talking about, asshole."

Roger laughed again. "Yeah, you probably don't. Be ready, Mick, or maybe we don't need you around after all."

Roger left the small observation room, closing the door behind him. Roger was in charge of surveillance, monitoring the security cameras that panned the island, the dock, the sky. Mick's job was to monitor the cameras and alert Roger of a security breach. Now he looked for a landmark. Something, anything to give him a clue where he was. Only the sun told him he was on the West Coast, north of California. Probably off the coast of Washington based on the angle.

Thank fucking Uncle Sam he'd spent enough years in the military to learn something—like how to make a sextant.

He also had a 24/7 visual on Lucy Kincaid. He touched the screen. "I don't want to hurt you, Lucy."

But he didn't see any other way. He'd be dead if he didn't act the part, and if Mick was dead he couldn't save Lucy's life.

NINE

KATE HAD RECEIVED a one-word response from Quinn Peterson: *Working*.

She hated waiting. Her entire life had become a waiting game. She pushed away from the console and heard something.

Her gun was in her hand without another thought. She leaped from her chair, moving to the door, putting her back against the wall. The hum of her computers distracted her, the movement of Lucy dancing on the screen drawing her eye. She took a deep breath, focused. Listened.

Footsteps on the metal stairs.

Someone was here. It wasn't Professor Fox. It was the middle of the afternoon and he'd be sleeping. And he wouldn't come to her room. He always used the intercom to summon her, especially after Kate had almost killed him when he startled her that first time.

More footsteps. At least three people. Possibly four. Kate closed her eyes. Boots. Army? Hiking? She'd heard that Dominguez's troops had been hiding out on the mountain after taking out a humanitarian aid convoy last month. The government didn't take kindly to criminals who stole so blatantly, so

Dominguez had a bullet with his name on it, from both his competitors and now the government. It was only a matter of time, not that Kate cared. She could get off the mountain whenever she wanted—by air.

A knock on her door. If this was the FBI finally coming for her, they wouldn't have been so polite.

"Kate Donovan? It's Dillon Kincaid. I'm here to talk about my sister."

Kate stopped in her tracks. The guy who said all those things online? Who, without knowing her *at all*, had seemed to get inside her head? How could Dillon Kincaid have found her? And how could he get to her in half a day?

"Kate, please let me in."

"Who's with you?"

"My brothers."

"How many?"

"Three."

"You have three brothers?"

"Yes."

"And you all came up here because you think I can lead you to your sister? Think again. I don't know where she is. Go home."

The doorknob turned. It was locked.

"Go away," Kate said. "I'll send all the information I get to Quinn."

But if I think I know where Trask is, I'm going after him myself.

"I'm not leaving," he said.

"Then sit out there all night. It gets cold when the sun goes down, even in June."

"I called in favors, traveled hours by plane, jeep, and foot, to find you. I think you know more than you're saying. I know you can find Lucy. I brought my brother Patrick. He's a computer expert, like you. He's the one who isolated your transmission and located you."

"Bullshit." Was the FBI planning her takedown right now? She needed to get the hell out of here. No, dammit! Kate didn't want to leave. She was so close.

"We're here, aren't we?"

"You're jeopardizing everything!"

"I didn't tell Agent Peterson where you were. He knows we know, but he didn't ask, I didn't tell. Please let us in."

She closed her eyes. She didn't know what to do. She didn't want help, but she needed it. The Baja island—had she been right? Wrong? Was Trask there, or was it another trap? She didn't know, couldn't see the truth anymore.

She was so damn tired. She missed Evan, she missed Paige. She hated being alone, but she didn't see any alternative.

She opened the door, kept her gun leveled at the man on her threshold.

Two guns were aimed at her head.

"Kill me and he still dies," she said, staring into the green eyes of the man she assumed was Dillon Kincaid.

"Put the guns down," Dillon said without taking his eyes from hers.

He was tall. Handsome. In shape, but no body-builder. He reminded her of Quinn, *GQ* good looks; a strong, square jaw; and intelligent eyes. Dillon stared at her, as if he could literally read her thoughts. She quickly appraised his dusty jeans, the dark green

T-shirt, and his mussed-up sun-streaked, light-brown hair that, though short, fell in waves across his forehead. But it was the intensity of his eyes, their focus and strength, that took Kate's breath away.

"Jack. Connor. Now." Dillon stepped through the door, toward her gun, no fear on his face. "Kate, please."

As soon as he entered, his eyes caught movement on the screen against the far wall. His expression changed, hardened. Worry clouded his face.

Kate lowered her gun, keeping her eye on the men Dillon called Connor and Jack. Brothers? Perhaps. Jack was all military, hard-edged. She knew the type. Connor had the same hard edge without the layer of dissociation. Cop, not military. Yet another man was behind them. Thinner, with fair skin and dark hair. His gun was holstered, and she instantly thought *Patrick, the computer expert.*

As soon as Jack and Connor lowered their weapons, she followed Dillon's eyes to the screen. Her dance over, Lucy was being shackled to a straight-backed chair by two men. She fought them, the freedom of her dance over.

Dillon walked to the screen. "Which one is Trask?"

"Neither," Kate said. "He won't show himself on camera." She paused. "I'm the only one who has seen him and lived."

Dillon turned to her. "Did you work with a sketch artist?"

"You don't understand."

"You didn't tell anyone? What if we can get his picture out?"

"The man I saw is a chameleon. Of course I gave a

description, even while I was on the run from my own government. Do you think I'm so callous that I would let women *die* in order to protect myself? Because of *me* they have his fingerprints. Because of *me* they have a description. Lot of good that did catching him!" Kate turned to the screen, jumping when one of the men slapped Lucy across the face.

"And because of me my two best friends died."

Dillon almost didn't hear what Kate had said. He tore his eyes away from Lucy on the screen and touched Kate's arm. All muscle. In her midthirties, her shortish hair was so blond it was nearly white, pulled into a haphazard hair band with loose strands falling out, tucked behind her ears. Her face was devoid of makeup, fresh and clean, worry lines creasing her forehead, her red lips dipping into a frown. This woman had so much pain and sadness in her face, taking the crimes of others as her own personal cross to bear.

Her computer beeped as Dillon was about to question her. Connor, Patrick, and Jack filed into the room. Jack remained at the door, on alert. Patrick sidled over to the computer system.

"What's that?" he asked.

"A message." She clicked on it. "From Quinn."

We're still checking your data. Hold.

"What is he checking out?" Patrick asked.

"The coordinates I sent about thirty minutes ago. But I think it's a trap."

Dillon asked, "What coordinates?"

Kate tensed, obviously feeling a touch of claustrophobia with all these men, these *Kincaids,* in her personal space. Dillon glanced around the functional room. It was large, but sparsely furnished. A bed in the corner. A nightstand. No personal effects anywhere. Two doors probably led to a closet and a bathroom. There was a whole wall of weights. And another full wall of computers and computer screens. Systems he didn't understand, but by the expression on Patrick's face, his little brother was impressed.

"Kate?" Dillon said softly.

In a move that surprised Dillon, Jack said, "I need to check on my men." He walked out, shutting the door behind him.

"Who did you bring?" Kate asked, panicked.

"Jack—" What could Dillon say about his brother when even he didn't know the truth? Dillon didn't even know if Jack still worked for the government, or if he was truly a mercenary. "Jack's a soldier down here. I contacted him and he and his unit helped us get up the mountain."

"The terrain is dangerous," Kate said, "but it's safe this far up. The observatory is university property, and they pay handsomely for the land."

"So what coordinates did you come up with?" Dillon repeated his question.

Kate motioned toward her computer. "Have a look."

Patrick sat down almost before she finished the invitation.

"I've been pinging constantly, trying to get a lock on the coordinates of the originating feed," Kate said.

"Pinging?" Dillon asked.

Patrick translated. "It's where one computer can

see if another on a network is online. A ping is sort of like calling a phone number and hanging up when you get an answer. You know someone is there, but you don't want to talk to them."

Kate smiled at the analogy. "Trask is good—very good," she said. "He has the feed going through numerous routers, using legitimate servers to mask his signal. I'm also working on the delay—there's a full minute-thirty-second delay, I think. But again, it's almost impossible to tell. The delay could be caused by one of the servers he's moving data through. He's sending the transmissions through a variety of hubs and nodes—virtually everything is a dead end."

"Wow," Patrick muttered. "Where'd you get this trace program? I've never seen anything like it."

"I wrote it."

"You?" Patrick was impressed.

"More or less. I improved it, I should say. The less you know the better. Quinn already told you I'm wanted by the government. Since they already want me for high crimes, a little hacking isn't going to increase my jail time."

Her words were light, almost self-deprecating, but there was a wistful quality that Dillon caught.

Connor spoke up. "But you think you might have found Lucy. Why are we standing here doing nothing? Let's get off this damn mountain and find her."

"Because I think it's a trap," she said.

"Why?"

Kate didn't answer.

"You have coordinates, but you don't want to do anything about it?"

"Do anything? What do you think I've been doing

for the last five years? Trask killed my partner. He's been killing women for sport for years. He's a genius and he's not going to let me find him until he wants me to, unless I can somehow outmaneuver him. He wants me to walk into a trap so he can kill me. He's gone underground because we have his prints— because of *me*. We have a physical description, and I think he's too vain to change his appearance. He's vindictive and powerful. He's not going to simply *let* me find Lucy, or any of his prey."

Patrick said, "But here you have your program— unbiased—tracing the feed through dead ends and nodes and landing at a live spot. The trace looks exactly the way it should look."

"I know the program *seems* to have found the live feed, but Trask plays a game of cat and mouse. The coordinates are the cheese."

"We have to do something!" Connor stared at the screen, watched Lucy helpless and fearful.

Dillon spoke. "Kate, she's our little sister. We have to follow every lead."

"By the time you get to that island, it'll be too late to get back here and retrace the steps. *If* it's a trap, or a phony lead, we've lost all the time we have. You can do what you want. I'm not going anywhere."

"You don't have to. She's not your sister. But we're going." Connor looked from Dillon to Patrick. "Right?"

Dillon was torn. He wanted to go to the island the coordinates pointed to. Lucy had said she was on an island.

But Kate was the one with experience tracking this

killer. She'd seen his face, been inside his head. Could Dillon trust Lucy's life to Kate's instincts?

Kate spoke up. "I sent the information to Quinn. He's looking into the data now."

"We can't wait for the FBI to act," Connor said. "Not when we're this close. What if he rushes it? What if this Trask knocks time off Lucy's clock, doesn't give us the full forty-eight hours to find her?"

Dillon glanced at the countdown.

33:50:02. 33:50:01. 33:50:00. 33:49:59.

His heart raced twice as fast as the countdown. He didn't want to wait, but he trusted Kate's instincts— on this, on understanding this killer.

"He won't jump the clock," Dillon said. "The countdown is part of the thrill."

"And you'd bet Lucy's life on your psychoanalysis? You haven't even met him!" Connor shouted.

Dillon took the jab, understanding his brother's frustration. "It's the anticipation. He's working himself up toward the final act." He turned to Kate. "Has he ever changed the countdown?"

"Only Paige," she said quietly. "She had twenty-four hours, not forty-eight. But that was a completely different situation. He . . . he had another girl, killed her when he captured Paige. We were close and he knew it. So the countdown was the same, he just killed two women."

"How did you track him then?"

"He wasn't as cautious then as he is now. We tracked him through his corporation, Trask Enterprises, which has several online pornography sites."

"What happened to the corporation?"

"The board of directors testified that they didn't know anyone named Trask, that Roger Morton was the owner/operator as far as they knew, and that someone from the outside had hacked into the company's equipment. We didn't catch anyone lying, but that's not to say someone didn't. Soon after, several people disappeared from the company. The corporation lost all its assets, but ultimately it owned the domain names and rights to all the big online porn sites and was able to refill its coffers. Quickly. Trask operates solely outside of Trask Enterprises, at least for now. The FBI is still tracking the company. Spending too much time doing it, in my opinion."

"He's bringing in money from all over the world. He's promised these people something," Dillon said. "He's not going to renege on his deal with them. He'll lose face, and they won't trust him down the road."

"But if Lucy *is* on that island, we can get her out before anything more happens to her." Connor's voice cracked. "You can stay, Dillon, but I'm going."

"Go," Kate said. "I never asked any of you to come here. I didn't *want* anyone to find me. You've already screwed me. As soon as this is over, I'm going to have to find another place."

"You're already giving up," Dillon said.

"I am *not* giving up."

"You're talking about when this is over. When Lucy is dead," said Dillon. "But if we *do* stop him this time, you won't have to hide anymore."

"You don't understand. Quinn didn't tell you everything."

"You might be surprised. He's been protecting you. You have friends you might not even know about."

Kate shook her head, not wanting to hear what Dillon had to say. And he couldn't push. He didn't have time to sweet-talk her, to coddle her and tell her everything was going to be just peachy. He didn't know if he believed it himself. But if they didn't do *something*, he'd never forgive himself.

Patrick spoke up. "I think these coordinates are valid. If we jam, we might make it to Hidalgo in four hours, maybe less, charter a plane and get to Baja in another four hours. That puts the countdown at twenty-five hours, giving us time to set up a rescue effort. It'll take the feds nearly that long to get permission for an op on foreign soil. We can meet them there."

"Do what you feel you must." Kate rubbed her eyes as if she had a fierce headache. "A few things you need to know. First, Trask will wire any facility to explode. He did it with Paige and others. Second, he kills on sight. He will give you no time to negotiate or plead. He shot Evan at point-blank range without hesitation."

"Who's Evan?" Dillon asked.

Kate didn't answer. "Third, he has four to six men surrounding him at all times. Trask doesn't like to lose his men, but they are casualties of war as far as he's concerned. He'll leave the wounded behind, possibly even shooting them so they can't talk. I doubt he trusts any of them, even Roger Morton, who's been with him since the beginning."

"We should wait until Quinn Peterson returns his assessment." Dillon remembered what Peterson had said about the last false lead and the lives that had almost been lost. Lucy was already in danger. Dillon couldn't send his brothers on a deadly mission without additional support.

"We don't have time," Patrick said, showing rare frustration. "Dil, I understand where you're coming from, but we have to move. We can't wait for the feds."

Kate pulled open a desk drawer and took out a laptop. "This is my extra portable. It has a four-hour battery, and an extra four-hour battery in the bag." She plugged the unit into her hard drive and started typing a bunch of commands.

"What are you doing?" Dillon asked.

"Giving Patrick everything I have. Everything except the trace program, which you wouldn't be able to run off this anyway without wasting battery life. You have the coordinates, maps, the connections he's used in the past. If I learn anything else, I'll communicate with you through this computer." She pulled another trick out of the drawer. "Here's a nifty device. Checks for explosives. Trask loves his bombs."

As Kate's hand brushed against her keyboard, a scream pierced the air. All four of them jerked their heads toward the screen.

Lucy was still tied to the chair. A woman stood over her. Dillon couldn't see her face, but she had short dark hair and was small and bony. Lucy's arm had been cut, the skin barely punctured, and blood slowly seeped from a three-inch incision.

"Dear God," Patrick said.

They heard Lucy's voice on the speakers. "Get away from me, you freak! Get away from me!"

The knife came up in the woman's hand and her profile was in view.

"No!" Connor screamed at the same time Lucy did.

The woman laughed, a low, barely audible rumble. "Just teasing," she said and kissed Lucy on the lips before walking out of view.

Dillon turned to Kate, whose face was ashen. "What is it?" he asked.

"It's Denise Arno. She's supposed to be dead. *She's supposed to be dead!*"

Kate punched her fist into her desk.

TEN

DILLON WALKED with Connor and Patrick as far as the edge of the observatory. "I wish you'd wait until we hear back from Agent Peterson. They're on top of this."

"We've been through this," Connor said. "You know how to reach us."

Jack motioned for his team. They immediately fell into position without a word.

Dillon stared at his twin. So much time had passed since they had considered themselves brothers. And they had been close—best friends as well as brothers.

Dillon wished he knew what had changed. He had hints, his years of experience, his counseling, understanding the delicacy and strength of the human psyche. But he didn't know enough to get into Jack's head. Jack's actions, however, gave Dillon hope. His help today had been invaluable, and Dillon would never forget it. Maybe later he and Jack could reconnect. When Lucy was safe and the family was back together.

"That Kate Donovan is a piece of work," Jack said. "Leave her. I don't think she's all there."

Dillon raised an eyebrow. "Since when did you get your psych degree?"

"Observation, brother. You don't need a fancy degree to see what's what."

"I'm staying until we hear from the FBI." Dillon slapped Connor and Patrick on the back. "Be careful. I know why you need to go. But stay in the loop. Remember that Kate thinks it's a trap."

"We're expecting anything," Connor said. "But you be careful, too." Connor looked worried and told Dillon to keep his backup weapon.

"Don't try to leave the mountain alone," Jack told Dillon. "I'll come and get you when I'm back in the area."

"Don't count on me being here." Dillon believed Kate was close to finding Trask, either through her computer or because Trask wanted her to find him. If she left, Dillon was going with her.

Jack turned and walked with his team, Connor, and Patrick down the mountain road. They disappeared from sight.

Dillon didn't know what made his twin tick, but he had ideas. A fierce sense of loyalty. A code of honor that wasn't exactly the same as their father's. Jack showed no fear, no remorse, and little emotion. Like an automaton. He did what he did—both good and bad—for a purpose, not because he enjoyed it. Unlike the man who had Lucy.

Trask imprisoned women for pleasure. And he relished the power he had over life and death, to be able to do exactly what he wanted without remorse, without repercussion.

Dillon remembered the tragic case of Angie Vance

earlier in the year. Her killer had suffocated her, laid on top of her body while she was dying, becoming sexually aroused while in physical contact with her dying body. Afterward she became garbage to him, disposed of in bags on the beach. A necessary cleanup after the act of murder.

Trask had the same basic fantasy—murder while in the process of a rape—but he wasn't the emergent killer who had raped and suffocated Angie. Trask was older. Orderly. Mature. Angie's killer had been aloof, with few friends. Trask had charisma, an ability to bring people, suspecting or not, into his fold. He had help in his killings, people loyal to him in the same way Jack's team was loyal to him.

Maybe Trask had been in the military? Maybe the men he surrounded himself with were indebted to him for reasons other than a common bond of hurting women. There was *some* connection between Trask and those who helped him. Military seemed the most logical, because these efforts relied heavily on strategic planning. But other groups had the same kind of bonding and ability to plan. Cops, for one. Any group of people who had been through a traumatic event. Had Trask saved these men at one time? From death or prison? Were they criminals? Had they gone to school together? Worked together?

Maybe finding out who Trask surrounded himself with would lead them to Trask himself. Starting with Roger Morton.

Kate had nearly lost it when she saw the woman Denise Arno on-screen. Kate knew her, but Dillon had been unable to get her to talk further. At least not with Patrick and Connor hovering in the room, putting her on edge. He had to return to her room, communicate with Quinn Peterson, find out what the FBI was doing. He had confidence in the system, unlike Kate Donovan. He'd worked in the system long enough to know that people like Quinn Peterson were wholly dedicated and committed to saving lives.

But Lucy wasn't Quinn's sister. And while Dillon had no doubt that Kate Donovan would do anything and everything to stop Lucy's murder, he also knew that her number one goal was to stop Trask.

After learning from Peterson about the failed sting operation five years ago, Dillon had glimpsed Kate's motivation. Yet something about Peterson's explanation didn't jibe with the woman he'd just met. She seemed too responsible, too smart to play vigilante, putting herself and two other agents in a dangerous situation without authorization.

Yet she had been continually breaking the law for five years by hacking into computer systems around the globe. For the purpose of finding a killer, Dillon reminded himself.

He suspected that there was a lot more behind what had happened five years ago, and that only Kate Donovan knew the whole story.

"I thought you'd go with them." Kate stood on the metal stairs outside her room.

"I told you I was staying."

"Pardon me for not believing you."

Had Kate been lied to so often she trusted no one?

"Remember the Dr. Seuss story of Horton the Elephant?"

A hint of a smile curved her lips. "And you're Horton?"

He smiled back. "I always liked his philosophy."

He followed Kate back into her room. Barracks, he should say. His eyes immediately found the screen where Lucy was . . . wasn't where she should be. In its place was an older, poorer-quality video.

"What happened?" Dillon swallowed, suppressing the panic that rose with the bile in his throat. Was Lucy dead?

"She's still alive." Kate wasn't looking at him. "I told you he's not going to jump the countdown."

"What happened?" he repeated.

"If you want to look at the recording, go ahead." Kate faced him, sadness etched in her vivid blue eyes. "It was more of the same."

Dillon looked up at the ceiling, his throat tight. What good would it do to watch his sister be hurt . . . be raped? The most important thing was finding her alive. Taking care of her, nursing her. He shook his head.

"I want to talk to Quinn."

"He hasn't gotten back to me since I sent the coordinates. That was over an hour ago."

"May I?" Dillon motioned to the keyboard attached to the lone computer that had instant messaging.

She nodded, looking at a host of other monitors that flashed code and programs Dillon didn't understand.

Peterson, it's Dillon Kincaid. I'm with your friend. What's happening?

Wait, I'll get Peterson.

Dillon didn't know to whom he was talking, so he didn't type anything further. "You knew that woman?"

She nodded curtly.

"Who was she?"

"Denise Arno."

"And?"

Kate said nothing.

"Kate," Dillon said, his voice sterner than he intended. She faced him. "I need to know everything. I believe you want to help, but my goal is not Trask. It's saving my sister. If you can't get behind that, then maybe you don't have your priorities straight."

"Don't talk to me about my priorities. Who are you to judge me?"

"I'm not judging you. But I need to know *everything* about Trask if we're going to stop him. This is my job. I get into the heads of killers. I begin to think like them. Breathe like them. I'm beginning to get a handle on Trask."

He continued, starting slow and speeding up as he went. "He's forty, plus or minus. He's from a wealthy family, used to privilege and getting whatever he wants. His parents were strict, probably excessively strict, and he resents authority because of that. I wouldn't be surprised if his father was a high-ranking public official, attorney, or in some position of authority that he enjoyed abusing. Trask wasn't born in a vacuum."

"So he was an abused child," Kate said sarcastically, rolling her eyes.

Dillon took a deep breath. He was used to that kind of comment from law enforcement. "He may or may not have been abused in the traditional sense. I feel no physical abuse, or if he was physically abused it was when he was very young. He likely had a volatile temper even as a young child, unable to own up to his mistakes. He feels no remorse for his actions, and I sense from reading the files Peterson gave me that he never has felt remorse."

"Oh please," Kate said, hand on her hip. "So he's insane? He's incapable of feeling remorse so he doesn't know that what he's doing is wrong? Lock him in a padded cell, give him some drugs, and declare him cured?"

"Don't put words in my mouth," Dillon said, his rare temper rising. "I never said he was insane."

"But—"

He put his hand up. "I'm giving you a rough profile of the man I think Trask is. Understanding his past, getting a sense of his character and personality, will help us find him and, more important, stop him. But I need more. I need to know about Roger Morton, and I need to know about Denise."

"Why?" she asked, honestly curious.

"The more we know about the people he surrounds himself with, the more we know about Trask himself." He took a step toward her. "Between the two of us, we can stop him . . . after we save Lucy."

He glanced at the countdown. 33:02:40.

"We don't have time to play games." Dillon sat at the desk chair, watched as Kate paced like a tigress, lean and rippling with suppressed energy.

"Denise Arno came to my partner, Paige Henshaw, a week before the ambush. Said she was running from Trask, that she knew about April—"

"April Klinger?" Dillon asked, remembering his conversation with Peterson.

"She's the reason we started our investigation into Trask Enterprises in the first place. Her family contacted us when a private investigator they hired to find April discovered that she was starring in online pornography movies. She'd been seventeen when she ran away, but was twenty at that point. The PI turned over a DVD he'd made of what appeared to be a snuff film, with April as the dead woman. It was so real—"

Her voice trailed off and she stared at the screen, where a woman was silently being beaten. Across the bottom of the screen flashed a disclaimer.

Role-playing fantasy rape. No one was hurt in the creation of this film.

She snapped back, her voice harsher. "Paige and I became certain April had been killed. We started investigating the company that housed the digital file that the PI had downloaded, Trask Enterprises. At first we had the support of the Violent Crimes unit—we couldn't locate April anywhere, dead or alive. For all I know, she could have been at the bottom of the Atlantic or chopped to pieces and fed to pigs in upstate New York. With no body, no evidence, no witnesses, we were stuck. Internal support waned. We were getting pressure to back off from upstairs. Other cases were more pressing. The Bureau even used my boyfriend, also an agent, to get me to drop it.

"But I couldn't get April's eyes out of my mind. She was dead. I knew it."

"What happened?"

"Denise contacted Paige, set up a meeting. Told us she knew that April had been killed, but she was too scared to talk about it. Gave us some information that alleged that Trask was bringing in girls from Russia to star in future productions."

Kate sat on the edge of her cot, squeezed her eyes shut, and rubbed her temples. Dillon resisted the urge to rub the tension from her shoulders. Kate wouldn't appreciate it, and right now he didn't want to do anything to upset her. She was already on edge. "Denise didn't make it to our next meeting. I used my computer skills and the Bureau's extensive network to hack into a secure server at Trask." She looked at him, put up her hand. "I know—don't say it. I could have jeopardized a conviction. But I was scared to death that Denise had been killed because she'd come to us. I couldn't do *nothing*.

"That's when I found her strapped to a chair. Naked. Live on the Internet, and damn, I was determined to connect this to Trask Enterprises and raid their company. But it wasn't them. Not on the surface. Someone was using their site, but it was obvious they were piggybacking on it.

"Paige and I had to find Denise. We told our boss what we learned and he said we didn't have enough to go on. But Paige talked to him, told him we had the warehouse under surveillance where Trask was supposedly going to be bringing in these Russian girls. We were supposed to have backup. But it never came. It . . ." Her voice trailed off. Dillon suspected that there was more to the story, but Kate jumped ahead. "We were essentially ambushed. Trask killed Evan and kidnapped Paige. Suddenly Paige was in the chair instead of Denise. I watched as my partner, my best friend, was raped, online where every pervert could see."

Kate stood and paced again, agitated, her hands moving constantly.

"And Evan was your boyfriend," Dillon said quietly.

She nodded.

"Why did you think Denise was dead?"

"NYPD found a body in the Hudson River. She matched Denise's description, but her face had been so brutalized, it wasn't recognizable. I was certain it was her. I had seen her beaten on the Internet. Why would Trask let Denise go? She could identify him."

Kate slammed both hands against the metal door. "But the bitch was working with him all along! I felt so damn *guilty* over Denise's murder. I believed her, believed everything she told us. She had bruises and worse. I honestly thought she was trying to do the right thing and we had gotten her killed. But she set Paige up!"

Dillon mulled the information over. "What kind of bruises?"

"When I thought she was dead? They were all over her face."

"No, the bruise you saw when she first approached you with information."

"Her throat. He'd attempted to strangle her."

"Is that why her voice is hoarse like that? On the feed?"

"Yeah."

"But her vocal cords should have healed by now.

There would have to have been extensive damage. Or ongoing trauma." Dillon frowned. Remembered another case he had worked on where women self-mutilated, or allowed others to do it, out of self-hate, and numerous other reasons, unique and personal: low self-esteem, the need to feel in control, the need to give to others something no one else would.

Dillon pictured the way Denise had treated Lucy on the screen. It wasn't an act. "Denise Arno hates women," he said. "Hates that Trask wants other women. I'm sure you've heard of autoeroticism."

"Where partners or solos bring themselves to the brink of death while engaging in sex." She spoke like a textbook.

"Denise would give herself, her life, to Trask except that it would end in her death. She despises the fact that Trask wants—needs—other women to fulfill his fantasy, because his fantasies always end in death."

Dillon pushed away the horrific image of Lucy dying while Trask raped her. If he thought about Lucy, he wouldn't be able to think like Trask. And that wouldn't do his sister any good.

"Denise is just as sick as Trask is," Kate said. "I don't really care *why* he does it. I just want to stop him."

"But we can't stop him if we can't walk in his shoes. He's smart. Logical, methodical, cunning. He's not going to slip up. We have to be smarter, shrewder. If we can't get into his head, we can't save Lucy. And I refuse to let my little sister die. This Roger Morton—he was in Peterson's file. He's been with Trask since the beginning, right?"

Kate nodded. "He's definitely wanted. He was at

the ambush. And he's on tape raping Paige . . ." Her voice trailed off. She was looking at Lucy on the computer, but not seeing her.

Dillon walked over to her, turned her face to look at him. "Does the FBI have a file on Roger? Can Quinn Peterson get it?"

"Absolutely. And I have all my early research."

"I need to see it. Now."

The computer beeped. Dillon and Kate walked over and he sat down.

Peterson here.

Dillon typed.

What's going on with the coordinates?

I'm working on it. We have a team mobilized, but it's going to take time.

How much time?

Two to three hours. We have to go in covertly because it's in Mexican waters. We don't have the time to go through official channels on this.

My brothers are heading there now. You'll probably beat them. You can contact Patrick through IMP@kincaid.com.

Call them back. We don't need civilians all over the place.

I couldn't have stopped them. K. thinks it's a trap.

I know. She told me. Kate needs to worry about her own ass. Is she there?

Yes.

Tell her I'm working on immunity. I'm doing everything I can to get her back. But Trask knows where she is.

She knows.

Dillon glanced at Kate. The hard expression on her face proved it.

"I wish Trask would come for me," she whispered.

"He knows where you are. He must have a reason for not coming after you."

"I don't think he knows *exactly* where I am. He knows how to talk to my computer, and he's probably narrowed down the region. But if he knew where I was, he would have taken me instead of Lucy."

"Why?" Dillon asked.

She said quietly, "Because he wanted me first. Paige saved my life. He grabbed her when our backup finally arrived." Kate looked at Dillon. "Paige and I dealt Trask a major blow. His freedom, his finances, his company. Payback."

"But why did he want you originally? You said he tried to kidnap you first?"

"I don't know. Maybe he planned on taking both of us. Like you said, he hates authority. I'll bet he really hates women in authority."

Dillon thought about that. "I think you're right, but there's another reason, maybe one we won't know until we talk to him."

"Shoot first," Kate warned him. "If you give him a chance to talk, he'll kill you."

Peterson typed:

And if she finds more information, send it. No vigilantes. I don't want to lose anyone. I have to run. The copter is ready.

Dillon closed down the IM, frowning. Maybe he'd made the wrong choice. Staying, trusting a woman he didn't know. The FBI was taking the information about the island off Baja California seriously. What if he was isolated here, unable to help when they found Lucy? She was going to be traumatized. She needed her family.

"She's not there," Kate said softly, as if reading his mind. "It was too easy."

"How can you be so certain?" Dillon asked, surprised at the quiet temper in his voice.

"Instinct."

"I don't know if I'm willing to trust my sister's life to your instincts."

"I don't blame you. But I didn't ask you to come here, and I certainly didn't ask you to stay."

Dillon walked to the far side of the small room, gathered his wits about him. Panic wasn't going to save Lucy.

"Where are your files on Roger Morton?"

She pulled open a file drawer under her desk. Every folder was neatly labeled and dated. "Where do you want to start?"

"At the beginning," he said.

ELEVEN

QUINN PETERSON RAN from the office, pulling out his cell phone to call his wife and let her know where he was going. Instead, he bumped into an assistant director from Quantico, Jeff Merritt. Quinn couldn't keep the shock off his face. "What's going on?"

"Ten minutes."

"Can't. We have a lead on Trask."

"Now."

Quinn swore under his breath, following Merritt into the office he'd just exited. Merritt glared at Joe Garcia until Garcia got the hint and left. Quinn wouldn't have followed Merritt except for one small thing: Merritt was his boss's boss.

"I told you," Merritt said as soon as Garcia shut the door, "that anything regarding the whereabouts of Trask must go through me first."

"I sent you my report."

"You sent me shit."

"Time is running out, Merritt. Can we have this pissing contest later? I have a helicopter waiting on the roof."

"Where did you get the intel?"

"I don't have time for this."

Merritt slammed his fist on the table. "Dammit, you're in touch with Donovan!"

Quinn knew the history between Merritt and Kate, and he wasn't about to get in the middle.

Jeff Merritt had been Paige Henshaw's lover.

He had been the one to push the Bureau into opening an investigation through the Office of Professional Responsibility. But Merritt didn't want to slap Kate on the wrist. He wanted her behind bars.

It didn't help that everything Kate had sent the feds had been dangerous dead ends. It wasn't her fault—she was being a good agent and sending everything, no matter how remote. But last year, Merritt had jumped the gun and nearly ended up getting himself and his team killed. That had renewed Merritt's vendetta against Kate.

"Put the past on hold, Merritt," Quinn said. "Trask is holding an eighteen-year-old girl captive and the countdown is under thirty-three hours. I don't have time for this."

"I'll bury you, Peterson."

Superior or not, Quinn refused to be threatened. He took a step toward Merritt. "Don't go there."

"Kate Donovan is a lunatic. She'll get you killed."

"You're just feeling guilty because you didn't believe her about Paige after the ambush."

Merritt reddened. "I have nothing to feel guilty about, except maybe leading my people into a trap with intel Kate Donovan submitted. This is a woman who led her partner into a dangerous, hostile situation. She's a vigilante. How can you be sure she's not working with Trask? How can you trust anything she says? She's a fugitive and she set Paige up to die. She also got her boyfriend killed in the process."

"Talk about rewriting history!" Quinn brushed past him. "Talk to me tomorrow."

He was almost out the door when Merritt said, "We have someone deep inside."

Furious was an understatement. "What?" Quinn slowly turned.

"Deep cover, complete silence. Last contact was two weeks ago."

"And you're telling me this *now*? You knew about the Kincaid girl twelve hours ago! Where is she?"

"We don't know."

"You have a guy on the inside and you don't know where he is?"

"He's supposed to check in every week, but Trask has intense security. He's missed check-ins before. Last message was that another show was scheduled. He didn't know where or when, just soon."

"Did you know about Lucy Kincaid?"

Merritt shook his head, but Quinn wasn't certain he believed him. "We suspected he was targeting a student at Georgetown."

"Why hasn't your guy taken him out?"

"Evidence, dammit! We have no proof."

"No proof? You have a man on the inside. He's an eyewitness. We have Trask's recorded voice. And this girl is obviously an unwilling participant."

"We have to find them first. I have to let my man run the op. He's our best hope. Trust me. He'll get her out if he can, then we can debrief him and get Trask."

"Who is he?"

"I can't tell you that."

"Fuck that, Merritt."

"Watch your mouth."

"What about a microchip?" Quinn asked. More often than not undercover agents had GPS microchips implanted on their person. It wasn't standard operating procedure, but for a deep-cover op like this Quinn would have insisted.

"Couldn't do it. Trask has a vigorous system of clearing his crew. We set up an extensive background for my man, even sent him to prison for six months to make contact with one of Morton's old buddies. We've invested a lot of time into finding Trask, instead of relying on a bitter, mentally unstable, renegade FBI agent who should be in prison."

"You want me to trust an unknown undercover who hasn't checked in for two weeks? Who just let a young woman be raped? Bullshit. You don't even know if he's still alive. My helicopter's waiting."

"Tell me where Kate Donovan is."

"I don't know."

"I know you've been working with the Kincaids. I know the brothers went after her."

"Then talk to them, because I don't know where they went."

"You arranged transportation to Hidalgo."

"Did I?"

"You're on thin ice, Peterson."

Quinn stared at his superior. He had several choice words for him, but limited his verbal assault. "You're after Kate because of what happened to Paige, and that's it. Revenge. But nothing you can do to Kate is worse that what she's been doing to herself."

"I'm after Kate Donovan because she disobeyed orders and got Evan Standler and Paige Henshaw killed. Her intel is shit and you know it."

"Her intel is all we have—better than what we've been able to uncover. Better than what your deep-cover agent has gotten us. Everyone went into that op eyes open, Merritt, and you know it. Paige was just as much to blame for the screwup as Kate. And maybe if your people out on the East Coast had taken them more seriously, they wouldn't have gone in without proper backup."

"Don't you dare put this at my feet."

"Put the shoe on, Merritt. It fits."

Quinn left. Taking a deep breath, he called his wife, Miranda, as he ran up the stairs to the roof, where the helicopter waited. Just hearing her voice would calm him down.

Jeff Merritt sat down at the computer in the task force room, looking for Kate Donovan's whereabouts.

He glanced at the computer screen where the Kincaid girl was restrained, naked. But instead of seeing the eighteen-year-old, he saw Paige.

She'd fought until the end, but she'd still died.

If only he had told her he loved her. Instead, they had fought.

"You have to give us backup! We're so close!" she'd insisted.

"You've been 'close' a half-dozen times and come up empty," he'd responded. "No more. Drop this case. You shouldn't be working in Violent Crimes anymore. Let me get you a job at Quantico."

Paige had glared at him. "I knew this was going to

happen. I knew you'd do this. That's why I didn't want to tell you."

"You would have *lied* to me? About something as important as this?"

"If I knew you'd get all Neanderthal on me just because I'm pregnant, yes. Please, Jeff. For me. One last time."

"Last time?" He'd snorted, having heard *that* before. "Is Kate pushing you to do this?"

"Of course not! But we both believe we have him nailed. He's going to show."

"Trask doesn't even exist."

"Yes, he does."

"Fine," he'd said. "You'll have your backup. But this is the last time, hear me? If nothing happens, you and Kate drop the investigation."

"Promise." Paige had smiled. "Eleven o'clock tonight. The warehouse on the corner of Sixth and Madison."

She'd given him a quick kiss and left.

Jeff Merritt stared at the phone. He hadn't believed Trask existed. He hadn't believed April Klinger was dead. Kate and Paige had had a bee in their bonnet because they couldn't stop the proliferation of pornography online. So they had created something that just wasn't there. The time, man-hours, and money they'd wasted going after a phantom named Trask.

Then and there, he had decided to put a scare into Paige. After that, she'd quit, take a nice quiet desk job, be a good mom to their child. A good wife to him.

That was five years ago. Now Merritt slammed his fist on the desk, eyes moist. He reached into his pocket and pulled out the diamond ring he'd been carrying all these years. He kissed the cold gem.

Paige was dead and it was his fault. But he wasn't alone in the blame. Kate Donovan was culpable, too.

And for that she would pay.

TWELVE

TRASK SAT ON THE DECK of the cabin he'd rented months before. The sun had long passed its zenith, but it was still hours from sunset.

Though he'd grown up on the opposite coast, he'd always appreciated the Pacific Ocean. Vast, endless, powerful. This particular island was different. Calm. No crashing waves, since he was in the middle of an archipelago, one of hundreds of small islands, most privately owned. Quiet, peaceful. He could retire here.

Retire? That was a long, long way off. He was in his prime, and he had no reason to give it all up now.

Still, he should have bought this island for his own private use when he'd first rented it as an escape five years ago. At first he'd told no one about it, so he had a secret place to disappear to every now and again. Away from Roger, Denise, and the others.

They were albatrosses around his neck at times, their identities known to the authorities. All it took was one slip and they'd be in custody. There was no doubt Denise would keep her mouth shut or kill herself. But Roger? He played the loyalty card often enough, but Roger would turn on Trask in a heart-beat to save his own life.

He had no one to trust. And it had always been that way. But the hypocrisy of others had really hit home when, at the age of thirteen, he'd discovered that his father—upstanding and righteous and the strictest bastard on the Eastern Seaboard—regularly visited prostitutes.

An only child, Trask was a master at blending into his surroundings. It was why he knew things he should never have known, learned the darkest secrets of the adults in his life. Not just his parents, but everyone he came in contact with. He was often in the room when conversations about him, or his peers, or his parents' peers took place. Conversations where his parents would have freaked out had they known he'd overheard them. They would have punished him severely for eavesdropping.

This talent had served him well from an early age, at home, at school, and even now with his lucrative business. He picked up on the nuances, the unspoken words, the truth among the lies.

He'd watched his father all the time. There was not much to love in the stern man. They'd lived on an estate, on more than an acre of land north of Manhattan, quietly wealthy. Old money. Antiques. Lush furnishings. Stonebridge Academy and the *right* friends. But because Trask was an observant child, he'd always suspected something about his dear old dad. Something dark clawing beneath the skin. A darkness he also saw whenever he looked into the mirror.

So he'd watched and waited. He could disappear for hours in the bowels of the city and his parents never knew. He'd mastered the security system years before—a child prodigy, the headmaster had called him when he was six—and had disabled the entire school's security system. His parents only trusted him because they'd whip him into submission.

He didn't fear his father's belt. It fueled the darkness inside.

One evening when he was thirteen, his mother had gone to one of her many charity events in the city. Trask was supposed to be safely stowed away at Stonebridge Academy. Thanksgiving break was over and his parents had driven him back there—doing so only because they had to meet with the school's headmaster.

Your son has a genius-level IQ, but a disturbing contempt for authority.

Because everyone in authority was an idiot.

His father had belted him and lectured him. Trask walked first to his dorm room, then changed his mind and crawled back into the Bentley's trunk while his parents continued to gab with the Stonebridge's idiot headmaster.

He'd thought about killing them, but he didn't want to get caught. A murder like that needed planning. Forethought. He'd need an alibi. But someday . . .

So Trask was in the trunk when his father drove to Manhattan's Upper East Side. After dropping off his mother at her charity event, he parked on the street. His father *never* parked on the street. Trask followed him as he walked up to a brownstone and a woman opened the door. She was young, in her twenties. She had huge tits.

Trask waited until his father was inside, then waited a little longer just to be safe, before breaking into the house by cracking the security code. He wanted to know exactly what his father was up to. Was he cheating on his mother? That information would be gold. Trask could use it to get anything he wanted.

He listened, following faint sounds to an upstairs bedroom.

There were more than two people in the room.

The door was closed but not latched. Trask quietly pushed it open a crack, just enough to see. Faint lighting illuminated the bedroom. His father was naked, a woman on her knees with his penis in her mouth. Another woman was behind him, rubbing his shoulders.

His father barked out an order.

"Down on your knees, bitch." He pushed the woman off his dick and she got on all fours. He mounted her from behind. It was then that Trask noticed a collar and leash around the woman's neck. His father pulled up on the leash and the woman's neck strained.

The other woman got a paddle and slapped Trask's father on his scrawny ass. Trask thought for sure his dad would whip around and deck her, but instead he groaned. "Harder, bitch."

She hit him again. Soon his father's behind was red. Welts began to form. The woman on the floor was gasping and crying out. Whether she was faking an orgasm or it was real, Trask couldn't tell. But she collapsed on the ground and his father rose, his large dick bouncing in front of him. He pushed the second woman down on the bed and mounted her. He went at her like a piston, the woman's head hitting the headboard, but his father paid her discomfort no mind. She didn't protest, taking the pain with the pleasure, his needs more important than her own.

The foul words out of his father's mouth shocked Trask. Never had the distinguished judge uttered the words *fuck* or *cunt* or *whore* within Trask's earshot.

Trask walked away when his father was done, but didn't leave the house. His dull but pretty mother wasn't the sharpest tack in the box, but she worshipped the ground his father walked on. She did as he commanded. And here he was, fucking two whores and getting spanked. What else did he do? And were these the only two women he screwed around with? Were there others?

Trask waited until his father left. Then he walked back up to the bedroom and watched as the two women showered together, fingering each other. He stood in the steamy bathroom when they stepped out of the shower.

One screamed, but the other looked at him with curiosity. "You're his son."

Trask nodded. "Are you're his mistress."

He looked older than thirteen, having filled out the summer before, though he still hadn't grown into his full height.

She laughed. "Oh, honey, I'm not his mistress. I'm his call girl, Mina."

He didn't say anything. Call girl? Prostitute?

"Are you a virgin?"

"No," he lied.

The women looked at each other. The talkative one

stepped forward and through his pants touched his throbbing dick. He came. He hated her.

"Wouldn't you like to learn about sex from someone who knows everything about it?"

"You're a whore," he spat out.

She nodded, smiled, her eyes flashing something he didn't understand. "Yes, I am. That means you can do anything you want, and if you screw it up I'll still tell you you're the best fuck in the world."

"I don't want my father's whores. I'll find my own."

The woman who'd first screamed—she was much younger than Trask had originally thought—stepped forward. "Your father owns this place. We come here when he calls us. Do you like to watch?"

"No."

They glanced at each other, then looked at his wet pants. "Give us your number and we'll let you know the next time we're here."

He'd never planned on meeting them. But a month later Mina phoned. He wasn't going to show up, but his curiosity got the better of him and he slipped away from school once more. He hadn't been able to get the idea of fucking the whores out of his mind. Maybe just once, he thought. But he would be in charge. He might be a virgin, but he knew what to do.

He hadn't expected what happened. He hadn't expected to be raped by two women at the order of his father, who'd watched the entire time. And when the game was over, his father had whipped him.

"Remember who you are. My son, nothing more. Without me, you're nothing. If you ever fuck around in my business again, I'll disown you."

The glass Trask was holding as he sat on the deck now shattered in his hand. He glared at it, angry with himself and angry at those damn women. They were dead now, long gone, no one would ever find them, because they no longer existed. He'd wiped them off the face of the earth.

And no woman has ever been in control since.

That's why Kate Donovan would die by his hand. She'd fucked up his life like no woman had done since those two whores humiliated him for his father. He wouldn't give up until he had her naked beneath him, and he fucked her dying body.

Kate slammed the folder shut.

"This is getting us nowhere."

She got up and paced. Dillon Kincaid was driving her crazy, and they'd only met a few hours ago. He was so damn *reasonable*. Logical, straightforward, focused. She couldn't stand sitting around and reading files she had practically memorized over the last five years. They knew Roger Morton's identity and background. A lot of good that did them. He'd disappeared. Probably had a new identity. Unless someone saw him, turned him in, they couldn't touch him.

She felt Dillon's eyes on her back. She turned to face him. "What?"

He looked like he wanted to say something else, but instead, pointed to the file. "Roger Morton is from a wealthy Northeast family."

"So?"

"Seems like an unusual background for being the CEO of a pornography company."

"Sociopaths know no economic limit."

"True. But why porn? How did he meet Trask? They were in it together since the beginning of Trask Enterprises thirteen years ago. Back when the Internet was still relatively new, and online porn just starting. They pioneered a lot of the webcam technology. The files say that Roger went to Stonebridge Academy and graduated in 1989, but there are no details. I don't even know where it is."

Kate crossed over to her computer. She regained her focus and did what she did best. Forget people, they were too unpredictable. Computers were logical. You couldn't love them and you couldn't lose them. Her hard drive might crash, but she always had a backup—like a clone—to download.

People bled. They died. They disappeared.

"Stonebridge Academy is in Connecticut. Opened its doors in 1909."

"College?"

"K through twelve. It's a boarding school."

"So Roger Morton went to what I'll assume is an expensive boarding school in Connecticut. Graduates in 1989. Trask Enterprises opens its doors in 1994. According to your notes, Trask started in pornography— films—but dumped them in 1998 when the Internet provided a better distribution mechanism."

"That's what we believe," she said.

"Where was Roger during those five years? There doesn't seem to be a college degree."

"We don't know. He wasn't in prison, he wasn't in the military, and he didn't own property under his name."

"What about his parents?"

"His mother's dead. His father disowned him after

Morton's association with pornography became public."

Kate snuck a look at Dillon while he flipped through pages in her file. He was dangerous. To *her*. He was a shrink, dammit, and here she was sitting in a pool—an ocean—of guilt and regret and vengeance. He could probably dissect her for an entire class of psychology students, enough fodder for an entire semester.

But he was also handsome. Classically, perfectly handsome. His light-brown, sun-streaked wavy hair had probably been slicked back before he'd started the trek up the mountain. He was tall, trim, and all muscle, like he worked out regularly but didn't live for the weight machines. She could see him as a professor, like Indiana Jones before he put on the hat.

Only Dillon Kincaid was even sexier, a small, imperfect cleft in his chin highlighting his otherwise sleek, chiseled face.

She turned her head. This is what two years of isolation with only a grumpy, seventy-year-old professor for company did to you. One hot, sexy guy in the right age range comes up the mountain and she gets all twisted up.

No, the real twists came from the fact that Dillon Kincaid was a shrink. Kate feared what he might figure out about her, even more than how much she was attracted to him.

There was no hope, no future. Certainly not for them. His sister would probably be dead in thirty-one hours, ten minutes. And Kate would never see Dillon Kincaid again.

A knock on the door had her reaching for her gun.

"Grand Central Station," she muttered, crossing the room.

She opened the door, using it as a shield, her gun out and ready.

Jack Kincaid stood there.

"Jack?" Dillon couldn't hide his surprise.

"My men went with Connor and Patrick, but I figured you two might still need some help."

Kate frowned. The shrink was bad enough, but she didn't trust the military goon, either. He came in anyway.

"Great," she said sarcastically, rolling her eyes.

She slammed the door shut, turned to the computer out of habit.

Lucy Kincaid was there. Naked. Tied to the floor.

"Dear God, not again," Dillon said.

"What god?" Kate said. Dillon turned to stare at her and she almost didn't say what was on her tongue. But she couldn't stop it. "If He's up there watching, He sure as hell doesn't care about any of us."

Dillon looked angry. She hadn't even known he could get angry. He seemed so even-tempered and in control, even when watching his sister onscreen. Then again, she always did bring out the worst in people.

But he didn't say anything. Instead, he left the room.

"Sensitive," she said, trying to laugh it off, but feeling like she'd crossed a line and could never go back.

"Never mind him," Jack Kincaid said, staring at her with dark, probing eyes. "Dillon is a saint." He took a step toward her and it took all Kate's training not to take a step back. Jack was no one to mess with. "Me, on the other hand, I'm no saint. But Lucy doesn't deserve to die to give some bastard cheap thrills, so you'd better not be fucking with us or you'll be following her to the grave."

THIRTEEN

As soon as their plane landed, Patrick got Quinn Peterson's message about where to meet. He relayed the information to Lucky and Drake, the two men Jack had sent with them after getting them a private plane and pilot. Patrick had a newfound respect for his mysterious older brother after Jack got them the plane, gave him two of his men, and then went back up the mountain. Patrick didn't understand him or his decision to stay clear of the family for the past two decades, but Jack's brand of honor and loyalty was rare.

The four men trekked two miles on foot to where Agent Peterson and a small group waited. Lucky stepped forward and pulled a paper from his jacket. "I've already mapped it out."

He'd been working on a map earlier in the back of the plane. "We're here now, the target is here." Lucky had the two points circled and pointed to a small red circle off the coast. "The island is two miles out, but I think we go in by sea. A copter would be too noisy."

"We have an unmarked Coast Guard vessel," Peterson said.

Lucky stared at him. "In Mexican waters?"

Peterson's face remained blank.

"We can get to the island inside an hour, rescue the target, and get back here," Lucky added.

"We have transport waiting at the embassy two hours away," Peterson said. "And a copter on standby. I just need to call when we have the target. But remember, we need to be careful. This could very well be a trap. Keep your eyes open."

"I have an explosive-detecting device," Patrick said. "It's primarily used for checking for explosives on commercial aircrafts and is calibrated for the most common explosive materials."

"Then you lead with me," Peterson said. "Trask likes bombs, but they're usually simple, time-detonated devices."

They left in the small, unmarked boat. There were nine men total: Peterson and his team of four; Patrick and Connor; and Jack's two men.

The island was small, not more than one square mile. If there hadn't been a large, dense grove of trees in the middle, Patrick would have assumed, from what he could see from the Coast Guard vessel's deck, that it was underwater half the time. It was also dark, the sun had already disappeared, leaving a spectacular glow on the horizon but doing nothing for their visibility, and they were running slow, without lights. The muggy weather stayed with them, even in the ocean. Saltwater coated their skin and sinuses. It was different here than farther up the coast. Hotter, humid, the air still, the waves warmer even at night.

"There." Connor pointed to a small inlet.

"No," Peterson said without elaborating. He motioned for the boat's pilot to slowly circle the island.

"What are you doing?" Connor demanded of Quinn.

"Recon."

"My sister could be dying!"

Lucky shook his head. "I don't think anyone's here."

They spent fifteen minutes circling the island before Peterson agreed to dock. They had to approach cautiously for fear of underwater rocks. There was a faint light in the center of the island, which was not much more than a mile at its widest, possibly a house or cabin. No boats, but that didn't mean anything. Lucy's captors could have left to get supplies.

Lucky stared at the brothers, his young face stern. "We go in low, quiet. Jack will have my ass if I get one of you killed."

"I was a cop," Connor said. "I know how to cover my own ass."

Patrick squeezed his brother's arm. Connor was tense, on edge. They all were.

Peterson spoke up. "Watch my commands. I agree with Lucky. Low, quiet, no rushing. Years ago Trask set a trap and we walked right into it. I don't want to walk into another."

They navigated the boat into the inlet. Peterson left two of his men on the boat, armed.

Patrick's gut told him Lucy wasn't on this island. It was too quiet.

Maybe she was on a nearby island. The map showed at least eight within a three-mile radius. Easy to get the coordinates wrong. After this, they'd have to hit each one and check. They might be close; they couldn't just give up and go home empty-handed.

They couldn't give up on Lucy.

A small, one-room cabin stood in the center of the island. A faint, yellow light illuminated the room. Patrick took out the EDD to check for explosives. Green. They slowly approached the structure. The needle wobbled toward the yellow. Warning.

"Hold it. There may be explosives."

Which could be a sign that Lucy was there.

Peterson held up a finger and motioned for his two men to walk around the cabin. They came back. "Nothing external. No electrical power to the cabin."

The blinds were drawn. A single door was pad-locked on the outside. Peterson checked the door frame for explosives. "Clear."

Drake and Lucky held back while Peterson's men cut the lock and opened the door.

At first, the smell hit Patrick. Then he saw her.

In the middle of the room was a naked female body, her face turned away from them. Her long black hair looked wet. A cell phone rested in the palm of her hand, as if she had tried to call for help.

Patrick's stomach clenched. *Lucy.*

"Lucy!" Connor ran in.

"Halt!" Peterson shouted and Patrick tried to pull Connor back as the EDD needle moved to the red zone.

When Connor touched the body, the head rolled away. He sucked in his breath.

It wasn't Lucy. It was another woman, just as young, just as innocent. She had been dead for several days.

"We have to get out," Peterson said. "I don't like this."

"Look at the wall." Connor pointed to the wall of the cabin. UNTIL WE MEET AGAIN, KATE was spray-painted in bloodred, along with a series of numbers that made no sense to Patrick.

The phone in the dead girl's hand rang.

There was a flash of bright light, and the cabin went up in flames.

Trask watched on his computer monitor as the men entered the cabin. He'd intended to blow the place as soon as they entered, but he'd been curious to see who they were. He would now get visuals to run through his database.

They didn't look like feds. There were two men, but there appeared to be a third outside the cabin. He wished he'd put up external surveillance, but he didn't have an unlimited power supply on that island. When he'd left the prostitute there three days ago as part of the trap, he'd needed the generator to keep the cell phone charged.

He'd never expected Kate to fall for the trap, and had she been the one to walk through the door, he wouldn't have blown the place. There had been a clue—one only Kate would understand—in the room that would lead her right to him.

But he didn't want the feds or some other pest to track him down and make him rush the show.

Okay, there was a fed there. The blond with the holster. The way he moved, issued orders, definitely a fed.

He'd been right about Kate from the beginning. She was smarter than most, she understood him. He'd already confirmed that she'd fed the government information and they'd acted on it. And she was still watching, waiting, knowing it wouldn't be that easy to find him.

Trask had to draw her out.

He saw her in cyberspace, among the hordes of people searching the Internet. She was sly, smart, focused. She had come close, before he'd been ready for her. He manually changed his frequency often now in order to thwart her.

But he was finally ready. Lucy Kincaid was the perfect bait. He'd send her another clue. Or maybe he'd just send her a message.

After he called the cell phone that sat in the dead girl's hand, Trask closed his eyes to avoid the bright magnesium flash.

Soon the cabin, and all evidence, would be ashes.

And if the feds died in the process, who the hell cared?

FOURTEEN

IT WAS DARK, a thin orange line along the western horizon that quickly disappeared as Dillon watched. He'd found this vista point a hundred yards from the main observatory, with a couple of old benches and a well-worn path. He could picture Kate sitting here watching the sunset and thinking about revenge and guilt and justice.

Kate had angered him. He didn't like that she'd gotten to him. It was the stress of no sleep and Lucy's danger that had fueled his anger and frustration. Kate was just the spark that had set it off.

His brothers hadn't argued about his decision not to go with them, probably because they felt that his presence would only hinder the operation. Maybe it would have. He didn't have their training, but he did have something they didn't: a key to the killer's mind.

Dillon had the utmost respect for law enforcement—he worked with them daily. But the one thing they too often lacked was the killer's motivation. The easiest way to track a criminal was to learn everything about his past, his family, his relationships, his associations. What drove a person to commit heinous crimes? Money? Fear? Lust?

The key was always there, in the past. Cops had too many cases and had to make too many quick decisions to take the time to process every step leading to the killer. That's where Dillon came in. When the evidence wasn't there, when there were no witnesses, when people were murdered and the police didn't know which direction to go, Dillon could focus the investigation. Give them tools to find the killer and take him down.

Every killer feared something. What did Trask fear? Poverty? Sexual dysfunction? Loss of freedom? Women?

He hated women, that was abundantly clear. But what about a fear of women? He subjugated them to beat down the fear within himself. He was physically strong, but he also had men around him to ensure that the women were kept under control. He restrained the women, even when they were too weak to fight. Rape was about power and anger, but rape as a show? That was ego. Proving over and over that he had control over these women, proving it in front of the world.

For the benefit of everyone, or just one person?

Roger Morton was from a wealthy family, privileged. Yet he became the CEO of a pornography business and was disowned. You didn't just walk away from millions of dollars to live out a sexual fantasy. There was money in porn, particularly online porn, but initially, Trask Enterprises had just been an upstart company and Roger couldn't have been pulling in huge sums of money until after the Internet grew exponentially over the years.

Did Trask have money of his own? Investors? If he

was wealthy in his own right, that held that he and Roger had known each other because they traveled in the same social circles.

Dillon was certain that Trask and Roger had known each other since childhood. It was not only logical considering the time line of Trask Enterprises, but there was a bond between the men that hadn't been severed even when they were forced to disappear after Kate exposed April Klinger's death.

Denise was a wild card. She was definitely the subservient in the relationship; she would do anything Trask asked of her. Yet she hated the women he brought in. Jealousy, deep and hot. What did she think of Trask's obsession with Kate?

The more Dillon thought about it, the more he became convinced that Trask was luring Kate into a trap he'd created just for her. He would reveal himself only to her, probably threaten someone if she didn't come alone. And because she had no fear of death—in fact, she welcomed it—she would go, thinking it would be worthwhile if she killed him in the process, regardless of what might happen to her.

It was that realization that calmed Dillon more than the time away from Kate's room. He knew what she would do; he would have to be watchful that she didn't take off without him.

From the corner of his eye, he saw Jack saunter down the path, fully armed, wearing the guns and ammo and equipment comfortably.

"She's trouble," Jack said, collapsing on the stone bench that afforded him the best view of the path.

"She's letting the past eat her alive," Dillon said.

He looked pointedly at Jack. "I'd always thought you'd done the same thing, but now I don't think so."

"Don't go there, Dil. Let's just do the op and go our separate ways."

"The op." Dillon shook his head, stared at the vast darkness around them. The temperature had dropped dramatically when the sun went down.

"You have to think of it as an operation. Distance yourself from the emotional complications."

"Lucy is my sister. I can't do that. It's not an operation. It's her *life*."

"I've dealt with a lot of life-and-death situations. You don't have to explain it to me," Jack said. "That's why it's even more important to separate your emotions from the job."

Dillon understood what Jack was saying—he'd heard it from Carina and Connor and other cops who went out and dealt in murder. If you got emotionally involved with the victims you wouldn't survive on the job.

But there was a reason doctors didn't operate on relatives and cops didn't investigate the murder of someone they cared about. You can't separate your emotions from people you know and love.

"Any word from your men?" Dillon asked.

"They checked in when they had the island in sight, then went radio silent. That was twenty-five minutes ago."

"Shouldn't they have gotten back to you by now?"

"Not if they're doing it right. Circle the island, verify security measures, find a safe place to dock, approach with caution. It's unknown territory; they can't just run in without reconnaissance."

Dillon hoped that they had found Lucy. Safe. That they were bringing her home. Maybe he could convince Kate to come back to the States and seek some closure for what had happened with her partner and her lover five years ago.

But Kate wasn't his patient, or his problem. She'd gotten under his skin, but that didn't mean he couldn't carefully extract her. He couldn't save every lost soul in the world. Look at Nelia. He'd never told anyone in the family that he'd flown up to Idaho two years after Justin's murder to talk to his sister Nelia with the purpose of bringing her home.

Nelia was nothing like he'd remembered. The light was gone from her eyes, and she told him she was dead inside. The only thing keeping her from suicide was the belief that she would go to Hell and never see Justin again. Faith? Perhaps, but it had done nothing to console her. And neither had Dillon. Everything he'd tried had failed.

When he'd finally suggested she see a psychiatrist so she could deal with her grief, she'd said, "I don't want to let it go. It keeps Justin in the small part of my heart that still beats."

Doctors should never counsel their own family. If they found Lucy, he could help with her immediate needs, but he would have to send her to someone else to heal.

When they found her. Because they would. They had to.

"What's she like?" Jack asked quietly.

"She's sassy. Smart. She has a scholarship to Georgetown. Knows four languages fluently and thrives in debate. Beautiful. Kind. She has a mouth on her, but what Kincaid doesn't?" Dillon smiled sadly. Lucy had their parents wrapped around her little finger, but her elder siblings received the brunt of her sarcasm.

"Why did you walk away from the family, Jack?"

"I had my reasons."

"Are they still valid?"

"My business, Dil."

"As always, Jack."

They sat in silent anger for several minutes and Jack changed the subject. "What do you know about this guy who has Lucy?"

"Not enough. I haven't met him. Psychiatry isn't a hard science. We base our interpretations on experience, facts, and personality, but human beings all react differently to stimuli."

"I get that."

"Trask is sexually damaged. I don't think he can truly enjoy sex without hurting or killing the woman in the process. He hates women, but I also think he fears them and the power they have or could have over him. It's deep and long-standing. Something happened to him in his youth, by an authority figure, possibly his mother. It twisted sex in his head."

"So it's his parents' fault?" Jack didn't hide the contempt in his voice.

Dillon took a deep breath. Hadn't he just gone through this with Kate? "I didn't say that. I'm trying to understand Trask. If I can understand him, then I can use that knowledge to stop him. Serial killers often have abnormal childhoods. Not all of them, but a huge percentage. Yet there are other children who are abused and lead tragic childhoods who never grow up to rape or kill. Trask would have showed signs of sociopathy from an early age. His parents may not have recognized it. The FBI notes on him indicate that he likely has a genius-level IQ. He has proven his intelligence by hiding his identity, his whereabouts, his Internet feed."

"Why Lucy?" Jack asked. "I mean, out of all the teenagers in the country, why her?"

Dillon hadn't thought about that. He'd been so focused on Trask and finding Lucy, he hadn't dwelled on a victim analysis.

"I don't know. They met online, he was prowling for someone. But Lucy might fit some profile only he knows about."

"What about the other victims? Are they all young and dark-haired?"

"They're all young, under thirty except for the FBI agent he killed." Dillon mentally reviewed the files. "They run the gamut from Caucasian to light-skinned Latinas. Brunettes, blondes, a redhead."

"What does that mean?"

"He's an equal-opportunity killer."

Kate stared at the link that popped up on her computer.

Click me, Kate.

She knew it was from Trask. She didn't want to click it. She had to.

The grainy video was of Connor Kincaid running into a cabin. There was a body on the floor. Patrick Kincaid came in behind him. Quinn Peterson was standing right inside the door throwing out soundless orders. *Get out,* he mouthed. A moment later, a bright flash, then nothing.

She dry heaved, her hand to her mouth. "No," she cried.

Hello, Kate.

She wanted to put her fist through the screen. Instead, she typed,

Bastard.

She almost heard his laugh through cyberspace.

Sticks and stones. You've come very close, Kate. I'll tell you how close but you have to promise me you won't bring anyone with you.

I don't need anyone else to kill you.

You humor me, Kate, darling.

Let Lucy go and I'll come. Alone.

Tsk, tsk. You think I trust you? I'll let Lucy go when I see you.

You think I trust you?

No. You can't trust me, Kate. But you already know that. Would you willingly trade places with Lucy to save her?

She answered without hesitation.

Yes.

I'm looking forward to killing you, Kate.

I'm looking forward to killing you, asshole.

There was a long pause and Kate feared she'd lost him. And there was no guarantee that he would let Lucy go, even if she did meet him.

She had to find his island and go in quietly. Unfortunately time wasn't on her side. It was dark right now, but the odds that she could find and get to the island before sunrise were not in her favor. A rescue in broad daylight? Virtually impossible. And there would be very few hours of dark left before the kill if she waited twenty-four hours.

"Dammit! What rock are you hiding under, Trask?" Her computer beeped.

Go back to time stamp 41:17:50. I had to manually reset my location because your program hit it. The data is all there. You're good, Kate. But I'm better.

"What are you reading?"

Dillon walked in without knocking. Had she left the door unlocked? With a tap on her keyboard, the onscreen text disappeared.

She didn't want to deceive Dillon, but she had no choice. If Trask knew she was working with someone, he'd change the rules. He had never jumped the countdown, but under pressure . . . ? She didn't know what he was capable of.

Yes, she did. He was capable of anything.

"Just checking my programs," she said.

"I'm sorry I stormed out like that."

"No apology necessary."

She pictured the video of his brothers walking into the trap. Her heart ached. She couldn't tell him, not like this. And Quinn . . . could they have survived the explosion? Was anyone left to get them off the damn island? Quinn was a seasoned agent, surely he had backup.

Her stomach flipped. She'd sent them the information. It didn't matter how many warnings she issued with it, how loud she screamed that it could be a trap, it was still her info and her fault those men walked into that cabin.

After last year, she was surprised they'd gone in at all. Two years, two traps. But what about now? What about her communication with Trask? Would they . . . could they . . . believe her?

And Trask had to know she'd sent the FBI that tip about the island. He'd had it rigged. He'd given her the false coordinates on purpose. From the beginning, he'd been monitoring her every step. He knew what she had done, who she talked to, where she had sent them. Trask would be expecting the cavalry when she showed up wherever he sent her. Unless he was orchestrating this charade all along. Feed her data, she cries wolf, the feds go in . . . nothing. Or a trap. And the girl still dies. Eventually her people would stop believing her.

Her mind was going in circles, but one thing was for sure: she couldn't tell Dillon about his brothers. It would tip her hand that she'd been in communication with Trask. And how could she explain that? Not until she knew more about when and where he wanted to meet, and what she could do to protect Lucy.

"You're under just as much stress as I am. Perhaps more."

"I'm okay."

He looked at her oddly. "Maybe you are, maybe you aren't. Right now I need to find my sister. What is your program telling you?"

"It's still working."

Frustration crossed his face and it took all of Kate's willpower not to tell him about her conversation with Trask.

"You're a computer whiz. Can you break into the Stonebridge Academy's computer system?"

"I don't know." She wanted to look at her data at the time stamp Trask had just told her about.

"Would you try? I think Roger Morton went to school with Trask. Maybe there's something in those records that will help us find his true identity. At the very least, we can capture the names of everyone who was at Stonebridge the same time as Morton."

How could she not? She bit her lip, torn.

She'd have to find a way to do both at the same time without Dillon noticing.

FIFTEEN

JACK CAME INTO KATE'S ROOM an hour later and Dillon looked up from the reports he was reviewing.

"I think I have him," Dillon began. "Not his identity, but where he went—"

"I have some news," Jack interrupted solemnly.

"What happened?"

"The cabin was wired—a magnesium burn. Fast and hot, but what really did the damage was the dry wood and accelerant in the corners."

"My God." Dillon shook his head. "Was Lucy there?"

"No, another girl, already dead. Unidentified."

"And Patrick and Connor, are they on their way back?"

"Back to San Diego." Jack sighed, showing a rare flash of helplessness. "Connor has some burns, but he'll be fine. Patrick is in a coma."

"Patrick?" Dillon couldn't imagine his little brother immobile. "How long has he been out?"

"Three hours. The feds have arranged for transport to the States. He's alive, but needs surgery."

Lucy missing, Patrick in a coma, Connor burned. Dillon glanced at Kate, her face pale. She quickly looked the other way, avoiding eye contact.

"And Trask?"

"They're no closer than we are." Jack stared at Kate. "Are they?"

Kate shrugged. "They have good people working for them."

"Few are as good as you," Jack said. "I think you know where they are."

Kate spun around in her chair. "If I knew where that bastard was, I'd be there. Do you think I'm holding out on you? Do you think I would jeopardize another innocent girl's life? Do you—"

Dillon put up his hand. "Jack, that was uncalled-for."

"Oh?"

"Do you have a basis for accusing Kate of keeping information from us?"

"Instinct."

Dillon looked from his brother to Kate and back. He was in a room with two people he didn't really know. The brother he'd shared the womb with, and a woman he'd just met.

"Jack, give me a minute."

Jack shrugged, left the room.

"You can't believe that I—"

Dillon put up his hand. "Kate, you are under intense stress right now. You're acting like Lucy is your own flesh and blood, and that means a lot to me. You're doing it because of duty and guilt and revenge—because of Trask—but you're also compassionate. You feel for my sister, and I won't forget that."

He took a step toward her, put his hands on her shoulders while she sat in her chair. She swallowed but didn't take her eyes from his.

"I also believe you will do anything you think is right to stop Trask from hurting Lucy or anyone else. Even if that means lying. To me, to anyone.

"Don't lie to me, Kate. I'm on your side. *We* are on the same side. Together we'll find Lucy. Don't play the maverick."

"I'm not," she said, her voice cracking.

Dillon ached for Kate, but not half as much as he hurt for what Lucy had already endured. What Lucy would suffer in twenty-four hours if they couldn't locate Trask's island.

"Trust me, Kate."

Her blue eyes searched his, full of agony and conflict. Any other time, Dillon would work on her, using his special talent to get her to open up. He wanted to, but he didn't have the time or energy to worry about Kate's mental health until after they rescued Lucy. He only needed her to trust him.

Kate diverted her eyes and Dillon suspected that she wanted to tell him something. Instead she said, "Before the colonel came in, you said you found something."

"Colonel?"

"Your brother. Jack."

"He's a colonel? How do you know?"

"The pin on his jacket."

Dillon had missed it, or if he had seen the pin, it

hadn't registered that Jack had the same rank their father had had when he'd retired.

"Trask?" Kate prompted.

Though he felt like he was being manipulated away from a conversation he needed to have with Kate, his discovery was important.

He showed Kate the files he'd been working with. "Roger Morton's classmates. I pulled all students in his class, the year before, and the year after. Since Roger and Trask have been together for a long time, and since Roger didn't attend college, I suspect they were in high school together. Stonebridge Academy is an elite boarding school for the rich and privileged."

"Logical, but that's a long way to look back."

"Not that long. Roger graduated high school in 1989. Eighteen years ago. A few years later, Trask Enterprises formed and a twenty-three-year-old was at its helm. No college education. The FBI couldn't find a prison or military record on him. Where was he for those five years? Apparently from these files doing absolutely nothing and living at home in Massachusetts. He wouldn't have had to work; his family is worth tens of millions."

"So why even start working at Trask Enterprises?" Kate said, beginning to follow Dillon's line of reasoning.

"Exactly. And who would hire someone with no practical experience to manage a business?"

"Nepotism. Friendship."

"Right. Roger's parents are in shipping, old established business. He could have worked for that company, but no. He did nothing until Trask opened up."

"I guess your theory makes sense, but Roger could

have met virtually anyone in those circles. His father could have called in favor after favor to get him a position."

"Nowhere in these files is there any record of the FBI interviewing Roger's father except for one notation that an agent went out after Paige Henshaw was killed, and Roger's father told this agent he'd disowned his son when he started the online pornography business. He also said he didn't know who Trask was."

Kate's eyes widened. "But they didn't ask the right questions."

"Namely, who were Roger's close friends during high school?"

"Makes sense." The brief excitement on Kate's face disappeared. "But it does us no good now! We can't get to Massachusetts and interview the man. We don't have the time."

"But Peterson has the contacts. He can get someone out there first thing in the morning." Dillon picked up a piece of paper where he'd handwritten fifty-six names. "And ask the father if any of these boys were close to his son. Trask's real identity is unknown to us, therefore he is probably using it to run a legitimate business or any number of things."

"And if we can get a photograph . . ." Kate's voice trailed off. She was the only person alive who had seen Trask in person.

"I'm going to call Quinn Peterson, okay?" Dillon held up his cell phone. The call could be traced, which was why Kate had only used her double-blind IM account to communicate with Peterson.

She nodded slowly, understanding that if Quinn

wanted to, he could turn over the records and the feds could burst in and arrest her.

"I trust him," she said.

Dillon left the room since the cell phone couldn't pick up a reception inside. The night was cold and he pulled his jacket around him. He walked to the vista where he and Jack had spoken earlier. He didn't know where his brother had since gone.

The reception was mediocre. "Kincaid?" Peterson said, white noise distorting his voice. "I'm on a military transport with Patrick."

"How is he?"

"Alive."

"Has he regained consciousness?"

"No."

Four hours now. That wasn't good. "Thanks for getting him out of there fast."

"I didn't expect you to call."

Dillon explained to him what he'd found in the files and about interviewing Roger Morton's father about associates in high school.

Peterson didn't say anything, but the crackle on the other end assured Dillon that he was still on the phone. "It's a good lead," Peterson finally said. "And we have nothing else. I have some men out at the island where the cabin exploded, looking for evidence, but everything was pretty much destroyed. Magnesium burns hot.

"Connor said Trask had to have been watching to know when to call the cell phone. That there was a camera across from the door.

"I'm sure it's melted, but we have the best people

looking at radio and Internet feeds. Time is not on our side."

"You don't have to tell me that," Dillon said.

"I'll send an agent out to Morton's house first thing in the morning. E-mail me the list of names and I'll get them out there."

Dillon hung up and heard a voice behind him. "Feds know anything?"

Jack. Dillon turned around. "Patrick hasn't regained consciousness. They're heading back to San Diego for surgery."

"I know. My team is on its way back to Hidalgo."

"And you?"

Jack's dark eyes narrowed almost imperceptibly. "I'm in it till the end."

Dillon raised an eyebrow. "I guess I just don't know what to expect of you."

Dillon's brother stared into nothingness. "I suppose I deserve that." He turned back to Dillon, a tic in his neck showing that he was angry. "I'm a lot of things, Dillon. But more than anything, I'm a man of my word."

Jack walked off into the darkness.

Mick had hoped Roger would forget or change his mind. He'd been physically ill since Roger had told him he would be next up with Lucy Kincaid.

He couldn't do it. He couldn't even get hard. Thinking about hurting her had him so twisted in knots he doubted he'd ever get it up again. He was perspiring and wondered if he'd eaten something bad.

Or maybe it was fear eating at him. He was about to do something that would get him killed. Get

Lucy killed as well. But he didn't see that he had a choice.

He'd used his homemade sextant at sunrise and sunset to figure out the longitude and latitude of the island. But if he was off by a fraction of a degree, he could send Kate Donovan miles in the wrong direction.

Did he trust his skills? He had to. He didn't have much choice at this point. He'd been trying to figure out a way to get Lucy off the island, but she was never unwatched. Denise, Trask, or Roger watched her at all times through the numerous cameras on the island. He was being watched, too. He'd had to be extremely careful, and he feared that between his caution and fear of exposure his coordinates were off.

But he had to do something until he found a hole big enough to rescue Lucy.

He had no way of contacting Merritt without Roger or Trask seeing the transmission. If they caught him, they'd kill him and Lucy before the FBI could make it to the island.

The only thing he had was knowledge. Knowledge that Trask had an open line on Kate Donovan. Though Mick didn't know why, Trask had been watching Kate closely, watching her every cyber move. If Mick could piggyback the transmission on the open channel, Trask wouldn't notice. *Probably* wouldn't notice.

If he did figure it out, Mick would be dead. But Mick was already staring at his death warrant. He didn't see any way out of this operation alive.

Mick used an old FBI training code from his Academy days. It meant nothing except to other graduates. A joke. Kate would get it.

Mick had never met Kate, but he knew of her. Everyone did. She was almost a legend. His boss hated her, but Mick liked her. You had to like someone who went balls to the wall when they believed in something.

She'd be able to decipher the coded message, and then hopefully recognize the numbers as time and degrees of sunrise and sunset. Then all she had to do was look up the data on the Internet to get the exact longitude and latitude.

She was smart. She had to understand. He just hoped she was smart enough not to come alone. She had to know that Trask wanted to kill her. Torture her first. Trask hated her. Whenever he spoke of Kate it was with a sick, twisted anger that showed in every molecule of his body, down to his black soul.

It would be brutal, worse than anything he'd done to those other women. Worse than anything she could possibly imagine.

The transmission had just gone through when the door opened.

"You're on, lucky boy," Roger said, slapping Mick on the back. "Watcha doing?"

It was innocuous in tone, but Mick didn't trust Roger.

"See this?" Mick pointed to a camera that was flickering. Mick had programmed it to flicker.

"What's wrong?"

"Don't know. I need to go out and check the wires."

"It's just a flicker. Come on. The show must go on."

Mick followed Roger, wiping sweat off his brow.

As soon as Dillon walked out to call Quinn Peterson, Kate went to the time stamp that Trask had told her would lead directly to his location.

Too easy. Right there was the primary satellite information. She traced the satellite and found the computer that was bouncing the webcam to it. Northeast of Seattle, Washington, near Mount Baker.

It took her a little time, and she kept looking at the door waiting for Dillon to walk back in. But after hacking into every ISP in that area, she found him.

Thirty minutes, but still it seemed too easy. He'd had to point her to the time stamp. Why hadn't her computer picked up on it? Had she messed up her program somehow? Had Trask planted the data and had her program ignored it because it wasn't a live feed?

She rubbed her head. This was more than she'd had before. And Trask had contacted her. Why would he send her on a wild-goose chase? The FBI, yes—he didn't want them around. But he wanted her. She'd known it since that night five years ago, and she knew it now.

She had the exact coordinates of the webcam that sent up the signal. That's where Lucy was. Dillon and Jack were off somewhere. She hoped they were sleeping, but doubted it. Lucy's screen had been quiet, and Kate packed her bag. Guns. Ammo. Emergency supplies. Check. Key to the plane. Check. Her codes and another laptop and a handheld. Her backup laptop wasn't as fast as the one she'd given to Patrick, but it was all she had left.

She hated leaving Dillon. She wanted to trust him. She wanted to trust *someone*. But bringing him along would most certainly get both him and Lucy killed. There was no way Dillon would allow her to intentionally sacrifice herself for Lucy.

Kate didn't see any other way to save her. If Trask even suspected that Kate was bringing in anyone, he'd kill Lucy. Without remorse, without hesitation.

Though she knew she could die, accepted it as part of her job, Kate didn't *want* to die. She'd worry about that when Lucy was free.

Movement on the screen. A man came into view. He looked familiar.

No. Not another rape.

She frantically typed on her computer.

I'm coming, you bastard! Don't touch her. You touch her and I'll send the fucking military to your location!

Nothing. He wasn't there. Damn him!

Lucy cried out, her voice vibrating in the small room. Kate muted the sound and prayed that Dillon wasn't on the other side of the door, that he hadn't heard his sister's pleas.

Something odd came over her computer terminal. At first she thought it was Trask responding. She stared at the series of numbers and letters. It looked familiar. Why?

She glanced up at the screen. That man with Lucy. He was familiar. Why? Was he a fed? She couldn't name him, but she'd seen him before, a long time ago.

She looked back at the code on her screen and it came to her instantly. The FBI training academy. A test code in one of their textbooks.

She wrote down the numbers and letters, then translated the code from memory. It was a simple code, something all trainees used to pass messages and have fun. It helped them see the patterns behind words and actions, not just learn to decode.

What did these numbers mean? They looked like degrees. Degrees of what? Or time. Military time. Wait. Both. The code had been backward, and now she saw that the numbers were definitely time of sunrise, noon, and sunset and degrees, which would be the degrees of the sun over the hemisphere.

But she didn't know what they meant—if Lucy was south of the equator, the numbers meant one location. If she was north, they meant something completely different.

She typed frantically in her computer, searching for an online nautical map that would give her the longitude and latitude that corresponded to these times and degrees.

If in the south, she was in the middle of the ocean. If in the north . . . eighty miles from the location Trask had given her. Same latitude, different longitude. Was it her mistake?

She recalculated the data Trask had sent her and the mystery data. No, she knew this stuff. And her numbers were right. That meant that Trask was either messing with her, or he was deliberately sending her eighty miles away.

Why? To keep her away from Lucy. In case she

brought in the feds. Once he had determined that she was alone, he'd bring her to Lucy.

He wanted Kate to watch her die. He'd get a sick, twisted pleasure in that.

Movement on the screen distracted her. She watched as the man on-screen climbed on top of Lucy. She typed frantically into the feed she'd locked onto with Trask.

> Get that man off Lucy now and I'll be there as soon as possible.

Nothing.

> Dammit you fucking bastard! Don't do this!

Nothing.

She kicked the desk. Who was she to be giving orders? Trask held all the cards. He knew where she was, but she didn't know exactly where he was. Which feed was right? What Trask sent, or this FBI code?

Why would he send her to the wrong place?

What are you thinking, Kate? He wants to control you. If you're nowhere near Lucy, he can do whatever he wants.

He'll never let her go.

The man on the screen leaned over Lucy. Kissed her. She tossed her head back and forth, straining to get away from him. This man was different. He didn't have the violent urgency to hurt Lucy that Roger had.

Did the FBI have an undercover agent there? An FBI agent who would rape to protect his cover?

She looked at the coded message again. An FBI training code from the Academy. Her gut instinct was that this man was, or had been, one of theirs.

She typed.

> Don't let anyone touch Lucy again and I'll meet you. Fair trade. If anyone touches her, you'll never get me. I'll go so deep you'll never find me.

He was there.

> You'd never be able to live with yourself.
> You're right. But you won't be the one killing me.

Nothing.

She watched the screen. The man seemed to be listening to someone off-camera, then he unzipped his jeans.

The man was leaning into Lucy, his face burrowed in her neck. But the expression on Lucy's face changed. Almost imperceptibly. As if she were listening intently. Would Trask notice? He wasn't a fool. Dammit, the fed was going to get himself killed. Maybe he deserved it.

Damn you, Trask!

Lucy didn't want to be raped again. The humiliation of being naked and exposed to a camera was almost unbearable, but she was alive. Yet every time she thought about what had happened that morning, she screamed inside, her mind trying to make sense of it, trying to accept it. Her heart was crying at the pain, the embarrassment, the deep wound on her soul that the one thing that was hers, all hers—her choice— had been ripped from her. And she'd never have it back.

She had never felt helpless before, not like this. When she was seven and Justin was killed she had known what had happened—her parents never lied to her about it—but she hadn't seen Justin dead, she hadn't been physically hurt. The pain from that time was emotional, mostly from an overwhelming sense of loss, like part of her was missing.

Now death was a reality, the defiling sex, the humiliation of the film. Her rape was going to be replayed for everyone, even after she was gone. It wasn't fair. She hoped that her family never saw, that they didn't know what had happened to her. She didn't think she could look them in the eye again.

More than anything, she wanted her mother.

Tears escaped from her eyes, and she hated herself for showing her pain and fear. She didn't want Trevor to know how much she hurt inside. She tried to keep a straight face, blank, block everything out, but it was getting harder and harder the longer she was restrained.

"Don't cry."

The man on top of her, the man she'd been able to block out while he kissed her neck and breasts, had noticed her anguish and she froze.

She tossed her head back and forth, trying to avoid his lips. Avoid his eyes. In the background she heard Roger say, "Fuck her already. People are paying for a show."

She heard his zipper. Felt him against her leg. He buried his face in her neck, his hands on her hips.

God no, please no, not again.

"I don't want to hurt you," he whispered, his voice barely audible. "I sent for help. You need to trust me. Watch carefully."

Trust him? Her rapist wanted her to *trust him*? Was this some sort of sick mental game, a bastardized version of good cop, bad cop? She'd never trust him or anyone here.

"Get off me!" she screamed as loud as she could.

From the door, "Do it already. Spread her legs. Show the camera." Then, muttered, "Amateurs."

"Please trust me," her rapist whispered in her ear. Then he raised himself up, looked down at her.

She closed her eyes. *Just do it. Do it and I hope you die a horrible death and burn in Hell for eternity.*

"Cut!"

It was Trevor's voice.

Roger intervened. "What? Come on, we're just getting going. Mick is a little slow to the task, but he's finally getting into it."

"Change of plans."

The red eye of the camera was off. Lucy's eyes widened. What was happening?

The man, Mick, stood up slowly. He turned to Trevor. "What the fuck?"

"You're pathetic," Trevor said. "Any other red-blooded man would have taken what was offered. Seven minutes to get that dick hard? What are you, a fag?"

Mick reddened. "I, I—"

"Just go. Monitor the cameras. Now."

"What's going on?"

"None of your business," Trevor said and watched him leave. "Denise!"

The woman who hated Lucy came into the room. She wore a business suit with a short skirt, heavy makeup, and her hair had been styled and teased.

To Roger, Trevor said, "You and Frank play out the rape game with Denise."

"Aw, come on, what happened?"

"Are you questioning me?"

"No, but—"

"Lucy will be back onstage in just a few hours. But I need to leave the island. I don't want any down time from here on out."

"You never leave in the middle of a show. You need to tell me what's happening."

"I need to tell you nothing."

Lucy listened to the exchange, unsure what was going on, but seeing this as an opportunity. Both Trevor and Roger sounded angry.

Watch carefully, the man who had almost raped her had said.

Something was happening.

And she would definitely be watching carefully.

For the first time, she felt a tickle of hope that she might get out of here alive.

SIXTEEN

"WHERE'S LUCY?"

Dillon walked into her room and Kate jumped, still uncomfortable having people around after so many years being alone.

He stared at the muted computer screen where Denise was being raped by two men. Kate had almost forgotten it was on. She'd been so intent on planning how to get off the mountain without alerting Dillon or his brother.

"I don't know. The screen went blank, then Denise came on. I'm not worried about her. She's doing this willingly."

"Are you sure?" Dillon frowned at the sick perversion playing out on the screen.

"I'm sure," Kate said. "She faked her own death and attacked Lucy. She helped set Paige up to be killed. You have any doubts?"

"I—"

"Trask Enterprises' biggest moneymakers were their rape-fantasy scenarios. That's where Denise got her start. Don't feel sorry for her."

Dillon couldn't help but wonder how Denise had gotten to this point in her life. What had happened to make her feel that her only choice, her only option, was to be used in such a vile, sick manner? She had no self-esteem, no self-respect.

Someone had destroyed Denise's ego years ago, and Dillon couldn't help but feel compassion for the abused woman, regardless of the crimes she'd committed.

"Why?" Dillon said.

"Oh, she probably has some tragic story in her childhood." Kate rolled her eyes as if she didn't believe it. "But that doesn't justify her actions."

"No, what I mean is why did he take Lucy off air?" Dillon feared he wouldn't have the next full twenty-four hours to find her. Though he didn't want to see her on the Internet, there was some comfort in seeing her alive. Now he knew nothing of her fate.

"I don't know," Kate mumbled.

Dillon stared at her. She was lying. He knew it as surely as he knew his name.

"Has he done this before?"

"He intersperses his 'best-of' shows with his live action. Maybe he was losing ratings because Lucy wasn't cooperating, so he pulled her off to lie to her, to convince her that if she played along he would let her go. How am I supposed to know?"

Dillon frowned. Something wasn't right. He hadn't met Trask, but he knew enough about his process to know that for him, it was about the end. The murder. Everything else—the money, pretending rape was consensual sex, even the legal online pornography he'd been associated with—was nothing compared to his need to control, rape, and kill women.

He wouldn't let one go. Ever.

"What did you see before he took Lucy off air?" Dillon demanded.

Kate stared at him. "Go check it out yourself," she snapped. "Go back to the twenty-four-hour mark."

Dillon strode over to her backup terminal, where she had digitally recorded Lucy's captivity. He found the time stamp and watched a man walk slowly into view of the camera. His hands clenched as the man fell on top of Lucy, touched her. Unzipped his pants.

For the first time Dillon wanted to kill someone. He'd been traveling from San Diego to Texas when Lucy had been raped the first time. He only knew about it because Quinn Peterson had called to tell him. He'd almost been relieved he hadn't watched it.

Dark agony crawled around his mind, suffocating his heart, making him see red. He could all too easily picture himself with the gun Connor gave him, pulling the trigger over and over, hitting this bastard square in the chest. Killing him for touching Lucy. Dillon's head pounded and all he could think of was murder without regret.

Then the man looked over his shoulder and the screen went black. Dillon fast-forwarded the recording. Five minutes of time passed before the screen went back up. Denise was there, fighting with two men as they tore off her clothes.

He shut off the monitor.

"He took Lucy somewhere."

"You don't know that. He's giving her a break. For the finale. Denise is a great actress. Her show will do well, prep the perverts for the end."

"Any more headway on his location?"

"No."

"Dammit, Kate, what aren't you telling me?"

Kate stared at him and Dillon ran a hand through his hair. He was grasping at straws, trying to find his sister in the proverbial haystack. Patrick was in a coma and Lucy was going to die.

And this woman—this renegade FBI agent—was holding back.

When she didn't say anything, Dillon left the room. He needed to talk to Jack and figure out what they were going to do.

Dillon was ready to sell his soul to the Devil for Lucy's whereabouts. But he had a feeling the Devil himself was behind Trask's evil mind, and wouldn't tell him a thing.

Roger walked into the room Trask had converted into an office. "Sixty e-mails wanting to see Lucy. They're not happy."

"Sixty out of eighteen hundred seventeen paid viewers?"

"Sixty in fifteen minutes."

Trask waved his hand. "They'll get off watching Denise. Why aren't you in there with her?"

Roger scratched his crotch. "I gave them a show. I'll be back. How long do you want us to go at her?"

"At least an hour. That'll keep these"—he tapped the stack of e-mails—"perverts jerking off."

"Why'd you pull Lucy?"

"I have my reasons." Not that he planned on sharing them with Roger. Roger had always told him Kate Donovan was a threat. *Give it up, pal. If you know where she is, go in and kill her. But don't play games. She's a wily bitch.*

Kate Donovan was no threat. She was as weak and vulnerable as any woman on the face of the earth. Just more driven than most.

Trask would take care of her and enjoy every second. He'd imagined too often her neck in his hands and his cock in her cunt. She would know the moment before she died that she was nothing but a source of pleasure for him and him alone.

And then he'd crush her windpipe and watch those blue eyes freeze in death.

"Watch Mallory."

"I always watch the new guys."

"There's something about him. He's . . . off."

"He checked out."

"Are you questioning me? Again?"

"No," Roger said slowly. "Why are you cutting me out? You messing around with Donovan again? Wait until after tomorrow night. We're still getting new viewers, we'll top two thousand by the last hour. I say we let everyone have a turn with her and then—"

"I'm the director," Trask said, his voice low. "Is she locked up?"

"Tight."

"Go back and fuck Denise. I have something to do."

Roger left and Trask opened the drawer and stared at the photograph of his father in his judge's robes. His face burned, remembering the humiliation this man had forced him to suffer.

Then he cut him off completely. His twenty-first birthday, cut off without one fucking dime.

His father was unforgiving. If only he'd had the

courage to kill him before being disowned, everything would have gone to him when the bastard croaked.

"Look at me now, Father," Trask said. "You rode on Mother's bank account. You were nothing before you married that stupid woman. Just pathetic. I have money, millions. You cut me off, but I came back even stronger. If you were alive, you'd be paying me to watch my shows."

His father was dead, and good riddance, but for once Trask wished he were alive. Just so Trask could turn the tables and do to him what he'd done to Trask.

Degrade and humiliate him. Hurt and abuse him.

But the bastard even stole that small pleasure from him.

Dillon couldn't find Jack. Where had he gone? They didn't have time for games, they needed to force Kate to talk. Dillon had a feeling Jack would be good at that.

If only Patrick were here. He could decipher her damn computer codes. She'd been working on something. Her demeanor, her tone, her body language said it all.

She'd lied to him. Dillon tolerated a lot, but he drew the line at lies.

He called Connor to find out how Patrick was doing.

"He's still in a coma," Connor said, his voice sounding surprisingly close. "We're in San Diego and they're prepping him for surgery."

"Surgery?"

"Pressure on his brain. They need to relieve it or there's no chance he'll survive."

Dillon paled. "Peterson didn't tell me that."

Connor sounded both angry and helpless. "Tell me you and that Donovan woman know where Lucy is. Tell me where. I'll be there."

"We're working on it."

"That's not good enough!"

Dillon let Connor yell at him. Dillon wanted to scream himself. "I know," he said quietly.

"Is Lucy . . . is she okay?"

"Yes."

"Peterson just left to go back to headquarters. He said you had a list of names that this Trevor/Trask character may be."

"It's a theory." Dillon filled Connor in, knowing that the process would comfort him.

"Call me when you find Lucy. Peterson has a plane fueled and ready at Miramar. It's all ours. I can be flying anywhere in less than thirty minutes."

"Call me when Patrick is out of surgery. How're Mom and Dad holding up?"

"Mom's in shock. Dad's being steadfast." Connor's voice broke. "He cried when he saw Patrick. I haven't seen him cry since Justin's funeral."

"I'm going to find her," Dillon said.

Connor didn't say anything.

"I will," Dillon repeated.

"We have twenty-three hours. Time is running out."

"Have faith." *Have faith in me.*

"When you get the coordinates send them to me. Don't go after him yourself."

Dillon tensed, rubbed his eyes. "I'll send them to you, but I'm going."

"You were right on the money about Kate Donovan and your profile of the bastard who took Lucy, but he'll kill you. Fuck, Dil! I don't know if Patrick is going to survive this surgery, but if they don't go in he'll definitely die. We can't lose Patrick and Lucy and you."

"I'll call you. Tell Mom and Dad I love them."

"Dil, you're not—"

Dillon hung up. Connor was right. He had no business going after Trask and trying to save Lucy. He could end up dead, and Lucy would still die.

But sometimes brains beat out brawn. Sometimes knowing how the hunter thought, knowing what he felt, meant more than knowing how to kill him.

The more Dillon read of his file, the closer he got to understanding exactly who Trask was.

The man who had Lucy had been unusually bright and industrious from early childhood, quiet, focused, and studious. But because of his above-average intelligence, school bored him—even private school. He turned to challenging himself, probably by hacking into computers. Working with his hands. His parents were not involved with his day-to-day life, and he was an only child. If he had a sibling, that sibling was much older. That fit. Especially if the sibling had achieved a lot, been perfect in his parents' eyes. He had big shoes to fill, and because he tended toward darkness even as a child, he messed up. He made mistakes and was punished for them. He was curious about his surroundings, so curious that he definitely got into trouble. Not with the law, but with his parents. Strict rules. Image. Wealth.

He thought back to his recent case where privileged teenagers killed for the thrill. Their parents were wealthy, focused on image and not the rules. In fact, the parents of the killing team had been emotionally distant and unconcerned about what their kids did— as long as they didn't tarnish the family name.

Had Trask tarnished his family name? Had he made an unforgivable mistake in his parents' eyes? Been disowned, like his friend Roger Morton?

Money was important to him. Hugely important. He thrived on moving money around, laundering it. He got a thrill out of making his fortune through the sex trade. Something that would embarrass his parents.

But he hadn't used his real name.

Or had he?

Dillon needed to look back at those original files from Trask Enterprises. There was something there, and since Kate had interviewed virtually every employee, the answer was probably trapped in her brain.

As soon as he entered Kate's room, he knew she was gone. Her *essence* had disappeared.

Along with her laptop, her backpack, and her PDA. "Dammit, Kate!"

He picked up a piece of paper with his name on it.

Dillon—

I know you won't understand, but please try. I can save Lucy, but only alone. You have no reason to trust me, but please, on this, you have to.

I won't let you bury Lucy. If you have a chance

*to put flowers on my grave, I'll know. If you curse
me, I'll understand.*

*Tell Lucy when she comes home that she's the
bravest woman I've ever seen and I wish I could
have known her.*

—Kate

She knew where Lucy was and was going after her
alone. Damn her! Renegade? Maybe idiot was a better word.

Dillon ran from the room. "Jack!" he called, not
knowing where his brother had gone, but figuring
he'd be invaluable in tracking Kate in the middle of
the night on this mountain. "Jack!"

"Over here."

Jack was in a grove of short, stubby trees, doing
what Dillon didn't know, and at this point didn't
care. "Kate went after Trask. Dammit, I knew she
was lying to me. Have you seen her? You've been all
over this observatory. She has to have some sort of vehicle."

"Vehicle? You could say that. She's probably headed
for the plane."

"*Plane?*" Dillon panicked. "We'll never catch up to
her in time."

Jack pulled a large square device from his backpack. "She's not going anywhere without this."

"It looks like a car battery."

"It goes to that fine little Stationair she has hidden
about a mile away. The plane won't fly without it."

SEVENTEEN

KATE LOOKED AT HER CONTROLS for the third time. What was wrong? She had fuel, but the plane just wouldn't start. She had no power.

Damn, damn, damn! She had just checked the battery last week. It couldn't be dead.

What was wrong with the damn plane?

The door opened. She swallowed when she saw Dillon Kincaid. She hadn't thought him capable of fury, but his face said it all.

He'd never been as angry in his life.

He held the plane battery in his hands. "Looking for this?"

"Let me go."

Dillon climbed into the turbocharged Cessna 206. He sat in the copilot seat, his tall frame filling the small cockpit.

"You are going to get Lucy and yourself killed. Maybe you deserve it. You think you do, so who am I to question it? But I will not have you getting Lucy killed in the process."

"It's not like that! He'll kill her if he sees me with anyone—"

"You've been talking to him?" The words were

quiet, but the fury vibrated in the plane. He dropped the battery at her feet.

"He contacted me. I told him if he pulled Lucy off-camera I would meet him. I'm trading myself for her! Don't you see that this is the only way? One hint of the feds anywhere and he'll kill her. I can't risk it."

Dillon grabbed her arms and lifted her from her seat. "You're not stupid, Kate! You think he's going to let Lucy go just because you walked into his lair? What are you thinking? You'll both be killed and he'll walk again! He wants you because you attacked his legitimate business. You embarrassed him. He's not going to give Lucy up. It's a game to him. It's fun. He wants to kill her."

"I know things he doesn't know I know."

"Oh, for shit sake." Dillon dropped her arms, leaned back into the seat, and held his head. "You're a fool, Kate. You're not going anywhere without me."

Kate was trembling when she pulled the gun out of her vest pocket. "I'm sorry, Dillon. I don't want to hurt you. Please leave my plane."

"You're going to shoot me and fly away? You wouldn't."

She nodded. "I'm not noble, Dillon. I'll take justice any damn way I can get it. I'm already going to Hell. One more death isn't going to change that."

Dillon leaned forward. His green eyes burned. "But you've never killed anyone in cold blood."

He snatched the gun from her hand. She couldn't have been more surprised.

"Impressive." Jack Kincaid stepped into the plane, sank into one of the two seats in the back. "I thought I'd have to intervene."

"Shut up," Dillon said.

"Don't do this," Kate whispered. "Please, I know what I'm doing."

"Don't talk to me right now. Just get this plane off the ground."

Jack grinned, stretched his legs as best he could in the small craft, and put his left hand behind his head, his right hand holding a pistol loosely pointed at Kate.

She hated having the gun aimed at her, but she could hardly say anything. She'd had a gun on his brother.

"I'll get a little shut-eye," Jack said and closed his eyes, but Kate didn't think they were really closed. "You two work out the details of the operation. Wake me when we get there."

"No." Kate shook her head. "No! You don't understand!"

Dillon grabbed her chin, turned her to face him. She didn't want to face his fury. He was too good for her. He wouldn't compromise his soul. He wouldn't kill in cold blood. And the only way to stop Trask was on his terms. Morals meant nothing. All that mattered was the end result.

Killing him.

She hadn't believed men like Dillon Kincaid existed. Yet here he was, handsome and smart and angry at her. With very good reason.

She so badly wanted to trust him. But he was a novice—a shrink, for Pete's sake—and not someone who could walk away from a gunfight. Jack Kincaid? Yeah, he might survive. But not Dillon.

Kate didn't want his death on her conscience.

"Tell me exactly what's going on," Dillon said, voice low. "I will know if you're lying."

And he would. She had no doubt that he could see inside her mind.

"My trace program found his Internet server but I didn't know it. He's been tracking my every online move. He sent me a message, directing me to the proper time stamp in my program, and I saw the satellite route, traced it to a location northeast of Seattle, in the Cascade Mountains near Mount Baker.

"Then I received a secure transmission off the same feed. It gave me time and degrees—essentially, all the information I needed to determine longitude and latitude. I looked it up and the coordinates were eighty miles away from where Trask wanted me to meet him. An island, west of the rendezvous point, just north of the San Juan Islands on the Canadian/Washington border."

"What game is he playing?" Dillon wondered out loud.

"It's not a game. The information was coded using an FBI Academy code. Something only agents would know because we learned it at the Academy.

"I realized that Trask was planning on meeting me away from where he has Lucy. Probably because he believed I would tell the FBI. So I have the element of surprise. I'm going to the second coordinates. Lucy said she was on an island."

"You need backup."

"Yes, but who's going to believe anything I say now? Your brothers and Quinn walked into a trap. If the feds go to the island, they'll most assuredly get Lucy killed. If they go to the mountain, Trask will know. He's expecting them, but he's not expecting *me* to come in alone. It's the element of surprise. Don't you see? I have to go to the second location first, get there faster than I told him I'd meet him. To see if Lucy is there. If she is, I can rescue her and then still have time to meet Trask on the mountain. If she's not there, then he kept his word and brought her with him. He promised to trade Lucy. I'll have enough time to get to the mountain location and save her."

"You can't believe him."

"I know that! But I can kill him."

"And he knows you want to kill him! You're blinded by revenge. You're not seeing the big picture, Kate; you're going to get yourself *and* Lucy killed."

Dillon stared at her, his eyes bright and almost wild. "Is that what you want? Do you want to look into that man's eyes as he rapes you? Do you want to give him the pleasure of strangling you? Or slicing your neck open? Because believe me, he gets extreme pleasure out of killing. It fuels him, satiates him, makes him feel like he has power. And because you screwed up his plans five years ago, revenge will drive him even further. You will not get off lightly. He'll bring you to the brink of death and back again, and never even let you beg for mercy."

Kate's eyes burned but she refused to cry in front of Dillon Kincaid or his arrogant military brother.

She turned from him, picked up the battery, and left the plane.

Dillon caught Jack staring at him. He rubbed a hand across his face, his temper still high. He didn't normally lose his temper. He didn't attack vulnerable women. And that's exactly what Kate Donovan was. For all her physical strength, her mental prowess, her training, and her determination, at her core was a vulnerable, lonely woman who was crying out for help. And he'd intentionally terrified her.

"What?" he snapped.

"Nothing."

Dillon didn't want the respect he saw on Jack's face. Instead he stared out the dark window. A flashlight bobbed around the plane and he heard Kate mumbling something. A metal door clicked shut. A minute later Kate jumped back into the plane, slammed the door closed, and locked it.

"Your death will not be on my conscience," she said. She sat down, flipped switches, and started the plane.

"What's your plan?" Dillon said, ignoring her comment.

"We have a full tank. I can go eleven hundred miles. There are a couple small airports I can stop at to refuel in northern Arizona. Might be a little tricky, but I'll figure it out."

"Tricky?"

"Avoiding customs, the fact that my license expired, little things like that. But I can talk my way around it."

"Shit," Jack mumbled from the back.

"You have a better idea?" Kate snapped.

"I know a place south of Red Rock where we can refuel."

"And they'll just refuel with no questions?" Kate smirked. "Good friends." She glanced at a map. "That's over eleven hundred ten miles. Cutting it really close on the fuel."

"It's twenty miles south of Red Rock. Take it or

leave it. Even with our added weight, you should be fine."

"Doesn't make me feel much better." She looked at the map. "Still, that's nine hundred miles from Seattle. We'll make that leg easy."

"How fast does this little prop go?"

"The Stationair is one of the best 'little props' Cessna makes. The 206 cruises at 164 nautical miles."

Jack did a mental calculation. "That's 188 miles an hour? That makes it about eleven hours when you factor in one stop to refuel. When does that put us in Washington?"

"About eleven thirty a.m."

Dillon said, "And you arranged this meeting with Trask when?"

"Two p.m."

"Where?"

She hesitated.

"Dammit, Kate!" Dillon slammed his fist on his knee, took a deep breath. "No more secrets. We're in this together, got it? Jack and I are not leaving your side. We need to find Lucy. That's our number one focus. Not Trask."

"You'd let him go to kill again?" she spat out.

"It doesn't have to be either/or. But the most important thing is to save Lucy. Or do you not agree?"

She stared at him, eyes wide. He saw when she realized what she had been saying. "Of course I agree," she said quietly, looking down.

Kate finished her preflight check. They started moving forward, rapidly increasing speed. The plane bumped and bucked on the uneven runway. Dillon had no problem with flying, but he couldn't see anything. The plane's lights only lit up the ground immediately in front of him.

"Do you know what you're doing?" he asked.

"I've flown this plane a dozen times."

"But there's a cliff—"

"I know." They were going faster.

Suddenly the ground gave way. They were airborne. Kate made a sharp turn to the right, turning a full 180 degrees. She checked her instruments as they continued to ascend.

"We don't have oxygen on board," she said, "so I'm going to keep it under twelve-five." She glanced back at Jack. "Red Rock?" she said, skeptical.

He nodded. "Straight as an arrow. When you hit the Nevada border, wake me."

"It'll take six hours."

"I haven't slept in two days." He closed his eyes.

"What's your plan?" Dillon asked Kate.

"I had planned on meeting Trask at a campground near Mount Baker, until I got the second coordinates. They're nearly two hours apart. I was going to check out the island first, but now that you're here you and your brother can go to the island and I can meet Trask on the mountain. It actually works out better."

Dillon shook his head. "You care about one thing. Killing Trask. Jack and I care about saving Lucy. If he brings her to the mountain, I want Jack there. And if she's on the island, I'll be there."

"Trask isn't going to screw with me. Not on this. I told him I wouldn't come unless he took her off-camera. Remember when Denise went on? He stood by his word."

"Yeah, but for how long?" Dillon asked.

She couldn't answer that.

"I'm not letting you out of my sight. You're coming to the island with me."

"How can you think I would jeopardize her life?" Kate felt sick to her stomach. Maybe she deserved it.

"Because I think you are so blinded by revenge that you can't see the whole picture. I also think we should call Peterson."

"No," Jack and Kate said in unison.

Dillon glanced at his brother. "I thought you were sleeping."

Jack opened his eyes and leaned forward. "I think Kate is a wack-job, but she's right about this."

"Thank you," Kate said sarcastically.

Jack continued. "This bastard so much as smells a fed, Lucy's dead. I know men like Trask. They have a sixth sense when it comes to the authorities."

"We can't act like a bunch of vigilantes. The FBI has resources, surveillance, and equipment. Manpower. I've worked with SWAT. They can come in low and quiet and no one will know they're there."

"They're not going to believe me anyway," she said. "Especially after the trap your brothers walked into."

"But Trask contacted you," Dillon said.

"Doesn't matter. It's my word they don't trust." Kate glanced at him, the green glow from the controls and gauges giving her face an odd, ethereal presence. "I'm surprised you even trust me. I almost got your brothers killed."

"Connor and Patrick are grown men. They did what they thought was right. And you were right about the trap," Dillon said. "You warned them."

"And this could be another trap. And another. If it weren't for the second set of coordinates I don't think—" She paused. Full disclosure. "I think they have an undercover agent inside Trask's operation."

"What?" Dillon exclaimed. "How can that be? Lucy was *raped*. They couldn't possibly allow that."

"Normally, I'd think not, but you're forgetting that Trask killed two federal agents. They want him as badly as I do." Kate stared at Dillon. "I'm the one who had to run from my country, blamed for Paige's death, yet the powers that be can infiltrate Trask's network and Lucy becomes collateral damage as long as they take down the organization."

"I can't believe that."

"Believe it," she said. "That FBI code is definitely in-speak. Possibly an agent who turned, or undercover. I think the latter. Because I recognized the man onscreen before Trask pulled Lucy."

Dillon shook his head. "This is ridiculous. A conspiracy theory run amok."

Kate looked at Jack. He agreed with her, she could see it in his eyes. "Jack agrees with me."

"Nothing surprises me," he said calmly.

Kate frowned. Maybe Dillon was right. How could she go into this alone? She felt like she was covering her ass, wanting to call Quinn Peterson and give him the information. So that *when* Lucy died she wouldn't feel guilty.

Nothing could stop her from feeling guilty.

"We'll call Peterson when we're in Red Rock," Kate said. "Give him the information. But I don't think anyone in the Bureau is going to believe me anymore. I've sent them out on too many wild-goose chases."

"But Peterson must know about the undercover agent."

"Maybe, by now, but there's something very odd about this setup. The FBI doesn't handle clandestine missions like this, jeopardizing civilians. And even if a civilian was in jeopardy and the agent couldn't save her, there would be some mechanism to know where the agent is. Like a GPS microchip implanted under the skin."

Jack snorted from the rear of the plane.

Kate ignored him. "Trask has been playing me for a long time," Kate admitted, the realization terrifying and angering her. "This time I *know* he's there. But I feel like the girl who cried wolf."

Dillon put his hand over hers. "No one is going to die. Not Lucy, not you."

She wished she believed him.

He forced her to look at him. She flushed under the intensity of his gaze. "I mean it, Kate. We're going to find Lucy and everyone is walking away alive."

EIGHTEEN

QUINN PETERSON GLANCED at the clock. Three fifteen in the morning. Six fifteen on the East Coast. Late enough to rouse his pal Hans Vigo from sleep.

"What?" Vigo asked.

"I need you to dig around for me."

"It can't wait?"

"No."

He moaned. "Okay, what?"

"Merritt has an undercover agent with Trask."

Vigo was silent. "Are you sure?"

"Positive."

"For how long?"

"Longer than he's had Lucy Kincaid."

"Fuck."

"You can say that again."

"Fuck. What do you want?"

"Who, what, when, and how."

"Why?"

"I know why."

"Paige."

"Bingo."

"Okay. Anything else?"

"Who do you trust up north?"

"No one."

"Seriously." Quinn tried to sound lighthearted, but failed.

"I am serious. Exactly where?"

"I need someone to interview Charles Morton. My records show him living in Boston."

"Boston. Abigail Resnick."

"I'm going to e-mail you a list of names. Kids who went to school with Charles Morton's son nearly two decades ago. What I need is for him to identify anyone Roger Morton was close to."

"Roger Morton, as in the man who raped Paige Henshaw and killed Evan Standler?"

"That's him."

"You're going to get fired. I have seniority, I'll probably just get my ass kicked and demoted to the basement to read cold case files. But you? You're already on the hot seat for working off-the-clock on the Butcher investigation."

"Water under the bridge. I'll take care of Merritt."

"The man's a serpent."

"I know."

"What are you thinking? That one of these guys Morton went to school with is Trask?"

"Yes."

"Why?"

"A forensic psychiatrist out here has this theory that—"

"I'm a forensic psychiatrist."

"The best, but you weren't working this case five years ago."

"True." Vigo sighed. "Okay, I'll call Abby."

"Abby?"

"Abigail," Vigo corrected. "She'll do it for me. Just cover her ass, Peterson. It's a mighty fine ass, and I don't want to see it bruised."

"Consider it covered."

Trask sat locked in his office doing research. Research Roger should have done. Perhaps on the surface Roger made a stab at checking out who Mick Mallory was, but no one was as good as he was. Trask prided himself on knowing everything about everyone.

And, to be truthful, he had been blinded by Mallory's performance on the last job. The guy had watched Rayanna die and hadn't done anything about it. Obviously he was who Roger said he was— an ex-con who had violated parole and didn't want to go back. He was willing to do anything.

But he'd supposedly been in prison for rape. Trask had given him the perfect woman—practically a virgin, restrained, beautiful—and he hadn't done anything. He'd approached her as if he wanted to be her lover.

That in and of itself wasn't a red flag. Perhaps Mallory was a bit sick in the head, an obsessive type who fixated on a woman over time. Women loved being fondled and admired, up to the point where a man showed his balls and finally did something about it. Then they cried rape and abuse and any other thing to get attention. Saying that they're scared.

Trask showed them what being scared meant. Some pathetic loser stalking his ex-girlfriend was child's play. Nothing. A jerk. But Trask knew fear, had tasted it, and he gave it back to the bitches times ten.

On the surface, Mick Mallory had served five out of an eight-year sentence for raping his next-door neighbor, Trina Bowers. There was a warrant out for him because of a parole violation, following Bowers home from work a month after his release. He fled, contacted Roger.

The contact had originally interested Trask. Few people knew Roger or how to contact him. But it was Skud McGinley who'd set up the meeting—Skud was an old friend from the early days of Trask Enterprises who'd been in and out of prison for a variety of drug-related charges, then got life for whacking his old man for the insurance money. He and Roger had kept in touch over the years, and Skud had met Mick in prison.

Trask believed it. Skud couldn't be bought, he was as ornery as they came. Hated authority. So if Mick was a plant, it had been planned for well over a year. He had to have been in prison at some point to meet up with Skud. That's deep cover, and Trask didn't think any of the FBI pricks had the balls to do any real prison time.

Everything checked on Mallory. So Trask went to look for Bowers. There were several of them in the country, but Mallory had been arrested in Massachusetts—Bowers should have lived there at one point. Trina—that was the name on the court documents, but those could be forged. Trina could stand for Katrina, Trinity, Christina, any number of names.

Court documents. He looked through the transcript. Looked legitimate, but he didn't have an original. And he didn't have time to send someone out to Massachusetts to pull the hard copy.

There was no Trina Bowers who would have been twenty-four six years ago. There was no thirty-year-old Trina Bowers in Massachusetts or the bordering states.

Then he found it.

"Trina" filed charges that Mallory had followed her home from her place of employment, a law firm in downtown Boston.

Branson, Ordello, Kimball & Associates.

Sounded legitimate, but no such firm ever existed.

The devil was in the details, and Mick Mallory had just been sacrificed by those details. Probably some FBI bureaucrat screwing up. No surprise there.

Did Kate Donovan know him?

No matter. Trask would serve his head on a silver platter to Kate. Then he'd make her watch Lucy die.

Don't rush, he admonished himself. He had more work to do. He pulled down the digital film of the feds who'd walked into his trap off Baja. They looked like cops, a little too rugged to be feds, but they were probably among the cream of that particular crop. They looked familiar, but Trask knew he'd never met either of them.

Trask ran their images through his photo-recognition program.

Almost instantly their identities popped up. He straightened, tense.

Patrick James Kincaid, thirty-two, San Diego, California, sergeant in the San Diego Police Department.

Connor Mateo Kincaid, thirty-five, San Diego, California, private investigator.

Lucy's brothers.

Something wasn't right. Why weren't the feds working on this? Why would they bring in outsiders? He'd sent the false Baja coordinates to Kate, which meant she was in touch with the Kincaid family.

Did that mean she hadn't called the FBI? Playing maverick herself? Why work with the Kincaid family? How had they gotten together?

He ran the third image through his program, wondering if the man was another Kincaid brother. Instead, he learned that the man was Quincy Peterson, special agent in charge out of Seattle. Peterson . . . the name wasn't familiar. He must be new, or hadn't been involved five years ago. Different team. Maybe the feds were falling apart. They'd trusted Kate Donovan's information and come up dry several times.

He smiled.

He'd done his research on Lucy and knew she was high risk—her family were cops and military, the epitome of authority.

In the beginning, nearly a year ago, he'd joined a Georgetown chat room and waited for the right girl. Listened, watched, conversed with the students. He'd picked Trevor Conrad as his identity because Trevor had planned on going to Georgetown all those years ago. Had he lived, of course. Seemed a fitting tribute.

In January, incoming freshmen started flooding the chat rooms. That's when Trask really perked up. Young, eager, excited. They assumed everyone in the chat room was a student, freely shared information about where they lived, what they planned to study, their families, their photos.

He and Lucy started talking about things they had in common, such as speaking French. It was fun to pull out his rusty high school French and use it with Lucy. It only took a couple of weeks before she was sharing everything about herself with him. He knew her real name. Her hometown. That her father was retired army and her mother had escaped from Cuba. He learned about her brothers and sisters and wondered if he should seek out another girl. A kid with that much firepower around her could be dangerous to him.

Then she sent him her picture.

Her resemblance to Monique was remarkable. The same long, thick wavy hair. The big brown eyes. The flawless tan complexion, though Lucy's was from her heritage instead of the sun. Tall, slender, with curves in all the right places.

So Trask decided taking Lucy was a challenge he was up to. Screw her family. He'd done this enough times without anyone, except Kate Donovan, getting close. They'd never find her. The pleasure of taking down such a noble and self-righteous family appealed to him.

If Connor and Patrick Kincaid were out of commission, either dead or injured, there were three viable Kincaids left since the oldest, a woman, wasn't in contact with the family. Jack Kincaid, thirty-eight, was in the military, and even Trask, who could break into virtually every secure computer network, didn't know where he was deployed. His file was beyond top secret. All Trask had was his rank, colonel. For all he knew, Jack Kincaid was working in Iraq or black ops in South America. He didn't even have a photograph of him.

Dillon Kincaid, thirty-eight, was a psychiatrist. Certainly no threat, and Trask hadn't spent a lot of time researching him other than knowing that he consulted with the District Attorney's Office on criminal cases and had his own client list. Trask had no use for shrinks. What good were they anyway?

Carina Kincaid, thirty-three, was a cop engaged to another cop. Where were they? Looking for Lucy? Staying home? Trask brought up their most recent photographs, stolen off Lucy's computer before he'd abducted her.

He hadn't seen either of them, but he kept their images in mind. Carina Kincaid and Nick Thomas were a potential threat simply because of their law enforcement background. He'd kill them on sight, minimize potential damage.

He pulled down Dillon Kincaid's photo as well to familiarize himself with the doctor. Just in case. You couldn't be overprepared.

First things first. Mick Mallory had to die.

And Trask decided how best to execute him. He could hardly wait until Kate showed up at Mount Baker.

He checked his computer. Yep, she was gone. She hadn't logged onto her computer for more than two hours. He didn't know exactly where she was in Mexico; he'd misled her hoping she'd slip up and tell him. But it would take her at least twelve hours to get to Washington and she said she'd be at the mountain by two o'clock. He still had plenty of time.

He went to find the infiltrator. They had a trip to take.

NINETEEN

DILLON'S CELL PHONE RANG and Kate jumped. They were flying low over the desert. Kate had turned off the transponder to avoid being detected by radar. It was still dark, though the sun was tinting the eastern horizon.

"Who is it?" she asked.

Dillon didn't respond. They hadn't spoken in more than four hours. He'd slept uneasily, his thoughts flowing from Lucy to Kate to his brother Jack, whose motives he still didn't understand.

Caller ID was unavailable. Dillon answered.

"Dr. Kincaid."

"Doc, it's Quinn Peterson."

"Is Patrick okay?"

"He's out of surgery."

"And?"

"That's all I know. I'm at headquarters. I have some information about your Stonebridge Academy theory."

"And?"

"Roger was close to three people in school. His roommate, Paul Ullman, is one. Ullman is a stockbroker for one of the big five in New York. Lives in a penthouse, high security, and nets five million a year. He's from old money out of Vermont, estranged from his parents, and takes care of his mentally ill sister, who's in an expensive assisted-living facility in Vermont.

"Adam Scott is a year older. Expelled with Roger and Paul over something Morton wouldn't disclose. My agent out there is going to make a trip to the school, should only take a couple hours for her to get there and report back. Might be something. Morton got Roger back into Stonebridge, as did Ullman's parents. But Scott never went back."

"Why?" Dillon asked.

"Morton didn't know. But get this: Roger's other close friend was named Trevor Conrad."

Dillon leaned forward. "Trevor Conrad? Where's he now?"

"Dead."

"Are you sure?"

"Died on campus apparently. In an accident. Morton clammed up."

"There was no Trevor Conrad on the list," Dillon said, fearing he'd missed an obvious connection when he was putting together the list of names for Peterson.

"No, but when the agent asked who else Roger was close to, Morton named the kid."

"And you're sure he was a student at the school?"

"Yes, according to Morton they were roommates the year of the expulsion. I'll let the agent know that we're interested in more information about Conrad."

"Could his accident have something to do with the expulsion?" Dillon pondered out loud.

"Could be. Morton threatened to call his attorney.

We don't have to jump through the hoops, my gal out there can threaten with the best of them, but she felt it would be easier to get the information from the school than from Roger Morton's father. Who, by the way, hasn't heard from Roger in more than five years. Agent Resnick believes him. The man hates his son."

"What is Adam Scott doing?"

"Morton didn't know. He's familiar with the Ullman family, so he gave Agent Resnick that contact information. All he knew about Scott was that he's from New York, his father was a judge, and his mother was from the established New England family of Mortimer."

"That should be easy to trace."

"I already have people on it."

"Thank you, Peterson."

"What has Kate discovered? We only have eighteen hours."

"I know." Dillon swallowed. "We're getting closer," he said.

"Close enough to get to the location? Shit, I don't have to tell you this but even if we find out where Lucy is it may take us hours to get to her location."

"I know," Dillon said quietly. "What about your people?"

Peterson didn't say anything for a long moment. "I think my boss has an inside man. I have someone looking into it. But . . . it's under the radar. I think it's an unauthorized operation and heads are going to roll."

That confirmed what Kate had said, Dillon thought.

"Will you let me know when you find out?"

Peterson didn't say anything.

"Peterson?"

"I'm watching a very interesting computer program," he said.

"Lucy?" Dillon's stomach clenched. They had shut down the computer to save the battery, checking on the status of the Internet feed every thirty minutes.

"No. A GPS satellite. Through your cellular service provider. You're moving fast, Kincaid."

"That I am."

"Where are you going?"

Dillon was torn. He wanted to tell Peterson. He trusted him. He knew he would do anything to save Lucy's life. Kate? He didn't know what she would do. Her drive was focused on Trask, not Lucy, no matter what her heart said. She wanted to wait until they were closer.

Dillon felt a hand clasp his shoulder. Jack's voice low in his ear. "Don't."

"Keep in touch," Dillon said and hung up.

He whirled around and faced Jack. "Or what?"

"We have a plan, we stick to it."

"I think we need backup."

"I think you're wrong."

Dillon looked out the window. It was dawn, the sun coming up on the right side of the plane. They were flying low; it looked like they were somewhere over Arizona. Deep canyons and high plateaus in red and gold gleamed in the morning sun.

It would have been romantic if he was with any other woman on any other trip.

"How did you learn to fly?" he asked Kate.

She glanced at him, said, "My boyfriend. Evan Standler."

"He's the one who died five years ago," Dillon said.

She nodded. "Evan had a small plane. Saved up every dime to pay for fuel. I put in enough time, got my license. I'll admit I haven't kept up on my license. It expired four years ago. But it's like riding a bike." She glanced at Jack. "But I'm sure the Colonel can pitch in if I get in trouble."

Jack winked.

Kate smiled. She was beautiful when she smiled, looking like the girl next door instead of a mercenary. "I always wanted to fly." She turned wistful. "I remember sitting on the roof of my grandparents' house and watching the sun rise. The birds would wake up, start flying around, and I wanted to join them. I've always thought the Wright brothers were incredible. I mean, to see a dream, work their asses off, and achieve it. Not many of us can say that. We could barely get off the ground at the beginning of the century, and way before the end of it we've put a man on the moon and the rover on Mars."

She sighed. "Originally, I wanted to join the air force. I needed a way to pay for college."

"Why didn't you?"

She glanced at him, smiled again. "A problem with obedience to authority." She looked over at Jack. "I think your brother understands that."

Jack just grunted and closed his eyes again.

"What happened to your parents?" Dillon asked.

"You *my* shrink now?"

"I'm making small talk."

"Right. *What happened to your parents? How do*

you feel about that?" She frowned, staring straight ahead, out the window.

Dillon tensed. "That's not fair, Kate. I haven't done or said anything to make you feel uncomfortable, other than question your motives and reasoning."

"You're right," she said quietly. "I don't know who my father was. My mother left me with my grandparents when I was five. Couldn't stand me."

"I'm sure that's not—"

"Don't placate me, Dillon," Kate snapped. "My mother was raped, okay? And I'm the end product. She went in twice to have an abortion but couldn't go through with it. When she left me with my grandparents she told me, 'I'm sorry, Katherine, I tried to love you but I can't.' " Kate took a deep breath. "I must look like him, because I look nothing like my mother."

"I'm sorry."

"I don't want your pity."

"It's not pity."

"I can't believe I said anything," she mumbled and fidgeted with the controls. "Shit."

"What?" Jack asked from the back.

"I don't think we're going to make Red Rock."

"It was those headwinds outside of Phoenix," Jack said. "They ate up the fuel. How long?"

"Fifty miles before I start getting really nervous."

"That's almost there."

"Almost ain't good enough."

"It'll have to be. I'd offer to jump and lighten the load, but you'd probably be shot down. My friends are a little sensitive."

"Great."

"Trust me, we'll make it," Jack said. "My license isn't expired."

Kate rolled her eyes.

"Nice friends."

"I have a lot. Surprised?"

"It sure isn't for your bedside manner."

"Ouch," Jack said. He leaned over and whispered in Kate's ear, "Just because I'm for hire doesn't mean the government doesn't hire me." He looked at the controls. "Ten degrees north, we'll come at Red Rock from the east, which should help with the fuel. The wind will be behind us."

"It'll add another fifteen miles that we don't have fuel for."

"Trust me."

"Right."

Dillon had always assumed Jack was still in the military, one way or the other. "Who do you work for?" he asked his brother.

"Mostly the good guys," Jack said, leaning back in the seat and closing his eyes again, but he wasn't fooling Dillon.

"So you're not in the military anymore?"

"What does it look like to you?"

"It looks like you won't answer my damn questions."

"Double ouch."

And he didn't answer Dillon's questions.

Stonebridge Academy had a gated entrance, ivy-covered brick walls, and a huge, stately brick mansion in the middle of the grounds, flanked on either side by long, two-story buildings. In the center was a large grass area where young men were playing polo. Sports for the rich youth, not the urban hellhole Special Agent Abigail Resnick had grown up in.

During the two-hour drive, which she'd done on personal time, Abigail hoped Hans Vigo was right and she wouldn't be answering to anyone for what she was doing. She didn't mind breaking rules—she didn't much care for rules anyway—but she didn't want to get caught.

She took the circular drive up to the mansion, but before she could get out of the car, a tall, distinguished man—*butler,* she thought—came down the stairs and held her door open for her.

"Thanks," she said and flashed him a smile that had melted icier men.

No dice. Heart of stone in this one.

"Who do you have an appointment with?"

She flashed her badge. "I need to speak to the headmaster. George Fleischer."

The butler frowned almost imperceptibly. She'd done her homework while on the road—gotta love wireless Internet—and knew Fleischer had been the headmaster for the last twenty-eight years.

"Follow me."

She did.

The inside of the mansion was even more opulent than she'd expected. She almost gawked. Her pathetic public school in the heart of Richmond, Virginia, was functional. Metal, wood, desks, graffiti. None of this Victorian furniture, oil paintings—which had to be real—or polished wood.

Instead of being embarrassed or intimidated, she grinned. "So, how much to send my kid here?"

"You have an applicant?"

"No. Just curious."

He didn't answer her. Maybe it wasn't just money. A poor girl from the wrong side of the tracks in Richmond sure wouldn't cut it here, nor would her kin.

She smiled wider. "Mr. Fleischer, please?"

"I will see if he's available. Please be seated."

She sat, watched where the butler went. Checked her watch. Ten minutes passed and she followed the same path. Almost immediately the butler emerged from down the hall.

"Ms. Resnick, I'm sorry, only students and employees are allowed beyond this point."

"Special Agent Resnick," she corrected, "and I need to speak with Mr. Fleischer now or I'll be back this afternoon with a warrant. And I won't be smiling."

"I don't threaten easily, Special Agent Resnick."

"And I don't make idle threats."

"What is this regarding?"

How to play it? Vigo had given her so little information, but apparently she had learned something juicy from Morton.

"Trevor Conrad."

The cadaver of a butler paled, if that was possible. "Wait."

He left again, but less than a minute later he returned and escorted her to a parlor. Not the headmaster's office, but private. Progress.

George Fleischer entered by another door, younger than she expected. If he was sixty, she'd eat her badge. He had dark, graying hair, was impeccably dressed in a tailored suit, and his eyes were clear blue and focused.

For the first time she felt a tad nervous. She had no authority to be here. But if he even smelled that she was hesitant, she wouldn't get the answers Vigo needed.

"Mr. Fleischer, thank you so much for taking the time out of your busy day to—"

"Stop the game. What's going on?"

"I don't—"

"You come in here and drop a name and expect us to jump through hoops? I demand an answer or I will call your superior."

"Fine. Call him. I'll wait."

He hesitated. Call his bluff.

"Perhaps you don't know that there is a warrant out for the arrest of one of your former students, Roger Morton."

"I didn't."

Liar.

"And in the course of investigating his whereabouts, I learned that he may be in contact with some of his old friends from this school. I was speaking with Charles Morton and—"

Fleischer's head shot up higher, if that was possible. "You spoke with Mr. Morton?"

"Yes, this morning. And he suggested that I come out here for answers. He's still angry with what happened with his son."

"His son was reinstated in school and graduated with his class. Mr. Morton has no cause—"

"He's not upset with the school. He and his son are estranged. He told me his closest friends were Paul Ullman, Adam Scott, and Trevor Conrad."

Fleischer nodded. "That would be my recollection."

"You would have a recollection about friendships formed nearly two decades ago?"

"You don't know Stonebridge Academy, do you? We are a premiere school for young men age five to eighteen. Our students go to the top universities; they are from the best families in the world—we have a prince from the Middle East among our students. The brightest and the wealthiest. I've been here for nearly thirty years. Roger Morton was nine when I took this post. I know him and his friends."

"Do you know why the FBI is looking for Morton?"

"I've heard."

"And we believe he's working with one of his old pals. We know where Ullman is."

"And you know Conrad died."

"What I want to know is why did you reinstate Morton and Ullman, but not Adam Scott?"

Fleischer looked distinctly uncomfortable. She had him. "A witness indicated that Mr. Scott was the ringleader. He was the oldest, and he claimed responsibility for the accident."

"So it was an accident?" She raised an eyebrow to show that she didn't believe him, and to give him a chance to explain. She didn't know how Trevor Conrad had died.

"We had no reason to believe otherwise. A thorough investigation proved that the boys had been experimenting—yes, against school rules—and the laboratory exploded. An accident."

"But it wasn't reported to the authorities."

"No need. We take care of these things internally."
That might explain why Conrad's records had been
expunged and therefore his name not on her original
list.

"So because Scott was the instigator, he was kicked
out." She made notes. "I need his most recent picture."

"I can't give you that."

"I'll be back with a warrant in four hours."

She turned.

"Wait. Just wait."

He left. Ten minutes later he came back with a thin
file. "Photo, last-known address, and parents. That's
all I can give you without a warrant, Ms. Resnick."

"Thank you so much for your help, Mr. Fleischer.
It's been a real pleasure."

TWENTY

QUINN PETERSON SLAMMED down the receiver after Hans Vigo called him about what he'd learned. As soon as they found Lucy Kincaid, someone was going to pay for the botched undercover operation.

What was Jeff Merritt thinking when he sent Mick Mallory deep undercover? Mick had been a damn good agent at one time, but when his wife was killed three years ago he'd developed a death wish. He was technically on psychiatric leave and Merritt had no business bringing him in on this case.

But more important than that, they now had a line on Trask's real identity. The agent Vigo had tagged to quietly work the investigation had uncovered huge news.

Merritt walked into the task force room without knocking. "What is so damn important that you demanded I drop a conference call with Virginia?"

Quinn knew he had to tread lightly. Merritt had his emotions involved and that was never good. Quinn knew that from firsthand experience.

"I have a line on Trask's identity."

Merritt couldn't keep the shock off his face. "And?"

"We think he's a friend of Roger Morton from grade school. Morton went to an elite boarding school in Connecticut. His father is a big shot, old money—"

"I know all about Morton. I interviewed the father myself. He has no idea who his son is running with. He disowned him, and our people know Roger Morton has never been home."

Quinn took a deep breath. "Did you ever interview the headmaster from the boarding school?"

"Why? He graduated nearly twenty years ago. Paige was killed five years ago."

"Dillon Kincaid read over all the files and he—"

"You mean the doctor I'm *this* close to getting an arrest warrant for?"

"*What?*"

"He's aiding and abetting a known criminal."

"Are you talking about Kate?"

"Do I need to pull you off this case?"

Quinn stared at Merritt. "Take a step back, Merritt. You're doing yourself a disservice."

"Don't talk to me."

For the first time, Quinn saw how pained Jeff Merritt was. His hair was out of place, his eyes had bags under them, and his clothes had been worn for well over twenty-four hours. Merritt lost the woman he loved to a sadistic killer. Quinn had almost been in those shoes. To think he nearly lost Miranda twice to a killer . . . but the fact that she survived didn't mean he couldn't understand what Merritt was going through.

"Jeff," Quinn said quietly, "I've been where you are."

"You know nothing."

"Guilt that you couldn't stop Paige from disobeying orders. Anger that she put her life on the line. Remorse that you didn't tell her you loved her the last time she walked out your door."

Quinn saw that he had hit the nail on the head with the last point.

"Dr. Kincaid is a consultant for the San Diego Police Department. This is what he does for a living. He figured out Roger's connection to Trask."

"And the Bureau is filled with incompetent fools? I'll tell that to your pal Vigo."

"The Bureau is overworked and understaffed, and you know as well as I do that as soon as Trask's trail dried up, we worked other cases. You know how it is."

"I've never stopped working Paige's murder."

"I know. And that's why you're too close. What were you thinking sending Mick Mallory in?"

"Mallory is the best damn undercover agent in the Bureau."

"*Was*," Quinn corrected. "Until his wife was murdered. He's mentally unstable and you know it. And how could he have let Lucy be raped?"

Merritt frowned. "He must have been in a position where he couldn't have helped her without blowing his cover. Last time he checked in there were six people, including him and Trask. Five men, one woman. He was waiting for the right time—"

"Right time for what?"

"I can't tell you that."

"You sent Mallory to assassinate Trask." Quinn shook his head. It all made sense now.

"It's not supposed to be a suicide mission."

"Since when do you have the authority to send in an assassin? Not to mention a man who isn't trained for it?"

"What makes you think I don't have the authority?"

He might, though if the operation blew up around them Merritt would be the scapegoat. Quinn had seen it happen before. But this time? Quinn highly doubted Merritt had any sanction for Mallory's assignment.

"I'm going to play it straight with you, Merritt, and I want you to be straight with me. Okay?"

"What?"

"Kincaid believes Roger is working closely with someone he went to school with. Trask Enterprises began five years after he graduated from high school, but Roger Morton had no job, no college, no friends. Kincaid got the list of every student at Stonebridge Academy who had been at the school with Roger. His father identified three who had been Morton's closest friends. One is dead. One is a stockbroker in New York. The other was expelled. I learned he's on the board of directors of six legitimate companies, but can't get a recent picture of him. My contact says that he owns stock in all the companies, sends his proxy to the meetings, and no one claims to have seen him. I have one old picture of him when he was sixteen, right before he was expelled."

Quinn slid over the picture of a blond teenager with icy blue eyes. "Kate is the only person who has seen him and is still alive. I'm going to get this to her."

"You're working with her." But Merritt couldn't take his eyes off the photograph.

"I want you to drop all charges against her."

"No."

"Give her immunity, Merritt, and don't tell me you can't."

"Paige died because of her."

"Paige died because of *him*." Quinn slapped his hand on the photograph of Adam Scott.

They were in a holding area of a small military facility. If it could be called a military facility. It looked more like a makeshift training camp in the middle of the desert. Red Rock, Jack had said, but Kate told Dillon they were at least twenty miles from Red Rock and she wasn't one hundred percent sure where they were without looking at her maps. Dillon didn't buy into conspiracy theories, but right now he would have believed virtually anything anyone told him about this place. Off the grid, Dillon thought. The men were not in standard military gear, and everyone knew Jack Kincaid.

Kate paced anxiously, like a caged tigress. "What's taking so long?"

Dillon couldn't say, so he didn't answer. Instead he asked, "What kind of place is this?"

Kate shrugged. "Looks like a private mercenary training camp, except that their equipment isn't surplus. State of the art. Did you catch a glimpse of the radar system at the airport?"

"No." Didn't look like an airport, either. One runway and a solitary building in the middle of nowhere. They were being held underground. "So is this run by the military or not?"

"Depends who you ask and when you ask it."

"You're as helpful as Jack."

"You really don't know what your brother does?"

"I haven't seen him in eleven years."

That surprised Kate. "Really?"

"Why are you surprised?"

"Because . . . I don't know. You seem close."

"We were, at one time." And seeing Jack again conflicted Dillon. They were different people today, with no way to regain what they'd had growing up. They'd grown apart, leading different lives, going down dramatically different paths. Dillon hadn't been faced with the choices Jack had, but deep down Dillon knew he couldn't walk away from his family forever, to only show up at funerals. His parents, his brothers and sisters, they were as much part of Dillon's life as his work.

"Jack joined the army right out of high school. He was going to put in the minimum years required to qualify for the free college education. Something happened his first tour. He's never spoken of it, but he became career military and chose to keep his family at arm's length." Dillon rubbed his face. "Before that, we were close. If you'd asked me twenty years ago if Jack would stop speaking to his family without an explanation, I'd have laughed. But it happened and we've learned to live with it."

"That doesn't explain why he's helping you now, when he doesn't even know his sister."

"Loyalty," Dillon said. "A sense of duty." He stared at Kate. "Very much the same reasons you've been hiding out and breaking the law—your loyalty and duty to your partner."

Kate stopped pacing for a minute and looked at him. He was standing by the door, looking out the lone window into a hallway that was gray and empty. Though the room was underground and air-conditioned, it was still blazing hot. June in the Nevada desert.

She wanted to argue with him, explain that it was more than simply loyalty that had her dedicated to stopping Trask. But he wasn't thinking about her. His eyes were far off. Thinking about the missing years with his brother? Or what future Lucy might—or might not—have?

"We're going to get her in time," Kate said quietly.

Dillon turned to face her. She was complex, and he couldn't say that he knew her. He couldn't even say that he would have made the choices she'd made in life. But something deep down in her core, which shone through in her vibrant blue eyes, told him she was all there. Not a renegade FBI agent, not a narrow-minded revenge nut, but a disciplined and trained federal cop.

It was the action that did it, he realized. She'd been pent up for two years at the observatory, on the run for three years before that. Yet six hours on the move and she had developed a calm—pacing notwithstanding.

"Lucy's a smart kid," he said, not knowing what to say about his sister. Dillon had been twenty when she was born. Already out of the house, in college. Planning on medical school. Even Patrick was thirteen years older than Lucy. She was practically an only child. She'd grown up fast—not only because of her older brothers and sisters, but because she'd seen death at an early age. She'd been seven when Justin—her seven-year-old nephew—was killed. They'd shielded her to some extent, but it had affected all of them.

"Smart and sassy and spoiled," Dillon said, his voice cracking.

Kate reached up and touched his shoulders. "Lucy is lucky to have family who loves her so much," she said quietly.

Dillon took Kate's hand. "You didn't."

She shook her head. "Maybe that's why I fight for the underdog. I'm okay, Dillon. I know you think I'm this fly-off-the-handle maverick, but I *am* okay. I accept that I could die. It's not a death wish, it's not being stupid. But if I go in with fear, I'll never be able to do my job."

"You don't have a job. You're doing this for revenge." Or was she? Maybe not revenge so much as justice. He began to see and admire Kate in a whole different light.

"Maybe. But I'm doing this because it's the right thing to do. Trask will kill Lucy without a second thought if the feds swarm the island. She won't have a chance. Either the house is rigged to explode or he'll put a bullet in her head. He doesn't want to be caught, but more than that he doesn't want her to live."

"You and Jack seem to agree on this."

"Jack's seen a hell of a lot more than I have." She searched his eyes. "So have you. You've been inside the criminal minds of sadistic men and women like Trask. You try to make sense of it to stop it. To be honest, I'd rather take my chances face-to-face than look inside their heads to figure out what makes them tick. But without men like you, we'd never be able to learn why. And maybe stop it from happening in the future."

Dillon touched Kate's cheek. She leaned into his hand and closed her eyes. For a brief moment, he felt her strength and vulnerability. Saw her loneliness, how weary she was of this hunt. But it was her vocation; she would not give up.

Dillon's phone vibrated and he pulled it from his pocket. A picture came in with a message from Quinn Peterson.

Show to Kate.

He turned the image to show Kate. "Know him?"

She stared, her face going white. "Trask." She swallowed. "Where did you get that?"

"Peterson." He was about to call.

"Don't. Text him. It'll take him longer to trace it, and we should be gone by then."

"I thought we agreed that Peterson needs to be clued into the two sets of coordinates." But he sent the text message. "He's not coming after you."

"Maybe not, but others will."

"Who?"

"Jeff Merritt, for one."

"Who's he?"

"He used to be my direct supervisor, Paige's as well. He and Paige were also . . . involved."

"Isn't that a conflict?"

She shrugged. "It happens. It wasn't a problem until he started pulling us off the Trask Enterprises investigation. It caused a huge problem between him and Paige and we—Paige and I—got reckless."

Kate sighed, ran a hand through her short blond hair. "Merritt was worried about her safety, and because of that pulled us instead of giving us backup. We were pissed. Paige went to him, and I thought she had gotten sanction, but . . ."

"What?"

"Nothing."

"Tell me, Kate."

She was obviously torn. "When we stormed the warehouse after getting the tip from Denise about the Russian girls being illegally brought in, I thought we had backup. Paige said—implied—that we were covered. But . . ." She shrugged.

"She lied."

"No," Kate said emphatically. "She didn't. I just didn't understand what she had planned."

"She lied to you."

"No, dammit!"

"She lied and died and you've been blaming yourself because you can't blame your dead friend."

"Paige was the closest thing I had to family! Mine was nonexistent. A mother who couldn't look at me, elderly grandparents who didn't talk to me, and when they died, I was shuffled from stranger to stranger. Paige . . . she was closer than blood. I'm not going to taint her name."

Kate's eyes were red, sweat glistened on her brow. "You don't know how she died. How she was brutalized. You didn't see her body, shredded. Blood everywhere. Her eyes—"

Dillon pulled Kate to him, held her while her body shook with soundless sobs.

The truth, at last.

His phone vibrated and Kate jumped back. She gave him an odd half-smile, embarrassed. He touched her cheek. "It's okay, Kate. I don't think you're weak. It takes a strong person to be honest with others, but the strongest people are honest with themselves."

He looked at the phone, showed Peterson's message to Kate.

Adam Scott, 39. Expelled from Stonebridge, disappeared for six years. We're tracking his finances now. There was a death at the school Scott and Morton attended—a kid named Trevor Conrad. We're looking into him as well as another guy, Paul Ullman, who was Scott's roommate. Tell Kate that Mick Mallory is undercover and will take down Trask/Scott first chance he gets. Be careful.

"Mallory," Kate muttered.

"Know him?"

"No, but I've heard of him. And he and Jeff Merritt were close. Merritt must have sent him in." She frowned. "I don't understand why. How do we have someone on the inside, but Trask—Adam Scott—still got to Lucy?"

"Good question," Dillon said.

"Give Peterson the coordinates. But," Kate implored him, "make him understand that they must use extreme caution. Not just for their safety, but for Lucy's." She didn't know if she was doing the right thing, but she'd agreed when they left Mexico that they would tell the FBI what they'd learned. She had to live up to her word. She wanted Dillon to trust her. To believe in her.

Dillon nodded, typed in the message.

Kate glanced at her watch, started pacing again. "It's been thirty minutes. They should be done."

"Impatient, impatient." Jack sauntered into the

room. "We're fueled up and I downloaded some maps of the area. It's just shy of nine hundred miles to a small airstrip outside Bellingham. It'll take me forty-five minutes to get from the base of Mount Baker to the campground. I also have a copter on alert. A pal of mine in Canada. He's going to meet us at the airstrip, take you to an island near the one you think Lucy is on."

"Why do we need a helicopter?" Dillon asked.

"I pulled down a map of the island Kate thinks Lucy is on. No way to land anything, even a copter—"

"We can't hit the island from above," Kate interrupted. "They'll hear. We need to take a boat and—"

Jack held his hands up. "Do I look stupid? I have a safe landing spot and a boat ready for you ten miles from the island. Hank will land the copter and get you situated. You'll be in communication with him, and if you need an emergency pickup he'll be there. I trust him."

Dillon raised an eyebrow but didn't say anything. Jack didn't seem like the type of man to trust anyone, yet he had this mercenary base—which might or might not be run by the U.S. military—in the middle of the Nevada desert, and a convenient pal up in the Pacific Northwest who just happened to have a helicopter.

"And you're going to take my plane?" Kate said.

"You mean Professor Fox's plane?"

She glared at him.

"It sounds like a good plan," Dillon intervened. "Let's go."

Dillon watched as Jack and Kate bickered about

the plan. He held back and looked at the message from Peterson.

I can't get clearance for backup yet, but I will be there. Be damn careful.

"Move it, Dil," Jack called back. "Time is running out."

Dillon tensed. Jack didn't have to tell him that. And with only the three of them—four if Quinn Peterson made it in time—Dillon didn't know if anyone was going to get out alive.

For eight hours Lucy had been locked in the bathroom. She drank water from the sink, but other than that had no food and felt drained. Defeated.

She slept on and off, laying down in the bathtub after an hour when no one came back for her.

What was going on? Why did they take her off the camera? She was grateful, but . . .

Grateful? Grateful that she had a towel and water and wasn't being raped? Pathetic, Lucy. Just pathetic. Was this the Stockholm syndrome? Was she going to do anything for them just so they didn't hurt her again? Thank them for the water?

Get a grip, Luce. This is like torture. Head games. Making you sweat it out, trying to break you.

She had slept through the sunrise, because when she opened her eyes the room wasn't dark, light was filtering in through the skylight. The dancing dust particles caught in the sunlight were surprisingly beautiful. For the first time, she felt hope . . . that she just might get out of this. That maybe God was watching out for her.

The door opened and she stifled a scream.

Denise was naked. Her face was swollen, her breasts cut and bleeding, and she was limping.

"Oh my God," Lucy said without thinking about how Denise had hurt her earlier. "Are you okay?" Stupid question. "Let me help . . ."

Denise stared at her as if she were insane. Maybe she was, but this woman was in pain. Blood ran down her legs. Lucy took off the towel she was wearing, unmindful of her nudity as she handed it to Denise.

That was when she saw Roger in the doorway. "You're next."

Lucy started shaking. She stepped back, almost fell into the tub.

Denise grabbed her arm and pulled her out of the bathroom and into Roger. Lucy jumped backward.

"I need to shower." Denise shut and locked the door.

Lucy stood there naked, Roger staring at her. She tried to cover herself.

Roger laughed.

"Come on, princess. Your fans are getting restless. Denise is used, they want fresh meat."

"Please, don't—"

"Save it for the camera."

He grabbed her wrists, pulled them behind her back. A man in the corner of the room made crude gyrations with his pelvis. She turned away.

Hope disintegrated.

TWENTY-ONE

AS SOON AS THEY WERE AIRBORNE, Jack offered to fly. Dillon was surprised when Kate relinquished the controls and sat in the back. She took out her laptop and booted it up.

Dillon glanced at his brother. "Thanks, Jack."

"Thank me when we rescue Lucy. Do you have an update on Patrick?"

"Same."

"Shit," Kate said from the rear of the Cessna.

Dillon got out of his seat and, hunched over, carefully made his way to the seat next to Kate. "What?"

"You don't want to see this."

"I have to."

She turned her laptop to face him.

Dillon stared at the screen, his heart pounding as his fists opened and closed.

He wanted to punch something. Someone. The bastard who was raping Lucy. He would kill him, so help him God. He would kill him with his bare hands.

But the rape was almost not as bad as the poll in the corner of the screen.

Vote Now!
How should Lucy "die"?
o Stabbing
o Strangulation
o Suffocation

The time stamp was 16:54:00. They had less than seventeen hours to rescue Lucy and they were still four hours out of Washington.

"Don't watch," Kate said, turning the laptop back to her. Her fingers typed quickly, Lucy's screen was minimized, and five minutes later she'd shut down her laptop. "There's been no further communication from Trask or the undercover agent, Mick Mallory."

"He's letting this happen."

"If he exposed himself, he'd be dead," Kate reminded him.

"I don't care." Dillon stared out the window but didn't see the desert or the bright morning sun. "The FBI doesn't even know where Mallory is. They don't know if he's dead or alive."

"We know he was alive last night."

"That doesn't make me feel any better. He's done nothing to help Lucy, and now—" He didn't state the obvious. Now Lucy was being raped again, and with each passing minute, her death drew closer.

"This might not make you feel better, Dillon, but for what it's worth, this is the first time in five years that I think we're going to stop Trask."

"Before or after he kills Lucy?"

Jack became tense as they approached the landing strip. He'd kept the controls after leaving Red Rock so Kate could get some sleep, but Dillon knew she hadn't slept a wink. She'd stared out the window the entire flight, checking her laptop every thirty minutes. Thinking? Planning? Regretting? Dillon wished he could find a way to talk to her, get her to share what was really troubling her. But he had Lucy on his mind, and he wouldn't be able to think until his sister was safe.

"What's wrong?" Dillon asked Jack.

Jack looked at him, surprised. "Nothing."

"You're worried about something."

For a minute, he didn't say anything. Then, low, "It's funny. We have barely spoken in twenty years and you can already read me. Because you're a shrink?"

Dillon shook his head. "Because I'm your brother."

Jack glanced at Kate, who appeared to be sleeping.

"I'm just running through the op. Adam Scott wants Kate on the mountain at two p.m. A little less than two hours from now. We're going to land in fifteen minutes. I have transport, but it'll be cutting it close. Still, I don't know what his game is. Why call her out to the mountain in the first place when his headquarters is eighty miles away?"

"If we can believe the second transmission."

"Kate does, otherwise she wouldn't go to the island. She'd come with me to Mount Baker."

Dillon nodded, weighed the information. "He doesn't know about the undercover agent, or that the agent contacted Kate. He doesn't know about Lucy signing to us that she's on an island. So he's leading Kate away from Lucy in order to isolate her, to make sure she didn't bring anyone. That she's alone. Then he'll either kill her there, or bring her to the island once he believes she's alone."

"And when she doesn't show?"

"He'll attempt to contact her to see if she was delayed."

"He isn't going to be on the mountain alone," Jack said. "That would be stupid."

Dillon shook his head. "No, he's holding the ace: Lucy. If Adam Scott is on the mountain, Lucy will be nowhere near it. He'll be in communication with his team. He'll call for her death in a minute if he thinks it'll buy him time or allow him to escape."

"I'll identify him, follow him. He'll be pissed because Kate didn't show, but he'll also be expecting a tail."

"Expect the unexpected," Dillon said. "He's not going to be alone. He has a trick, something that he will use to get to Kate. To force her to come with him. He could have another woman. Or I could be completely wrong and he will bring Lucy with him."

"I always expect the unexpected," Jack said.

"Lucy's not with Trask," Kate said.

Dillon glanced over his shoulder. She was staring at her laptop. "She's still onscreen."

Abigail was surprised when Vigo met her at the airport at two Eastern time.

"Surprise," Vigo said and flashed his award-winning grin.

Abigail refrained from grinning back. The man was incorrigible. "What are you doing here?" She slid into the passenger seat, grabbing the dashboard when Vigo pulled quickly from his parking place.

"Peterson asked me to run Ullman's finances and clients. Surprise, one client is Adam Scott. Double surprise, Ullman is the stockbroker for all the corporations on which Adam Scott sits on the board. And for a triple play, Ullman carries his proxy."

"So he definitely knows something."

"I'd say he knows everything. We may need to bring him in. Consider him armed and dangerous."

"So why did you come up yourself?" Abigail asked.

"Peterson wants the best on this case and, well, that's me." He smiled again and Abigail laughed.

At Ullman's Madison Avenue highrise, Vigo and Abigail flashed their badges and security cleared their weapons. "Let's get up there before one of Ullman's friends calls that we're here."

Paul Ullman had a spacious contemporary office with white carpets and black-and-silver furniture, against the backdrop of the Manhattan skyline. Abigail winced at the shine, polish, and prestige. "Phony."

Ullman himself was a short, wiry man of thirty-seven with black, slicked-back hair and dressed in an impeccably tailored Italian suit. He walked into his office via a side door, immediately clasped the hands of Vigo, then Abigail. "So sorry to keep you waiting," he said, then, all in one breath, "I was in a meeting, couldn't get out, I hope you don't mind."

"We haven't been here long," Abigail said.

"Good, good, please sit down." He motioned toward a black leather couch in the corner. "Please." He sat on the arm of the chair across from the couch. When neither agent sat, he stood, his hands shoved in his pockets, rocking back and forth on the balls of his feet. "What can I help you with?"

"You're Adam Scott's stockbroker and carry his proxy for all his boards, correct?" Abigail said, cutting immediately to the heart of the matter.

Ullman blinked rapidly several times. "Scott? Um, I'd have to check—"

"You went to school with him, I'm sure you remember him."

"Of course, but I—"

"When was the last time you saw Mr. Scott?"

"I don't know. Years. We do business only through e-mail and correspondence."

"When was the last time you corresponded with him?"

"Um, I don't know."

"Do you know what the penalties are for laundering money?"

"Laundering?" Ullman paled even more, if that were possible against his already ghostly pallor. "No, I'm a legitimate businessman, I don't do that. You can check my records."

Vigo spoke up for the first time. "We will, thank you very much."

"I, um, my company. My lawyers. I would need to see a warrant."

Vigo frowned, started searching his pockets, pulled out an envelope. "You mean like this?"

Ullman snatched the papers, read them, his mouth working but no sound coming out. "I, I . . . I need to get my attorney."

"Do you remember Trevor Conrad?"

"I'm not talking to you without my attorney."

Vigo put his hands up. "That's your right, of course. Just don't leave the room while you call him. And while you're at it, Special Agent Resnick will take a little look at your computer. It's covered there, in the warrant. Page two."

Trask listened to his attorney.

Not good. For five years they hadn't been able to trace him, and now all of a sudden the feds knew about Trevor Conrad.

Worse, they knew his real name. And that fucking bastard Paul Ullman was going to talk.

He shouldn't have used Trevor's name with Lucy. It had been arrogant, cocky. He could see that now, but at the time it had been fun. Part of the game.

He would adapt. He always did.

"Kill him."

"The feds are with him now."

"I don't care. Find a way. You always find a way."

He slammed his phone shut.

In fifteen more minutes Kate would be here. She'd better show. He was in no mood for any bullshit.

At least Ullman knew nothing of importance. Except the truth about Trevor's death, but even he wasn't stupid enough to talk about that.

Trask opened his computer and hacked into Ullman's accounts. He needed to save most of his money before the feds cut him off. He'd lost millions of dollars a few years ago when they'd uncovered one of his accounts. But they'd never made the Ullman connection before.

This was definitely going to be a problem.

He turned and faced the restrained fed in the backseat. Mick Mallory stared at him with hatred.

Trask laughed, went back to his computer.

Hate. What a wonderfully empowering emotion.

Quinn Peterson had just landed in Seattle when his cell phone rang. "Peterson."

"It's Vigo. Good news, bad news, worse news."

"Give me good news. I need some."

"We have all Adam Scott's finances. Paul Ullman has been laundering money for years. We've seized his accounts, have computers and e-mails that I'm transporting to Quantico right now."

"Fabulous. What's the bad news?"

"Scott transferred more than half the accounts to unknown sources before we could seize them."

"Someone tipped him off."

"We think the attorney, but we can't prove it."

"What's the worse news?"

"Ullman is dead."

"*What?* You were supposed to sit on him!"

"We did!" Vigo said defensively. "He went to meet with the attorney—we obviously couldn't sit in. But we flanked the room. He came out of it, nodded to us, went over to his balcony, and jumped."

"Jumped?"

"Thirty-six stories, right there on Madison Avenue. Splat."

"Innocent bystanders?"

"He hit a parked car. Totaled it."

"Anything else about Trevor Conrad's death?"

"We're on our way to talk to his parents."

"Keep me informed."

*   *   *

Jack circled around the meeting location. He saw a Hummer but no Adam Scott, no people at all. They could be inside the vehicle—he didn't have a good view of the rear seat because of the shaded windows.

The coordinates Scott had sent to Kate were for a closed campground at the base of Mount Baker. An avalanche during the winter had made this area treacherous, so park rangers had closed it off until they could clear the roads. The work was nearly complete, but the road hadn't been opened to the public yet.

Scott had told Kate there was a cabin at the site, but there was no cabin.

Though Jack had backup a few miles away, for this leg of the operation, he was on his own.

Just the way he preferred it.

Jack faded back into the trees and waited. He was good at it.

Trask glanced at his watch. Kate had five minutes.

He slapped the leg of the man next to him. "I would tell you I was sorry, but I'd be lying," he said. "You're nothing but a fucking, stupid cop. They're better off without you."

Mick Mallory didn't respond, barely moved. He couldn't, of course, as he was drugged and barely coherent, his mouth taped shut, and his feet and hands restrained.

"The irony of this whole situation is that April Klinger's death was an accident. I didn't mean to go that far. She completely consented. Not to being strangled, of course, but to being raped. I *paid* her for it. She signed a contract." Trask looked out the window. Saw nothing but trees and bark and two unused campfire pits.

Would Kate show?

Yes. Unless something happened, she would come.

He logged onto his pocket PC and checked the cue. Kate wasn't online, hadn't sent him any messages.

"April was unusually beautiful. I admire beautiful women. Really, what else are they valued for except their physical appearance? Which is exactly what they want. They like having men lust after them. They love showing their bodies to the world. My actresses enjoyed every minute because in the end, women are simply whores here to service our needs."

When his father disowned him, Trask plotted his murder. He would kill the judge, find a way to regain his inheritance—through his mother, who would welcome him home no matter what.

Then he came up with an even better idea. He'd been working on the side distributing snuff films— mostly fake, but a few real gems nonetheless—when he saw the future of the Internet. To have a system where anyone could simply download a murder appealed to him.

In a few short years, he had made a fortune. Making his money from online pornography was nothing compared to the first film he'd produced.

Of a judge being spanked by two whores.

Trask had embellished it, but used much of the same choreography as real life. Found someone who looked, more or less, like his father.

When it was complete, he put it on the Internet and sent his father the link. Watched online as the message was opened, the link clicked.

A month later Judge and Mrs. Scott died in a car accident. Their deaths stolen from Trask. He'd wanted his money and instead got nothing.

When his father disowned him, it wasn't in word only. He cut him off completely, changing his will.

The bastard.

Trask pushed the foul memories of his dead father away and logged onto his own webcam. Lucy was there, alone. He called Roger.

"What the fuck is going on?"

"We had to take a break. Frank almost killed her when she kicked him in the balls."

"Why weren't her legs restrained?"

"We wanted to try something different."

"I'm the director, remember? This is my show. Keep her tied down and don't be stupid. Give Frank a few minutes to cool off, then get him back in there."

He slammed his cell phone shut, looked at his watch.

Kate was late.

He slapped Mallory next to him, and his victim moaned. "Show's on, Mick. Get your ass in gear. I think Kate is playing with me, and I don't like being jerked around.

"Wait until she sees what I have planned for her."

He took out a syringe and injected the contents into Mick's arm. "This should wake you up."

TWENTY-TWO

THE NOISE OF THE HELICOPTER made it impossible for Kate and Dillon to talk, which was probably for the best as they both thought through the plan. Dillon put aside the trauma Lucy had suffered and focused on the rescue. The pilot was landing on an island less than a mile from Lucy's suspected position. A boat was waiting for them. They would pose as lost tourists if necessary, but Dillon felt that the disguise wouldn't work if one of Trask's men saw them. Trask—Adam Scott—would most certainly have done his homework. He knew what Kate looked like, and Dillon wouldn't be surprised if he had files on all the Kincaids, including himself.

If they were wrong about Lucy's location, then they'd lost hours of time. It could be a trap, or it could be a wild-goose chase.

But Trask had given Kate a location only eighty miles away. Close enough that Dillon believed that Lucy *could* be on this island, or one nearby. And that they had time to save her.

He looked at his watch: 2:10. Less than ten hours and she would be dead.

Dillon considered what he knew of Adam Scott.

Expelled from high school for the mysterious death of a student who had supposedly been his best friend. A lab explosion? He wondered what was missing from the story. His two friends, Roger Morton and Paul Ullman, had been reinstated to the school, but not Adam. Because of the school? Or perhaps Adam's parents? Or maybe the school was covering up a crime, claiming it was an accident and handling the "punishment" themselves.

Scott had been seventeen at the time, only a year away from graduation. He must have received a GED because four years later Scott had graduated from Georgetown, according to new information from Peterson. That knowledge of the university would have been enough to fool Lucy.

He had Roger Morton in charge of pornography, and Paul Ullman laundering money through a variety of companies. Peterson said they were still uncovering tens of millions of dollars in accounts, half of which Scott had siphoned off almost immediately after Ullman had been questioned by the FBI.

"If only we weren't on a fishing expedition," Peterson had lamented. "We could have shut down the accounts before talking to Ullman. But even then, we didn't know the extent of his tentacles."

Still, according to Peterson, Scott had taken a huge financial hit when the FBI had seized his accounts earlier in the day. He had enough money to disappear, but his conduit was closed. There was no other way to launder the money coming in from his current operation, and future operations were in jeopardy.

A small consolation for what Lucy had gone through.

Dillon glanced at Kate. Her profile was stunning. Hard lines softened by large blue eyes and a small, aristocratic nose. Her face was completely devoid of makeup, her skin tan and smooth, her hair sun-bleached even lighter than her natural blond shade.

She was all muscle, lean and athletic, from hours of working out each week. Except for the soft curves of her breasts and hips, she had no fat on her body.

A sliver of something hit Dillon in the chest. Something about Kate . . . she was unlike anyone he'd met. *Born in hate* she'd said. Unloved by a mother who'd been raped, misunderstood by grandparents too old to raise an active girl. Dillon suspected she was a tomboy, rough-and-tumble as a kid.

Kate was an anomaly. She thought that he had her pegged, that he'd analyzed and classified her. But she went beyond classification. She was too complex and driven. A hero in many ways, Dillon thought. Living every day of her life in search of a man who brutalized women. It didn't matter, he realized, why she did it—guilt, revenge, duty. What mattered was that she did it, and that she kept at it even at the expense of her own happiness and freedom.

Few people would feel the need to get involved, even when tragedy slapped them in the face. Kate, on the other hand, jumped in with both feet, determined to end Adam Scott's reign of terror.

She was scared, but her fear didn't stop her. She knew she could die, but that realization didn't slow her down. And she was doing it for a girl she'd never met: Lucy.

Kate turned and caught him watching her. He held her eyes, and she didn't turn away. The strength and vulnerability he saw on her face, under her skin, in her heart moved him like nothing else could.

Lucy had hope because of Kate Donovan. Dillon would make sure they both got out of this alive.

Hank, the pilot, said, "There's our landing spot. I came around from the north so we wouldn't be detected if they have a scout. Five minutes."

"Ready?" he asked Kate.

"More than ever," she replied.

There had been no movement for twenty minutes after the rendezvous time Adam Scott had given Kate. What was his game?

Jack considered heading to the Hummer. He could look underneath, see if it was rigged with a bomb. But what if Trask was watching from the tree line? What if he was waiting for Kate to get antsy and show herself? Jack had already done periphery surveillance, but he didn't know exactly who he was up against. He had to assume Trask had a plan.

He watched the Hummer closely. It bounced, very slightly. Someone was inside.

The door opened. Jack looked through the scope of his rifle.

Two men emerged. One was Trask. The other man was handcuffed and didn't look completely conscious. His head lolled back and forth, but he was moving forward.

Trask had a gun to the man's head. Who was he? A setup? The undercover fed Kate had told him about? Someone else?

"Kate Don-o-van," Trask called out mockingly. "Come out, come out! Or do you want another death on your conscience? Because I certainly couldn't care less about killing this traitor."

Trask paused. Jack didn't move, lying low in the pine needles.

Scott spoke, his voice echoing in the silence. "Kate, show yourself or this fed dies. Then the girl."

Jack didn't move.

"You want to kill me, don't you? If I don't check in, the girl will die. Painfully. Roger knows how to avoid all the major organs. She'll bleed to death. Slowly. Like your dear friend Paige."

The bastard grinned. "Paige. I almost wish I could kill her all over again."

Jack's finger rested on the trigger. He couldn't take Trask out. The Hummer partly obscured the target. Jack was a good shot, but if he missed—and at this distance he couldn't be guaranteed a clean kill— Trask would order Lucy killed.

Trask frowned, grabbed his pocket, and extracted a phone. His face clouded and twisted as he listened to whoever was on the other end.

He shot the hostage in the back.

Jack didn't fire. He had a less than fifty percent chance of hitting him and Jack wasn't willing to risk Lucy's life with those odds. Dillon and Kate hadn't had enough time to get to the island. Jack made the difficult decision to let Trask go.

The killer jumped into the Hummer and sped off.

Jack waited a good five minutes. He heard the vehicle leave, didn't hear it stopping or idling. Didn't mean that Trask couldn't stop the car and backtrack, hoping to lure Kate out with the half-dead man face-down in the dirt. Jack proceeded cautiously.

He reached the fallen man. Checked his pulse. Faint, but steady. The wound was bleeding slowly. From the location Jack suspected the man's right kidney was destroyed, but he was alive and would probably live if he had surgery.

Jack pulled out a cloth and applied pressure to the wound, securing it with tape from his emergency first-aid kit. He called his pal who was waiting a few miles off. "I need a copter at my location ASAP. Man down, critical."

"ETA ten minutes."

Jack turned the man over, searched his pockets for ID, and found none. No identification of any kind.

"Lucy."

The man's voice was faint, but Jack couldn't miss his declaration.

"What?" Jack slapped him. "Buddy, wake up. Help's coming. What about Lucy?"

"Sorry." He hadn't opened his eyes and Jack didn't think he was fully conscious.

Shit. Was Dillon walking into a trap just like Patrick and Connor had?

Jack needed to get to his brother. He didn't harbor any illusions that they'd be best friends again, but they had an understanding, and dammit, Jack didn't want Dillon to die.

They circled the island. Dillon was unusually silent, and for some reason that bothered Kate.

The air was warm, but the water was icy cold coming down the Strait of Georgia. The fog had burned off, it was midafternoon, and the day was clear, bright, and beautiful.

Kate wished it was gray and misty. What happened to the rainy city? What happened to gray skies? She'd never believe what people told her about the Pacific Northwest again.

"Are you okay?" she asked, pretending to look at a map while she scanned the shoreline for any hint of people, particularly people with guns.

"As okay as I can be under the circumstances."

He had on sunglasses, and Kate wished she could see his eyes. They spoke to her in a way he didn't, saying things his words couldn't express. But with the shades, he looked harder, more focused. More like the life Kate wanted to leave behind, instead of the future that for the first time she thought she might have. After they saved Lucy.

She was ready to give Trask up. The FBI had his real identity, they wouldn't let go until they had him in prison. Quinn Peterson told Dillon they'd hit his financials. It was only a matter of time, and for the first time Kate was okay with that. The most important thing was to save Lucy Kincaid. Then maybe she could face the OPR and appeal for leniency. Rebuild her life.

Rebuild it with a man like Dillon Kincaid.

Not that she harbored any illusions that Dillon would want to be a part of her future. It was more the idea of a man *like* Dillon Kincaid in her life. A man who was steady, self-confident, smart, and *not* a cop. She needed to rethink her life and her choices and decide what she wanted to do, what she could do, when this was over.

But for now, she put those thoughts aside. She might not survive. She accepted that. But she'd give her life to ensure that Lucy *did* survive. And Lucy's brother.

"There," she said pointing to a rocky spot on the shore.

"That cliff?"

She nodded. "We'll scale it. It looks solid." She glanced at him. "Can you?"

"Yes."

They'd passed a dock on the opposite shore, but there were no boats. Because Trask was attempting to meet Kate at the base of Mount Baker? Or because no one was here? It was safer to land on this side of the island, where the dense trees and bushes gave them cover.

"If the numbers sent by the undercover agent were even a fraction off," Dillon said, "we could be miles from her."

"I know. But we're close. I feel it."

Kate tied the boat to a water root, made sure it was secure, and pulled herself up by a branch that hung over the water. She shimmied along the branch to the short cliff, then used roots and vines to work her way up the fifteen feet to the top.

Dillon followed her path, agile but heavier than Kate. The vines she used started to pull under his weight. He was only a foot from reaching the top when a vine gave out and he was suspended over the water, holding on to a branch that dipped, threatening to break.

"Grab my hand," Kate said, laying flat on the ground and reaching down as far as she could.

"I can do it," Dillon said, trying to pull himself farther up the weak branch.

"Grab my hand," Kate repeated.

"I weigh a hundred pounds more than you."

"Dammit, Dillon, I can handle it. Give me your hand."

The branch dipped and his sunglasses fell into the water. He swung toward her. She grabbed his arm, holding it in both hands as his feet sought purchase in the rock. His toes found just enough hold to help her bring him up over the edge.

He laid on the ground next to her.

She jumped up, offered her hand. He took it and she helped pull him up. They stood face-to-face, breathing hard, her black tank top covered in sweat and dirt, his green T-shirt molded to his body.

He touched her chin. "Thanks," he said quietly.

"This way." She motioned toward the thickest part of the trees, grabbing the backpack she'd dropped when helping Dillon up the rock face.

They ran low through the thick trees and bushes, which shielded most of the sunshine, making the island dank and cool. The branches and sharp leaves scraped their bare arms along the way, but they didn't slow down. A branch hit Kate in the lip and she bit back a cry.

"You okay?" Dillon said softly, turning her around to face him.

She dabbed her lip with her finger, came back with blood. "Stupid trees."

He pulled the corner of his T-shirt up, held it to her lip. His hair had turned even wavier in the damp air coming off the water. Without gel to tame his bangs, they fell across his eyes, making him look far more attractive than he had any right looking. Than she had any right even thinking about.

He was close, too close. Smelling of sweat and adrenaline, all male. That's what this was, the excitement and fear of the operation. And she'd been alone for too long, and now . . . the first man she saw excited her. Reminded her that she was a woman, that she missed having someone hold her.

She stepped back, stumbled, and he caught her, his eyes staring at her, questioning, wanting, needing.

Or was that her own need reflected in them?

"What's that noise?" he whispered.

She listened. A low hum. Faint. Steady.

"A generator," she whispered back, heart pounding. "This is it."

She pulled out her gun, instinctively taking the lead. Dillon followed right on her heels.

Mick Mallory was on his way to surgery when he regained consciousness.

"Stop," he said, his words slurring.

"Sir, you've been shot."

"I need to make a call."

"You need surgery. Nurse! Ten cc's of—"

Mick reached out and grabbed the doctor's wrist. "I'm FBI. Undercover. I need to call in. I have information—" he started coughing.

The doctor hesitated, then pulled out his cell phone. "Can you use this?"

Mick grabbed the phone. His fingers didn't want to work. He handed it to the doctor and told him what number to dial. "Hold it," he said, motioning to his ear. His head pounded and his entire body felt like it burned from within.

The doctor held the phone like Mick asked.

"Merritt."

"It's Mick."

"Where are you?"

"Hospital. No time." He repeated the coordinates he'd sent to Kate Donovan. "He set a trap for Donovan, but she didn't show. She must have gotten my message."

"Why didn't you send the message to me?"

"No time," he repeated. "I don't know what happened. Someone brought me to the hospital, but he didn't tell me his name and he left."

"Dammit. Are you okay?"

"Am I okay?" He blinked up at the doctor but couldn't really see anything.

The doctor pulled the phone away and spoke. "I don't know who you are, but this man is going in for surgery. He has a bullet in his right kidney."

"Where?"

"Bellingham General."

Merritt ran to the roof while on the phone. "I need a copter, then a plane to Seattle. ASAP."

Paige's murderer was in Washington right now. Finally, he had a chance to make everything right. Finally, the hope of not waking to Paige's phantom screams every night.

I'm sorry I didn't believe you, Paige. But I'm going to make it right. I promise.

Kate Donovan had better not fuck this up, or he'd have her head as well.

TWENTY-THREE

THE CABIN WAS on a raised foundation, twelve stairs leading to a large deck. They'd circled it once, found one man patrolling while chain-smoking cigarettes.

Kate and Dillon communicated by hand signals and eye contact.

I'm taking him out. Kate motioned toward the man who now stood against a tree, facing the opposite direction.

Dillon shook his head, but Kate ignored him. He tensed, not knowing what she had planned. He trusted her, but the stakes were too high and the chance of error too great.

She circled around and he almost lost her in the undergrowth. She moved like a cat, lean and low, limbs working in unison.

She came up to the man from behind, grabbed his neck, and twisted.

Dillon heard the crack forty feet away.

The man crumpled to her feet and she disarmed him. Behind a tree she checked ammunition, then returned to his location.

"Don't feel sorry for him," she said. "He raped your sister."

"I don't," he answered.

She stared at him. "I know what you're thinking."

"No, you don't."

She couldn't know. Even *he* didn't know what he thought about the last two days. But nothing would surprise him, even Kate's ability to kill a man without hesitation.

She'd been trained to do it. She didn't do it for pleasure. Sometimes murder *was* justified.

"We don't know how many people Trask has here," she whispered. "We need to assume at least six. He couldn't have gotten back from Mount Baker by now, but"—she glanced at her watch—"we're getting into the window where he may show up."

"We need to get Lucy to the boat as quickly as possible and over to the island where the copter is waiting."

"Don't wait for me."

"Dammit, Kate!" She was still focusing on Trask. "We have enough on Adam Scott to stop him. Don't do this."

She stared at him, her eyes softening a bit. "I can swim, Dillon. We don't know what condition Lucy is in. Get her to safety. I'm not going to be stupid. I promise." She squeezed his hand. "Don't wait for me."

He touched her face. He needed to touch her. To give her a connection to something good and real and whole.

"There are people who care about you, Kate. Don't forget that."

She swallowed, nodded. Did she have tears in her eyes?

"Let's go."

They'd already decided that Dillon would get to Lucy and Kate would cover them.

They crept up the deck, keeping low, listening.

A sliding door opened.

"Ollie!"

A female voice.

"Dammit, Roger, I don't know why he's not—" the door closed and they couldn't hear anything except muffled voices.

Dillon pictured Lucy as she'd been on the video. There was a window in the room where she was being held. The window had some sort of shade covering it.

Kate motioned for him to go left, around the back side of the deck.

They split up. He circled around the deck, looking at the windows for one that looked familiar. One entire side of the cabin, which he avoided, was a wall of windows overlooking a narrow inlet. Lucy must be in the rear of the cabin.

He rounded the corner, his heart pounding, completely focused on his sister. There were two shaded windows. He pictured the film. There had only been one window where Lucy was kept, based on the shadows and quality of light. Which one was Lucy behind?

Cautiously, he peered around the edges of the first window he approached. It was dark inside, the filtered afternoon sun casting shadows through the slit less than a quarter-inch wide.

A bed. A dresser. Nothing else. He listened. A female cry from the room next door.

Anxious, he treaded lightly to the second window. There was no slit for him to see through. He listened. Nothing.

Then, a woman screamed.

Lucy.

He swallowed his panic. Carefully, silently, he tried the window. Locked.

"Stop! No, no, no!" Lucy cried from inside.

Dillon quickly studied the window. One sheet of glass, double-paned. No gentle tap would break it.

He retrieved Connor's gun from his pocket and slammed it into the window. Before it finished shattering, Dillon jumped through it.

Kate heard the scream followed by breaking glass.

She ran back to the main door, opened it. It was, surprisingly, unlocked.

Click.

"Kate Donovan." The voice was low and husky.

She turned. Denise Arno held a gun aimed at her.

"Roger!" Denise called.

Kate swung her leg up without hesitation. She made contact with Denise's hand at the same time the gun went off. The heat of the bullet brushed by her face.

She let her momentum take her around instead of fighting for her balance. She rolled out of the way a split second before a second gunshot came from down the hall.

She fired three times at Denise, then twice at the shadows in the hall. From the corner of her eye she saw Denise go down, blood coating her chest.

Gunfire rang out from the hall. Dammit, she hadn't put Roger out of commission.

Who else was here? Where was Dillon? Where was Lucy?

Another gunshot, this time from the back of the cabin.

Dillon!

A man was naked and on top of Lucy.

Dillon heard himself cry out. The man looked up, startled and confused. He fumbled for a gun that was far beyond his reach, crawling off Lucy as he tried to stand.

Dillon strode over and kicked him in the face. The man grunted, rolled over, reached his gun in the corner.

Dillon aimed his gun and fired. Again. Again. He saw blood but didn't make the connection.

The man screamed out and clutched his leg. "Fuck! Fuck!"

Dillon picked up the bastard's gun and pocketed it, then brought out the knife Jack had given him before they'd split at the small airport. He slashed the ropes binding Lucy.

"Dillon, you're here. You're really here!"

"Lucy, we have to get out. Now."

She nodded, silent tears running down her face.

Dillon pulled off his T-shirt and handed it to his sister. Shaking, she put it on. It hung to her thighs. She started for the door.

"No," he said quietly. He picked up the camera and threw it against the wall, where it broke, pieces falling to the threadbare carpet.

He led Lucy to the window and eased her over the broken glass before following her out.

He didn't want to think about the gunshots he'd heard moments before. He didn't want to think that Kate was dead.

He had to get Lucy out.

He also had to find Kate.

Torn, he took one look at Lucy's face and knew she couldn't do it on her own. Kate was strong and trained. She was a survivor. He had to believe that.

Lucy was a terrified eighteen-year-old. He would get her to safety, then come back for Kate.

He helped Lucy over the deck railing. "I have a boat."

She nodded, trusting him implicitly.

"You're going to be okay, Luce. I promise."

She nodded again, tears running down her face. Her entire body shook.

Dillon took her hand and they ran low through the trees. He heard no more guns. He heard no more shouts.

Each step was torture as he realized that he was running away from Kate. That she could be dead, dying, in need, and he was leaving her behind. Maybe she'd gone for the boat. She could run faster alone than he could with Lucy. She could be at the cliff already.

The thought propelled Dillon forward. Less than ten minutes later they reached the edge of the island.

Kate wasn't there.

No time to go back. Dillon said to Lucy, "Trust me."

Lucy only nodded, her large brown eyes looking left and right. Terrified.

He picked her up and tossed her into the water, away from the rocks at the base of the cliff. He followed. Together, they both swam to the boat and climbed in.

He scanned the cliff. *Dammit, Kate! Where are you?*

"Who are you looking for? Were they following us?"

"Someone who's been helping me find you."

Kate was nowhere.

Dillon cut the lead rope and started the motor. He'd get Lucy to the copter.

Then he'd go back for Kate.

Kate checked Denise's pulse. Nothing. She was dead.

The man outside was dead.

Gunfire was coming from two places in the cabin. One down the hall where she'd heard breaking glass. The other from the nook that turned into a kitchen.

She was behind a heavy wood table. She'd heard the scream, the gunfire, the breaking glass.

Please, Dillon. Get Lucy out now!

"Where is she?"

A man she didn't recognize came out of the kitchen.

She needed to take her time. She had half a clip left. She couldn't afford to waste the bullets. The gun she'd taken from the dead man outside had already been emptied.

Where was Roger Morton?

Roger emerged from the hall. "Someone took the

girl. I'm going after them." He ran past Kate's hiding place.

The other man called out, "Where's that bitch who killed Denise?"

"Hell if I know, she probably escaped with the girl!"

Roger left through the sliding glass doors and the second man hesitated, then followed.

Kate immediately left her hiding place and went to the room down the hall where Lucy had been held captive. Déjà vu hit her again as she stared at the broken camera, the broken window. *Paige.*

A naked man, bleeding, crawled toward her in the doorway.

She shot him in the head, imagining that he was Trask and she'd been in time to save Paige.

She jumped out the window, saw movement in the trees. A naked chest. Heard the startled cry of a girl in a dark green shirt.

Dillon had given his sister his shirt.

She had to buy them time to get to the boat.

She ran around the deck making noise. She fired into the air, then ran into the second man.

He was young, couldn't be more than twenty. The realization startled Kate. She'd been expecting Roger.

But being young didn't make him less of a killer. He raised his gun.

She was faster. Three pumps into his chest. He didn't get a round off.

"Richie?"

Roger's voice came from around the cabin. He emerged from the direction Dillon and Lucy had run from.

He saw Kate. "You fucking bitch!" He raised his gun. "I should have known it was you."

Kate dove for cover, off the deck and into bushes. Hot, burning pain hit her upper arm and she bit her tongue to keep from crying out.

She pulled her tank top over her head—she had the black one over a white one—and tied it around her arm where Roger's bullet had sliced cleanly through her skin. She leaned against a tree to catch her breath.

"Where's the girl?" Roger called. Close. Too close.

Kate stood, got her bearings, exposed herself, and fired once, twice.

She missed, but Roger fell to the ground, giving her enough time to run.

Away from Dillon and Lucy. To give them time to get the hell off the island.

She could swim. She didn't want to think what the salt water would do to the bullet wound in her arm, but maybe she'd be lucky. Maybe she'd get to kill the bastard who'd raped Paige and Lucy and a half-dozen other women.

She counted the shots she'd fired in her head.

Dammit, she only had one bullet. She'd better make it count.

She ran.

Trask watched on the webcam as the man jumped through the window and kicked Frank in the face.

When he received the message that the outer perimeter had been breached, he'd tried to reach Roger. Nothing. What good was he if Trask couldn't count on him when it mattered? Roger had used his silence twenty years ago to demand trust. "I never said any-

thing about Trevor, did I? I never said anything about
Monique. You can trust me, you know that, right?"

Fucking idiot.

Now his prize had been stolen. Frank was dying.
For all he knew Roger and Denise were dead, too.

And Dillon Kincaid—the last man Trask thought
would come after Lucy—had shot Frank and destroyed his show. He took his girl. Monique.

No, no, *Lucy.* Monique was already dead.

Trask slammed his hand on the dashboard of the
Hummer. He was at the docks at Anacortes, but he
didn't dare go out to the island now. Not with
the feds this close.

That fucking Mick Mallory. He must have figured
out where they were. Alerted someone.

Kate. She'd been in contact with the Kincaids. Her
fingerprints were all over this travesty.

Damn, damn, damn! First his money gone. He'd
lost more than half his wealth in minutes. Minutes!
Then his people.

He should never have trusted anyone. Hadn't he
learned that before?

His father. The whores. His own mother turning
her back on him after he was expelled. Roger and
Paul, weak, needy fools.

No one had ever stood by him. He could only de-
pend on himself. Everything he knew, everything he
was, was due to *his* intelligence, *his* foresight, *his* vision. No one had seen the potential of the Internet
until he had launched his online pornography company. No one saw the potential of fantasy role-playing
until he did it first.

Because he understood the darkest fantasies of

human nature. He harbored them. He'd harbored them his entire life.

Everything was crumbling, but Trask felt free for the first time in years. Everyone he had mistakenly trusted was dead. Now he could go after Kate Donovan on his own. No cameras, nothing but her and him and his hands on her neck.

He'd keep her alive for a long, long time. Long enough to crush her soul before he watched her blood flow.

But first he had a need. Lucy had been stolen from him. In nine hours she should have been dying underneath him.

Someone else would fill her role. An understudy.

He looked around the dock. The day was warm and bright, hundreds of people out in boats and walking along the dock, shopping, taking in the sun.

He spied a lone woman. A little old for him. But she had short blond hair like Kate. Tall and skinny. Walking toward her sporty little car.

He got behind the wheel of his Hummer and followed her. She would go home eventually, and he had backup recording equipment in his car. If she had a family, he'd kill them first. If she lived alone, all the better.

He hoped she lived in the country where her screams couldn't be heard by neighbors.

TWENTY·FOUR

DILLON STEERED THE BOAT toward the island in the distance where help waited. He swallowed anger and a deep, intense protective rage he'd never felt before. He gently touched Lucy's hair as she huddled in the bottom of the boat, under a damp wool blanket Kate had taken from the helicopter and stuffed under the seat. Lucy shook uncontrollably, her face buried in her hands.

"Lucy, you're safe. I promise."

"You know." She looked up at him, blinking in the harsh sunlight. Her voice trembled, the pain and anguish evident in those two words.

"Yes." He couldn't lie to her.

Tears streamed down her face and she closed her eyes, burying her face again.

He gently, cautiously, touched her cheek. She was bruised, but her external injuries would heal. He remembered what Kate had said in her note when she had planned to leave without him.

"Luce," he said, trying to keep his voice calm, "you're the strongest, bravest woman I know. We're going to get through this, okay?"

She nodded but wouldn't look at him.

She was scared and hurting. He was trained to help people deal with tragedies, their fear, their overwhelming sense of hopelessness. Intellectually he understood what Lucy was feeling: the humiliation, the fury, the helplessness, the terror, the injustice. Wanting to live and die at the same time.

But he didn't know *how* she felt. He'd never been a victim. He'd never been physically and emotionally terrorized by a sadistic killer.

He wanted to take and internalize her pain. Yet for the first time he felt ill-equipped to offer the right words or guidance. She was alive, and that meant everything to Dillon and the Kincaid family. But what did it mean to Lucy?

As he neared the island where the copter waited, he saw three men standing on the shore. As he came closer, he recognized Jack. Quinn Peterson. The pilot, Hank.

How could they, four men, possibly know how to help Lucy?

He tossed the rope to Jack, who tied it off. That's when he saw a tall, lean woman standing with Quinn Peterson. Her long black hair was pulled into a high ponytail and her face was ruddy from being outdoors.

She stepped forward. "Miranda Peterson. May I?" She nodded toward Lucy.

"Please be careful."

Miranda looked him square in the eye. "I know exactly what she went through." Then she stepped into the boat.

"My wife," Peterson explained. "Lucy is in good hands."

Dillon didn't need to ask questions to connect the dots.

Jack said, "Trask shot and left for dead an undercover agent. I dropped him at the hospital before coming here. Where's Kate?"

"Back there. Where's Trask?"

Jack paused. "I had to let him go. I didn't know where Lucy was, and I didn't want to risk exposing myself and having him call for her execution. He's driving a yellow Hummer and I already gave the plates to Peterson."

"I ran them," Peterson said. "Registered to Denise Arno."

Dillon started for the boat. "I'm going back."

"Not alone," Jack said.

"I'm going, too," Quinn said. "Miranda will take Lucy to the hospital."

"You go with her," Jack ordered Dillon. "Peterson and I will go back to the island."

Dillon slowly burned. He'd been the one who'd left Kate behind; he wasn't going to just walk away. If she died, how could he live with himself? He'd made a choice, the only choice he could make, but that didn't mean he wouldn't finish the job.

Miranda led Lucy from the boat. She wrapped her in a second wool blanket. "We'll be at Bellingham General," she said. "But Lucy wants to go home."

Dillon felt all eyes on him.

Lucy was safe. Alive.

Kate was in trouble.

"We'll get Kate, then regroup at the hospital," Dillon said.

No one argued.

*   *   *

Kate ran.

She'd hidden on the far side of the island, but Roger had closed in on her and she'd had to run again.

Roger Morton was chasing her through the dense growth on the island. Her arms were cut, and the gunshot wound throbbed. Her makeshift tourniquet had slowed but not stopped the flow of blood. It didn't help that she was running, pumping blood faster and faster through her veins. Her chest burned, but she had to escape.

Everyone else was dead.

She was covered in blood, but she couldn't think about it. The blood came from killers and rapists; she must not feel remorse. Not for Denise, the woman who set her and Paige up for Trask. Not for the young man she'd killed, who would have killed her without remorse. Not for the man whose neck she'd broken.

Roger was unharmed, and she had one bullet.

Stupid, stupid, stupid! But her emotions were raw, on the surface, and walking into that cabin was like walking into Paige's graveyard. She'd fired over and over, not thinking, not being smart.

Maybe she deserved to die.

No.

Dammit, she'd finally saved one. She had destroyed Trask's operation. She had hope that he would be found and Paige could rest in peace.

That she could live in peace.

"Kate, I'm going to fuck your dead body. You know that, don't you?"

Roger's vicious words cut through the air. Close, so close.

He would do it, too.

"The island's not that big, babe. The water's cold. You're losing blood. Come to me. You won't survive in the water. You know it."

Psychological manipulation. She *would* survive. She wouldn't let Trask win. Or Roger.

One bullet. She wiped sweat from her brow. Her short hair fell in her face; she'd lost the small band that had held it back. With one arm, she pushed it back.

One bullet. She listened. Heard a twig break.

Five feet. One bullet. She'd better not miss.

She jumped up.

They came at the island from the dock. The fastest way to get to the cabin and to Kate.

Dillon led the way, having visually mapped the island when he and Lucy escaped.

"Kate!"

He heard another man calling for her. On the far side of the island, away from the cliff. She'd led them away from the boat so Dillon and Lucy could escape.

Dillon swallowed heavily, glanced at Jack and Peterson. They had the training, but now they considered him part of the team.

He nodded, led the way toward the voice, Connor's gun in his hand.

"I'm going to fuck your dead body, you know that, don't you?"

The voice was closer. Roger Morton by the sound of it. The cabin loomed in front of them. Jack put his finger to his lips and quietly ran up the porch stairs as Peterson and Dillon ran past.

". . . you're losing blood. You won't survive . . ."

Kate had been shot. Dillon ran faster, his body and mind focused on one thing. Saving Kate.

He saw Roger Morton facing away from him. His attention focused on a small grove of trees.

Kate jumped up, gun in hand, only feet from Morton.

Morton aimed.

Dillon fired.

Morton and Kate fell.

Had he shot Kate? *Please God, no.*

Dillon ran to her.

Kate saw Dillon at the same time that Roger aimed his gun toward her. Instead of firing her own weapon, she collapsed, hugging the ground. She heard the shot at the same time, felt a thud as Roger Morton fell. She scurried to the other side of the tree, not knowing if Morton was faking it, dead, dying, or if it was just a flesh wound.

She peered around, saw Roger's face.

"Fucking bitch!" he said.

Alive. Definitely alive.

"Kate!"

Dillon. Running toward her.

Roger still had his gun. He was so close she could almost touch him. Bleeding from the leg. He used the tree to brace his back, then stood.

Aimed his gun at Dillon.

Dillon dove and tackled Roger, whose gun fell into

the dirt next to Kate. She grabbed it, aimed it toward the fighting men as they rolled in the dirt.

Almost immediately, Dillon had Roger beneath him and slammed his fist repeatedly into his face, his rage almost out of control.

"You. Hurt. My. Sister." The words came out in grunts with each physical impact.

Quinn Peterson was only steps behind Dillon. He paused a moment, watching. No one wanted to deny Dillon his revenge.

Ten long seconds later Quinn stepped in and intervened. "I got it from here," he said quietly to Dillon.

Dillon stared at Roger's bloodied face and his own hands. He swallowed, his chest heaving with exertion and anger. He stood, turned to Kate.

She lowered her weapon. His face gradually changed as he walked over to her, knelt in front of her, pulled her into his arms, and held her tight.

"I thought I hit you." His words were an agonized whisper. "Are you okay?"

She nodded into his bare chest. She put her hands on his flesh. His heart pounded into her palm. His breathing was labored from running and attacking. His arms squeezed her, holding her up. Protecting her. Keeping her safe and making her feel for the first time in her life that she was not alone.

Quinn Peterson handcuffed Roger and pulled him up. Roger swore and threatened them. "I'm going to call in the Coast Guard and have them pick us up at the dock. I'll process Morton and call you later."

Jack Kincaid came down from the area of the cabin. "Four deceased. One female, three males."

"It's not over," Kate whispered.

"What?" Dillon asked, pushing her away from his body to look her in the eye.

She shivered, missing the heat of his body. "It's not over. Adam Scott is still out there. And he's not going to stop until we stop him."

TWENTY-FIVE

DILLON WALKED into Lucy's room. Miranda Peterson was there, sitting at her side, talking softly to her. He couldn't make out the words, and she stopped as soon as he entered.

"Dr. Kincaid," Miranda said with a nod.

"Dillon," he said, not taking his eyes off his little sister. She looked so pale, so young. That his vibrant, sarcastic, wonderful little sister had been hurt clouded his mind and tightened his heart.

He crossed over, gave Lucy a smile. "Hey, Luce."

She didn't smile back. He swallowed thickly. "Hi." Her voice sounded so strange.

He was at a loss for words. He was a trained psychiatrist and all he wanted to do was hug her and tell her everything would be fine. But it wasn't fine and he couldn't lie to her.

"I called home and told everyone you were safe."

Lucy didn't say anything. Dillon continued. "We're going to take you home tomorrow morning."

"Fine," she said, her voice far away. "I'm really tired," she added, turning away from him.

"The doctor gave her a mild sedative," Miranda explained.

Dillon said, "Okay. I love you, Luce."

He turned for the door. Behind him, he heard Lucy's voice. "Thank you, Dil."

Miranda followed Dillon out. He rubbed his moist eyes, wishing he could trade places with his little sister. Miranda touched his arm.

"I know I don't have to tell you that it will get better with time," she said to him.

"I hate that she's suffering."

"Give her space. You want to help, she knows that. But you have to give her time to sort through what happened on her own."

"I just wish I could go back to Thursday morning and change everything," he said.

"You love her. That's what she needs. Love. And time. Watch her, care for her, she'll let you know when and if she wants to talk and who she wants to talk to. Every woman is different. You can't put rape survivors in the same box."

"I know that in my head, but in my heart—"

"She's your sister. You can't be her brother *and* her shrink. She'll respond to your love and concern much better if she doesn't think you're waiting for her to fall apart."

The elevator doors opened and Dillon turned to see Carina walking briskly down the hall.

Carina ran straight into Dillon's arms, hugged him tightly. He returned the hug, letting his tears finally flow.

"Oh God, Dillon, it's over."

Dillon didn't correct her. In the back of his mind he couldn't help but think about Adam Scott waiting for his chance to get to Kate.

Carina stepped back. "Where's Lucy?"

"In here." Miranda led Carina into the room.

Through the doorway, Dillon watched Lucy reach for Carina, hug her tightly, and cry.

He turned away and saw Quinn Peterson approach. "How's Lucy?" he asked.

"Alive. Safe. Thanks for asking Miranda to help."

Quinn said, "Miranda knows what it's like to survive Hell. Lucy is in good hands."

Dillon rubbed his eyes, tired and weary. "What did Roger Morton have to say?"

"Not a word. Called his lawyer. We have him isolated. No phone calls, no visitors. I'm going to let him sit today and go back at him tomorrow."

"But he could have key information about Adam Scott's location."

Quinn nodded. "Probably. But he's not talking right now, and I can't read his mind."

"I want to talk to him."

"I don't think that's a good idea." He nodded toward Dillon's hands, which were scraped and red from the beating he had given Roger.

"There's other ways to get information."

"You're not going to beat it out of him."

Dillon almost smiled. "No, not really my style."

"Tomorrow morning. You can sit in on my formal interview with him. Hopefully his attorney will tell him to turn on Scott in the hopes of cutting a deal."

"A deal?" Dillon exclaimed.

"I didn't say we would. We're talking the difference between life and death, not life and ten years. Roger Morton is never going to be a free man."

"There are no leads on Scott?"

"Your brother Jack gave us a good description, so we used a forensic artist to update the old school picture we have based on Jack's comments. It's being sent to every law enforcement agency in the country and he's now an FBI Most Wanted. I have a pair of agents in New York tracking down family and friends. His parents are dead. Car accident eight years ago."

"Adam Scott is a methodical killer. He would have had a reason to kill his parents."

"Money. Except that his father had disowned him years before, severed all ties with him. We don't know why. So Scott received nothing from the estate. I have financial and legal experts going through the records, starting from when Scott was expelled. We're going to try to piece together his past, but the car accident may be just that, an accident."

"It'll take weeks," Dillon said. "We don't have weeks. He's going to go after Kate."

"He's waited for years to go after her. He's patient," Peterson said.

"True, but his entire network has been destroyed. He doesn't care about Morton and Denise and the others on the island. It's his financial network. Not being able to launder money through Ullman. Having his identity known. His legitimate assets seized. This is about revenge now. Payback." Dillon frowned.

"What?"

"He has nothing to lose. Before, he had time and money to play with her. But now he's going to be scrambling to stay one step ahead of us. His picture is all over the media. His money's been cut off. He probably has alternate identification, but he isn't going to leave the country without first trying to kill Kate. He sees her as the reason for his failure and will feel an urgent need to make her pay so he can rebuild. He has patience, but less than you think. I don't think he ever knew where she was in Mexico."

"But he said—"

Dillon shook his head. "He's a liar. You can't believe what he says. If he knew where she was, he would have gone after her instead of Lucy. He smoked her out, made her—and you—believe he knew where she was. That makes her a sitting duck because now he *knows*. He's been savoring this revenge for five years."

"We cut off some of his money and resources, but he didn't lose a fraction of his assets then."

"But a *woman* thwarted him. A *woman* figured out his game. That eats at him like nothing else. To him, women are receptacles to serve him. They only exist to give him pleasure. They are worthless and lesser humans."

Peterson grabbed his vibrating cell phone off his belt loop. "Peterson. Okay, I'll be right there."

He said to Dillon, "Mick Mallory is in recovery. I have clearance from his doctor to talk to him. Want to sit in?"

Dillon followed Peterson to the elevator and they went down to the second floor. "Jack believes Adam Scott was using Mallory as a hostage to lure Kate off the mountain, or to see if she sent backup. Scott must have seen what happened on the island—we have checkpoints set up all around the San Juan Islands and he hasn't shown. We found an abandoned boat in Bellingham that has evidence that Lucy was on it. We think he left the island to meet Kate in the mountains, and either one of his people told him about the raid on the island, or he watched it on the webcam before you destroyed it."

Peterson glanced at Dillon. "He knows who you are now."

"I think he's always known who I was. And everyone else in the family. He wouldn't have gone after Lucy without knowing. But why her?"

"I should be asking you that question."

"If I had to guess it's because she reminds him of someone. Or she was a challenge. Or she was easy." Dillon rubbed his face. "Seriously, I think she responded to him online, the easy part, and he researched her, learned about her family. Considered Lucy a challenge. He despises authority. His father was a judge. He was expelled from school. He's never worked for anyone other than himself. He's always been in charge, even when he was younger. He doesn't take orders or advice from others. Every decision is his, but when things go wrong he'll be the first to blame the other people involved. *They* aren't worthy, *they* aren't smart enough, *they* don't see his vision."

Mick Mallory was on a respirator, the monitors tracking his heart and lung function. "Jack said his kidney?"

"His right kidney is gone. Fortunately he can survive with one. He lost a lot of blood. Your brother saved his life. He would have bled to death."

"Is he conscious?"

"Yes."

They walked into the room.

Peterson stood next to the bed. "Mallory, wake up."

The man opened his eyes. He was forty with a short military cut and hard brown eyes. His face had been through an ordeal prior to being shot, but he might have been handsome if not for a three-inch scar across his cheekbone.

"Who are you?" His voice was scratchy.

Peterson flashed his ID. "SAC Quincy Peterson, Seattle. I have a few questions."

Mallory stared at him. "Did you find the girl in time?"

"Yes," Peterson said.

Mallory's entire body seemed to relax. He closed his eyes, let out a long breath. "I'm sorry."

"When did you go undercover in Scott's operation?"

"Scott?" Mallory opened his eyes, questioning.

Peterson explained how they had learned Trask's real identity, then repeated, "When did you join his operation?"

"I'm not allowed to tell anyone but my supervisor."

"Merritt?"

Mallory nodded. "It's bad. I know it's bad." He looked at Dillon. "Who are you?"

"Dillon Kincaid. Lucy's brother."

"I didn't want to hurt her."

"But you would have. Had Kate not made the deal with Adam Scott, you would have raped her to protect your cover."

"Kate? She got my message in time? I was afraid

Trask—Scott—had intercepted it and that's how he knew I was undercover."

"Kate got your message. Can you explain what led to your being shot this afternoon?" Peterson asked.

Mallory frowned. Sweat formed on his brow, and his heart monitor started beating faster. "He called me off. I . . . I didn't want to hurt her. I really didn't. But if I exposed myself, I would be dead and who would have protected her?"

"But Scott figured out who you were anyway."

"At first I didn't know. He said he had a job to do off the island and needed me as backup. I thought, this is my chance. Except he had a fail-safe plan with Roger Morton. If he didn't check in, Roger was to kill the girl and disappear. I wouldn't have enough time to get back to her. And I didn't know if Kate had gotten the message or understood it. So I went with him.

"He told me all about Kate Donovan. How she had put an end to his legitimate business and he had to re-sort to illegal porn. How he set a trap for her. That no one would believe her anymore because of all the false leads. He pulled Lucy off-camera to entice Kate to come.

"Then he told me that I was the bait. He decked me before I could reach my gun, disarmed me, and then drugged me."

"Where does Merritt fit in all this?" Peterson demanded. "This was not a sanctioned undercover operation."

Mallory started coughing. His heart was racing and sweat poured from his skin. Dillon said, "He needs a doctor. He's going into shock."

Peterson stopped Dillon from pressing the call button. He leaned forward. "Mick, talk to me. What's Merritt up to?"

"He . . . revenge. For Paige. He wanted me to kill him."

Dillon pulled his arm from Peterson's grip and pressed the nurse call button. Almost instantly one came in, checked Mallory's vitals, and paged the doctor.

"You need to leave," she said.

"Where's Scott going now?" Dillon asked Mallory.

"I don't know! I—" Mallory flopped on the bed. Two doctors rushed in and pushed Dillon and Peterson out of the room.

"Shit," Peterson said, running a hand through his hair.

"Kate's in trouble."

"She's in more trouble than from a killer on the run. I heard from my people in San Diego. Merritt is up here and he's going to take her into custody."

"No. She saved Lucy's life!"

"There's nothing I can do about it tonight, but tomorrow I'll call in every favor I have."

"She didn't do anything."

"She needs to answer for her actions, face the Office of Professional Responsibility. They'll decide whether to prosecute or not."

"But prison?"

"Merritt is high-ranking. I'll do what I can. He crossed the line sending Mick Mallory into a deep undercover job. I'll push Merritt, maybe get something we can cut a deal with."

Peterson went down and Dillon went up three flights of stairs to where Kate had had her arm sewn up. She sat on the edge of her bed, alone. She was still wearing the white, bloody tank top. Her arm was bandaged. She was dirty, pale, and so tired it was all Dillon could do not to gather her in his arms and hold her.

"How's Lucy?" she asked.

"Alive. Thanks to you."

"And you." She sighed. "No word on Scott?"

"No." Dillon sat next to her, took her hand. "How are you feeling?"

"I'm fine. The arm was nothing. More messy than anything. I just want to find a place to take a hot shower."

"I have a hotel reservation."

"What about Lucy? Aren't you going back to San Diego?"

"She's going back in the morning. She's resting now. Peterson put a guard on her door. My sister Carina is with her now."

"And you're not going?"

"I'm going to talk to Roger Morton tomorrow morning. He called for his attorney, but Peterson and I are going to tag-team him. I've had experience interviewing killers."

Dillon took a deep breath. "You need to know something. Your boss, the one you told me about, Merritt, is coming here. He wants to arrest you."

"I expected it."

Dillon turned her chin so she was forced to look him in the eye. "I will do everything in my power to make sure you don't go to prison. Quinn Peterson will call in every favor. My brother Jack seems to know everyone on the planet. I'll ask him to call the president of the United States if we have to."

A tear slipped out of the corner of her eye and Dillon wiped it with his thumb. Put his thumb to his lips and tasted her agony.

"I think you should do the right thing, face the board and tell them everything that happened five years ago. Including what you told me on the plane. That your partner wasn't honest with you from the beginning. I know she's dead, and she's not here to answer the charges for herself. But she was your best friend. She would not want you to go to prison for something that wasn't your fault. You acted to the best of your ability and knowledge. No one can expect anything more."

"I—"

Dillon put his finger to her lips. "But," he said, his voice low, "if you think the deck is stacked against you, if you think you can't face it, I'll help you disappear."

"You'd do that for me? Why?"

He didn't know why. A torrent of emotions assaulted him, feelings he'd never had. He'd never been an emotional man. He was reasonable, intelligent, professional. Reason over feelings, logic over emotion.

But here with Kate Donovan, his feelings refused to remain buried. He just didn't know what to call them. He'd never experienced them before.

For a person who made his living working with other people's emotions, Dillon was at a loss to understand his own heart.

"You saved Lucy," he said simply.

"You'll help me out of duty," she said flatly.

"No, not duty. It's more than that."

She stared at him. "What? If not duty, why would you break the law to help me?"

"You've shown me more about myself than I've ever seen. You pushed me. You trusted me. You trusted me even when everyone you've trusted has let you down."

"You're a man who inspires trust," she whispered, glancing down. "But do you trust me?"

He pushed her chin up again, his eyes falling to her lips. A small cut on her upper lip where the tree branch hit her was already healing. He leaned over and kissed it lightly. Then he kissed her again. Her hand came up around his neck and held him to her, a sob escaped her throat.

He swallowed her sob, kissed her again, opening her mouth, tasting her, pulling her tongue into his mouth. His arms went around her back, holding her. She molded perfectly to his body, her small breasts pushed flat against his chest, her hand clutching his hair.

He reluctantly pulled back. "Let's go."

"They haven't released me."

He smiled. "I'm a doctor. I'm releasing you." He pulled her up, held her close. "Let's see about that hot shower."

Jeff Merritt started to walk into Lucy Kincaid's hospital room and was stopped by a broad man in quasimilitary garb.

Merritt flashed his badge and started to walk past.

The man put his hand out and held him back. "You can't go in there."

"I need to debrief the girl," Merritt said.

"You are not allowed in there."

"Out of my way, soldier."

The man shifted his stance, from protective to offensive. "You need to leave," he told Merritt.

"I don't take orders from local law enforcement," Merritt said. What did these people think he was? Some two-bit cop? He was an assistant director in charge in the Federal Bureau of Investigation. He had more authority in his little finger than they had in their miserable lives.

The door opened and a woman stepped out. She shut the door firmly behind her and frowned at them. "What's going on here? She's sleeping."

"I'm in charge of this investigation. I need to speak with the victim and get a statement."

"Hell no," she said, crossing her arms.

Merritt fumed. "And who are you?"

"Detective Carina Kincaid, San Diego Police Department. You're not talking to Lucy until she's ready."

Merritt needed to find out what the girl knew, what Adam Scott had said or she had overheard. He had to find Scott. He couldn't rest until that part of his life was over. He was so close, but once again Kate Donovan had fucked it up.

"If Scott abducts another girl, it's on your conscience."

The woman raised an eyebrow at him. "Go away."

Merritt turned and left. He'd already tried to see Mallory, but he was in emergency surgery. Internal bleeding. He might not make it. Dammit, why couldn't Merritt have spoken to him first? He might know something important about Adam Scott's next move.

He flashed his badge at a nurse. "I need Katherine Donovan's room number."

"One moment." The nurse went to a station and looked it up. "Five-fifteen," she said.

He smiled. "Thank you." Finally, someone who responded to authority.

Merritt closed his eyes as he waited for the elevator. He was so close to avenging Paige. The two people responsible for her death were within reach. Kate Donovan and Adam Scott.

He pushed aside memories of his own culpability. He hadn't believed that Kate Donovan had found Paige that fateful day five years ago. He was so furious that they had gone against orders, that one agent had died and one was abducted, that he believed Kate was just blowing smoke to save her own ass.

Then, on the computer screen, he saw her jump through the window. Saw her pull the knife out of Paige's chest. She ran, and the cabin exploded.

Sweat formed on his brow. If he had believed Kate then, would they have been able to save Paige? He didn't know.

But if Kate hadn't disobeyed direct orders, Paige wouldn't have been in that position in the first place. If he had sent backup, even more lives would have been saved.

"God, I miss you, Paige." He remembered how much he'd loved her spunk, her courage, her beautiful, exquisite face.

And then the image of her brutalized body, the

rapes and the stabbing, assaulted his senses and he pounded his fist on the elevator wall.

For five years revenge had been in the forefront of his mind. And now half of it would be complete.

He'd bring Kate up on charges. Going through the Office of Professional Responsibility was merely a technicality. He could keep her in prison until they made their findings.

But first he had to figure out how to smoke Adam Scott out of hiding. Using Kate Donovan as bait.

He squeezed the small DVD player in his pocket. He would show her what she'd been responsible for. Make her work with him. Because now the ends most certainly justified the means.

He opened the door of room 515.

It was empty.

TWENTY-SIX

THE HOTEL WAS on the water, ten stories up, and Kate opened the sliding glass doors to let in the cool, fresh breeze even though the sun had set long ago.

Dillon handed her the backpack from the plane. She didn't know how he'd gotten it, but the idea that he'd thought she might need something was endearing.

He touched her face and she melted inside. She couldn't imagine him wanting her. She probably had more baggage than all his patients combined. But she would take it, at least for tonight.

"Do you mind if I shower?"

He shook his head, kissed her. "I'm going to get you something to eat."

"The hospital fed me dinner."

He grimaced.

She laughed. "Hey, it wasn't bad. I'm used to worse food from Professor Fox's observatory." She took his hand, squeezed it. "Don't leave."

He kissed her again. "I'm not going anywhere."

Kate hadn't been intimate with a man in a long, long time. She hadn't thought she missed it. After watching Trask and his games, she thought she'd never want to have sex again.

But here, with Dillon Kincaid, she saw everything good sex could be, between two people who wanted to please each other.

"Shower," she murmured into his lips, pulling him along with her.

She backed into the lush bathroom. A single white rose sat on the black marble counter. She picked it up, smelled it, savored it.

"You?"

Dillon took the rose, touched it to her nose, then put it in a water glass.

"How hot?" he asked, turning on the shower.

"Very hot."

"Ouch."

She grinned and pulled off her tank. She saw Dillon's gaze travel down her body. She had a lot of little scars here and there. "I've sort of abused my body. This," she pointed to a long faded diagonal scar down her side, "was made by a skinhead when I went undercover back in my irresponsible youth." She found herself laughing. She hadn't been able to think about her previous years in the FBI without thinking about Evan and Paige. But now, recounting the good she had done seemed to free her.

"And this," she stepped out of her jeans and pointed to a round, gnarled scar on her upper thigh, "was a bank robbery. Hostage situation. I went left, should have gone right."

She stepped over to Dillon. The bathroom was already growing steamy from the hot water. "Does my body disturb you?"

"Disturb?" He grinned lopsidedly. "I wouldn't use that word."

He unclasped her bra smoothly, dropped it with her soiled clothing. He gently touched her shoulders, his long fingers trailing down her breasts, touching the little scars on her stomach, the bigger one on her side.

"You've had your appendix removed," he said, touching a very faint one-inch scar on her abdomen."

"I was thirteen. I thought I was having menstrual cramps. It burst."

He frowned. "Dangerous."

"I survived."

"You're a survivor."

He kissed her.

"Take off your clothes," she commanded.

He pulled the borrowed shirt over his head. His body was long and lean, but his muscles were hard and tight. He had several nicks on his chest where the branches on the island had hit him. She kissed one, then another, then another.

He dropped his pants and backed her into the shower.

"Damn, that's hot," he grimaced.

She sighed, content. The hot water hit her abused body, making it ache even more before easing her pains. She groaned, then allowed the massage jets to pound her muscles. She caught Dillon watching her.

"What?" she asked.

"You're beautiful."

She glanced down, feeling embarrassed and excited at the same time. She'd been told she was pretty, but coming from Dillon it came with a heart of sincerity, a frank and honest and unsolicited comment.

"Thank you." She smiled up at him. "You're not too bad on the eyes yourself."

He kissed her, then reached for the shampoo and poured a quarter-size pool into his large hand. "Turn around, please."

She complied, tilting her face up toward the ceiling to avoid spray directly in her eyes. Dillon rubbed the shampoo into her hair, his long fingers massaging her head from the crown to the base. The rich lather smelled fabulous, but what was more luxurious was Dillon's attention. Slow, strong, steadfast. Focused all on her head, her neck, rubbing and massaging the tension out of her body. She felt the pressure of the last two days—the last five years—spiraling down the drain.

"Oh, God, that feels good," she murmured. "Where have you been?"

He whispered in her ear. "Waiting. For you."

An erotic shiver slithered through her body. Dillon rinsed her hair, then picked up the soap and facecloth. His strong, talented fingers massaged her body, leaving her feeling limp, languid, like a jellyfish.

"I'm not going to be able to move," she said on a sigh, kissing his wet shoulder. She moved her mouth to his neck, the taste of his skin a new and exciting flavor.

She took the soap from him, rubbed the bar against his body. Building up a lather that she took across his chest, his shoulders, his back. Down his sides, to his narrow waist and flat stomach. Dillon may not have been in an occupation that required staying in shape, but he had no problems in the body department. His abdomen had a defined six-pack, and his thighs were solid muscle. She wanted to touch him for hours.

Dillon slowly turned her around so he could rub her shoulders. She put her hands on the tile wall as his talented hands hit still-tight muscles. He kissed her neck softly, his tongue leaving a trail of desire in its wake.

"Dillon," she breathed.

He kissed her earlobe. "I want to make love to you," he whispered, his voice low and sexy.

"Please."

He shut off the water, reached out, and pulled in a large, thick white towel. He wrapped her body, then picked her up and carried her from the steamy hot bathroom to the startlingly cool bedroom.

Goose pimples rose on her skin. "I shouldn't have opened the balcony door," she said.

Dillon sat her on the bed, crossed the room, and closed the door. Then he returned, pulled down the comforter, removed her towel, and put her between the sheets. He climbed in after her, pulled the comforter over them. "Warm?"

"Getting there."

She wrapped her arms around his neck. He was staring at her with an intensity she hadn't seen in him before. Something shifted inside her, from casual lust to serious desire.

Dillon wasn't a man to have one-night stands. Dillon was the type to have serious, discreet, and long-term relationships. Kate couldn't help but wonder why he wasn't married. He was prime. Handsome, sexy, smart, and compassionate.

"What are you thinking?" He stared at her.

"Why you're not married."

"Who says I'm not?"

She almost hit him, then saw a smile curve around his lips.

"That was mean," she said, trying not to smile back.

"I'm not married, never been married."

"Why not?"

"I don't know. I've been pretty focused on my practice."

She touched his face, ran her hand through his hair, then pulled him to her lips. Kissed him lightly. Over and over.

The light kisses turned hot, their breath entwined, their hands moving to touch everywhere. Exploring as only new lovers can. Cautious, wanting to please, wanting to bring out the best in each other, and in themselves.

Dillon sank into Kate. He wasn't a man who gave in to his passions and wants. He thought things out, never acted without looking at every contingency. But with Kate, he let his needs take over, an intense and heady desire for her. A feeling that if he let her go, she would vanish and his world would be a darker place.

Her limbs wrapped around him, her heart beating rapidly beneath his chest. Kate had a fierce passion and focus in everything she did, and now it was all directed at him. He kissed her over and over, not able to bring her close enough to satisfy the growing need inside him.

Her hands seemed to be everywhere, on his back, his waist, his ass. Her touch electrified him. He wanted nothing more than to make love to her. Slowly. Methodically.

In bed, Dillon had always been a gentleman. He painstakingly made sure that the woman with him enjoyed herself. He always led the dance, directed the movements.

He tried to slow the pace, to make sure Kate was relaxed and comfortable and ready for him.

Kate would have none of that. Every time he slowed down, she sped up. His mind was a whirlwind; his body wanted her now.

She kissed him repeatedly as her hands roamed, pushing him away.

"What's wrong?" he said, surprised.

She grinned. "Nothing's wrong." She pushed off the comforter, which had become tangled in their legs. Then she climbed on top of him, straddled him. "If you don't make love to me right now, this very minute, I am going to burst."

He swallowed, felt her hands clasp his erection, watched as Kate slowly slid down.

He took her hands into his, watched the pleasure spread over her expressive face. Her short, layered blond hair hung in her face, damp from their shower, making her look natural and even sexier.

"Dillon," she sighed heavily.

It took all his willpower to let her direct their lovemaking. He wanted to go slow and soft, to show her affection. She drove him forward, not giving him time to rest. His release was imminent.

"Kate," he said.

She opened her eyes, now bright with passion, and stared at him. "What?"

He rolled her onto her back and pulled out. She blinked, confused. "What's wrong?" she asked.

Dillon swallowed, not sure what was going on between them, but wanting to make sure Kate knew this wasn't a game to him.

"This isn't about the finish line," he said, his voice thick with desire and frustration.

A startled look crossed her face. He didn't want to hurt her. He wanted to show her what love could be. What it could be between them.

He kissed her swollen lips. "Let me show you what making love can be."

Kate welcomed his embrace. His kisses told her he wanted her. She relaxed under his attention. She'd been so close to release when he pulled back. Maybe that was it. Prolonging this night, the limited time they had together. She pushed aside the thoughts of the morning, when they would part. She might never see him again. She told herself that was okay.

She was lying. But they had the here and now. She wasn't going to waste it.

Dillon's mouth found her breast and she moaned. His tongue played with her nipple, bringing it to full attention. Then he moved to the other side. Her hands grabbed at the bedsheets, a swirling sensation building again inside her. His hands were warm; everywhere his fingers touched made her hot. Light and purposeful, his mouth went from her breasts to her navel, back up again.

"Dillon, I want you."

"I want you, too, Kate." But he didn't make any move to speed things up.

"Fast is good."

"Sometimes," he murmured into the space between her breasts. He looked up at her, his chin resting on her chest. "Slow is good, too."

"I can't wait."

He smiled seductively. "You mean, you don't want to wait."

"That, too."

His eyes blazed. "I'm savoring you, Kate. Won't you allow me that?"

"I'm already undone."

"That's an old-fashioned way of saying you're hot and bothered," Dillon teased.

"I don't believe you." She smiled at him, sat up in the bed, and wrapped her arms around his neck. "Yes. I'm hot and bothered. I want you to make love to me. Now."

"Demanding, too." He kissed her, his own breath labored. So he was as turned on as she was. "I *am* making love to you, Kate. The minute we stepped into that steamy shower, I started to make love to you."

He kissed her again. "Kissing you." His tongue circled her lips, went down to her neck. "Tasting you." He lightly bit her earlobe. "Eating you."

She sucked in her breath as his fingers parted her thighs and felt the hot wetness between her legs.

"Touching you." He swallowed heavily.

"Making love is more than having sex," he whispered in her ear. "It's a full-body experience." His hands roamed up her body, clasped her head from behind. "From your head."

He kissed her, his breath hot, labored, wanting. His mouth moved from hers, back to her hard nipples, down her stomach, never stopping. He brushed his tongue against her clit, making her jump. Then he licked each inner thigh, first the right, then the left, and she squirmed, grabbing his head with her hands. Trying to bring him back to that spot in the middle that needed—demanded—his direct attention.

But he had other things on his mind. His mouth found her toes, pulled them one by one. She gasped. No one had kissed her toes before. His thumbs put pressure on the bottom of her foot, sending bolts directly to her hot core, and she gasped.

"Oh, God, Dillon." She could barely speak, her mouth dry.

"Down to your feet," he said.

He climbed on top of her, his erection reaching for her, his face inches from hers.

"Making love," he whispered into her lips, "is much, much more than having sex."

Then he slid into her, filling her, their bodies drenched in perspiration and desire.

Slowly, they moved together, finding their rhythm. Kate was losing herself in Dillon, giving her body, her heart, her soul over to him. Everything she was from this day forth was because of him. He had showed her things about herself she hadn't realized, understood her in ways she didn't know she missed.

She moved beneath him. His hands found hers. He raised his body, his face intent on hers. "Kate," he gasped.

"I'm with you," she whispered.

They came together, sealing a bond neither had sought or expected.

Dillon pulled Kate to him, holding her tight, his

hand over her rapidly beating heart. They didn't need to speak, not now.

Their mouths found each other and they continued to explore.

Sleep came much later.

Trask stared at the terrified face of the woman beneath him. She was restrained, and his hands encircled her neck. He tried to imagine Kate Donovan beneath him as he attempted to rape the woman.

He was failing, limp and unable to take her. Instead of Kate, he pictured Mina, that wily blond bitch who had hurt and humiliated him for his father's pleasure. As soon as she came to his mind, his cock softened.

He remembered killing Mina and her whore friend. The blood. Red and wet. He smelled copper, felt the slickness of their pathetic lives coating his body. He'd stolen back the power. He was free of them.

Kate Donovan had taken his prize, Monique. *Lucy.* He would find her. Kill her with his bare hands. Then he would regain his strength, be able to do whatever he wanted.

He began to harden. He released her neck and she gasped for air.

"Stop." Her voice was almost gone. "Please, stop. I'll do anything, just don't kill me."

Her pleas further excited him, but he'd prefer it if she fought him. Like he knew Kate would as soon as he had her.

He pushed himself into her and she tried to scream, but with her bruised larynx it came out a gasp. She pulled at her restraints, egging him on.

"That's it. Fight me, bitch."

She stared at his face. He wasn't wearing a mask. The realization hit her. She saw her death in his eyes.

Trask wrapped his hands around her neck as she thrashed. He pressed hard, felt the bone break. Watched her eyes as she knew she was dying.

But he still had trouble.

"Fuck you, Mina!" *No, Kate.*

The woman beneath him scratched at his gloved hands, her eyes wide. He watched a blood vessel swell in the corner. Burst.

He kept slamming himself into her after she was dead, but no relief came.

TWENTY-SEVEN

A KNOCK ON THE DOOR woke Dillon and Kate. They were still entwined from the night before, naked, but Dillon had pulled the comforter on top of them in the middle of the night.

"I don't want to move," Kate said.

He kissed her neck. "Don't."

He slid out from the sheets, slid his jeans on, and crossed to the door.

"Who is it?"

"Quinn Peterson."

"One minute."

Kate moaned and got out of bed. She grabbed her pack and went into the bathroom.

Dillon opened the door. "Come in."

Peterson entered. "Merritt's on his way over. Where's Kate?"

"Why? What's the rush? Doesn't he have more important fugitives to pursue? Does he know where Adam Scott is?"

"I tried to talk him out of it, but he's adamant."

"I'm not going to let Kate be arrested."

"You don't have a choice."

"Dammit, Peterson, I thought you were going to

do something about this!" Dillon ran his hands through his hair. "She's the one who found Lucy."

"Merritt is questioning that. He's floated the theory that she intercepted a transmission meant for him from his undercover agent and because of that four people died and Adam Scott got away because of her maverick ploy."

"That's bullshit and you know it. Mallory told us he sent that message to Kate."

"Mallory's in ICU and unable to talk."

"This Merritt has it in for Kate. He isn't going to listen to the truth. He's already made his mind up."

"I agree. Where's Kate?"

"I don't know."

"Dillon, don't do this. I need to talk to her."

Kate stepped out of the bathroom in clean jeans and tank. "I'll go into headquarters on my own terms," she said.

Peterson raised his eyebrows but didn't say anything.

Dillon took Kate's arms. "You don't have to do this. Remember what I said."

She smiled sadly at him. "I remember. And this is the right thing to do. Full disclosure, and let the chips fall. I'm ready to tell the truth. But I don't know if anyone will believe me."

"I believe you."

"If you want to piss Merritt off, we should leave now for headquarters. We'll just miss him," Peterson suggested. "That way you're turning yourself in."

"Sounds good to me," Kate said.

"I'm working double time trying to get him off this case," Peterson said. "He's not thinking straight. But

I have to smooth the way at Quantico and that's not an easy task."

"I appreciate it, Quinn. Really."

"So hang in there. All I need is time, okay? And you're in my jurisdiction. I'm not letting him take you out of it."

Kate was packing up her equipment when her computer beeped.

Dillon and Quinn both crossed over and watched as she retrieved a message.

There was no return e-mail or identification.

"It's him," she said.

> Kate:
> You took my lead actress, so I had to find an understudy. Click here. The show must go on.
> Trask.

She glanced up at Dillon and Quinn. They both nodded. She clicked the link.

The digital video had been set up in the corner. Adam Scott didn't try to hide his face. A woman with short blond hair had been tied to a bed. She was pleading. Scott wrapped his hands around her neck.

Cut.

The next shot was him raping her, putting his hands around her neck again.

Kate frowned. "A glitch?"

"No," Dillon said. "He edited the video."

"Why?"

Dillon watched closely. Something was off about the tape. It was only five minutes long. At the end

Scott gave out a primal scream as he pummeled the dead girl's body.

Cut.

"I need to see it again," Dillon said.

Kate played it again. Dillon watched closely. "Stop."

She froze the frame. "I don't see anything."

"There." He pointed to the lower right-hand corner, where Trask was mounting the girl.

"I still don't see anything."

"Can you enlarge that frame?"

Kate typed on the keyboard. The frame enlarged four times.

"I don't see anything."

"He's soft. He can't rape her. Now run the film enlarged."

They focused on Scott's shrunken penis. Now the digital splicing was obvious. He had deleted parts of the video, probably those showing how he'd managed to get himself hard enough to penetrate her.

"He might have said something he didn't want us to hear," Dillon surmised, "or done something to himself to enable penetration. But he never climaxed."

"How can you tell?"

"It's a guess, but he has no condom on. When we find the victim forensics will be able to tell. But it was really the rage on his face. He was angry that he couldn't climax. This girl wasn't giving him what he needed. Either because it's not live, or because he has severe sexual dysfunction. Or both. Maybe having the show live gives him the sense that he's playing a part. And"—Dillon clicked on the original message—"look how he signed his name."

"Trask," Quinn and Kate said in unison. "But he knows we have his real identity," Quinn added.

"Trask is his public persona. It's who he thinks he is, or who he wants to be," Dillon said. "Adam Scott is weak. Adam doesn't fight back. Adam was abused. Trask hasn't been abused. He's in charge. *He* fights back. He hurts those who hurt him."

"You're not giving me some crap about a split personality," Quinn muttered.

"No. Adam is fully aware of who he is. For him, it's image. He needs to think of himself as strong, successful, virile. That's Trask. I think his sexual dysfunction is growing because we know who he really is. While we don't know enough about his childhood to figure out what caused this, he doesn't know that. He assumes we know everything."

Dillon looked from Quinn to Kate. "You're not safe, Kate. Not until he's caught."

"He can't get to me," she said.

"Did you get a good look at that woman?" Dillon asked.

She nodded. "She looks just like me."

When Kate Donovan walked into the Seattle field office heads turned. She entered with her head held high, her pride intact, but inside she was scared. She hadn't seen or spoken to Jeff Merritt since the day Paige had died, when he'd told her he'd track her down to the ends of the earth.

There was nothing he, personally, could do except bring her in front of OPR. They would launch an investigation—one she knew had been going on for years—into the op that had gotten Paige and Evan killed. She didn't know what they believed or what they knew. Even if they believed her that Paige had told her they had backup, Kate had broken protocol by not briefing the backup squad herself.

She had trusted Paige.

She had run five years ago because she was scared and angry. Mostly scared. And Jeff had been wild-eyed, overcome with grief she knew all too well. She had watched Evan die in front of her.

She'd intuitively believed that the only way to clear her name was to find Trask—Adam Scott—and prove that he was the brutal killer she knew him to be. She'd done that over the years, but still Merritt wanted her head.

Because Paige had died and he blamed her as much as Adam Scott. He didn't know the truth. She hadn't wanted to hurt him at the time, but he wouldn't have believed her anyway. How could she have ruined the reputation of her dead partner? It had seemed so much easier to run and work outside of the law.

But now? She just wanted it to be over.

Quinn let Dillon stay with her in an interview room. "I'll be here the entire time."

She shook her head. "Merritt won't allow it."

"Then I'll be right outside."

Again, she shook her head. Dillon frowned.

"I can't let you do that. You need to go home with Lucy."

Dillon took her hands, squeezed them. "Lucy is in good hands. Carina is with her. She's going to be overwhelmed as it is when she sees everyone. And we haven't told her about Patrick. We didn't want her to know until she regained some strength."

"Dillon, I'm not going to walk out of here tomorrow or the next day. Merritt is going to find a way to detain me. I don't know what tricks Quinn has up his sleeve, but it's going to take time. And I'm going to have to face the Office of Professional Responsibility at Quantico."

"What do you want?"

"What do you mean?"

"You face the OPR, you tell them everything, and they clear you."

"You have an active fantasy life." But she smiled.

"Are you going to ask for your job back?"

She blinked. She hadn't thought about it. "I don't know."

"Whatever you decide to do, do it for you. Not because of me, or Paige, or Adam Scott. Make the decision that is best for you."

She thought about what she wanted. She really didn't know. For so long she'd been alone with her computers. She'd learned so much, taught herself, much of it illegal—like hacking into private corporations and the government. She would have to tell the OPR everything about what she'd done. She had no idea what they would do. Maybe they would clear her of charges on Paige's death, but what about the crimes she'd willingly committed in her pursuit of Adam Scott?

"I could go to e-crimes," she said. "If they'll have me. I had an offer from them five years ago to transfer out of the VCMO unit. Don't know if it's still open, but I'm a lot better now than I was then."

She frowned.

"What?"

"Adam Scott was even better. He manipulated me through the computers. He knew exactly what I knew. Maybe I'm not as good as I thought."

"You're incredible. Patrick was impressed, and he's the best I know."

"I'll think about it."

Dillon kissed her hand. "I'm not going to leave you, Kate."

"I'm okay. I'm not going to blame you for being with your family right now." But she would miss him.

They held hands across the table, the silent connection giving them both strength they needed.

Quinn Peterson entered. "Merritt's here and he's pissed. I told him you walked in and surrendered. Are you ready for this, Kate?"

She nodded, not taking her eyes from Dillon. "I'm ready."

"You'll have to leave, Dillon. When we're done, I'll call over to the jail and have Morton transported here for the interview."

Reluctantly, Dillon stood. "How long?" he asked Quinn.

"An hour, maybe a little more." He glanced at his watch. "It's eight right now. If you have something to do, meet me here at ten."

"I'll be back, Kate. I promise."

Kate watched Dillon walk out the door and her resolve began to chip away. Quinn sat on the edge of the table. "I'll be here for the formal statement," he said. "Just tell the truth, the good, the bad, and the ugly, okay? We'll find a way out of this."

Jeff Merritt opened the door and slammed it shut.

"Kate Donovan," he spat out.

"Jeff Merritt," she said with equal disdain, looking him straight in the eye. He was short and lean, blond, with a goatee but no mustache to go with it. Kate couldn't believe that five years ago she'd thought he and Paige made a cute couple. The guy was dangerous.

"I don't know how you can live with yourself," he finally said.

Peterson interrupted. "Let's do this by the book."

"Leave."

"No."

"Dammit, Peterson, you're already on thin ice."

"Agent Donovan has a right to representation. I'm that person. And in case you're forgetting, this is *my* field office."

"In case you're forgetting, you work for me."

"Don't pull rank."

"Don't be an asshole."

Quinn didn't move. Finally, Merritt sat down and took out a tape recorder. He slammed it on the table.

"ADIC Jeff Merritt and SAC Quincy Peterson are interviewing former Special Agent Katherine Donovan regarding the murders of SAC Evan Standler and SA Paige Henshaw, as well as civilians Denise Arno and Oliver Johnson."

Kate slammed her fist on the table. "Denise was not an innocent civilian! She's been working with Adam Scott from the beginning."

"You'll have a chance to tell your story, Ms. Donovan. For now I'll take your statement and you will answer my questions. Understand?"

She fumed. She hated this arrogant prick.

"Understood."

Dillon arrived at the hospital as Lucy was getting ready to leave.

"Where have you been?" Carina admonished. "We're already late for the plane."

"How'd Lucy do last night?"

A cloud crossed Carina's face. "She had nightmares. Miranda is a saint. She calmed Lucy down instantly, knowing exactly what to say, when to be tough and when to be kind."

Jack walked around the corner. Dillon was surprised to see him. "I thought you left."

Jack stared at him a moment. "I had some things to take care of. I thought I'd head back to San Diego with you, if it's all right. I have some time."

Dillon nodded. "Thank you. I'm not going back right now."

Carina frowned. "Why?"

"I have things to wrap up here." When Carina didn't say anything, he added, "I'm sitting in on the FBI interview with Roger Morton at ten."

"Lucy needs you."

So does Kate, Dillon thought but didn't say. "Lucy is in good hands. I need to do this, Carina. Adam Scott is still out there."

"You're not a cop," Carina snapped, irritated. "The FBI has taken over the investigation."

"Which they fucked up five years ago," Jack interjected.

"I have a strong sense about Scott," Dillon said.

"The FBI has its own profilers," Carina argued. "It doesn't need you."

"I'm sorry you feel that way, Sis, but I'm staying. I'm going to talk to Lucy and then go back to FBI headquarters."

Jack nodded. "You do what you have to in order to find the scum who hurt Lucy. And I'll make sure he doesn't hurt her again."

Now that his real name and image were known to the authorities, Trask had to plan carefully. Fortunately he had always thought this day was inevitable. While he couldn't travel as freely as he wanted until he underwent plastic surgery, he knew what superficial changes to make to his appearance to blend in. He didn't need that much time. Just long enough to get to Lucy again and use her to lure Kate Donovan into a trap.

He realized that the reason the bitch he'd followed home from the docks wasn't good was because she looked like Kate but wasn't Kate. Kate would fight and scream and claw at him. She wouldn't beg for her life. She wouldn't tell him she'd do anything he wanted. Instead she would try to get away. Just the thought of her fighting him gave him a hard-on.

And Lucy—she was *his*. She had volunteered to meet him. She was everything he needed. He might not kill her, not right away. Use her to get to Kate and kill her, purge Mina and all the whores from his body. Once that happened, he'd be free. He could have the life he'd envisioned with Monique. Where he was in charge and she did what he said. He'd just have to be very careful not to accidentally kill her. He might have to take a few whores on the side. But Lucy would learn quickly that she had to behave or she'd be dead, too. Fear would keep her in line.

He downloaded all the messages from Mick Mallory's PDA. Some were cryptic, but he began to build an understanding that Mallory and his supervisor, Jeff Merritt, were acting on their own. Mallory had been sent to kill him.

What a fool. Mallory should have known immediately that Trask was untouchable.

With his network broken, he didn't know everything that was going on. He went online to see if Kate was surfing around, trying to locate him. Saw that she had downloaded the video. He smiled. Good, now she knew what her fate was. Make her scared. She'd fight him all the more.

But he didn't know where she was. Her mountain hideout was inactive. This frustrated him to no end, and he ended up calling his attorney, the one who had warned him about Ullman's betrayal yesterday.

"Where's Kate Donovan?"

"How should I know?"

"That's what I pay you for."

"Don't call me, Adam."

"You're my attorney! I pay you to talk to me."

"I have to advise you to turn yourself in. There's a warrant for your arrest."

"Fuck that, and fuck you!"

"Turn yourself in and I'll be able to help you."

"You'll help me *now.*"

"I can't do that. They're watching. Closely."

"You're a fool."

He slammed down the phone. He had a fake ID

and passport all ready, but he wasn't done. He had to find Monique and Mina.

Lucy and Kate.

And what about that shrink Dillon Kincaid? Who would have thought a fucking *doctor* would have it in him to shoot a man in cold blood? Frank didn't even have a gun on him.

Trask called the hospital. Maybe this would be easier than he thought.

"This is Connor Kincaid," Trask said. "My sister Lucia Kincaid is a patient. She's being released today and I don't want to miss her."

"One moment."

He waited. Then the nurse came back on the line. "I'm sorry. Ms. Kincaid has already been discharged."

Discharged? Where would she go? Of course, he thought.

Home.

Trask went online and bought a ticket for that afternoon. One-way to San Diego.

TWENTY-EIGHT

QUINN MET DILLON in the lobby of the field office and led him into the rear. "Morton's on his way over."

"Where's Kate?"

"She's cooling off in an interview room. She and Merritt went at it. Verbally," he added.

"I want to see her."

Quinn glanced at his watch. "Ten minutes, if you want to be in with Morton."

"Come get me."

Quinn led Dillon to the room where Kate was being held. There was a plainclothes guard at the door. "Merritt insisted," Quinn said before Dillon could ask.

"She's not going to jail."

Quinn shook his head. "We're keeping her here overnight. It's not very comfortable, but better than going to Seattle PD and being processed." He cleared Dillon with the guard. "I'll be back when Morton arrives." He left Dillon alone with Kate.

Kate jumped up and ran into his arms. He held her tight. A wave of relief that she was okay, that she was safe, washed over him. And something more—a deep need to be with her.

He kissed her repeatedly, then held her at arm's length to take in her appearance fully. She looked more like a cop than when he'd first met her two days before, but weariness clouded her expression. "Are you okay?"

She nodded. "You came back."

"I said I would."

"How's Lucy?"

"She has Carina and Jack taking her back to San Diego. They'll take care of her."

"Jack?"

"He's staying until Scott is captured."

She nodded. "You think Lucy is in danger."

"Absolutely. Both you and Lucy."

Kate sank into one of the chairs around the conference table. Dillon sat next to her, turning his chair so they were knee to knee and he could hold her hands. "Why does he want me now?" she asked. "I understood his frustration before—Paige and I slowed down his operation, forced him to go underground. I can see that he wanted revenge. But now we know who he is. He has the money to disappear—why doesn't he just disappear? It doesn't make sense."

"It does make sense," Dillon said. "You're thinking about this logically from *your* experience. But Adam Scott has a different background. It's personal."

"I never knew him before we started investigating April Klinger's disappearance."

"What I mean is, for *him* it's personal. You remind him of another woman who took something from him. Maybe he was unable to fight back or reclaim what he lost, so he's put you in her role. On the surface, he can convince himself that he's getting back at you because of what you stole from him—his legal porn operation, his freedom of movement, and now Lucy. But it's an act. What he really wants is revenge on someone he could never get revenge on. By killing you, he's avenging his own failures, hurting the person who hurt him."

"I guess that makes sense. But if I were him, I'd lay low for a couple of years and come after me when I'd least expect it."

"That's logical, and up until now Scott has been smart. But we've exposed his identity. We took away his support—Roger Morton and Denise Arno. And remember, for him this is not so much a *game* as a *show*. He sees himself as Trask, the actor. Onstage. Performing. His public persona is much different from his inner person. In fact, on the surface Trask is amiable, charismatic, attractive. Inside, where he's Adam Scott, he's dark and twisted. He's been able to keep them separate—meaning, if we saw his dark side, we'd recognize it immediately. But Trask the actor has taken over. A man who can trick teenage girls into meeting him. A man who probably didn't seem like he'd hurt anyone. He looked *safe*. But in exposing Adam Scott, the weaknesses and insecurities that he has long suppressed are coming out. That's why he couldn't rape the woman last night. That's why he couldn't climax. It was in his face—the rage, the frustration, and fear."

Kate sighed, squeezed his hands. "I just want this

to be over. I want Lucy to feel safe again. I want to get my life back."

"Quinn said you and Merritt had it out."

"Merritt's an asshole. He honestly believes that I intentionally brought Paige into a dangerous situation and did nothing to save her. And I told him the truth—that Paige had assured me he'd authorized backup. I thought there were agents surrounding the building, ready to act. He didn't believe me."

"But Quinn does."

"I think so."

"You're doing the right thing, Kate. And no matter how long it takes, I'll stand by you."

She touched his face, then dropped her hand when Quinn Peterson walked into the room. "Morton's here," he said.

Dillon stood. "Are you going to be okay?"

She nodded, gave him a quick smile. "I'm okay."

Dillon asked, "Did they find the girl in the video?"

"Not yet. I sent the file to the lab to see if they can find any personal information from the images. It appears to be her own bedroom, very feminine. A double bed. She's likely single, so unless an employer or relative calls, or she has a roommate who wasn't home last night, we might not find her for a couple of days."

Dillon followed Quinn down the hall, around the corner, and through a secure door into another interview room. Two guards stood next to a chained and seated Roger Morton. Quinn motioned for them to step out.

"Where's my lawyer?" Morton sneered as the cops closed the door.

"I'm sure he's on his way. We informed him of this meeting."

Morton's dark hair had begun to gray and he sported the beginnings of a beer belly. He was muscular with a thick neck and hands. He played with a class ring on his left pinky finger. He was neither handsome nor ugly, an average guy who worked out to build the muscles, but as he aged the muscles were turning into flab. Purple and black bruises had formed on his face from Dillon's attack the day before. Dillon couldn't muster any sympathy for his injuries.

"I'm not talking. Told you that."

"I know what you told me yesterday," Quinn said. "I'm giving you a chance to make a deal."

"Talk to my lawyer."

"I will." Quinn tapped his fingers on the table. "But if you cooperate and help us find Adam Scott, we'll make a deal. A good deal. If you don't, it's special circumstances murder. Death penalty."

"Bullshit. You don't have me for murder."

"We have a witness from five years ago who has given us a sworn statement regarding the events in the warehouse that resulted in the deaths of two agents."

Morton leaned forward, chains clinking. "If you have a sworn statement that is at all accurate, it has a criminal stating that Adam Scott killed that guy in the warehouse, not me. I know that Kate Donovan is not a reliable witness." He snorted.

Quinn tensed. "You were there. You are an accessory to murder. We have you on tape raping eight girls."

"Women," Morton corrected. "Consenting women."

"Lucy did not consent," Quinn said. "Paige Henshaw did not consent."

He shrugged. "I didn't kill them. What's rape? Five to seven?"

"Kidnapping, use of a weapon during the commission of felony rape, you'll be getting far more than seven years."

Morton stared straight ahead.

"You don't get it, do you? Adam Scott is leaving you to take the blame. The evidence at the cabin on the island points to you as being an equal partner in Trask Enterprises, including murder, rape, kidnapping, money laundering, e-crimes, and that's just the major-ticket items." Quinn leaned forward. "Scott gets away with your money to sun himself on some Caribbean island and you are left having to answer for his crimes."

For the first time, Dillon saw a flicker cross Morton's face.

"So Scott gets away and you go to prison. Seem fair to you? Especially since, as you say, you didn't kill anyone."

"I didn't," Morton insisted. "And you're not going to get me to say I did."

"You attempted to kill Agent Kate Donovan."

Morton snorted. "She was trespassing."

Quinn stared at him and shook his head. "That's not going to fly, Roger. You had kidnapped and raped a girl on the premises. Probable cause." He leaned forward again. "Mick Mallory survived. I already have a statement from him. So between Mallory, Donovan, and Lucy Kincaid, I have three eyewitnesses."

"Mallory?" Morton looked skeptical.

Dillon spoke for the first time. "You didn't know he was an undercover FBI agent?"

By the look on his face, this was the first Morton had heard of it. "That's a fucking lie."

Quinn shook his head. "We had an undercover agent inside and Scott learned his identity. He left the island with Mallory with the purpose of killing him and luring Donovan into a trap, but someone saw the attack and got Special Agent Mallory to the hospital in time."

"Bullshit," Morton said. "Mallory watched Trask whack that bitch—" He stopped himself.

Quinn raised an eyebrow. "Continue."

"Fuck you."

Morton leaned back in his chair and glared at them.

Dillon glanced at Quinn, then said to Morton, "I understand why you want to protect Adam. You've been covering for him for a long time. Ever since he killed Trevor Conrad."

Morton's eyes flickered. "I don't know what you're talking about." There was no passion in his words.

Dillon didn't have all the details, but he'd begun to piece together the complexities of Morton's relationship with Adam Scott. He started fishing, knowing that the waters were ripe. "You, Adam, Paul, and Trevor were best friends. Palled around together at Stonebridge, rich boys with the world in your palm. Cocky. But Adam was always a little different. He had a dark charisma. You did things you probably wouldn't have done because of him egging you on.

After all, you wouldn't be a man if you didn't push the envelope."

Dillon leaned forward, stared Morton in the eye. "Trevor balked. I think he knew something about Adam that he didn't like. Planned to talk to the authorities about it. And Adam killed him. The explosion in the science lab was to cover up the murder."

The look on Morton's face told Dillon he wasn't far off in his analysis. He pushed deeper, putting himself into Adam Scott's mind. What would he have asked his best friends to do? What would have repelled one of them so much that he would have risked everything to talk to the police?

"You all raped a girl, but Adam killed her. Probably strangled her while having sex. Maybe it was an accident. Maybe not. But Trevor freaked."

Dillon watched Morton closely. He was off this time. Damn, he thought he'd nailed the connection, what Adam lorded over Roger Morton and Paul Ullman to get them to commit felonies. Morton himself wasn't hard to sway; he was already predisposed to a life of violence. He was a classic power rapist. Without Adam Scott, he probably would have ended up in prison at some point in his life. He was abusive and treated women as objects. But he wasn't the brains behind Trask Enterprises, merely a figurehead.

But Adam Scott. He had dark fantasies that had developed early in his life, fueled by strict parents. But that wasn't the reason Adam turned to murder. He was sexually dysfunctional. And if he *had* killed a woman during sex when he was in high school, that meant the cause of the dysfunction had occurred even earlier in his childhood, likely at the onset of puberty.

Morton wouldn't know how to cover up a crime. That was all Adam, the genius. And maybe it was strictly Adam's crime that they were covering up.

"Maybe you had nothing to do with the rape. Maybe Adam told you about it. Boasted. Maybe he needed help getting rid of the body."

Morton squirmed. Dillon didn't smile, though he felt some small pleasure in weaving through the facts and conjecture and nailing Roger Morton. He certainly would lose at poker.

"What was her name?"

"You're fishing." Morton's voice was weak.

"We've reopened the investigation into Trevor Conrad's death," Quinn said. "We'll exhume the body and with technology today, it's very easy to determine the cause of death even after twenty years in the ground."

That wasn't always true, but Morton didn't know that.

"It was an explosion. Not much left of Trevor."

But Morton was losing some of his cockiness.

Quinn turned back to Adam Scott's disappearing act. "Scott took a federal agent to Mount Baker in an attempt to draw Agent Donovan out. He shot him in the back while you were back on the island. He knew about the raid on the island, but he didn't warn you, did he? He just walked. Left you, Denise, the others to take the rap. He had a huge head start. You could have escaped. *But he took the only boat.*"

Morton frowned. Didn't say anything.

"What we want is your cooperation. We want the names and whereabouts of Scott's victims' remains.

We want every known hideout of Scott. Bank accounts, property, the works. Everything you know."

He didn't say anything. Thinking.

Dillon glanced at Quinn, got the nod. "What I want to know is why?"

"Why what?" Morton asked.

"Why Lucy?"

He shrugged. "She's hot. Just like—" he stopped.

"Like who?"

Something clicked in Morton's head. He straightened his back. "If I give you something, something really good, that will solve a major case for you, what do I get in return?"

"It depends on the information," Quinn said.

"I need something better than that."

"You give us everything on Adam Scott, tell us what happened with Trevor Conrad, and cooperate from here on out, I'll put in a good word."

"A good word?" Morton laughed, leaned back. He knew he had them on the hook. Dillon feared that the conversation was turning away from them and that they wouldn't get anything.

"I'm not a U.S. attorney," Quinn said. "But I can make a recommendation to deal, simple felony rape instead of kidnapping, conspiracy to murder, manslaughter, and a host of other charges the lawyers will pile on when they know they can get the death penalty."

Quinn stared at Morton. "I can also tell them that you're a vicious prick who rapes teenagers and watches as they die. I can nail you for Henshaw's murder even though the man wore a mask. You were there. We have your prints. We have a nice federal prison down in Florida. Cuban gangs run it. They won't like it that you hurt one of their own. And I'll make sure every guard knows exactly what you did and who you did it to."

Morton squirmed. "I'll tell you what. I'll give you one thing, then I want an attorney in here who can make me a deal before I give you everything. Got it?"

Quinn nodded.

"Does the name Monique Paxton mean anything to you?"

Quinn shook his head, then stopped. "Paxton? You mean Senator Jonathan Paxton?"

Morton nodded. "He was some low-level politician at the time. Monique was fucking Adam. They were hot and heavy for a couple months. One night things got kind of rough. She ended up dead. I mean, if she was just some whore from the wrong side of the tracks, no one would care. He could have dumped her body and no one would have looked too closely at anyone. But it was *Monique Paxton* and he couldn't just drop her on her daddy's doorstep. He called me, and I had Trevor with me. I don't know why he called me—I was hours away. But his parents were out of town for the weekend. So I went down, brought Trevor, and we took care of her. But when Trevor saw the news on Monday about how this politician's daughter was missing, he sort of flipped. Adam didn't tell us who she was at the time. Trevor wanted to confess, the stupid prick. Adam convinced him not to, but didn't trust him. Got Paul to help get him to the lab, then rigged it to explode. But he was already dead."

"How?" Quinn asked.

Morton shook his head. "Nope, nothing more. I want a deal on the table or you get nothing more from me."

Dillon spoke quietly. "And Lucy looks like Monique."

"They could be fucking twins."

TWENTY-NINE

"SENATOR PAXTON?" Dillon asked.

"New York," Quinn said. "His daughter disappeared more than twenty years ago. Ironically, his political career took off soon after. He was a state representative, then ran for attorney general on a strong public safety campaign. Won, parlayed that into the governorship eight years later, and then, when there was an open seat, ran for the Senate. He's been there for four or five years now."

"And his daughter was never found."

"Not to my knowledge. I think I would have heard. The FBI was involved, and it was a case that we studied at the Academy. Can someone vanish off the face of the earth? The only way anyone can disappear is to completely assume another identity, be reclusive and live in the middle of nowhere and see no one, or be dead. The conventional wisdom was that she was dead, but there were no signs of foul play, no evidence, and if I remember currently no known boyfriend in the picture. So if Roger Morton is telling the truth, Monique never told her father she was dating Adam Scott. Never brought him home. And since he wasn't a student at her school—he went to an all-male boarding school in Connecticut—he wouldn't even have been looked at unless one of her friends had mentioned him."

"So Adam Scott got away with murder," Dillon thought out loud. "Was she the first? If it was truly an accident like Morton said, he may have learned that he experienced more sexual satisfaction during scarfing. Only instead of using a scarf or cloth, he used his own hands."

"How does that fit in?"

"Consider this. He kills Monique while having sex. They're going at it, probably consensual at first. He puts his hands around her neck and feeds off the fear on her face. He isn't *planning* on killing her. But the excitement of her fear keeps him going too long. He climaxes, but she's dead. From then on, he can't climax without killing. And considering his actions last night, he's even having problems with that."

"So Trevor Conrad is going to go to the cops and he kills him. Blows up the lab at school to cover up the crime."

Dillon nodded. "And Paul Ullman and Roger Morton are under his thumb. They aided and abetted. Even if Morton is right and Scott killed Trevor, and they only helped cover it up, Scott would still have control over them. They knew. And Monique Paxton was a high-profile victim. Her father was a politician. Not something they'd be able to walk away from easily, even with their family money."

"I need confirmation before I can go to the senator. At least a location where her remains are buried."

"They weren't buried," Dillon said solemnly.

"Why do you say that?"

"Adam Scott would have obliterated her remains. There may be traces, but my guess is that he burned the body and spread the ashes, or used some sort of chemical to quickly eat away the flesh."

Quinn nodded. "Because there was physical evidence on the body."

"Exactly. His sperm, his DNA, skin under her fingernails, marks on her body. He had to literally destroy her to save his life. His DNA isn't in the system. Whether he subconsciously knew he was going down this murderous path, or it was a natural sense of self-preservation, Adam Scott vanished Monique Paxton." Dillon glanced at Quinn and said, "I think it's safe to give Senator Paxton the news."

A man approached them. He was shorter than average with graying blond hair, a goatee, and dark circles under his eyes.

"Merritt," Quinn mumbled.

"You interviewed Morton without me?" Merritt said without preamble.

"It's my case, my jurisdiction," Quinn said.

"I told you *nothing* happens on this investigation without me being informed." He glanced at Dillon. "Who are you?"

"Dillon Kincaid."

"The victim's brother? What the fuck is he doing here?" he screamed at Quinn.

"I'm not going to get into this with you right now," Quinn said, keeping his voice low. "I've already talked to my superior about you sending Mick Mallory in to assassinate Adam Scott."

"That's a lie!"

Quinn raised an eyebrow.

"Peterson, I'll have your badge."

Another man approached, younger, in a three-piece suit that fit stiffly. "Agent Peterson?" he asked formally.

"What is it, Carl?"

"A message. It's important."

Quinn took the paper and swore. Merritt gloated. "This isn't over," Quinn said. "You're not going to railroad her."

"I'm not railroading anybody. I simply want her in jail where she belongs." Merritt turned and walked off.

"What?" Dillon asked. "You won't put Kate in prison."

"I'll do everything I can to keep her out," he said and handed Dillon the note. It was from the director of the Office of Professional Responsibility.

Quincy Peterson, SAC, Seattle Field Office, FBI:

We are remanding Katherine Donovan, SA, Arlington Field Office, into your custody pending resolution of ongoing investigation. You are to produce SA Donovan at headquarters in Washington DC Monday, June 10, 2007 at 0800 for a formal debriefing and interview.

SA Donovan is considered a flight risk and must not be allowed to leave on her own recognizance.

Dillon frowned. "But this is good, right? You have custody of Kate, not Jeff Merritt."

He nodded. "I just didn't expect it to happen so quickly."

* * *

Kate had been sitting in the interview room for hours. A secretary brought her lunch, but she only picked at it.

She hated being caged.

Her room at the observatory was smaller than the interview room she was being detained in, but she had the freedom to come and go as she pleased. Knowing she couldn't leave this building unnerved her.

She finally sat after pacing for what seemed like hours. When Dillon had walked in this morning after seeing his sister off, she had been surprised and grateful. And deliriously happy. After last night, she had feared that the connection they'd made would be short-lived. Dillon had a life, a career, his family in San Diego. A family who depended on him. Who was she to claim him? Who was she to want him to stay with her instead of returning home?

But she didn't want him to go. She couldn't stop him, of course, but deep down she wanted him with her. She was strong—she would face whatever happened with the OPR. She owed it to Paige, to Evan, and to herself to tell the complete truth to the best of her knowledge.

"I'm sorry, Paige," she mumbled. But Dillon was right. Paige would never want her to live like this— on the run, in fear—to protect her name. And Evan deserved to be recognized as a hero for his actions, coming in at the last minute to try and save the situation, calling in the police. Their sirens chased Trask away and saved her life.

"Thank you, Evan," she said. Evan would have liked Dillon, and that thought gave her peace. She had loved Evan dearly. He was smart and fun and dedicated. But Evan would never want her lying to protect Paige or anyone. And he would want her to be happy, just as she would if the situation were reversed.

Who wouldn't like Dillon? she thought, remembering the way he had savored her body. Each kiss focused, planned, with the purpose of driving her wild. And he was smart. God, she loved smart men. Men who didn't just survive on their brawn or common sense, but *intelligent* men who she could have a conversation with and not feel like she was talking to a brick wall.

That he had returned, for her, gave her even more confidence that she would find a way out of this mess. She'd probably lose her job—had probably lost it already. She certainly hadn't been receiving a paycheck for the last five years, living on her small savings, taking odd jobs, and relying on the kindness of Professor Fox. But if she could clear her name, come out of hiding, she could get another job. Maybe not in the FBI, but there were police departments everywhere.

Even a few in San Diego where Dillon lived.

And if she didn't want to be a cop anymore, she could go into computer security.

For the first time in five years, she saw hope in her future.

Dillon walked in and came straight to her.

"How are you doing?" he asked, taking her hands.

"I'm going stir-crazy."

He gave her a half-smile.

"What happened with Morton?"

"He's willing to deal."

"Are you serious?"

"Absolutely. Quinn's putting it together with the U.S. attorney right now."

"Wow. Does he know where Adam Scott is?"

Dillon shook his head. "He didn't say one way or the other, but my guess is no. He was agitated when Quinn started pushing him about Scott getting off completely and leaving Roger holding the bag. If he knew anything for certain, I think he would have said something. But maybe there's something he knows that will lead us to him."

He motioned for her to sit down. "What's wrong?" she asked as she sat.

He sat next to her, squeezed her hands, leaned in for a kiss. She pulled back, knowing something was happening.

"What's wrong?" she repeated.

"The OPR set the hearing for next Monday."

"Tomorrow?"

"A week from tomorrow."

"That's good."

"Are you sure?"

She nodded. "Absolutely. I need to tell them everything."

"You're in custody until then."

"Custody?"

He took a deep breath. "Merritt wants to transport you to the local jail until you fly to Washington, D.C."

She started shaking. "And?"

"Quinn is battling it out now. He's taking personal responsibility for your actions."

"Meaning I run and he gets screwed."

"Something like that."

"That's okay. I'm not going to run." She held Dillon's face in her hands. "I'm tired of running. I'm going to face the OPR and tell them everything. Then whatever happens, I'll know that I told the truth."

He leaned forward and kissed her. "I'm not leaving you, Kate."

"I could be in prison."

"I'll wait."

She stared into his intense green eyes. "You would, wouldn't you?"

He nodded, kissed her again. "You're not alone, Kate. And you'll never be alone again."

A knock on the door interrupted a more passionate kiss, then it opened.

Quinn walked in, sat down across from Dillon and Kate. "You're in my custody, Kate. I've sworn up and down to the director of the OPR that you're not a flight risk."

"I'm not."

He nodded, turned to Dillon. "I have some news."

"About Scott?"

"Not exactly. I'm going to San Diego tomorrow morning. To interview Lucy."

Dillon shook his head. "Why? You have enough evidence, you don't need to make her go through that again."

"We've been analyzing her messages to and from Adam Scott. He said some cryptic things that we think she might have the answers to. In addition, we need to find out what she heard or saw while on the island. She may know what his plans are without knowing she knows. I shouldn't have to tell you that interviewing the victim is crucial in an investigation like this."

"You have plenty of evidence without Lucy!" Dillon slammed his hand on the table, displaying a rare burst of anger. "She's been through Hell. Just yesterday she was raped. I can't—"

"You don't have a choice, Dillon. I'm going down there and I'm going to ask her to talk to us. She doesn't have to, I know that, but it would help. We have to stop Adam Scott. If we don't, Lucy will never be safe again. Neither will Kate. He's not going to rest until they're dead. You know that, Dillon. *You* told me that."

Dillon knew Quinn was right, but he hated the thought of Lucy having to recount her abduction and rapes. Kate squeezed his hand.

"I'm going," he said.

Quinn nodded. "I expected you would."

"And so is Kate."

Quinn raised an eyebrow.

"She's in your custody, isn't she?" Dillon said. "And I'm not leaving her up here where Jeff Merritt can get at her, or where Adam Scott might find her."

Quinn looked at Kate. "Okay?" he asked her.

Kate smiled seriously, nodded. "When?" she asked.

"Tomorrow morning. Early. Until then, you need to stay here."

"I'll stay with you," Dillon said.

Quinn shook his head. "I've given you both as much latitude as I can. I wish I could do more, but please don't push this."

"It's okay," Kate told Dillon. "Really."

Dillon didn't want to leave her. But at least she was

coming to San Diego. He'd show her what a family was, how they stuck together, how good a family could be. Show her the family she'd never had, a family that maybe she'd like to be part of. With him.

"Are you sure?" he whispered.

She nodded. "It's only a few hours. I'll see you in the morning, okay?"

He kissed her lightly on the lips, wished he could keep her with him all night. "Tomorrow morning."

THIRTY

IT WAS AFTER MIDNIGHT when Dillon spoke to Jack on the phone. "How's Lucy?"

"She'll be okay."

"That's not telling me anything."

"She knows about Patrick. She became hysterical, insisted she had to see him. Carina didn't think that was wise. She ended up giving Lucy a sedative to get her to sleep."

Dillon frowned. "I think you should let her see Patrick."

"What good will that do?" Jack asked. "She's already beating herself up over what happened. Seeing him like that will make it worse."

"I don't think so. She needs to focus on someone other than herself. Her imagination over what might have happened to Patrick will be far worse than letting her sit with him for a while."

"He's in a coma, Dillon." Jack stated the obvious.

"Seeing Patrick, sitting with him will help Lucy. Taking care of Patrick will give her mind a chance to stop thinking about what happened to her. It'll give her a break. Keeping her locked in the house on sedatives, under what can be the stifling love and concern of the family, where all she can think about is the rape, is emotionally exhausting."

"Are you sure?"

"Yes. Look into Mama's eyes. You'll see a reflection of pain and suffering. Lucy sees the same thing, and that fuels her guilt and anguish. If she wants to see Patrick tomorrow morning, take her."

"All right. But I'm telling Carina it's your idea. She's damn protective of Lucy. She's acting more like the bodyguard than me."

"That's Carina." Dillon paused. "I'll be coming home tomorrow."

"I thought you were staying up there with Kate?"

"She's coming with me."

"Really."

"So is Quinn Peterson. He needs to talk to Lucy."

"Debrief her."

"Essentially."

"Do you want me to prepare her for it?"

"No. I don't want her imagining the questions or trying to think up what she's going to say. I'll meet you at the hospital at noon. That'll give Lucy time with Patrick, which should calm her."

"You're the boss," Jack said.

"How's it going with Mom and Dad?"

"You're not talking about Lucy, are you?"

"No."

Jack paused. "With Mama, it's like I never left. Dad . . . you're the shrink, you figure it out."

"He's acting like you betrayed the family and him, personally."

"Bingo."

"Can you hang on a couple more days?"

"Think you'll find Scott by then?"

"I think Scott will find us. Be diligent, Jack. He wants Lucy and he'll kill to get to her."

It wasn't yet dawn when the door to her room opened.

The fog of sleep disappeared immediately as Kate jumped up. The fluorescent lights blasted on and Kate blinked rapidly. She reached for a gun that wasn't there.

Merritt. And two cops. "What's going on?" she asked.

Merritt nodded to the cops, who approached her. "You can't do this," she said. "I'm not going anywhere with you."

"No, you're not. Sit down."

"What do you want?" she asked.

It wasn't until one of the cops took out handcuffs that a tingle of fear crept up her spine.

One cop held her while the other handcuffed her to the chair and the table. Why the table?

So she couldn't move.

"I want to show you something." Merritt dismissed the cops, and they left.

"Where's Quinn?"

"It's three in the morning. He's probably at home with his wife."

Merritt had a briefcase in one hand. He placed it on the table, opened it, took out a DVD player. While it booted up, he said, "I watched Paige die."

She didn't say anything.

"Then I watched you. And all I could think about was that I wished you had been in Paige's place."

Her stomach churned.

"You had no one. Evan had been killed. Your grandparents were dead. No one knew where your mother was, or even who your father is. No siblings, few friends. Paige had everything! A family who loved her. Lots of friends who cared for her. *Me.*"

He leaned over and for a moment Kate believed he was going to pull out his gun and shoot her.

"Paige was pregnant when she died. You thought she was your best friend? She didn't even tell you. *She told me the week before she died.*" He turned from her, punched some buttons on the player.

Paige was *pregnant*? Kate was shocked. Paige hadn't said anything. Not even hinted about it.

She'd thought they'd been best friends. Closer than sisters. But Paige had been drifting back then. Focused on the job. And Jeff. Had Kate missed the clues? Not only about Paige's pregnancy, but about the reality of their relationship?

"Why do you think I wanted her pulled off the investigation?" Merritt said. "But no, you pushed, pushed, pushed."

"I never pushed Paige on the investigation," Kate said. "She told me you said everything was a go. She lied about the backup. Maybe *you* wanted her pulled, but she was going full-steam ahead."

"Paige never lied to you!"

"Yes, she did!" Suddenly Kate remembered something about that fateful investigation five years ago. What Evan had said. *Kate, get out. There's no backup.* How did he know? Had he been following them? Or had he been privy to inside information? Kate had told Evan everything about the investigation. He knew where she was going and why. He wouldn't have come there unless he knew she was in danger.

"Unless you lied to her," Kate said slowly. Maybe Paige believed she'd convinced Merritt to give them support against Trask. But he never had. He didn't want his pregnant girlfriend to push it. Maybe he placated her?

But that didn't make sense, either. Why would Merritt intentionally pull backup and jeopardize their lives?

Unless he thought the whole sting was a fraud and they weren't in danger? But that would mean he had inside information—inside information that wasn't even true. Or he really believed there had been no real threat in the first place.

"Don't even go there," he said with venom.

He stepped away from the computer screen. Kate stared as she saw Paige naked on a thin mattress, and a masked man—Adam Scott—naked and towering over her.

Kate couldn't move, couldn't swallow, couldn't even breathe. Scott raped her, his hands around her neck. He was strangling her. But not completely. He gave her enough air to live, leaned up, and suddenly there was a knife.

Without preamble, he slit her neck. Not deeply, but the blood poured out. In a frenzy, he sliced her. No deep stab wounds, just numerous, repeated slices as she screamed, the sound hollow and tinny coming out of the player's speaker.

Then he took the knife and planted it deep in her chest.

Kate watched the life disappear from Paige's eyes, saw the terror embedded in her face.

She lay like that for nine minutes and thirty-six seconds. Kate knew that because of the counter in the corner. Merritt said nothing, and Kate couldn't stop watching. Blood soaked into the mattress.

Paige, oh God, I didn't know you were pregnant. Why didn't you tell me? Did you lie to me—or did Jeff lie to you?

She saw a shadow on the side of the film, then heard shattered glass and watched as a younger version of herself jumped through the window, looked around. She felt like she was there again, finding the booby trap, watching the digital countdown. She'd often had nightmares of those damn green numbers counting backward, and she always woke up in a sweat when it reached 00:00.

Then her aiming her gun at the camera. For the split second she was full face in the camera, she looked crazy.

No wonder the FBI thought she was dangerous.

The screen went blank.

Merritt leaned over her and whispered, "Now you know exactly how Paige died. I hope it gives you nightmares for the rest of your pathetic life."

"You bastard," she said between clenched teeth.

"I've had to live with that for five years. Watching the woman I love be raped and murdered. Because of you."

She had been taking the blame for so many years that she almost said she was sorry. She *was* sorry because Paige didn't deserve to die. None of the women Scott murdered had deserved that brutal end. But the truth was, she'd thought they went into that warehouse with full backup. She'd thought Merritt had sent in a full team. Paige had told her they were covered. She had had no reason to doubt it.

And Evan had come in, at the right moment.

But no one else had followed. Because there was no one else.

Had Evan followed them, fearing something was wrong? Had he died because he thought she and Paige had gone vigilante? Had he died thinking she'd crossed the line?

Evan had said something before he died. Something that had made no sense until now.

"It's a setup, Kate. Get out."

She'd always thought he'd meant Trask was setting them up.

She stared at Merritt. Maybe it was someone closer to home.

Why would Merritt want them dead? Was it her . . . or Paige? Or had he made a fatal mistake he was still trying to cover up? Or maybe it wasn't a setup in the traditional sense, but Merritt's own twisted way of proving to Paige she needed to quit field work.

Merritt suddenly stood. He tapped buttons on the DVD player and set Paige's rape and murder to play on a loop. He pushed the machine out of her reach.

"Enjoy the show."

Then he walked out.

THIRTY-ONE

KATE COULDN'T STOP watching Paige's murder. Even when she finally closed her eyes, she still heard the screams. The sound was worse than the visual because the terror and pain somehow sounded more real.

And even when she closed her eyes, she saw that knife come down repeatedly.

I'm sorry, Paige, I'm so sorry.

She laid her head on the table and sobbed. The recording was twenty-six minutes long. She'd watched it seven times. It had just started the eighth playback when the door opened.

"Kate?"

She looked up, her eyes blurry, unfocused. *Dillon.* Never had she been so grateful to see anyone.

He rushed to her side, glanced at the screen. His jaw tensed as he watched Adam Scott slice Paige's neck. He slammed it closed, cutting off her scream.

"What's going on, Kate?" He tried to pull her from the chair to hug her, noticed the handcuffs. "Kate?" He knelt in front of her, holding her damp face in his hands. She shook in his arms.

"How'd you get this?" he asked, trying to conceal the anger rippling through his body.

"M-Merritt brought it in."

"When?"

"A couple hours ago."

"Good Lord, Kate." He held her. She leaned into him, wanting him to hold her close, closer. *Don't leave me, Dillon.*

"Why didn't you call for someone, sweetheart?"

She closed her eyes, shook her head into his chest. Breathed in the warm, masculine scent of woodsy soap. "I guess I deserved it."

Dillon held her at arm's length. "Dammit, Kate, you don't deserve it and you know it!"

Her lip quivered and he kissed it. Kissed her over and over. Held her close. Her heart rate began to return to normal.

"I'm so glad you're here," she whispered.

"I need to get someone to take off these handcuffs. Will you be okay for a minute? Peterson is at his desk."

She nodded, sniffed, tried and failed to smile to reassure him. He held her chin. "Kate, stop torturing yourself. Okay? What happened five years ago was a tragic accident. It wasn't your fault."

She nodded again, unable to talk. She took a deep breath and put her head back on the table.

"I'll be right back," Dillon said and ran out.

A pang hit her hard in the chest. Merritt's words came back with a vengeance.

You had no one. Evan had been killed. Your grandparents were dead. No one knew where your mother was, or even who your father is. No siblings, few friends. Paige had everything! A family who loved her. Lots of friends. Me.

The loneliness of her life hit her hard. Dillon Kincaid was everything she wanted in a lover, everything she wanted in a man. But he also had a family, something she'd never really had and knew she wouldn't fit into. How could she? She had no practice with people. No friends, no family. Growing up she'd been a loner. Not because she didn't want to make friends, but because people thought she was odd.

And she was. She was a computer geek before computer geeks were fashionable. A tomboy well into her high school years. And when her grandparents died, the foster homes were a blur. She didn't act up, but she moved every six months because of other problems. One woman had a job and was transferred out of state. Another couple needed room to keep a family of children together. An elderly woman died in her sleep.

Kate wanted a family, but every time she got attached, something happened. With Evan, she thought she had everything she wanted.

But he was dead, too.

Now she felt too old to learn how to be part of a family. Five years of virtual solitude didn't make it any better.

Were these feelings for Dillon real? They'd been forged in adrenaline, in the hunt for a killer. When Adam Scott was found, could they have something? Something that lasted?

Kate didn't know. But she didn't want to let Dillon go. She was a loner, but she no longer wanted to be. She wanted to be with Dillon.

Quinn Peterson stormed in, Dillon on his heels.

"Merritt just nailed his coffin shut," Quinn said, crossing over to her and using a master key to release her from the handcuffs.

"Paige was pregnant," she said.

Quinn's eyes flickered. "Merritt told me the other day."

"I didn't know."

Dillon sat next to her, took her hands, and rubbed them in his. "You have to do something about Jeff Merritt," Dillon told Quinn. "He can't get away with doing this to her."

"He won't," Quinn assured them. He ran a hand over his face and Kate realized he hadn't slept the night before, either.

"Did something else happen?"

"I got a call at two in the morning that the police in Anacortes found a woman dead in her house. Paula Corbin. She'd been found by her sister who came by, worried because Paula wasn't answering her cell phone or her house phone. The description matched the recording Scott sent to Kate, so I went out and confirmed that it was our gal. The FBI is working with the local police on collecting evidence."

"What else?" Dillon asked.

"I talked with the head of the OPR this morning. She said that there's paperwork missing from the Trask Enterprises investigation. Someone took them after the fact—there are references to certain documents that are nowhere to be found."

"Why?"

"Because someone made a mistake."

"Merritt."

"Possibly."

"Remember how I said Paige lied about the backup? I think Merritt lied. I think he was trying to scare her into quitting. Because she was pregnant."

"But why would Merritt jeopardize her life if she were pregnant?"

"I don't know. Maybe he didn't think we were on to something. There were a lot of people who thought we were making a mountain out of a molehill, that April Klinger wasn't dead and we were wasting resources."

"That's clear from the reports—in fact, that's all that's clear."

"I have a copy of everything that's supposed to be in those files," Kate said.

"Where?"

"Mexico. I kept computerized files of all my reports out of habit. I have them all on CD."

"I'll send someone to retrieve them."

"Someone trustworthy. If Merritt had anything to do with that sting going bad—"

"You don't have to say it, Kate."

"Thank you for everything you've done for me."

"Where's Jeff Merritt now?" Dillon asked.

"He had a flight out this morning to Washington. I'm going to alert the OPR about this latest situation. I imagine they'll be doing something about it." Quinn looked at Kate. "Are you going to be okay?"

She nodded, glanced at Dillon. Felt warmth, strength, and love pouring from him into her. "I could use a shower."

"We have a full bath in the break room. I'll show you where it is, but we only have thirty minutes before we have to leave to catch our flight to San Diego."

Trask watched the Kincaid family from afar for nearly twenty-four hours. Jack Kincaid, the military brother, was the most dangerous. He was everywhere Lucy was. To get to her, Adam would have to find a way to take Jack out first.

Connor Kincaid pretty much stayed at the hospital with the other brother, Patrick. The female detective lived nearby. The sheriff went home with her. The parents were old, they wouldn't be a problem.

The shrink who screwed up his plans was nowhere. Trask searched the Internet, found out that Dr. Dillon Kincaid owned a house only a few blocks from where Lucy Kincaid lived. He drove by several times, but it was dark. Had he stayed in Washington? Why? Was Kate still there? Did the doctor and Kate have something going on? Or was the shrink trying to get Roger Morton to talk?

Trask wished Roger had been killed along with everyone else. He didn't trust him. The bastard would turn on him in a flash. If he'd been able to get to him, he would have killed Roger himself. But there was no way he could show his face.

He'd darkened his hair a bit, nothing drastic because he didn't want the dye job to be obvious. He wore sunglasses, stuffed cotton in his cheeks, and put on colored contacts. Brown. The overall effect worked to tone down his appearance, making him look more average. If someone who knew him looked twice, they might recognize him, but at first glance he could pass as a stranger.

All he needed was one chance.

He'd never considered a woman a threat, except for that bitch Kate Donovan. But now he had the upper hand where she was concerned.

He knew exactly how to draw her out.

The only people living at the Kincaid house were Lucy, her parents, and Jack Kincaid. How long was Jack going to stay watching Lucy? Soon it would be just Lucy and her old parents.

Adam didn't want to wait, but he was willing to. He had money—a fraction of his wealth, thanks to that idiot Paul Ullman, who didn't have the brains to avoid the feds and let him know what was happening so he could transfer more funds.

He'd wait, but if he saw an opportunity he would act.

He drove by the doctor's house again. Still dark. When would he be coming home? He wouldn't be staying up north indefinitely.

But since the house was vacant now he had a place to hide. To put the finishing touches on his plan.

As soon as he had Lucy Kincaid again, he'd put her back online. Send the link to Kate.

Kate Donovan would walk right up to his door. And then he'd kill her and take Lucy with him, to serve him forever.

THIRTY TWO

LUCY WAS BACK *in the cabin. Tied to the floor. Trevor Conrad stood over her; Roger and Frank flanked him.*

"You're dead," she said, but no words came out.

Roger and Frank disappeared, but Trevor remained. "I'm not."

He poured gasoline all around her and picked up a phone.

"Patrick," he said, "I have your sister."

Patrick ran through the door. "Lucy!"

"It's a trap! Run!"

The room exploded. Patrick flew through the air, his head bandaged. He landed in the wall. She smelled smoke and heard Trevor laughing at her.

Sharp steel sliced her neck.

Dillon jumped through the window, his face and hands bleeding. He grabbed Trevor by the neck and began to strangle him. Trevor took the knife and cut out Dillon's heart.

Lucy jumped from bed, still half asleep. Frantic, she ran around her room, feeling the windows and the door. Cool. There was no fire. Her neck burned. She flipped on the light and looked in the mirror.

The wild eyes that stared back couldn't possibly be hers.

The bandage that had covered the wound on her neck was in her hands; the red welt throbbed and bled. She stared at her hands. Blood coated her fingers.

Her door opened. Jack stood there. "Lucy. It was just a nightmare."

He crossed the room, concern on his face. Lucy must have looked frantic. She would never have imagined that Jack could be worried about anything.

Jack took the bandage from Lucy's hands and together they walked to the bathroom. In silence, he cleaned the wound and reapplied the bandage. "Do you want to tell me about it?"

She shook her head. "I need to see Patrick."

"Are you sure?" He looked at his watch. "It's only seven."

"Now. I have to make sure he's alive."

Jack hesitated, then said, "All right."

Lucy relaxed. "I just need to get dressed. I'll be downstairs in ten minutes. Okay?"

He nodded and left.

She sat in the bathroom for several minutes, gathering her strength, trying to push that awful vision from her mind. Her heart was beating so fast Lucy wouldn't have been surprised to see it leap from her chest.

The dream had seemed so real.

Kate felt a million times better after a hot shower. She dressed in the same clothes she'd worn the day before, and went back to the interview room. No one was there. She found Quinn and Dillon in Quinn's office. Both of them were on the phone.

Quinn hung up first.

"Any word on Adam Scott?"

Quinn shook his head. "Yes and no. He's disappeared again. My agents out in New York have managed to track down some of his identities, but they're old. We were able to put together his past movements, but we don't know where he went. He could still be here in Seattle—or he could be halfway across the world."

"What about the yellow Hummer?"

"We found it at the airport, long-term parking. We've brought it in as evidence, but there's nothing to tell us what his plans are."

"You think he flew somewhere?"

"He didn't leave the parking ticket in the car, but security cameras indicate that it went through the kiosk at ten forty-five Sunday morning."

"Right after Lucy left with her family."

"I flew her out of a private airport. She wasn't at Sea-Tac."

"Maybe he wasn't following Lucy. Coincidence?" She frowned and sat down across from Quinn and glanced at Dillon, who was watching her. He hung up his phone.

"That was Jack," he said. "He's taking Lucy to the hospital. We'll meet them there at noon."

Quinn pulled out some notes from a stack in the corner. "You and Dillon arrived at the island about two p.m. He brought Lucy to the helicopter at two fifty-six p.m. By the time we went back, found you, it was after four."

"I can buy that he watched Dillon rescue Lucy. I think he would have monitored her online virtually the entire time he was gone. So he knew what happened, he couldn't reach his people, he disappeared. Why not go to the airport right then? Why wait until Sunday morning?" Kate pondered.

"You think he was waiting for a chance to grab Lucy again?"

"Yes."

"But he must have seen the security on her. Jack Kincaid could intimidate Osama with one look."

"Right," Kate said. "But he's patient. He isn't going to do anything stupid. And do you think Jack Kincaid is going to stay in San Diego forever? That man is itching to get back to whatever it is he was doing in Mexico in the first place. A week, if that. He'll leave her in good hands, I'm sure. But eventually everyone will become complacent. They'll assume Adam Scott left the country. And when they least expect it, he'll get Lucy. We stole her from him. His ego took a huge blow. He's not going to sit by and do nothing."

"We're not going to get complacent," Dillon said. "I know what Adam Scott is capable of. He'll wait a day, a week, a year to get to Lucy. And to you. But I don't think we'll have to wait a year."

"Why?" Quinn asked.

"Because he's been dealt a huge blow. That's eating at him. We have Roger Morton in custody. Eventually, we'll get information from him. Scott doesn't know what or when. He's fuming—betrayal by his supposed friend, Kate rescuing Lucy, Lucy back home." Dillon paused. "I think he's already in San

Diego." He opened his cell phone. "I'm going to warn Jack."

Trask followed Jack and Lucy to the hospital. Visiting her near-dead brother perhaps? Interesting. Add another dynamic to the situation.

Just how loyal was Lucy to her family? What would she do to save them? She would be home soon enough, and he needed time to plan the next move.

He quietly broke into Dillon Kincaid's house.

Trask walked through the small bungalow. He admired the doctor's taste. Not quite minimalist, simply sparse, classic, and dark. Dark furniture against hardwood floors; luxurious rugs in the living room and dining room. The kitchen was well-appointed, with gourmet cooking utensils and state-of-the-art appliances. The master bedroom continued the dark theme, navy blue bedding and window treatments. The second bedroom had been converted into a home office.

Though the house was not even fourteen hundred square feet, it was well laid out. Particularly for his purposes. Set far back from the street with a long, narrow front yard and a long, narrow backyard. The garage was in the rear, detached.

Perfect.

Trask sat down at Dr. Kincaid's computer and logged onto his private server. The feds hadn't found it; even if they had, they wouldn't be able to track him here before he was ready to reveal his location. He took out his equipment, set it up in Kincaid's bedroom.

He couldn't have planned this better had he tried.

All he had to do was wait, and with the doctor gone he could stay here indefinitely as long as he was careful. One of the many Kincaid clan members could be checking on the house, though so far he hadn't seen anyone drive by. He wouldn't use the lights. There was food in the refrigerator and pantry. Enough to sustain him for some time.

He had three options. Wait until Lucy was free of her military bodyguard. Wait until Dillon Kincaid came home and use him as bait. Or find a way to kidnap Lucy from the hospital. Out of her house she was far more vulnerable. Trask wouldn't take his chances head-to-head with Jack Kincaid, but a well-placed bullet in the back of the head could stop any man.

Lucy walked into Patrick's room alone—Jack was waiting right outside the door.

She closed the door, feeling for the first time like she could breathe. She loved her family, appreciated everything they were doing for her, but the last two days had been suffocating. All these people who loved her and they were trying not to walk on eggshells around her because they wanted life to return to normal as much as she did. But they'd seen what had happened to her. They couldn't pretend they didn't know. Nothing had been left to their imagination. They had feared the worst and seen it happen. She couldn't look at them without the guilt crashing down around her.

All she wanted was to be alone. But at the same time, she never wanted to be alone again.

Her heart beat with the rhythm of fear, which saturated her blood and made her doubt that she'd ever be able to reclaim her life.

She stared at Patrick in the hospital bed, her pulse racing. His long lanky body seemed to have shrunk. He had on an oxygen mask and an IV gave him nourishment. He was in a coma, because of her.

Not being dead hadn't really sunk in. Death had come too close, and she was still trying to wrap her mind around her mortality. She couldn't think about being raped, maybe later. Maybe much, much later.

Dillon had risked his life to save her. Jack, a brother she barely knew, had come home just for her. Patrick was in a coma because of her.

She'd been so stupid. No, stupid didn't cut it. She'd been irresponsible. She deserved everything that had happened to her. She had listened over and over to the warnings from her family about strangers and the Internet, but never in a million years had she thought anything would happen to her.

You didn't deserve anything that happened, Lucy.

It was Dillon's soothing, commanding voice in her head.

None of this is your fault.

She didn't know if she believed the phantom Dillon, but somehow it made her strong enough to cross the room and sit next to Patrick's still body.

His head was bandaged, and for some reason that bothered her more than anything. It made everything more real. That he'd had brain surgery because of the explosion that nearly killed him. That he was in a coma and might not survive.

She ached for Patrick, and for herself. For what she had done to her family.

What Adam Scott had done.

Intellectually, she knew she had to stop blaming herself. Emotionally, she couldn't. Not yet.

Lucy took Patrick's hand. Suddenly, the urge to talk, to tell Patrick everything, hit her. He couldn't look at her with pity, he wouldn't tell her everything would be all right. He wouldn't offer her food or suggest that she get some sleep.

"Patrick," she whispered, "it was so awful. At first I didn't want to die, I wanted to fight and hurt them back. Then, later, all I wanted to do was die. And I hate that. I hate that I was giving up when you and Dillon were working so hard to find me. You had more faith in me than I had in myself. I'll never disappoint you again."

THIRTY-THREE

JACK WAS STANDING outside Patrick's hospital room when Dillon arrived at noon.

"How are they?"

"Lucy's been in there for nearly four hours," Jack said, nodding to Kate, who stood next to him. "You were right, Dil. She's calmer since she's been here."

Dillon nodded, relieved that he'd been right. So much of psychology was second-guessing human nature, trying to understand people better than they understood themselves. Anticipating what they needed before they realized they lacked anything.

"Quinn got us an office so he could talk to her in private. We have it for two hours. I thought questioning her in a normal environment, instead of taking her to FBI headquarters or a sterile room, would help. Why don't you take a break?" Dillon suggested to his brother.

"I'll check in with my troop," Jack said. "Don't leave the hospital. If you're right and Adam Scott is in San Diego, he could be watching this building."

Dillon watched Lucy through the observation window as she spoke to Patrick. Dark circles framed her large brown eyes, her skin pale, her hair pulled harshly back from her unadorned face. But she was holding up.

He stared at Patrick, his head bandaged, immobile in the hospital bed. It was the first time he'd seen him since the explosion, and Dillon's eyes burned.

Kate took his hand and squeezed it. "You okay?"

He nodded and tapped on the window. Lucy glanced over her shoulder, a brief look of terror crossing her face. It disappeared quickly, but Dillon couldn't help but fear that she'd be living with that panic for the rest of her life.

He motioned to her. It was obvious she didn't want to leave Patrick. Lucy kissed Patrick's hand and whispered something in his ear, then met Dillon outside the door.

"What?" she asked.

"Let's go for a walk."

"Can I go back and see Patrick?" she asked.

"Of course."

She relaxed a fraction, glanced at Kate as they started down the corridor.

"Lucy, this is Kate Donovan," Dillon said. "She was instrumental in helping us find you."

Recognition lit Lucy's eyes. "Carina told me you were with Dillon on the island."

Kate nodded.

"Thank you." Lucy's voice was a whisper, and she dipped her head.

Dillon opened the door of an office at the end of the hall. Lucy stared and said, "You're the FBI."

Quinn nodded. "Quinn Peterson."

Lucy frowned, looked at Dillon. "What's happening?"

"Quinn wants to ask you some questions."

She shook her head. "No."

"Lucy, I know this is hard for you. And we're not going to talk about what they did to you."

"You know it all anyway," Lucy said, her voice quivering. "Everybody knows."

Dillon wanted to address that fear of Lucy's, but not now. "What we need to know is how Trevor Conrad found you online, what some of his messages meant, and if you heard or saw anything that might help the FBI find him."

She shook her head again. "I don't know anything." She bit her lip.

"You might not think you do," Dillon said, "but something you know might fit with something we know."

She didn't say anything.

Kate took Lucy's hand. "Lucy, he's out there and he's angry. You beat him. He didn't kill you. *You've won and he's lost.* That doesn't make him happy. If we can't stop him, you'll never be able to reclaim your life. Do you want to be scared forever?"

Lucy bit harder on her lip. Her hand went up to her neck, where the bandage was hidden under a high collar. She glanced at Dillon, then at Kate.

"Okay," she said, her voice a squeak.

Kate looked at Dillon, and as much for his benefit as Lucy's, she said, "I told you that Lucy was the bravest woman I've ever known."

Two hours later, while Dillon walked Lucy back to Patrick's hospital room, Kate frowned at Quinn. "Well, that didn't get us anywhere."

"We had to do it," Quinn said. "And we were able to establish a better time frame. Analyzing the messages from Trevor Conrad will greatly help e-crimes develop better programs to spot online predators."

Kate sighed. "Not that it will do any good. Neither the FBI nor local law enforcement has the resources to police the Internet."

"Maybe not, but it will give people the tools to police it themselves."

"What I don't understand is, how did a smart girl like Lucy get sucked into his trap?"

"And she'll never be able to forgive herself for it," Quinn said.

"It just proves that it doesn't matter how smart or careful you are; if a predator wants you he'll find a way."

"You sound defeatist," Quinn said. He raised an eyebrow. "What would you suggest? Hiding out in the mountains of Mexico?"

"Touché." Kate played with her fingers. "I never thanked you for standing by me for the last five years. I'll never forget it."

"I had a sense of what drove you." Quinn paused and Kate looked up at him. "You did the wrong thing for the right reasons. It's going to be okay next week."

"I hope so. For the first time I'm looking at the future. I'm hoping I won't be looking at it from behind bars."

Dillon met up with Kate in the parking lot. "Where's Quinn?"

"He had to take a call." Kate motioned over

toward the edge of the parking garage, where Quinn sat on the cement railing for better reception.

"Jack's going to take Lucy home. Why don't you come with us?"

Kate tensed. As much as she wanted to be with Dillon, she didn't know if she was ready to face the Kincaids. She'd met most of them over the last few days, but together? They were a force.

"Quinn and I have the airline records from every flight leaving Sea-Tac from the time the Hummer was seen entering long-term parking until this morning. We have surveillance footage from the security checkpoints and we're going to try to figure out where Scott went. If he's not in San Diego, we need to alert authorities wherever he may have landed."

"I'll go with you. Six eyes are better than four."

She shook her head. "Go with your family."

Dillon took a step closer. "What's wrong?"

"Nothing."

He didn't say anything, but his eyes spoke volumes.

"Lucy needs you," she insisted.

"You're making excuses. Why don't you want to meet my family?"

"Now is not the right time. They have too many stresses on them."

"Why is meeting you a stress?"

"Your mom doesn't need to entertain company."

"Why do I think you're pushing me away?"

"I'm not."

"Yes you are, Kate."

"Am not!" Oh, God, she sounded like a child.

"Kate." He pushed her chin up, forced her to look at him. "Don't do this. I want to bring you home."

"Dillon, the Kincaids are . . ." She couldn't think of the right word. "Overwhelming. There's so many of you."

"We're not going to all jump on you at once."

"I feel like an outsider. And I'm going to remind them of what happened to Lucy."

"Stop right there. Give my family credit. They'll like you for you."

"I don't know how families act. My grandparents died before I even hit puberty, then foster care and all that crap. I just don't know if I'm ready."

"Kate." Dillon forced her to look at him. He kissed her.

She swallowed. "Why now? Can't we just hold off for a day or two?"

"You're shaking."

"Am not."

"Kate, I love my family, and so will you." He backed her into the car and said, "You fit right in. We have a couple cops, a PI, Connor's dating a prosecutor. Jack's in the military. But we don't have an FBI agent." He leaned over and kissed her. She sucked in her breath, not expecting the onslaught of emotions that hit her from his short speech.

"My family will love you as much as I do," he whispered in her ear. "Please let me take you home."

She wrapped her arms around him, held him tight. "I don't deserve you," she said.

"Right back at you, Kate."

She laughed. It felt good to laugh; it had been way too long. "Let me work the case, okay? It makes me feel useful."

"Then I'll join you."

"Why don't I meet you there later?"

"For dinner?"

"No, I don't want to put your mother out."

"I'll cook."

"You cook?" she asked, wide-eyed.

"Absolutely. My mother taught me. Said the quickest way to a woman's heart was cooking."

Kate laughed again. "Okay, you have a date. I'll be there in a few hours."

"Are you sure you don't want me to join you?"

"Yes." She paused. "You, um, don't live with your parents, do you?"

Dillon smiled seductively. "Nervous about sleeping together under my parents' roof?"

Her eyes widened. She couldn't imagine a man of Dillon's confidence and prestige living at home.

He laughed, kissed her. "I have my own house, Kate. But the expression on your face was priceless."

Dillon rode with Jack and Lucy back to the Kincaid house.

"Did anything I say help?" Lucy asked.

"Yes."

"I don't believe you."

"Lucy, sometimes it's the smallest details that help in catching a criminal. I'm very proud of you."

"Is Patrick going to get better?"

"The doctor's are hopeful," Dillon said cautiously.

"You're lying to me again."

"I'm not lying to you, Lucy. Patrick is healthy. The surgery was hugely successful. They believe he will recover. But the human brain is still a mystery. It might take some time."

"Or he might never come out of the coma," she said defiantly.

"He might not. But I don't believe that. And you shouldn't, either."

After Dillon checked in with his parents, made sure Lucy was okay, and informed everyone that he was making dinner for a special guest that evening, he walked the four blocks to his house.

He could hardly wait for Kate to come home with him that night. He understood her hesitation—the Kincaid's *were* a bit overwhelming to outsiders. But Lucy was home and safe. Jack had returned, even if it was only temporary. And while Patrick was still in a coma, the doctors assured Dillon that everything looked promising for him to make a full recovery.

Dillon wanted to introduce Kate, the woman he loved, to his parents. It surprised him how quickly it had happened, but he was nearly thirty-nine years old. He hadn't been in love since med school when he dated the same woman for three years. That time, it had taken him months to realize that he was in love. Now, he knew it without reservation. Dillon loved Kate Donovan. She was just going to have to get used to it.

He turned the corner and saw his small, comfortable bungalow. Kate would fit in here, with his family, but she also might want her old life back. Maybe move back to Virginia and reclaim her job. He would support her in whatever she decided, but more important, he would be there with her.

He walked up the porch stairs, unlocked his door. It didn't budge. "Damn," he muttered. He always bolted the front door when he was home, primarily using the kitchen door as his entrance and exit since it was closer to the garage. When he left on Thursday, he must have gone out the back door.

He strolled down his driveway. The small rose garden he cultivated along the drive needed pruning. He might need to hire a gardener to tend to the landscaping, especially since he planned on spending a lot of time on the opposite coast. Frankly, he'd been too worried about Lucy to remember anything that day. He took the steps two at a time to his kitchen door. Unlocked it, entered, bolted it.

A smell hit him. Food. Had he left garbage in the house? He wouldn't be surprised; he had left in a hurry and it had been four days.

He crossed the kitchen and opened the cabinet door beneath the sink and pulled out the small, lined trashcan he used. He was about to pull out the garbage bag to take it outside when he saw an empty can of chili on top.

He hadn't eaten chili in ages. Someone had been in his house.

Quietly, he put the trash back under the sink. Every nerve was on alert and he listened to the sounds of his house. The silence. A creak.

The sound of someone breathing behind him.

Dillon slowly turned around. He didn't see anyone.

Then Adam Scott stepped into the kitchen from the dining room.

He had a gun.

"Adam."

"Trask to you."

Dillon couldn't get out the door; he'd bolted it when he entered. Out of habit. For security.

But that didn't help when the killer was already inside.

"What do you want?" Dillon asked. He gave his kitchen a quick once-over. Nothing was out of place.

Except that his butcher block of knives was no longer on the counter next to the stove. Scott must have been here a while. Not just in Dillon's house, but watching the Kincaid family. Anger ran through Dillon's veins. The arrogance of this bastard! But that also told Dillon that Scott had another flaw, one he planned to exploit.

"Not you. You're a means to an end. Thank you for being so predictable."

Dillon dug deep into his training and well-honed instincts. Adam Scott was here for one thing: Lucy. Because Lucy was bait. For Kate. "You'll never get to Lucy."

Scott laughed. "You don't know women very well, do you?"

Dillon knew exactly what Scott meant and he fumed. Lucy was intensely loyal, and an unscrupulous person could easily manipulate her guilt and fear. Scott would certainly not be above inducing a damaged woman to make a dangerous choice. He made his life out of it. Dillon wanted to believe Lucy was stronger than that, but right now she was too vulnerable.

"But you don't really want Lucy," Dillon said.

"Think again."

"You want to bring Monique back from the dead."

Scott's face twisted in shocked frustration. "I knew that backstabbing asshole would talk."

"I saw a picture of Monique, back when she went missing. She was beautiful. She looks very much like Lucy.

"How long did it take you surfing the Internet, manipulating teenagers, getting them to send their picture, before you found Lucy?"

"I'm not stupid, Dr. Kincaid. I know exactly what you're trying to do and it won't work. You've never met anyone like me, so your machinations won't work. I enjoy what I do. But it's all about the money."

"I agree, money motivates you. Probably because your father disowned you and took everything that was rightfully yours. You were an only child, you wouldn't have had to share with anyone, but—" Dillon recalled the notes Quinn had on the Scott family, "—he left his sizable estate to a museum."

Scott scowled. "You've been working with the feds. They're probably having a field day trying to figure out where I'm going."

"They believe you were coming here to San Diego. You know you'll never get to Lucy, even if there was some way you could contact her. She's protected by a bodyguard, and the police are patrolling the house regularly."

"But they weren't watching your house, were they?" Scott snickered.

"But you really don't want Lucy."

"Right, right, I want the fictional Monique." Scott attempted to look bored and amused, but failed. In his cold eyes, Dillon saw the truth.

"You want Kate."

Scott laughed, but his hand tightened around the gun. "Kate. She'll come to me on my terms." He cocked an eyebrow at Dillon. "And how well do *you* know Kate? Hmm? I noticed you just came back from Seattle. Didn't come back with your poor little sister. Screwing around with Kate, perhaps?"

Dillon would not allow Scott to bait him. "You want Kate because she outsmarted you."

"Kate is alive by accident. I would have had her five years ago if that guy hadn't run in and distracted me."

Dillon shook his head. "Kate is smart. She took down your legitimate business. Forced you into hiding. Cost you money. But that's not the real reason you hate her."

"Really?" Scott tried to look nonchalant, but his complexion had reddened.

"You hate her because she reminds you of a woman who humiliated and demeaned you." Dillon was taking a gamble, but he was ninety percent confident he was right about Adam Scott.

He said softly, "You were raped. Tied down and raped by a woman. The weaker sex. But you were weak. You couldn't fight back. Maybe you didn't want to. Maybe you liked it, and you hate that you liked it."

"Shut up!"

Scott lunged for him. Dillon dove right, toward the breakfast nook. He fell over the table, but tripped Scott. The killer stumbled, but stayed upright. Worse, he kept hold of the gun.

Dillon turned and, using all his strength, pushed the table across the nook and into Scott's body. Scott grunted, wedged between the table and the wall. Dillon jumped on the table and grabbed Scott's wrist, slamming it on the table to loosen his hold on the gun.

He didn't see the knife in Scott's left hand.

Dillon screamed at the searing pain in his thigh and grabbed at the wound. Scott pulled out the knife, pushed Dillon off the table, and hit him across the face with his gun.

Dillon rolled over, panting, trying to assess whether the knife wound was serious. Hot blood coated his fingers. He tried to force his mind away from the pain and think like a doctor. He didn't think it was deep.

He got up on all fours and Scott kicked him in the kidney. His vision blurred.

"You fucking shrinks know *nothing* about me. *Nothing.* You got that?"

Scott grabbed Dillon by his shirt collar and pulled him up, the gun cocked and touching the back of his head.

Dillon had no choice but to go where Scott led him, through his house and into his bedroom. He pushed him onto the bed and clicked a handcuff onto one wrist. The other end was hooked onto the headboard.

Scott smiled, but there was only sick humor in his face. "We have a call to make."

"Don't hang up or your brother dies."

Lucy started shaking uncontrollably. Trevor Conrad was calling her. Why? Hadn't he hurt her enough?

"Wh-what?"

"Listen. You have thirty minutes. Leave your house alone. Walk directly to your brother's house."

"Which brother?" Dillon, Patrick, and Connor all lived within walking distance.

"The shrink!"

Trevor had Dillon? That wasn't possible. Why did he want her to come? To rape her? To kill her? She couldn't do it.

What if Dillon was already dead?

"What do you want?" she asked, stalling.

"That's none of your business, Lucy. But if you're not here in thirty minutes, your brother will be dead. And if you tell anyone, he'll die in extreme pain."

"Let me talk to him. Please!"

He hung up.

She stared at her phone. What was she going to do?

There was a knock on her door and she stifled a scream. "Come in," she called.

Jack walked in. "Everything all right?"

"Yes," she lied. Could he tell something was wrong? She almost laughed at the absurdity of that thought. Wrong? Everything was wrong and had been for days. No one would know why. "I'm going to take a shower."

"Okay." He paused, looked around the room, and left.

Her phone beeped and she opened it.

New pix message.

She retrieved it.

"Oh, dear God, why are you doing this to me?"

Dillon was handcuffed to his bed, blood on his lip and streaked over his shirt. The message read: *Come alone, he lives. Tell anyone, he dies. Could you live with yourself knowing you killed the man who risked his life to save you?*

THIRTY-FOUR

QUINN STARED AT KATE across the table of the task force office that had been set up four days ago when the FBI had first learned that Trask had kidnapped Lucy Kincaid.

"Earth to Kate."

"Sorry. Daydreaming."

"About?"

"Dillon."

"Why didn't you go to his house with him?"

She sighed. "I made a mistake. You have enough people here to go over these records. You don't need me, do you?"

"No, I don't."

She gave him a mock frown. "I should be hurt by that."

"Go see Dillon. It'll make you feel better. I'll call you if we learn anything about Scott."

"Thanks." She paused.

"What?"

"Can I borrow a car?"

Dillon tore a wide strip off his shirt and, using his free hand and teeth, tied a tourniquet around the knife wound in his thigh. He assessed the damage. Not deep, but it still hurt like hell.

Scott had left as soon as he sent Lucy a picture of Dillon. Dillon wished he could have communicated something to Lucy to keep her safe, but he feared she would walk right over out of guilt. All he could hope for was Jack keeping her under lock and key. He wouldn't let her just leave the house alone.

Scott came back into the bedroom.

"Leave Lucy out of this," Dillon told Adam Scott.

"She only has ten more minutes. She didn't send anyone over. No patrols out front. No one lurking in the bushes. Smart kid. But nowhere near as smart as me."

"What do you really want?" Dillon asked. It wasn't money. While money was vitally important to Scott, he wouldn't risk being caught for it. He had lost a lot to the FBI, but he still had millions squirreled away. Enough to buy a new identity and disappear.

This wasn't about money. It wasn't just about the humiliation he'd suffered by having his sick webcam shut down, or even about his father disowning him. In fact, Dillon didn't think it was about Lucy.

It was about Monique—bringing her back from the dead—and it was about Kate. Lucy was a tool. A trap.

"You really do want Kate."

Scott stared at him, his hard face unmoving. Shrugged.

"You don't need Lucy."

"I need to give Kate proper incentive. And I like Lucy. She'll be properly submissive once I train her."

"We'll never stop looking for her. You know that."

"Makes it more of a challenge. Of course, I could

just kill you all, then no one would be looking for her. In fact, she wouldn't even try to escape." Scott seemed to seriously ponder this option.

"Lucy won't come."

But Dillon knew she would. The guilt over Patrick's condition would compel her to make sure the same thing didn't happen to him. Dillon wished he could have talked to her, but Scott had left the room while making the call, after taking his picture as proof of his words.

"Yes, she will. I've been watching your family for the last twenty-four hours. I know she spent hours at the hospital with your younger brother. With your commando brother around her all the time, I couldn't get her out of the house on my own. I used to have plenty of men who would have stormed the house and taken her for me, but Kate killed them all." He smiled oddly at Dillon. "You killed one of them, too, didn't you?"

"Yes."

"You shot an unarmed man. How does that make you feel, Doctor?"

"I have no feelings on the matter. He was raping my sister." He did have feelings, strong feelings. He would have done anything, killed anyone, to spare Lucy.

Scott just nodded thoughtfully. "How did you hook up with Kate Donovan in the first place?"

"Mutual friend," Dillon answered cryptically.

Scott didn't like that answer. "How does it feel to have sent your brothers into a trap?"

"Trap?"

Scott was jumping around, trying to keep Dillon off-guard.

"In Baja California. They walked right into it. Boom. Noble of you, to let them take the lead. Poor Patrick."

Dillon didn't fall for the bait. "This is between you and Kate. Leave Lucy out of it."

"You don't get it. Monique and I will disappear as soon as I kill Kate." Scott frowned rubbed his eyes. "Lucy and I will disappear."

"How did Monique die? Were you having sex and just got carried away?"

"It was an accident."

"You couldn't get hard, could you? So you had to play games."

"Shut up."

"You were soft. Maybe she teased you. You hit her. Saw her scared. Scared of you. That turned you on, didn't it?"

"Women like it rough. Monique loved our games."

"You got turned on when she was scared, were able to finally get it up and into her, then what happened? Your dick grow limp again? Couldn't climax?"

"I said to shut up." Scott was pacing.

Dillon knew he had him. He kept pushing, biding time. Jack would begin to get suspicious when Dillon didn't show up with the food he'd promised to bring for dinner. Jack would come check on him, see the blood and disarray in the kitchen.

Dillon just had to keep Adam Scott focused on him, not Lucy.

"So you put your hands around her neck. Squeezed. She was terrified. She would have begged you to stop, but she couldn't talk. You loved that. Finally you could have an orgasm. You achieved what seems so effortless for normal men. Victory, right? You were in charge, on top of the world. But you held on too long. Squeezed too tight. Monique was dead.

"How did you feel? Knowing you killed her for your own short-lived sexual pleasure?"

Scott backhanded him. "You know *nothing* about my relationship with Monique. I loved her."

"Funny way to show it."

"I've learned a lot in the last twenty years. I don't kill anyone by accident."

"What about April Klinger?"

"You're not going to get me spouting off about April. That's Kate's game. She's got that bee in her bonnet. If it weren't for that bitch April, no one would have investigated Trask Enterprises."

"Adam, I think—"

He hit him again. Dillon swallowed blood, coughed. "*Call me Trask!*"

Scott shook his head, started pacing again. "You people and your ethics. It's so easy to be me. I'm not encumbered by rules and morals. Morals are for idiots. Lucy is going to walk right into your house because she thinks she can save you. The only reason you're not dead now is for insurance." He took out a knife, stepped closer to Dillon. His purpose was to terrify and demoralize. Dillon kept his face blank.

Scott pushed back the rage that had coated his face while Dillon had pushed him about Monique. He said in a low voice. "As soon as I have Lucy, I don't need you."

"I know that. Lucy knows that, too. She's not going to walk into a trap."

Scott laughed. "You don't know women very well.

They are, by and large, stupid creatures. They have all these feelings and fears running around in those insipid brains of theirs. I know exactly what she's thinking. She's blaming herself for everything that's happened, probably thinks she's stupid. She'll do *anything* to make it up to her parents and that brother of yours in the coma. She's not going to think anything through. Women are incapable of reason. Even Kate, who I'll admit is smarter than most, doesn't always think logically. I mean, she was so devastated by that bitch Paige's death that she ran away!" He frowned. "Made it a little harder to find her."

"You never knew where she was. You bluffed."

Scott smiled. "You'll never know, will you? Kate was pretty good with the computer. Even I began to admire her savvy. But I'm better. I've always been better. Kate leads with her heart, thinking she can save the world when she should be more concerned about saving herself."

Dillon's jaw clenched involuntarily, and Scott noticed.

"You like her, don't you?"

"I love my sister."

"Kate."

"I barely know her."

Scott shook his head, smiled. "Interesting." He took out his cell phone, pressed a few buttons.

Suddenly, the knife came down hard on Dillon's free hand. He screamed out of pain and surprise, his arm jerking in response. The knife pierced both sides, then Scott pulled it out and Dillon tried, and failed, to bite back a second scream.

"Thanks," Scott said, pressing buttons on his cell phone. "Let's get this party rolling, shall we?"

Twenty minutes earlier, Lucy had gone to shower. Jack liked long showers, but something didn't seem quite right. He pictured her in her bedroom when he last talked to her. She had been holding something.

A cell phone.

He went to check on her. She'd been acting a little . . . strange earlier. He didn't want to make anything of it; if anyone had the right to act odd it was Lucy. But his instincts told him she was being deceptive.

Jack always trusted his instincts.

He heard the shower at the end of the hall. She'd been in there too long. He didn't want to break into the bathroom and scare her. Especially after the rape.

But he suspected that Lucy would think that way, that he would give her privacy, not worry if the shower was running . . .

He rapped loudly on the bathroom door three times. "Lucy? It's Jack. How are you doing?"

No answer.

Jack tried the knob. Locked. "Lucy? Open up. Now. Or tell me to go away and I will. I need to know that you're okay."

No answer.

Jack slammed his boot down hard on the doorknob and the old lock broke.

Steam and moisture escaped the room. Jack pulled back the shower curtain, for a split second thinking Lucy had killed herself.

But she wasn't there at all.

THIRTY-FIVE

KATE DROVE to the Kincaid family house using the directions Quinn had given her off the Internet. Something was bothering her and she couldn't figure out what.

All she wanted was to see Dillon and tell him she was sorry she'd been so weird about meeting his family. The fact that he wanted her to meant everything to her. She would just suck it up and put on a happy face and do it for Dillon.

The Kincaids lived in an older, well-maintained middle-class neighborhood of post–World War II houses. Small bungalows interspersed with more modern two stories. Large, deep front yards and lots of trees.

Movement to the right caught her eye. A jogger?

She looked at the house numbers: 340, 342, 344. That was it, the modest two-story house with a yard bursting with color.

Someone was lurking outside the house.

She slammed on the brakes and jumped from the car.

That was no jogger. Someone was jumping over the

fence. Not into the Kincaid backyard, but coming *from* the Kincaid backyard.

Kate ran, caught sight of the suspect. Long dark hair in a ponytail. Five foot seven, one hundred thirty pounds.

Lucy.

"Lucy Kincaid! Stop!"

Lucy looked over her shoulder. "No. Go away!" She ran faster.

Kate sprinted after her, tackled her on the front lawn two houses down.

"Get off me! Get off me!" Lucy screamed. "He's going to kill him. Let me go!"

Kate held her firmly, but pulled her into her lap, pinning Lucy's arms to her sides. She didn't want to hurt her, but there was no way she was letting Lucy go.

"Lucy, stop. Why are you running?"

Lucy stopped struggling. "Trevor is going to kill Dillon. You have to let me go. Please." Her voice quivered in panic and fear.

Kate's heart pounded. "You mean Adam Scott?"

"Right, Adam. He has Dillon."

"How do you know?"

Out of the corner of her eye, Kate saw Jack run from the Kincaid house, gun drawn. He saw her and Lucy and made a beeline for them.

"I saw. He called me."

"Adam Scott called you?"

"Yes. Thirty minutes ago. My time is almost up. He's going to kill Dillon! I have to save him."

"Why do you think Adam Scott has Dillon?" Kate asked as Jack stood next to them, his eyes scanning the area. Her entire body tensed. If it was true . . .

"My phone."

Kate loosened her hold on Lucy, who reached into her pocket and handed Kate her phone. Kate opened it, looked at the last message sent.

Dillon, shirt and face bloodied, handcuffed to a bed.

"Get her inside," Jack said.

"Come on, Lucy. Let's go inside." Kate helped her up.

"No! I'm supposed to be at Dillon's house right now! I'm going to be late."

"Is Dillon there?" Kate asked.

"He said he'd contact me when I got there."

"This is Dillon's house," Jack said. He pointed to the nightstand. "That's Justin, our nephew, in the photograph on the nightstand."

Scott had contacted Lucy at 4:50 that afternoon. He had probably been waiting for Dillon when he arrived home.

It was 5:20 p.m.

Kate stood. "This is going to end right now. I'm going."

"No," Jack said. "He'll kill you."

"Not right away." She stared at Jack. "You take Lucy back to the house. I'll go in."

"No way am I letting you go without backup."

Jack was right. "Okay," she agreed. "I need a layout of Dillon's house."

"Let's go inside and talk to my dad. I've never been in Dillon's house."

And at this moment, Kate knew Jack regretted it.

Inside, Dillon's father, Pat Kincaid, drew a makeshift

blueprint while Kate called Quinn and told him what had happened. He was calling in a local SWAT team.

Kate looked at Pat's drawing. "Are these two the only doors?"

Pat nodded. "Front and back. The back leads right into the kitchen. The dining room separates the kitchen from the living room, then there's a short hall here, his office here, a bathroom, and his bedroom here."

His bedroom was in the rear of the house.

"Where are the windows?"

Pat drew them in. "Three, one large window on this wall, and two narrow windows on either side of the bed."

"I'm going to the front door. Alone. He won't let me in if he sees anyone. Jack, as soon as Dillon is alone in the bedroom, you go in through this window"—she indicated the one in the rear—"and get him out."

"What about you?" Jack said. "You can't go in there unarmed, and he's not going to open the door without a hostage."

"He's cocky. I keep my hands up, he'll open the door to me. Or unlock it. We can wait for the SWAT team to get into place, but I don't think we have that much time."

"You think he's going to kill Dillon?" Pat said somberly.

"As soon as Dillon is of no benefit, yes. But right now he's safe. Without a live hostage, Scott knows he can't win."

Lucy's cell phone rang. It sat in the middle of the table.

Kate caught her eye. "Answer it. Tell him your brother Jack is sitting outside your bedroom door and you can't get out. Buy time."

Lucy nodded, shaking. She answered the phone. "Hello."

"You're late."

"Jack is sitting outside my door. I can't get out."

"Climb out the window."

"I'll try, but—"

"Five minutes or Dillon is dead."

Suddenly, an earsplitting scream came from the phone. Kate sucked in her breath.

Dillon.

Then another scream.

Dillon sat on his hand to stop the bleeding. He'd been dizzy for a minute, the pain clouding his thoughts. But he had to push past it. The worst of the pain was gone, only a violent throbbing in his palm that reminded him of the unexpected attack. It matched the throbbing in his thigh.

Scott had left the room as soon as he pulled the knife from Dillon's hand. Dillon had never felt so helpless in his life. Was Lucy going to walk into the trap?

Stay away, Luce. Don't do it. Don't worry about me.

He'd find a way out. He had to.

He pulled at the handcuff, but his hand was too big to slip out. He had nothing but books in his nightstand drawer. No paperclips or pins to try and pick the lock. Not that he'd be able to use his left hand. Already his fingers were numb and felt thick. The tendon may have been severed.

But that was the least of his problems.

He looked around his spare room. If Lucy came, Scott had to have some other place to take her. He wouldn't keep her here—someone would eventually come to the house, looking for him or Lucy. If Lucy didn't come, as soon as he was missed tonight Jack or Kate would call or come by.

Scott wouldn't kill Lucy, at least not right away. She had become Monique, the girl he'd killed all those years ago. But Kate? She stood no chance against Scott's rage. Scott viewed her as his personal demon in the flesh, the woman he had to destroy to regain control of his life. It wasn't logical to anyone but Adam Scott, but Dillon saw Scott's twisted reasoning. He prayed Kate didn't come looking for him.

As for him, Dillon knew he could die and Adam Scott wouldn't feel an ounce of remorse.

Kate called Quinn from her cell phone while Jack drove his SUV the long way to Dillon's house, parking around the corner so if Scott were looking he wouldn't see them.

"We're in place," she told Quinn. "He gave Lucy five minutes. It's already been four."

"He's not going to kill Dillon. That was a threat to get Lucy to move."

"You don't know that."

"He needs a hostage, Kate. Don't be reckless. SWAT ETA is three minutes."

"Dillon's already injured, Quinn. I can't let him bleed to death. I'm going. I'll count on SWAT being in place."

"Kate—"

Kate slammed her cell shut, looked at Jack. "Ready?"

He nodded. He was letting Kate approach first. Then he'd go through backyards into Dillon's, go directly to his bedroom and get him out.

Kate had a knife and a gun. She would kill Adam Scott without hesitation if she could. But first she had to assess the situation. Scott loved explosives. She wouldn't put it past him to wire the entire house and blow them all up.

No, he wouldn't kill himself. He was much too arrogant for that. That knowledge could buy her some time.

She pushed the fear that Dillon was seriously injured—or dead—from her mind. The scream had been sudden, brutal, solely to torment Lucy and force her to act. Scott would kill Dillon, but not until he had another hostage.

She took a deep breath and walked up the porch steps. She saw movement behind the blinds and resisted the instinct to draw her gun.

The door opened before she knocked, a gun aimed at her chest.

Adam Scott, the man she'd dreamed of confronting for the last five years, stood there, surprise on his face.

He had darkened his hair, wore brown contacts to hide his ice-blue eyes, probably to elude security when he left Seattle. But face-to-face, there was no doubt that this was the man who had shot Evan and kidnapped Paige. This was the man who had killed an innocent woman Saturday night because he couldn't kill Lucy. This was the bastard who was holding hostage the man she loved.

She itched to shoot him. Only days ago she would have lunged at him, knowing she'd die at the same time he did.

But today she had a future and she wasn't willing to sacrifice herself without a fight. Yet there was no way she was letting Adam Scott walk out of this house alive.

He smiled.

"Well, I was right about something," he said.

"What?" she asked.

He didn't respond. He grabbed her arm and she jerked back.

"Don't touch me," she said.

He pointed the gun at her head. "Get in. Now."

She stepped across the threshold. He spun her around, held her by the neck, looked right and left outside the house. "I know you didn't come alone."

"Aren't you smart."

"But it doesn't matter." He disarmed her, finding both her knife and gun. She'd expected as much. But at least the weapons were in the house. He put the gun in the small of his back and the knife on the top of a bookshelf. She wouldn't be able to reach it easily.

He patted her down again, pinching and hurting her on her thighs, her stomach, her breasts. She didn't cry out.

He pushed her onto the couch. "Where's Lucy?"

"I came instead."

"I'm killing you," he said matter-of-factly. "I want Lucy."

"You can't always get what you want."

He punched her with his fist. Her head snapped back and she winced, but didn't speak.

"She'll come. I'll cut off her precious brother's hand, and she'll come."

"She can't. Jack is sitting on her. They'll never let her out of the house. If Dillon has to die, they accept that."

"Do you think I'm stupid?" He stared at her incredulously.

"On the contrary, I think you're one of the most brilliant killers I've ever faced. Putting you in prison will be very satisfying for me."

He laughed. Kate raised an eyebrow but didn't speak. Everything Dillon had told her about Adam Scott swirled around in the back of her mind. His huge ego, deep arrogance, hatred of women, sexual dysfunction. And, above all, that he didn't believe he could be caught. He'd walked free for too long. He thought he'd never face imprisonment.

"You're right. I didn't come alone. The feds are all over this place. So kill Dillon, kill me, but you'll be captured or dead."

"You do think I'm stupid. The feds would never sacrifice a civilian for the 'common good.'" He laughed again.

"You killed two federal agents. One civilian is collateral damage."

"You're good, but I don't believe you." He shook his head, a smile still on his cold, hard lips. "But it doesn't matter. Even if they are willing to kill Dillon Kincaid, they're not willing to kill a couple dozen innocent civilians."

He leaned over to where he had his computer set up on a table. The fear Kate had kept restrained as she walked into this situation began to seep out. He had a program running, but she couldn't see what it was.

"See, I've been around with not much to do over the last day or so. Except make a couple bombs. One of them is in the engine of a black SUV I noticed parked in front of Lucy's house. Belongs to Jack, doesn't it? Wonder where it is now."

He tapped a couple of buttons.

An explosion rocked the house.

Scott shook his head, a satisfied smirk cutting across his lips. "Well, Kate, you weren't lying. You didn't come alone. Hope Jack got out of his truck in time. Or not."

He held out the cell phone he'd taken from her pocket.

"Call whoever you brought with you. I want Lucy Kincaid. Now. Or I'll continue blowing up targets all over San Diego."

THIRTY·SIX

"WHAT THE *HELL* was that?" her father exclaimed. Deep concern clouded his face.

Lucy feared the worst. Jack and Kate and Dillon, who had saved her life, were all in jeopardy. What if they died because of her? Because she'd been so stupid as to get involved with that evil man Trevor Conrad in the first place.

"I'm going to my room," she said, jumping up.

"I'll come with you," her mother said, distracted. They heard sirens in the distance.

Carina and Nick came in through the front door. "What happened?"

"I don't know. There was an explosion."

"We heard. There's smoke coming from about a block away from Dillon's house. Agent Peterson just called us about the hostage situation."

Lucy's cell phone rang. Fear squeezed every cell in her body. It was him, she knew, telling her everyone was dead. And it was her fault.

"Lucy!" Carina exclaimed. "Who's that?"

She shook her head, tears in her eyes. Carina picked up the phone. "Who's this?" Relief crossed her face, quickly replaced by fear. "I'll take care of it." She hung up. "Adam Scott planted a bomb in Jack's truck. That's what exploded."

Lucy's mother cried out. The anguish in her voice added heavily to Lucy's guilt. She backed away from her family. She had to get out.

"Who was that?" Nick asked, putting a hand on Carina's arm.

Carina accepted Nick's quiet strength, doubly glad he was with her now.

"Jack. He's alive," Carina said. "We need to get out of the house. We don't know where else this bastard has planted bombs. I'm taking you all to police headquarters, where I know you'll be safe."

"I'll drive," her father said.

"No. No Kincaid cars. He's been in town for over twenty-four hours, he knows what you drive. I'm calling a taxi, and we'll walk to the park on the corner."

"Mama, I'm so sorry," Carina said when she saw the stricken look on her mother's face.

Rosa nodded. "It's okay. Everyone is okay right now. Everyone will be okay."

Carina called the taxi. "Okay, let's go." She looked for Lucy. "Lucy!" Carina called. When she got no answer, she ran upstairs. "Lucy! Come on!"

A minute later she called down. "Is Lucy down there?"

"No," Nick said.

They searched the house quickly, but Carina knew Lucy was gone.

Carina tried to call first Jack, then Agent Peterson. Neither picked up, but she left the same message for each of them.

"Lucy is gone. I think she's headed to Dillon's house."

Kate was at a loss.

Adam Scott was willing to kill dozens, hundreds of people, right here from his computer.

The power went out in the house.

Adam laughed.

"They think that if they shut down the power they can stop me? I have four backup batteries for a total of twelve hours of juice. Enough time to do anything I damn well please."

"They'll never let Lucy come. I'm here. Take me. It's what you wanted, isn't it?"

"Take you? *Take* you?" He stared at her. "You want me to fuck you? To tie you down?" He took a step toward her. "To cut off your air?"

He grabbed her throat with one hand. She grabbed his wrist, but she was seated and he towered above her. She couldn't get up to kick him, and she couldn't stop him from cutting off her air.

She couldn't breathe.

His voice was low. "You'll feel my cock penetrate that tight hole of yours. Fill you up. And the last thing you'll know as you lay there dying is that I will be taking intense pleasure in fucking your body. You are a worthless whore, just like the rest of them."

He released her and she took deep breaths to refill her lungs. Her vision returned, but her throat burned. She swallowed several times before she could talk.

"Fine," she said, coughing. She had to stay out of his reach. Scott was strong, but it was his rage that worried her more. Yet it was also his rage that she could defeat him with if she was smart. And careful. "I'm not worried. I watched that recording you sent. You can't even get it up."

He pistol-whipped her, and she fell across the couch. Her vision blurred. She would be no help to anyone if she got herself killed before Dillon escaped.

"You fucking bitch."

"Go ahead. Try me." She squeezed her eyes shut, took a deep breath, opened them. Better.

He shook his head. "A willing participant is no fun. That fucking whore Denise liked it. She'd do anything I asked her to. What's the fun in that? I could have killed her and she wouldn't have cared. Yeah, she was an actress, she pretended she was scared, but she liked it. She came back for more. But Lucy . . . you took her from me. You and that fucking shrink."

"Why Lucy?"

"Why not?"

"You had to have picked her for a reason."

"You are so transparent! Buying time, trying to get me to talk. Do you think I'm going to break down and spill my guts and tell you what a miserable childhood I had and how I want you to stop me? I like my life just the way it is. And there are a lot more people out there like me than you think. I put up the disclaimer, but do you really think those people don't know what they're watching? Ha! They know, and they love it. I'm just better than them, better because *I* act out their fantasies. They want to be me.

"I'm rich. Even with your pathetic attempts to seize my accounts, I have millions all over the world. You'll never find it all. This glitch is just that: a temporary lull in the action.

"Don't ever think for one minute that I don't love every minute of what I do." He stared at her. "When I took Paige, it was you I wanted. But you know what?" He leaned forward, inches from her face. "She gave me the only thing a woman is good for, sex."

Kate's booted foot kicked up between his legs, connecting squarely with his balls. The pain that crossed his face was real, but he recovered quickly. As she rolled away, trying to get up off the couch, he grabbed her, threw her to the floor. Her head hit the hardwood floor and that stunned her long enough for him to climb on top of her. She was on her stomach, and he pinned her down. His arm came around her neck and he held her.

"Maybe not such a willing participant, after all," he growled into her ear. "Too bad I can't take both you and your boyfriend with me. I'd like him to watch."

"I don't have a boyfriend."

He laughed in her ear, then bit her neck so hard she screamed. "I was surprised, too, but Dr. Kincaid doesn't have a very good poker face."

Out of the corner of her eye she saw movement in the kitchen.

Scott saw it, too.

He pulled her up, produced a knife in his hand. It was at her throat.

Jack stood in the threshold between kitchen and dining room, gun drawn.

"I'll kill her," Scott said calmly. "Don't move."

"Give it up now, Scott."

"Trask! My name is Trask!" He held Kate close to him. "I think I'm holding the cards."

Scott took a step toward Jack dragging Kate with him. She provided him with a shield, dammit! She squirmed and felt the knife cut into her throat.

"Get out," Scott told Jack.

Jack didn't back off.

Scott pushed the knife deeper into her throat. Kate tried not to make a sound, but a cry escaped her lips.

Go, she mouthed to Jack. *Now.*

It was obvious he was torn, but he backed out of the kitchen.

"Out the door, soldier," Scott ordered.

Jack complied, a tight anger across his face. Scott bolted the door.

He bolted the door, Kate thought. That meant Jack had a key. Had Colonel Kincaid given him one? Or had he gotten it from Dillon? Was Dillon safe?

He had to be. Jack wouldn't have left the house with his brother still in danger. Would he?

With Jack gone he pulled Kate back over to the computer in the next room. "I set the next bomb to blow up in five minutes. Whoops, three minutes, ten seconds. Unless I stop it, it'll blow. You destroy my computer, it will blow. You hinder my escape, it will blow. Hell, I might just let it blow for fun."

"Doesn't give me the incentive to let you escape."

"Hmm, probably not. Except that it's this house that's the next to go. And your doctor friend is bleeding to death in the next room."

"Not anymore."

Dillon's voice to their right startled Scott for only a fraction of a second. But that was long enough for

Kate to take advantage of him dropping his arm just a hair. She brought her arms up between his knife arm and her neck, pushing them back. The sting of another cut to her throat didn't slow her; they didn't have time. She whirled around, kicked him square in the chest.

Scott threw the knife at Dillon who anticipated the move and turned back into the hallway. The knife hit the wall inches from where Dillon had been.

Scott turned back to Kate, her gun in his hand. He wouldn't hesitate to kill her, especially since he had an ace in the hole: bombs.

Kate dove at the same time Scott fired, seeing movement from the hall.

Dillon tackled Scott from behind and they both hit the floor hard.

"He has a gun!" Kate shouted.

Dillon grabbed his hand as Scott tried to turn the gun toward him. He slammed it against the wood floor. Once, twice. The gun fell from Scott's grasp and Kate retrieved it. Scott reached down and twisted his fingers into the hole in Dillon's hand.

Dillon cried out, tried to regain his hold on Scott, but the killer kicked him and jumped up. He glanced at his computer and laughed. "One minute forty-five seconds and it blows."

He opened the front door.

"Get the computer!" Dillon shouted at Kate. "Stop the bomb."

Kate grabbed the computer while Dillon went after Scott. He lunged forward, knocking Scott off balance and causing both of them to roll down the porch stairs. Dillon landed on his back, winded. Scott clambered up and Dillon grabbed his foot, pulled him back down.

Scott grunted, but he wasn't seriously hurt or bleeding. He had an edge over Dillon whose wounds had started bleeding freely again.

He heard a shout from the side of the house. Sounded like Jack.

Dillon tried to climb on top of Scott, to keep him on the ground until Jack arrived. Then, out of the corner of his eye he saw a dark-haired woman run across the lawn.

Lucy.

"Get out of here!" he shouted.

Scott kicked Dillon in the head and got up. He staggered forward, saw Lucy only feet from him. *Monique.* She'd returned for him.

He smiled. "You're late."

He took a step toward her.

She pulled a gun from under her sweater. Aimed it at Scott.

"Monique, you won't kill me."

She stared at him as if he were insane. That angered Adam more than anything. "Monique!" he said sharply.

"My name is *Lucy Kincaid*."

"Monique, it's me. Adam. I'm sorry. I didn't mean for it to go so far."

She pulled the trigger. The bullet pierced him in the chest. His mouth dropped open.

"Why, sweetheart. Why?"

She pulled the trigger again. Again.

Adam dropped to his knees. He was dead before he fell face first into the dirt.

"Lucy, stop!" Dillon called, stumbling up. Jack ran at him, held out his hand to pull Dillon up. "Thanks, bro," Dillon said. Jack nodded curtly, then turned to where Lucy had her empty gun pointed at Adam Scott's dead body.

Kate ran from the house. She had Scott's laptop.

"Run!" she yelled. "I can't stop the bomb!"

Jack removed the gun from Lucy's hand, grabbed her around the waist, then started for the street.

Local and federal police were pulling up in front of the house. Kate waved them off.

"There's a bomb! Get away!"

The explosion lifted them all off the ground as they ran. They hit the lawn across the street.

No one moved.

Slowly, Kate rose to her knees, shaking her head to get rid of the ringing, but it stayed with her.

Dillon. Where was Dillon?

Sirens, shouts, and screams filled the air. The last time Kate had seen Dillon was in the front yard. Had he heard her? Had he run far enough? Had he even been able to run?

"Dillon!" she shouted, her voice hoarse from Adam Scott's hands. She cleared her throat, coughed. The crackle of fire consumed the house that had been Dillon's. The firefighters were frantically setting up to try to save the neighboring homes.

"Dillon!"

She sat up, looked around. She saw Jack huddled over Lucy on the ground twenty feet away. They were both moving.

Dillon, where are you?

She couldn't lose him now. They hadn't had any time together, dammit! It wasn't fair!

Kate stood, pushing back the nausea that threatened. People ran back and forth, SWAT and feds and local police and fire crews. Debris covered a body in Dillon's front yard. Her mouth fell open and she cried out.

No, Dillon, please no.

She stumbled back across the street and a firefighter stopped her.

"You can't go there."

"No, no," she said, staring at the body. It wasn't Dillon. The body wore beige slacks. Like Adam Scott had been wearing.

"Kate."

She heard her name and turned slowly around. There. Dillon. Up against a car parked across the street. She ran to him. Touched his face. Kissed his swollen lips. Buried her face in his neck.

"Oh, God, Dillon. I thought—" She couldn't say it. She wouldn't say it.

"I know." His voice was weak.

She sat back on her knees and saw his leg was bleeding extensively. "Medic!" she shouted as loud as she could. "Medic!"

"I'm okay." He closed his eyes.

She laughed nervously. He was *not* okay. "Oh, Dillon." She tore her shirt and tied it around his thigh.

Lucy limped over with Jack at her side.

"Is he okay?" she asked.

Dillon nodded. "Luce, I'm fine."

Kate was concerned about the pallor of Dillon's skin. He'd lost a lot of blood. She checked his vitals.

Strong. Of course. Dillon was the strongest soul she knew. "Scott is dead," Kate said.

"I know," Dillon replied. He opened his eyes, searching for her. She clasped his uninjured hand, tears of relief falling freely.

"I'm not sorry I killed him," Lucy said defiantly. Her eyes had a pained, faraway expression.

It would hit her later, Dillon thought. No one could kill another human being, even an evil bastard like Adam Scott, without conflicted emotions.

Jack asked Kate, "What about other bombs?"

"I didn't see any more set up, but we need to get this computer to the FBI immediately."

Quinn Peterson ran over to them. "Where's Scott?"

"Dead," Kate said.

"In the explosion?

Kate and Dillon looked at each other. "Yes," they said in unison.

Jack led Lucy away and Quinn said, "An ambulance is on its way. Hang in there." He went to coordinate the authorities.

Dillon squeezed Kate's hand as hard as he could. "I don't think I'll be making dinner tonight."

"Damn." She leaned over and kissed him.

He touched her throat, where bruises were beginning to form, where dried blood coated her neck. "He hurt you."

"Well, he hurt you, too," Kate said. "Now he's dead."

She sat against the car next to him, put her head on his shoulder. "I'm sorry I made such a stink about meeting your family."

"I'm sorry I pushed you too hard."

"You didn't. I was just scared. But that fear was nothing compared to the thought of losing you. I don't want to lose you, Dillon."

"You won't, Kate. I love you."

Jack walked over to them. "Carina has Lucy and there's an ambulance on the way." He glanced over at Dillon's burning house. The first fire truck had arrived. "Your house is a goner."

"I won't need it for a while," Dillon said. "I'm heading out to Washington for a couple weeks."

"You are?" Kate asked.

"I told you I'd stand by you through the hearings."

She smiled through her tears. "You meant what you said and you said what you meant."

Dillon nodded. "One hundred percent."

THIRTY·SEVEN

THE FOLLOWING MONDAY MORNING, Kate walked into the scheduled hearing in the Office of Professional Responsibility. She was nervous, she couldn't help it. Even with Quinn Peterson's assurances and Dillon waiting for her outside, she knew she had to answer some serious accusations.

Nervous, but ready. More than ready to put the past behind her and live for the future.

She was surprised when she walked in and both Quinn Peterson and Jeff Merritt were sitting at the conference table. Quinn hadn't told her he'd be here; the last she heard he had returned to Seattle. Merritt had lost weight, his skin was pasty, and he had no gun in his holster.

A gun—and badge—sat in front of the director of the review committee, Madeline James.

"Sit down, Agent Donovan."

She sat. It was the first time someone had called her "agent" in . . . years.

"Regardless of what Mr. Merritt is about to say, this committee has determined that you will have to answer for leaving the country when you had been ordered to report for a debriefing after Special Agent

Paige Henshaw was murdered. Though you have been forthcoming about your illegal activities since, hacking government computers is still a crime and one we cannot take lightly.

"But it has also been decided that you may return to active duty provided you complete a probationary period as punishment for your crimes. We've decided that should you stay with the Federal Bureau of Investigation, you must return to the training academy, all sixteen weeks, and successfully pass every test as if you were a new recruit. Afterward, you will not be allowed in the field for a minimum of one year. Instead, you will be required to teach a class in e-crimes at the Academy."

"And if I don't want to return?"

"Then you'll be a civilian."

She glanced at Quinn, but his face was unreadable. She looked at Jeff Merritt, frowned.

"You mean," she asked for clarification, "I will be free?"

"If you mean you will not be serving prison time, yes. You'll be free. But if you choose not to return to the Academy, you'll lose your rank, your pension, and your gun permit, and will not be allowed to work in law enforcement or touch a computer for a period of two years."

Madeline James continued. "Your crimes were serious, but the committee has determined that there were extraordinary circumstances that would likely not be duplicated should you return to the FBI."

She nodded to Merritt. "You may speak."

"Paige is dead because of me," he said. "I have resigned from the Bureau."

Kate didn't say anything. But the final pieces of the puzzle began to click into place as Merritt spoke.

"When Paige told me she was pregnant, I told her to quit. She had always been a little reckless, and I felt that the two of you together were dangerous. You pushed the boundaries, but Paige was the one who really crossed the line. Over and over. That undercover operation seven years ago? Before you were partners? Paige went in against orders. I covered for her then, lied, so she wouldn't be reprimanded or fired.

"But then she became pregnant. With my child. And I knew she wouldn't stop her recklessness. I asked her to leave the field. I could have gotten her a position anywhere—at Quantico, at the laboratory—something safer. She refused.

"I was the one who canceled the backup the night you and Paige confronted Adam Scott. I honestly didn't believe you were in danger. I thought you were just meeting the girl, Denise Arno. You had called Evan before you left and told him I'd cleared backup. But he heard from someone else that they'd been put on a different assignment, so he followed you to the warehouse. He saw what was happening, called it in, but by the time anyone arrived it was too late. He rushed into the warehouse to help cover you and Paige—"

"He sacrificed his life to save mine," Kate whispered.

"When Paige was kidnapped I covered up my decision. With Evan also dead, it was easy. Easy to put the blame on you. And when Paige died"—he closed his eyes, shook his head—"I would never have intentionally put her in harm's way. She told me you were meeting Denise Arno alone and she had evidence. I didn't know it was a trap."

Madeline James spoke. "As Mr. Merritt knows, he is under investigation for his actions. Do you have anything else to add to your previous statements?"

Kate shook her head.

"And your decision about accepting our offer of probation?"

"May I have a couple of days?"

The director consulted a calendar in front of her. "I'll expect an answer Monday morning, which is the start of the next training session at the Academy. You'll report at oh eight hundred at Quantico, or you will meet me in my office at oh nine hundred to sign your resignation."

Kate stood, nodded to the committee members. She couldn't look at Jeff Merritt before she walked out the door.

Dillon watched Kate approach. He'd been waiting on a stone bench outside the J. Edgar Hoover Building. It was sweltering on this last day of June. He forgot the ache in his thigh and hand as soon as he saw Kate, though he couldn't tell by her expression what had happened. She'd told him she might be in there for hours, but only thirty minutes had passed.

He stood, took her hands.

She kissed him lightly. "Sit. You shouldn't be standing."

"I'm fine, Kate." But they sat down next to each other, hands entwined. "Well?" he asked, surprisingly impatient.

"I have two choices. I can quit, no repercussions except I can't work in law enforcement or on a computer for two years. I'd be a civilian again. Or, I can be on probation and earn back my rank."

"Probation?"

"I have to go through the Academy. Sixteen weeks." She groaned. "It was hard the first time around."

"You're smarter now."

"The tests didn't throw me. Do you know how many miles I have to run each day?"

"You're in great shape."

"I was in better shape when I was twenty-three."

"So that's it? Go through the Academy again and you're reinstated?"

"Well, I can't go in the field for a year. They want me to teach e-crimes at Quantico."

A huge weight lifted from Dillon's heart. She was free. He'd been so terrified she'd go to prison, no matter what Quinn Peterson had told him.

"Jeff Merritt admitted he'd pulled backup off our meeting and then covered it up. He resigned."

"What do you want to do?"

"Sixteen weeks is a long time. I'd only be able to see you on Sundays, if that."

He kissed her. "I'll be here every Sunday."

"You would?"

He nodded. "I love you, Kate."

She relaxed, rested her head on his shoulder.

"What do you want to do?" he asked her again.

She paused, thinking. "I'd like to go back. I think I have something to offer."

"I know you have something to offer. When do you have to start?"

"Monday."

"That gives us a week."

"Enough time for a little vacation in San Diego. I think your family misses you." She frowned. "How's Patrick?"

Dillon looked over at a statue of a man he didn't know. Possibly J. Edgar Hoover himself, or maybe a military war hero.

"He's still in a coma."

"I'm so sorry."

"It's not your fault, Kate."

She sighed uneasily. "Maybe not, but you love him and I hate that you're hurting inside."

"Patrick is strong. The doctor's believe he'll have a full recovery. Sometime." But with each passing day, the chances he'd come out of the coma grew slimmer. "Lucy's with him every day."

"Do you think that's okay? For her?"

"I don't know. She seems to be holding it together. And maybe—maybe he's the only one she can talk to."

Kate leaned into him, swallowing heavily. Her tension filled Dillon's own body and he shifted in his seat, forcing her to look him in the eye.

"What's wrong?"

"I don't want to take you from your family. They love you so much."

"Do you love me, Kate?"

She stared at him, startled. "How can you ask me that? I told you I do."

"No, you didn't."

"Yes I did! I told you last night after we made love—"

"Actually," he interrupted, "it was *while* we were making love and I don't count that. Look me in the eye."

She did. He saw worry there. But he also saw her love.

"I love you, but—"

"No buts. Tell me again."

She started to smile. "I love you."

"Good. Then we'll make it work."

"But—"

"Shh."

"Dillon, are you sure?"

"I've been a forensic psychiatrist for eleven years. I've had my hand in some high-profile cases. I think I might be able to find a job on the East Coast. Besides, Lucy is starting Georgetown in two months. I think I'd like to be here while she is."

Kate looked relieved. "Maybe it will all work out."

"I *know* it will all work out."

Dillon took her face in his hands, kissed her. "Let's start our vacation right now."

"You want to get a flight back to San Diego?"

"No, that can wait a few days. I want to get back to the hotel." He kissed her again, holding her lips hostage for a long minute.

"Um," she murmured. "That's nice."

"That's an understatement."